PRAISE FOR THE BOOKS OF

UNEXPECTED ENLIGHTENMENT

The action is non-stop, with child's play, schoolwork, and danger all churned together. Lamplighter introduces many imaginative elements in her world that will delight....
—*VOYA*

The British boarding school mystery meets the best imagined of fantasies at breakneck speed and with fully realized characters.
—Sarah A. Hoyt, author of *Darkship Thieves*

L. Jagi Lamplighter, a fantastic new voice and a fabulous new world in the YA market! Rachel Griffin is a hero who never gives up! I cheered her all the way!
—Faith Hunter, author of the *Skinwalker* series

The Unexpected Enlightenment of Rachel Griffin, a plucky band of children join forces to fight evil, despite the best efforts of incompetent adults, at a school for wizards. YA fiction really doesn't get better than that.
—Jonathan Moeller, author of *The Ghosts* series

Rachel Griffin is curious, eager and smart, and ready to begin her new life at Roanoke Academy for the Sorcerous Arts, but she didn't expect to be faced with a mystery as soon as she got there. Fortunately she's up to the task. Take all the best of the classic girl detective, throw in a good dose of magic and surround it all with entertaining, likeable friends and an intriguing conundrum, and you'll have *The Unexpected Enlightenment of Rachel Griffin*, a thrilling adventure tailor-made for the folks who've been missing Harry Potter. Exciting, fantastical events draw readers into Rachel's world and solid storytelling keeps them there.
—Misty Massey, author of *Mad Kestrel*

Other Books by

L. Jagi Lamplighter

For an up-to-date list, see http://ljagilamplighter.com/works.

The Books of Unexpected Enlightenment

The Unexpected Enlightenment of Rachel Griffin

The Raven, The Elf, and Rachel

Rachel and the Many-Splendored Dreamland

The Awful Truth about Forgetting

The Unbearable Heaviness of Remembering *(forthcoming)*

Guardians of the Twilight Lands *(forthcoming)*

... and more to come.

The Prospero's Children Trilogy

Prospero Lost

Prospero In Hell

Prospero Regained

THE FOURTH BOOK OF UNEXPECTED ENLIGHTENMENT

THE AWFUL TRUTH ABOUT FORGETTING

L. JAGI LAMPLIGHTER

BASED ON THE WORKS OF MARK A. WHIPPLE

ILLUSTRATIONS BY JOHN C. WRIGHT

Wisecraft Publishing
A publishing company of the Wise

Published by Wisecraft Publishing
A publishing company of the Wise

Copyright © 2017 by L. Jagi Lamplighter

ISBN: 978-0-9976460-3-0 (print)
ASIN: B076J2MZPX (e-book)
First edition
Revision 2.2.4 2018-03-06

Edited by Jim Frenkel

Cover art by Dan Lawlis
https://danlawlis.wordpress.com

Interior illustrations by John C. Wright

Typeset by Joel C. Salomon

Cover design by Danielle McPhail
Sidhe na Daire Multimedia
http://sidhenadaire.com

Chapter headings are set in RM Ginger, © 2009 Ray Meadows, licensed under CC BY-ND 3.0; see https://fontstruct.com/fontstructions/show/258661 for details.

CONTENTS

DEDICATION

To Jane Warner Brown Lamplighter
Whose stories of wonder lit the lamp.

AUTHOR'S NOTE:

This volume follows the revised edition of the first two books.

There are some differences.

Most notably, Valerie Foxx is now Valerie Hunt.

ONCE THERE WAS A WORLD

THAT SEEMED AT FIRST GLANCE MUCH LIKE OTHER WORLDS

YOU MAY HAVE LIVED IN OR READ ABOUT,

BUT IT WASN'T....

CHAPTER ONE:

ROANOKE IN THE SNOW

"HEY, CUTIE." GAIUS VALIANT GRABBED RACHEL GRIFFIN'S HAND AS she left the dining hall after dinner. The older boy leaned toward her and winked. "We're going to break some rules. Okay?"

"Certainly!" Rachel's pupils widened. "I'm game. What are we going to do?"

"Come and see." He grinned, touches of his native Cornish tones coloring his London accent.

Hummingbirds of happiness fluttering within her, Rachel fastened the toggles of her red wool duffle coat and pulled on a fluffy hat, knitted to look like a snowman. Grasping his hand, she followed her boyfriend outside into the cold darkness.

Snow was falling, blanketing the campus. Through the dark, bare branches of the trees, windows glowed in the towers of the seven dormitory halls. Tiny flakes danced in the air, lit by the wisplight from the lamps along the commons. In the glow of this lamplight, students laughed and threw snowballs or lay on their backs, waving their arms to leave snow-fairy impressions in the snow.

Everything was eerily lovely and strangely hushed.

It was Wednesday, the fifteenth of November, and the first snow of the year was falling. That morning, Rachel had woken up in London, in the flat of her older sister Sandra. What was supposed to have been a quiet visit—a chance for her to mourn the death of her otherworldly friend, the Elf—had gone spectacularly awry. Rachel, Sandra, and their mother had been kidnapped and dragged to the Temple of Saturn in the ruins of the ancient city of Carthage, where they were nearly sacrificed to the demon Moloch.

After their return to London, Rachel had spent a day and a half with her family, before returning to Roanoke Academy for the Sorcerous Arts in the late afternoon—which was still early morning here in New York. At lunch, she had found in her postbox an envelope from Detective Hunt with information about the family of Old Thom, the ghost whom Rachel and Gaius had met Halloween night at the Dead Men's Ball. When she shared the contents of the envelope with the aged shade, Old Thom had become so transfixed with joy that he dissolved into a beam of light. It was on her way back from that strange, uplifting encounter that she had spotted the first dancing flakes of snow.

Old Thom was not the only ghost under her care. After classes and throughout dinner, she and her blood-brother, Sigfried the Dragonslayer, had talked of nothing except the plans of the Die Horribly Debate Club—as their group of friends now called themselves, to Rachel's dismay—to return the shade of their late friend, the Elf, to her original home. Since hearing her first fairytale at the age of three, Rachel had longed to travel to some otherworldly place. She could not wait to see Hoddmimir's Wood, the World Tree, and the forest which grew up from the canopy of another forest that made up the Elf's home.

Sigfried was even more gung-ho. He had urged their friend Nastasia Romanov, the Princess of Magical Australia, to cut classes and take the Elf home today. The princess, however, had insisted that they should make the trip over the Thanksgiving holiday, when they were allowed to leave campus. That made sense, but to Rachel and Sigfried, both of whom were impatient to go, the delay came as quite a blow.

After all the recent drama, the peaceful swirling snow lifted Rachel's spirits. As she and Gaius walked down one of the paths that ran the length of the commons, she glanced sidelong, through the flakes gathering on her lashes, at her boyfriend. Gaius's coat was old and worn, with fraying sleeves. His chestnut hair was drawn back into a queue that was tied with a black ribbon at the nape of his neck. She knew he was short for his sixteen years, but he was at least a foot taller than she. As he walked beside her, he gave her a wide, cheerful grin that made her feel simultaneously tiny and beautiful.

She wondered what he would do if she scooped up an armful of snow and threw it at him, but she was too shy to try.

They walked along the commons toward the forest path that led to the docks. Powdery coldness landed on Rachel's nose. From the nearby lily pond that lay between them and the forest came the blare of a tuba.

"Must be Oonagh," Gaius chuckled. "No one else plays enchantments with a tuba."

"Oo! Cuz!" cried out a high voice with a thick Irish accent. "I've caught it!"

In the light of the wisp-lamps, two girls with red hair, both wearing capelet coats with double rows of brass buttons down the front, scrambled around on the frozen surface of the pond. The girl in navy blue, with dark coppery tresses that fell below her waist, was playing a tuba. Twinkles of indigo light came from the brass instrument's mouth and drifted out across the pond. The girl in the teal coat, whose hair was shoulder length and closer to the color of a bright new penny, held a large, upside-down glass jar pressed against the ice. Rachel recognized the girls as Oonagh MacDannan and her cousin, Colleen.

Colleen MacDannan looked up from where she knelt on the ice, face aglow with cold and mirth. "Oh, Gaius, look! My cousin's summoned an ice sprite, and I've caught it!"

Gaius and Rachel moved forward, hand in hand, to where Colleen crouched beside the topiary fountain in the middle of the pond. The fountain was currently off, but the leaping dolphins cut from living evergreens peeked out from beneath their snowy caps. Coming up beside Colleen, Rachel and Gaius bent over to see what she had captured. Inside the jar, swirls of snow formed a little humanoid shape, its tiny face pert and curious. The figure dissolved into a windy gust of snowy flakes, it reformed again. Wings like large snowflakes jutted from its shoulders, beating against the glass.

Rachel's lips parted. The little creature was both beautiful and mesmerizing. Gazing at it, she felt as if she could hardly breathe.

Gaius squatted down. "I think it's a frost jack. Aren't ice sprites bigger?"

"Could be a snowkarl," offered Rachel, peering down in sheer delight.

"No, you eejit," laughed Oonagh. She also had a thick Irish accent. "Snowkarls are native to northern Europe. There aren't any in America."

"Oh." Rachel bit her lip, embarrassed. "It's nice that they are letting us out in the snow."

"Why wouldn't they?" asked Colleen.

"Siggy told me," Rachel replied, feeling increasingly more awkward, "that during Monday's rainstorm they made everyone go back to the dorms and locked the buildings down."

"That's because of the Heer of Dunderberg and his lightning imps," replied Oonagh, setting her tuba on its case. "The school is afraid, now that the storm goblin's free, that he'll seek revenge. They want to keep the students safe." Looking up into the swirling whiteness, she added cheerfully, "So far no thunder or lightning, so we're okay."

Catching Rachel's hand, Oonagh pulled. "Come on! I see another one."

The two girls raced through the snow toward a spot where flakes were swirling beneath the last few indigo sparks of Oonagh's summoning enchantment. When they reached it, three tiny frost jacks twirled and danced on the ice. The two girls leapt at them, but without a jar, there was not much they could do to restrain them. They dissolved into snow and wind, vanishing out of their hands. Laughter, like tiny ice crystal chimes, rang out, mocking them.

"Over here!" Oonagh jerked Rachel in another direction. She called solicitously, as one might to a young child. "I see some more! Let's catch them, shall we?"

Rachel narrowed her eyes and glanced back at where Colleen stood, her face flushed and pink from more than the cold, gazing up all doe-eyed at Gaius.

"Oonagh," Rachel asked dryly. "Do you remember the time that you and my sisters and I all went to Ross Castle together, in Killarney?"

"Course, I remember!" The older girl laughed. "That trip was the craic!"

"I was six at the time."

Oonagh grinned. "You were such a wee dote!"

Rachel's voice became extremely dry. "I'm not six anymore."

"Sorry?" the older girl paused and peered at her. Rachel felt as if Oonagh was seeing her for the first time.

"You're distracting me." Rachel pulled her hand away and crossed her arms. "So your cousin can chat up my boyfriend. I know she fancies him. Though why she needs your help, I haven't a clue. They live in the same dorm. Can't she try to nick him there? On her own time?"

"Rachel." Oonagh gave her an apologetic smile. "You know you're too young to date a boy like Gaius Valiant. He's a senior. You're a freshman—an extra young one at that."

"What? Is there an expiration date? Can't have a boyfriend unless I'm properly ripe, like a pear or something? I'm not jam. Or a pie."

"Sweetie, be reasonable." Oonagh gestured at Rachel's tiny, boyish figure. "You may not be six any longer, but you still *look* six. Oh, okay, nine. You're far too young for... well, the things older boys want to do."

"Gaius is very chivalrous," Rachel raised her chin and spoke quite properly. "He does not do anything we would be ashamed to do in front of Sandra."

"Och! That's hardly fair to the boy, now, is it?" Oonagh put her hands on her hips, her coppery locks flying. "I reckon Gaius is old enough to do quite a few things I wouldn't do in front of your elder sister, and I'm quite fond of Sandra. Besides," she leaned toward Rachel, wagging her finger, "everyone knows you're only waiting around for that Dragonslayer boy to break up with the girl from Dee Hall, so you can date him."

"What? Sigfried?" Rachel cried out, outraged, her English accent even more pronounced. "I wouldn't date him if he were the last boy alive!"

"Why not?" Oonagh leaned forward, grinning wickedly. "He's extraordinarily handsome. Sigfried Smith, though young, may be the fairest boy on campus."

Rachel murmured, "Other than Vlad."

"Who?"

Rachel's cold cheeks grew pinker. "The Prince of Bavaria."

"You're on a first name basis with Vladimir Von Dread?" Oonagh gawked. "Doesn't matter how easy on the eye *that* one is. No girl in her right mind would date him!" She shivered. "Far too intimidating."

What might Oonagh's expression might be, Rachel wondered, if she were to announce that Von Dread was dating her sister and wanted to make Sandra Queen of Bavaria? Oonagh thought the world of Rachel's older sister, whom she had looked up to for years. Rachel pressed her lips together, resisting the impulse to brag.

No one would learn Sandra and Vlad's secrets from her!

Oonagh leaned toward her, smirking. "Are you sure about young Mr. Smith? He's quite the fair one! Good teeth, too."

"There's more to boys than their teeth," Rachel replied stolidly. "Siggy is my blood brother. It would be like dating Peter! Or you dating Liam or Conan or Ian."

Oonagh made a face, "Yuck!"

"Exactly. I am very fond of Sigfried Smith, but it's not that kind of fondness. Besides, spending time with Siggy is like trying to hold onto a fire hose at full throttle. He's bonkers! Gaius, on the other hand," Rachel continued seriously, "is a very clever boy. He's smart and witty and interested in a great many things. He's a good listener, too. A person you can tell secrets to. Sigfried doesn't listen to anything."

Oonagh's eyes danced. "So that's what you want from a boy, eh? Someone who will listen to all those big secrets you little freshmen keep?"

Rachel Griffin, who knew secrets that could destroy the world, did not reply.

"Rach, let's go," Gaius's voice called from the pond.

Rachel rushed back to where he stood by Colleen. Oonagh followed. The four of them looked down at the frost jack trapped under the glass. They watched it form, dissolve, and form again. With the snow falling past the wisp-lamps, landing on their hair and coats, the world around them began to seem distant and dreamlike. Soft icy chimes rang in her thoughts, calling her to....

A shiver ran through Rachel. She shook her head vigorously. Watching a fey creature was not like watching a pet mouse or a chipmunk. The fey were dangerous, even a little one caught in a jar. She took a wary step backward.

"What will happen to the frost jack?" Rachel's gaze was still trapped by the swirling fey.

"Och, 'tis bad luck to keep one of the wee folk imprisoned!" said Oonagh. "We just wanted to see it. We'll be settin' it free soon enough."

"Good," murmured Rachel.

"Let's go." Gaius took her hand and squeezed it.

Yanking her gaze away from the bell jar, Rachel smiled up at him and returned the squeeze. Together they continued down the tree-lined path that led through the forest to the docks.

. . .

They reached the ruins of Bannerman's Castle and walked through the arch and down the stairs toward the snow-covered docks. A tall gentleman in a suit and tie stood beside the dark waters of the Hudson. It took Rachel a moment to recognize Gaius's friend, William Locke. William looked so distinguished in his business attire, she never would have taken him for a college student.

Gaius greeted his friend with his customary lazy grin, as if he were an amused spectator, casually observing the little dramas of life. Locke towered over him. Yet the older student seemed genuinely pleased to see the younger boy.

"Hello, Miss Griffin." William Locke turned to her and nodded, inclining an eyebrow in an expression of scientific curiosity. William was an American and sounded like one.

"Hallo, Mr. Locke." Rachel curtsied, holding the skirts of her black academic robes.

"Any luck?" asked Gaius.

"We were too late." William bowed his head gravely. Turning to Rachel, he explained, "An Unwary teen disappeared while flying a drone from the west bank of the river." He gestured to the left at Donahue Memorial Park, a grassy area next to a small marina visible on the far west shore, just north of Storm King Mountain. "A team from O.I. joined the Agents investigating, so I came out to aid the operation. Sadly, the ogre had already... er... found him."

"Oh!" Rachel pressed a hand against her mouth, horrified.

She gazed down river curiously, a sudden longing stirring within her breast to see this deadly monster brought to justice.

"Are we here to help catch it?" she asked hopefully.

Her hand inched toward her calling card. An ogre was exactly the kind of opponent for which Sigfried and Lucky had been searching—an enemy that deserved a thrashing, something they could burn with impunity.

"Alas, I fear there is little we can do." William shook his head. "Even the experts have trouble dealing with that ogre—it leads a charmed life—and they are already on the case."

"Oh." Rachel gazed across the river in dismay. She longed to be allowed to join the hunt. The notion of possible danger did not disturb her. If it might save other victims from being devoured, she wanted to help.

"Let us put that sad matter aside, shall we?" continued William. "I believe Mr. Valiant has something special planned for you."

"For me?" Rachel looked back and forth between the two young men, her disappointment offset by surprise. "Where?"

"Have you jumped before?" Gaius asked, grinning.

"Not by myself," she replied quickly. "We're not allowed to jump if we are underage." The laws against it were very strict.

"But you've done it?" asked Gaius.

"You mean with someone else? Loads of times," said Rachel, "Though most recently going to and from being kidnapped."

"You won't be scared? Good."

"Not jumping with you, no."

Gaius squeezed her arm and put his other hand on Locke's shoulder. "Let's go, William."

Pure white light flooded everywhere. Rachel could not feel Gaius's hand or even her own body. Then the light faded, and sensation came flowing back.

It was no longer dark; nor was it snowing. It was early evening. The three of them stood on a street surrounded by rundown Victorian houses. The buildings were windowless and moss-covered. A biting wind swept down the road, carrying the odor of rotting trash. Rachel shivered and stepped closer to Gaius, who put an arm around her shoulder. He and William nodded at each other and began walking forward. Ahead lay a sprawling maroon and blue house with boarded windows. Some inner walls must have collapsed, because the cone-shaped roof of the turret lurched at a disturbing angle.

"Where are we?" Rachel clutched her boyfriend's arm. "Why is everything so ugly?"

"Detroit," William stated. "The economy fell apart here some years ago. This section of town was abandoned."

Rachel looked around. "But… I thought the economic downfall was just a façade, a tale spread around to explain the damage done during the Battle of Detroit."

"Some of both," replied William. "A real financial crisis was adopted as the cover story for the devastation."

"Battle of Detroit?" Gaius looked from one to the other. "Was that recent? We haven't gotten to the Terrible Years yet in True History. I think that comes next semester."

Rachel said, "It was the largest battle between the Wise and the Terrible Five, during the Terrible Years. It was a horrid battle. The Wise won but only barely."

"Was that Egg fellow there? If so, I imagine the battle was truly terrible," said Gaius.

Rachel shook her head. "Back then Mortimer Egg was just a hapless student who had not yet been possessed by Azrael. The demon was still inside my grandfather's old friend, Aleister Crowley. If anything, however, Crowley was worse. He had been a superb magician before Azrael possessed him. Egg was just… Egg."

"Crowley was at the Battle of Detroit," said William. "He had a dramatic duel with Aurelius MacDannan. They say the whole sky was filled with lightning and darkness and flashes of pure white fire. The other four of the Five Terrible Ones were there, as well: Baba Yaga and her chicken-legged hut destroyed sections of Brush Park. Morgana le Fay and the Morthbrood fought General Ernest O'Keefe and the American Sorcerous Militia in Brightmoor—both the Fifth Thaumaturge Brigade and the First American Enchanters were there. Koschei the Deathless single-handedly defeated the Second Canadian Alchemists, who had come down to help. He devastated the Hamtramck area."

William gestured off into the distance, perhaps pointing at the neighborhood to which he referred. He continued, "To this day, more than a quarter century later, there are places in Hamtramck where nothing will grow. The leader of the Terrible Five, Simon Magus, arrived with Veltdammerung supporting him—not just cultists, such as Miss Griffin has fought, but the supernatural forces as well: Unseelie, trolls, Jotuns, and the like. It was they who killed the lion's share of our forces."

"Who's Aurelius MacDannan?" asked Gaius.

"Oonagh and Colleen's grandfather," said Rachel. "He was a splendid sorcerer. He could do things no one else has ever been able to do, pull lightning out of power lines, for instance. Unfortunately, he died in that duel... killed by Azrael. Or at least, no one ever saw him again."

William nodded. "A great many people died that day. Three-quarters of the American Wise over the age of twenty-one were killed. My own older brothers and sister died. Siblings I never had a chance to meet."

"My great-uncle Cadellin died that day as well," Rachel said softly.

Gaius rocked back on his heels. "I... had no idea it was such a devastating battle."

William asked, "Have you ever wondered why the American Wise are more modern than the Wise of the rest of the world, who frankly are still living in the Nineteenth Century? Why the Americans are more permissive, more familiar with technology? It's because of the Battle of Detroit. It killed such a large portion of our older generation that many of our old traditions were lost and much of our former culture."

"I had no idea," Gaius repeated, slightly shaken. "In other words, the Battle of Detroit did to the American Wise what World War I did to the English aristocracy?"

"Precisely," William nodded again. "Ironically, it was because the American Wise—particularly my father and Iron Moth—had been investigating technology that our side won at all. Our iron weapons gave us an advantage against the Unseelie. It was the only battle of the Terrible Years that the Wise won, other than the final battle at Roanoke."

"Where my uncle Emrys died." Shivering from the extreme cold, Rachel looked around at the dilapidated houses. "But then why are we... oh!"

Even before they took another step forward, a smile began tugging at her lips as she anticipated what was to come. Sure enough, as they moved, the obscuration in front of them popped, and the dangerously-listing Victorian mansion vanished, along with the rundown buildings to either side. Instead, before them rose the shining black and silver skyscrapers of Ouroboros Industries.

Chapter Two:

Too Dangerous To Know

The three Roanoke students walked along a shrub-lined path leading between the skyscrapers. It was still bitterly cold, but the wind was not as strong here, making it seem warm in comparison to the street. To the left, sunlight glittered off a gigantic geodesic dome, larger than any mundane sporting stadium.

"What's that?" Rachel raised her hand to shield her eyes.

"Our degossamerization dome," replied William.

"Really?" she murmured, sliding her mask of calm into place to keep her eyes from growing as large as saucers.

William looked down at her. "Do you know what degossamerization is? I believe it is not studied until sophomore year."

"Of course." Rachel quoted from a dictionary in the library of previously-read books available in her perfect memory. "*It is the process of bathing an object in the light of the full moon to remove the gossamer-like impermanence of conjured items or alchemical talismans, so as to make them permanent.*"

"Very good."

"Sandra's a splendid conjurer, and my mum is a whiz at alchemy. I know all about degossamerization." With a casual air that required all the dissembling skills she had learned from her mother to achieve, she asked, "I don't suppose we could have a look?"

"I'm afraid not," replied William. "The process is proprietary."

I wager it is, thought Rachel smugly.

She gazed at the dome, but she made sure that William's face was visible in her peripheral vision so that she would be able to examine his expression later—without tell-tale clues, such as her gaze resting on his face, alerting him to her interest in his reaction.

"Father thinks O.I. bought up moon rocks after the Apollo missions and found a way to use them to perform degossamerization through alchemical infusions."

"Clever idea." William stroked his narrow chin thoughtful.

"Wonder if it would work."

"I've been quite curious about the magical properties of moon rocks," Gaius said cheerfully, tossing his chestnut ponytail over his shoulder. "Any chance O.I. could secure one?"

William smiled very slightly. "If you want to experiment on a moon rock, Gaius, I am certain either Vlad or I could procure one for you. Write down a list of the experiments you wish to perform, and we shall see what we can do."

Gaius looked quite pleased. "I'll do that."

"Wait here. I'll be right back." William strode purposefully into the nearest building.

As they waited for him to return, Rachel leaned toward her boyfriend and whispered, "What are we doing here?"

Gaius gave her a lazy smile that reminded her why she loved him. "I want to show you something. I've been working to set this up ever since you told me about how you tried to stop that airplane. But William was busy with the secret project—the one that saved you in Tunis."

"For which I am very grateful." Rachel curtsied, lifting the skirts of her robes as she bobbed. Straightening, she asked Gaius, "What is it that you want to show me?"

He grinned widely and drawled, "You'll see."

"Oh-kay."

Her curiosity burned so hot that she wondered if she might spontaneously combust. To distract herself, she stared at the degossamerization dome.

"Impressive building, isn't it?" asked Gaius, tilting his head back to see the whole geodesic dome. "Biggest degossamerization plant in the world, right?"

"The only one, so far as I know," she replied.

"Wait." Gaius frowned. "O.I. isn't the only company that degossamerizes stuff. We do it at school. Isn't that why conjuring and alchemy students stay up all night every full moon?"

"Yes. Exactly." Rachel nodded. "We—and everyone else in the world—do it the old-fashioned way. Depending on how solid you want your talisman to be, it takes thirteen months to get a proper one. Or a great year, if you want a truly smashing one."

"Great year? Wait. We learned this." Gaius leaned back on his heels and ran a hand over his hair. "Um...ah! The time it takes for the moon to come back to the same position in the Zodiac, right? About eight normal years to make one great year, if I recall. And if you miss a single full moon... all the work is for naught, right? That must really suck."

Rachel nodded. "Mr. Fisher lost one of the great talismans he had made for the Six Musketeers—one of the items that had defeated the Terrible Five—that way. He didn't get it outside under the full moon one month and—poof—the magic was gone."

"That's a shame!"

"It is one of the reasons conjurers often study enchantment as well... they want to be able to perform enough weather magic to ensure a clear sky on moonlit nights. Anyway," Rachel continued with a gesture at the dome, "it takes the rest of us a great year. Yet since the early seventies, Ouroboros Industries had been mass producing magical devices for purchase by the general public."

"Mass producing...? You mean they use magic to produce their washing machines and vacuums?" asked Gaius.

Rachel shook her head. "No, I mean Flycycles, flying umbrella platforms, and kenomanced bags, such as my friend the princess carries around that has a whole house inside it."

"Don't enchanted talismans have to be made one at a time, by hand?"

"Ordinarily. And yet — according to my father — O.I. has demonstrated over and over the ability to respond to market demands and customer complaints in under six months. It's assumed that they had found a way to use technology to produce moonlight, but no one knew for certain."

She did not add that even her father, the head of the Wisecraft's clandestine Shadow Agency, had not been able to figure out their method.

"Under six months instead of eight years!" exclaimed Gaius. "That's big! I imagine that they can sell a whole lot more enchanted gear than their competitors, right?"

Rachel nodded. "More than that, our current economy relies it taking eight years of cloudless full moons to make conjured gold indistinguishable gold taken from the earth. If they can make all the gold they wanted in a couple of months..."

"They could make a killing and, if they're not careful, flood the market."

"Exactly."

With her gaze resting on the dome's shining interstices, gleaming in the light of the late afternoon sun, Rachel recalled her recent conversation with William. She slowed down the moment when she mentioned the moon rock. It had been merely an instant, but the corner of her eye had caught a look of scientific curiosity that had flashed across William's face at the mention of her father's theory. This meant his interest in her father's notion had not been a ploy.

Rachel grinned. She had just done what the Wisecraft had not been able to do in over a generation. She had narrowed down the possible options for how Ouroboros Industries performed their mysterious alternate degossamerization process. It was not moon rocks.

She allowed herself a brief, victorious smile. Her father would be impressed... if he ever bothered to notice her. She had been so hopeful when they returned from fighting the demon Morax, two days ago, that she and her father would finally have a chance to sit down and talk. She longed to tell him what had happened to her the previous time she had been kidnapped, when she had saved him from the demon Azrael. Alas, the promised conversation had not occurred.

Father and Sandra, both Agents of the Wisecraft, had spent a long time quietly speaking to each other at the far side of her sister's flat. Then, before Rachel could have her promised turn with him, he had been called away. Sandra and her mother had tried to make it up to her, but it was not the same.

Rachel thrust aside that sorrow. She had Gaius's surprise and the trip to Hoddmimir's Wood to look forward to. No girl could be too sad with the prospect of a journey to the home of the Queen of the Lios Alfar ahead of her—not to mention this mysterious trip of Gaius's. She bounced up and down on the balls of her feet, eager to discover the nature of his surprise.

The glass door slid open by some unseen magic. William Locke strode out carrying nametags on lanyards. He handed them to the younger students, and they followed him into the building, showing their new tags to the guard at the door. Once inside, Gaius pulled off his long black academic robe and tossed it over his arm. Underneath, he was wearing jeans, a flannel shirt of Black Watch tartan, and a tan London Fog jacket. Rachel thought he looked rather dashing in his street clothes. She found it a bit unnerving to see him dressed this way, however, like coming upon a boy in his pajamas. She did not remove her robes, but she did shed her red wool coat.

As they walked down the hallway, they passed a large alcove in which rested a wreath surrounded by photos and bouquets of flowers. The photos were all of the same man, showing him smiling and surrounded by family and friends.

Seeing Rachel's interest, William paused and said, "That is a memorial for Henry Maxwell. The member of our Rapid Response Team who died at Carthage."

"Do you mean the one who was crushed—" Rachel swallowed, "—when the demon threw him into a column, and it fell on him?"

Locke nodded solemnly.

"I am so sorry," said Rachel. "The others who were hurt. Did they recover?"

"Two are still in the hospital, but it is believed they will make full recoveries."

"I'm glad."

Rachel stared at the face of the man in the photographs. Some of the photos also showed a woman and two little children. The thought of their father never coming home made Rachel's heart constrict. It reminded her how dangerous her own father's work was—which perhaps should have made her less angry with him. *But it did not.*

Instead, she felt all the more upset that he had not paused to hear the important things she had to tell him while he still had the chance. As she looked at the photos, however, something else struck her. It was entirely thanks to her mother, Siggy, and Zoë that she was here at all, to stand here and look at this memorial. If her mother had not whistled and freed her from the paralysis spell; if her friends had not jumped down from the dreamland; it might be her picture that was propped up on a memorial, surrounded by flowers.

The idea of dying did not frighten her. Rather, what troubled her was how helpless she had felt after Serena O'Malley had entered Sandra's apartment. There had been nothing she could do to defend herself, no one whom she could have called for help. It was the second time she had been paralyzed by an enemy. If she counted the time Sandra muted her, that made three battles where she had been entirely helpless.

Rachel was tired of being helpless. She wished she were more powerful, or, at least, that there were someone who was both willing to protect her and strong enough to do it.

But there was no one.

Just before the elevator, William paused and spoke to a secretary seated at a desk that overlooked the lobby. Turning back to Gaius and Rachel, William said with a twinkle in his eye, "Seems we're half an hour early. While we wait, would you like to see one of our labs?"

"Would I?" Gaius made a sound halfway between a gasp and a laugh. "That would be a yes. As if you didn't know."

William stopped, peered into one room, and then closed the door again, shaking his head. "That one is proprietary. We're working on improved communication methods for the Wise. Father and Iron Moth are quite protective of their prototypes."

"You mean, to catch up with cell phones?" asked Gaius. William winced and nodded. "For centuries, we were ahead on instant travel and communication. Now we are lagging seriously behind in the communication department."

"What's wrong with calling cards?" asked Rachel.

Gaius leaned toward her and said softly, "Have you ever been sitting in class, and someone's voice came out of your calling card, disturbing everyone?"

Rachel blushed. Was he referring to something she had accidentally done to him. "Yes."

"That doesn't happen with mundane phones. We have something called voicemail."

"I'm sure we can find something I can show you both." William rounded a corner and looked in another door. "Let's see... ah! Here's one that's safe for us to see."

Locke opened a door, and the three of them entered. Inside was a large laboratory with a number of work stations. Scientists in lab coats, both men and women, bent over their work. Their equipment varied from unfamiliar mundane devices that clicked and clacked, to hissing Bunsen burners and glowing soldering irons, to large, orange tricorne mirrors, such as alchemists used. The air smelled of various chemicals, of hot, melted metal, and, oddly, of garlic. In the center of the room was a device consisting of two long, narrow rectangular, metallic boxes attached to each other and seated atop a wheeled platform.

"Rail gun!" Gaius headed straight for the device—which was at least as large as a cannon—and stroked its sleek gray side. "What does it shoot?"

"That's precisely what we are working on," explained Locke. "This is an order for the King of Transylvania. He wants...."

Another man strode into the lab. William stiffened, and Gaius gasped. Rachel spun around to get a better look at the newcomer. As he took off his hat and tossed it onto a hat rack, she saw that it was a tall, broad-shouldered young man—a young man she knew.

"Blackie!" She ran over to greet her second cousin and then stopped abruptly, recalling with a shudder that his memory had been damaged.

"Do I know you?" Blackie Moth asked in his clipped, midwestern accent. He had a shock of dark curly hair, a pointed goatee, and steel-gray eyes.

Rachel knew some people had visceral reactions to seeing a crippled or deformed body—such things did not trouble her. The thought of a crippled memory, however, sent a spasm of horror throughout her being. It took all her dissembling skills to force her face into a smile.

"I'm Rachel Griffin." She curtsied, ducking her head until she could school her expression. "Your second cousin."

He pulled out a notebook, opening it to a family tree. "You are related to me... how?"

"Your grandmother, Lady Nimue Griffin Moth, was the sister of my grandfather Blaise Griffin, the late Duke of Devon."

"Ah. I've heard of you." He traced the tree, pressing his finger against a place on the page. Each word was short and clipped, which is exactly how Rachel remembered him as speaking before his accident. He looked at her frankly. "I didn't realize you'd be Oriental."

Rachel gave him a kind smile. "My mother's half-Korean."

It felt strange to say that, after so many years of believing that her mother was a quarter Korean. She still felt a bit dazed by the realization that she had somehow been wrong about the identity of her great-grandmother for her whole life. Before returning from London, she had asked about her real great-grandmother, but her mother knew almost nothing about Grandpa Kim's mother. Ellen Kim Griffin had only ever met her step-grandmother.

Gaius leaned back on his heels. "I think you mean that Rachel's Asian."

Blackie scowled, "I ain't buyin' into that newspeak nonsense. 'Specially as their word-alchemy sucks mothballs."

"Word alchemy?" Gaius leaned farther back than he had meant to and had to step back rapidly to regain his balance.

"They try to move the essence of an idea from an old word to a new one, leavin' behind the qualities they don't much like. Isn't that alchemy?" asked Blackie. "Only to make it work, they have to endow the original words with the essence of hatred and vitriol, in order to get folks to stop usin' em. Turn 'em into swearwords. Look at: Oriental, Colored, cripple, retarded. Perfectly good words, ruined."

"I... never thought of it that way," said Gaius, who was looking decidedly uncomfortable.

Blackie continued, "Homeless now means what used to be meant by bum or tramp. And let's not even get into what happened to that little word that used to mean full of fun."

"They're just trying to be kind," countered Gaius. "Does this 'word-alchemy' do anybody any harm?"

"Sure does. Perfectly good older books suddenly banned, because now they have swearwords in 'em that weren't swearwords when they were written," spat Blackie. "Bah. You should have heard the nonsense words the American Sorcery Council wanted to use to replace *Unwary*—*Mundie? Muggle? Flobbit?* Thank goodness the Wise actually showed some wisdom and voted it down."

This last comment caused Gaius to snort with amusement, though he was still a bit red in the face.

Rachel listened, but she did not weigh in. She had always vaguely thought that *Asian* was a word for people and *Oriental* was for rugs or gardens—though she knew both words had been used differently in ages gone by. She was amused to notice, however, that, even without his memory, Cousin Blackie had retained his talent for turning an innocent conversation into something that caused offense. Rachel's grandmother, Lady Devon, had once described him as having the manners of a mutt who ran into the house after capturing a rabbit—so that when he shook the creature to snap its neck, he also broke the household crystal.

Blackie turned to William. "Where's your better half?"

"You mean Vlad?" asked Gaius.

Blackie snorted dryly. "Not Dread. Coils. Fine gal. Head for science."

Her cousin must have meant Naomi Coils, William's girlfriend. William nodded pleasantly. Gaius, however, looked distinctly uncomfortable, though maybe he was still unnerved by the previous conversation.

"She's well," William replied. "I shall tell her you asked after her."

"How's Granite doing at MAAT?" Gaius asked. Leaning close to Rachel, he whispered, "Blackie's younger brother was a senior at the Upper School last year, but this year, for college, he transferred to Minnesota Academy for Alchemy and Thaumaturgy."

Rachel leaned over and whispered back, "I know. He's my second cousin."

"Oh. Right."

Aloud Rachel said, "William, weren't you thinking of going to MAAT, too? At least that's what S—" Her voice cut off.

"I did think about it, but I felt Roanoke had more to offer me, overall," replied William.

He did not ask her what she had been planning to say, which was for the best—because only after she had begun to speak had Rachel recalled that she had only known about his plans because she and Sigfried had been spying on his conversation with Sandra.

"What does MAAT have that Roanoke does not?" Rachel asked curiously. "I thought the other academies only offered a portion of our curriculum."

"That is true when it comes to sorcery," William replied. "But Minnesota Academy for Alchemy and Thaumaturgy also offers mundane sciences not taught at Roanoke."

"Oh!" exclaimed Rachel. "Yes. I guess that makes sense."

"MAAT is almost a training program for O.I.," said Gaius, gesturing at the laboratory around them. "A great many of the graduates end up here."

"It's the only school in the world that mixes magic and technology," said Blackie. "Outside of Bavaria, anyway. And to answer your question, Valiant, my brother Granite's doing well, when he can be bothered to go to class. He's been there only three months, and he's already running a gamblin' ring. Spends too much time on non-scholastic pursuits, if you ask me."

There was a moment of silence.

Gaius turned and gestured toward the rail gun and the surrounding lab. "So you are involved with this research?"

"Yep."

"And you're working on rail guns?" prompted Gaius.

"Yep."

"Ammunition or the weapon itself?"

"Yep."

Rachel sighed. Even back when he had his entire memory, Blackie had never been a big conversationalist, but he used to be more forthcoming than this.

She turned to William, who was leaning against the wall with only his shoulders touching the plaster; the rest of his body formed a straight diagonal line, as if he were propping up the building. He was smiling a rather sardonic smile. As he turned his head to glance

at something in the lab, his dark brown hair fell forward, and Rachel noticed for the first time that his ears were slightly pointed. It made him look quite dashing.

She quickly looked away. It would not do to fall in love with yet another of Gaius's friends. *Not that she was in love with Dread!*

"Blackie, you mentioned Transylvania?" she asked.

"The king requested a weapon to fight his vampire menace," William replied, his unexpected ears again hidden beneath his hair. "Blackie here is part of a team working on developing a rail gun that fires garlic."

"Still in the exploratory stages. Won't be ready any time soon," said Blackie curtly. "We're experimentin' with a few approaches: compressed garlic mixed with metal shavings to form the sabot, a sintered hollow projectile with garlic juice inside, and endowing our current ammunition with essence of garlic via alchemy. So far, this last one is the most promisin'. Wanna find the cheapest way to hurt those blood-suckin' 'louts."

Gaius's eyes widened. "You need a *rail gun* to shoot vampires?"

"Suckers are tough."

Rachel giggled. Blackie just looked at her.

"Besides," Blackie added with a shrug, "it was a good excuse to design this prototype. Eventually, I hope to build a much bigger one —for flinging stuff into space."

"Siggy wants to go into space," noted Rachel.

Blackie grunted, "If we get the bigger model workin', we'll fling 'im up there for you."

"Can you tell us more—about this project?" asked Gaius, gesturing at the gun.

"Well...." Blackie slid his hands into his pockets and tipped back on his heels, thinking. "One option is to try foamed metals, but our zero-g lab is not yet a hundred percent operational. Another option is gravomancy, which looks promisin,' but gravomancers are rare. We're recruitin' as we speak."

"Foamed metals!" Gaius's eyes lit up. "I've read about those. So you'd fill the pores with garlic-infused gas?"

They talked in detail about the experimental work, using many terms that Rachel did not know, some of which were not in any dictionary she had memorized. While she did not begrudge her boy-friend the time spent learning about things he found fascinating, she did not wish to be alone with her thoughts, which were growing darker.

Who had robbed her cousin of his memory? What power was re-sponsible for his terrible loss? Could it be someone upon whom she could sic Sigfried and Lucky? She imagined this mysterious entity, its head aflame, while Lucky and Sigfried roasted marshmallows.

The thought of Blackie's loss of memory was too disturbing. Casting about for a pleasant subject, Rachel recalled something she had overheard the Agents say back in September.

She turned to Locke. "That glowing umber stuff your Rapid Response Team used to capture the demon in Tunis?" she asked. "That was the same stuff that caused you to abandon your plant in Miyagi Japan, wasn't it?"

William and Blackie exchanged glances. "How did you know—"

Gaius cut them off with a laugh. "How does Rachel Griffin ever know anything?" He spread his hands. "It is one of the world's great mysteries."

Rachel smiled slightly, secretly delighted by the boys' reactions. "What is that stuff?"

William smiled dryly and gestured at Blackie. "Here's the man to ask. It was his research that made it possible. A high price to pay, but at least we are putting it to good use."

Rachel turned to her second cousin. "Was it the work you were doing when you lost your memory? The same project William worked on last summer?"

Blackie nodded. "I was tryin' to reproduce an experiment Locke and Dread performed their freshman year."

"Oh?" asked Rachel politely.

"The two of them blew up the forest behind Roanoke Hall," stated Blackie. "I'm told they still have trouble gettin' magic to work there, even today."

"Hang on!" Rachel whirled around to face William. "The ex-plosion that left that barren spot behind the main hall? That was *you*?"

Locke covered his mouth with his fist and cleared his throat. "I believe it was. Yes."

"As Siggy would say, 'Ace!'" laughed Rachel.

"You mentioned this Siggy earlier. Before I schedule him to be flung into outer space, who is he?" asked Blackie.

"My blood brother."

"Guess that makes 'im my blood-second cousin then." Blackie pulled out his notebook and opened to the family tree. Grabbing a pen, he asked, "What's his full name?"

"Sigfried Smith the Dragonslayer," Rachel replied with the proper amount of archness.

"The kid who killed a dragon in the sewers of London?" Blackie wrote the name beside Rachel's and put the little book back in his pocket. "Even I've heard of him."

Rachel continued, bright-eyed. "Siggy and I have been ever so curious about the exploded area. We wondered if the same method could be used to stop magic or produce wards."

"It can be used to freeze demons," Blackie replied. "Unfortunately, we haven't proceeded beyond the one application. Most of my notes conveniently disappeared during my 'accident.'"

"Accident or... Rachel's heart sank.

"Erased by the Raven?" she whispered.

"You mean the Guardian?" Blackie asked, a strange look in his steely eyes. "Don't think we're supposed to talk about him."

Of course, it was the Raven.

That took the wind out of the sails of her elaborate plans for revenge. She could not hate the Raven. She could, however, hate whatever drove him to do such a thing. The demons? The chaos outside the Walls of the World? Whatever it was, she felt certain that the Raven would never rob someone's memory for his own benefit.

"Why not?" asked William. "Talk about the Guardian, I mean." Blackie crossed his arms. "He'll make us forget."

"Not me," Rachel shook her head. "I can't forget."

"Can't? Not even if the Guardian wanted you to?" asked Blackie skeptically.

Rachel nodded solemnly.

William asked. "Because of the Rune that the elf-woman gave you?"

"I thought you said it was okay to tell the others," Gaius explained quickly. "Now that she's...." He faltered, not uttering the word *dead*.

"I did. It's all right." Rachel absently touched the side of her head, where the silver Rune was tattooed to her scalp, under her hair. "But it's probably better not to tell too many folks."

"Perfect memory, huh?"

Blackie grunted. "Can't say I'm not envious, but I imagine it's a burden, too."

"Why?" asked Rachel, surprised.

Blackie shrugged. "Can't forget pain? Can't forget sorrow?"

"I... suppose," Rachel swallowed, her mask of calm sliding into place to hide how close to home his comment had struck. She thought of the trouble she had been having as the emotions she had tried to cast returned to haunt her. Pushing that matter aside for another time, she flashed the young men her brightest grin. "But the joy stays fresh, too."

"Maybe." Blackie did not look convinced.

"Are you planning to continue your research?" she asked. "To find more uses for the original experiment?"

Blackie regarded her for a moment. Then he took a piece of paper, wrote on it, and handed it to her. On it, he had written:

This is a sample of my handwriting.

Rachel read it and then nodded, puzzled.

"Take a look at this." Blackie drew a folded piece of paper from his pocket and handed it to her. Rachel unfolded it.

Blackie watched her. "Found that when I woke up in the lab without my memory. First thing I remember seeing."

The note on the folded paper was written in Blackie's handwriting. It read:

I, Blackie Moth, attest that my memory was removed with my permission. Furthermore, I charge myself not to investigate the reason it was taken or to continue my current line of research.

Some things are too dangerous to know.

Coracinus Nefarious Moth

CHAPTER THREE:

YE SHALL KNOW THE TRUTH

"YOUR MIDDLE NAME IS *NEFARIOUS*?" GAIUS ASKED AFTER RACHEL, stunned by the content of Blackie's note, handed it on to him. He looked extremely amused.

Blackie shrugged. "Pop's humor runs dark."

"Nefarious is as nefarious does, eh?" Gaius drawled, his eyes sparkling with humor. "Except when you're Nefarious, regardless."

Blackie snorted dryly, "Think you're the first person to mock my name?"

"I'm not mocking you!" Gaius protested, spreading his hands. "I'm envious. We both have Latin names, but Gaius means 'Boy' or perhaps 'Man of the Earth' and was the name of practically every single Roman ever born, while yours means 'Black Nefarious!' Clearly, I received the short end of that stick."

Blackie's lips twitched slightly, but he stopped short of actually smiling.

"Though I guess you need a distinctive first name to go with Moth," Gaius continued airily. "Isn't just about everyone and his neighbor named Moth in the World of the Wise? Dean Moth. Nurse Moth. Your family. That singer whose son goes to our school, what's his name, Marble Moth? Isabella Tiger Moth and her siblings? That super-tall proctor with the cowboy hat at Roanoke, Coal Moth, and his younger siblings, also named after rocks, except for Ignatius— who was probably originally called Igneous."

"Marigold Merryweather Moth," murmured Rachel, thinking of her classmate, Rowan Vanderdecken, who was a descendant both of Merry-Merry Moth and, as it turned out, of her now-departed ghostly friend, Old Thom.

"Who?" Gaius asked. "Oh, right! That girl who married the

captain of the Flying Dutchman. And there's the one we learned about in Math, Easterly Moth. And we covered so many Moths in True History that I couldn't list 'em if my life depended on it. Truly, I'd die a Mothless death! I'd wager that over nineteen percent of the people we've studied in that class have been named Moth—most of them named after mist or sea foam or some other physical object. What's it with all these Moths?"

"We're the most far-flung family in the World of the Wise," Blackie replied dryly.

"Weird that you are so common, yet I'd never even heard of the Moths before I came to school," said Gaius.

"That's because the Unwary branches of the family have other names," replied Blackie, "like Smith, Wright, and Brown."

"Wha—" Gaius's eyes narrowed suspiciously. "You mean the Smiths are a branch of the Moths?"

"Yup," replied Blackie.

Gaius turned to William, as if he thought the older boy would confirm that Blackie was pulling his leg, but William merely nodded.

"Is Sigfried Smith a Moth?" asked Gaius.

Shaking herself free of the shock of Blackie's note, Rachel murmured, "I'm pretty sure Siggy made up his name."

Gaius drawled, "I understand Smith and Brown. But what is so great about little flying night insects?"

Rachel and the older boys all laughed.

"You've got it backwards," Rachel giggled. "The night insects are named after Moth, because they are his creatures. Lord Moth is the right hand man of Elf King Oberon, along with Puck, Lord Mustardseed, Lady Peaseblossom, and Lady Cobweb."

"Ooooh," Gaius's eyes grew wider. "From Shakespeare."

All her dissembling training failed to keep Rachel from laughing in her boyfriend's face. "To the degree that King Henry the Fifth and Richard the Third are 'from Shakespeare', yes."

"Moth is a real person?" asked Gaius.

"He's a real elf," Rachel nodded.

"My mother was one of the elven Moths, a great-granddaughter of the original Lord Moth," said William. "My father met her at Blackie's father's wedding, when the Old Branch of the family showed up."

Now it was Rachel's turn to go wide-eyed. "You mean, showed up… from Under Hill?"

William nodded calmly.

"Blimey," Rachel whispered softly. No wonder he had pointed ears: William's mother had been a fey creature. "Does she live here in Detroit?"

"The mortal world is a difficult place for those accustomed to faerie," William replied without any change of expression. "She returned to her homeland soon after I was born."

"I'm s-so sorry."

"It's something William and Vlad and I all rather have in common," Gaius quipped merrily, though a shadow haunted his eyes, "being motherless."

"Even if William has merely misplaced his," Blackie observed dryly.

William spread his arms, unruffled. "I will try to do better next time."

Gaius handed the note back to Rachel, who read the words again. Their full meaning struck her. Her hand, holding the note, began trembling with wrath.

"This is total rubbish!" Her voice snapped with righteous fury. "Nothing can be too dangerous to know! If it were, how could I know everything?"

Blackie asked, "Who wants to know *everything*?"

"I do," raged Rachel, waving the note about.

"No value to that," opined Blackie. "No one needs to know the total number of eyelashes on all the fruit-flies in the Amazon."

Rachel blinked. "I'm not sure fruit-flies have eyelashes."

"Not my point," Blackie took his note back and folded it. "And you know it."

Rachel turned away, seething. As she gritted her teeth, she remembered something—an event that had never occurred. She had been standing in the Memorial Gardens gazing down at the Comfort Lion, the house cat-sized lion that was the familiar of her roommate Kitten Fabian—That part had happened. Then, in her recollection, the little tawny beast gazed up at her with his intense golden eyes and said, *"Ye shall know the truth and the truth shall set you free."*

That last part had never happened. But she remembered it. A shiver ran up Rachel's spine. *How could that be?*

Spinning around, she addressed the three young men. "I have a question for you scientific gentlemen. What's the difference between knowing *everything* and knowing the *truth?*"

All three looked intrigued.

"That is interesting!" Gaius leaned against the wall and rested his jaw on the palm of his hand. "Up until now, I had thought your desire to know everything was an excellent goal. But Blackie rather does have a point about fruit flies and their eyelashes—or lack thereof. At the very least, knowing about Amazonian insect eyelash numbers definitely sounds rather less important than knowing the *truth.*"

"Knowin' the truth tells you which falsehoods to avoid," stated Blackie. "Truth is power. Know the truth about an enemy, the whole truth, and you can destroy him, leavin' no clues."

Rachel's eyes grew big as Blackie spoke. Talking to him was almost as disorienting as talking to Sigfried, only Siggy always looked delighted whenever he advocated violence. Blackie looked deadly serious. She sneaked a glance at Gaius, but he was merely nodding his head.

"I must disagree with our friends," William said dryly. "I believe that knowledge is valuable for its own sake. What you do with the knowledge is an entirely different matter."

"Fair enough," agreed Gaius.

William added, "How you use your information is a measure of your intelligence. A man of sufficient brilliance can make use of anything—even the number of eyelashes on Amazonian fruit flies." He paused, considering. "Well, maybe not that, but... most things."

"I'm sure William could think of a use, even for that," grinned Gaius.

Gaius now stood beside William, his shoulders resting on the wall, his back straight, just like his older friend. The two young men, one short, one tall, standing side-by-side in identical poses, looked so cute that Rachel had to struggle not to sigh wistfully.

Blackie grunted, unconvinced. "Even if you could know everything, Cousin Rachel, you wouldn't have any use for all that knowledge."

"I jolly well would!" Rachel shot back. "I would put it in a library. My dead Elf friend predicted that I might someday build something called the Library of All Worlds—where information from many worlds could be collected."

Briefly, Rachel described the idea that her Elf had suggested for a cross-world library. All three young men gave her their undivided attention. She spoke to them in a calm, business-like manner, cool and collected, but, inside, her heart soared. It made her feel so grown up—being here, away from school, and speaking so seriously with these older boys.

"So that is the idea, though I have no idea where to put the library itself," she finished, "but I guess that will sort itself out in time. Maybe, since Gaius wants to help me, we could ask Vlad to house it in Bavaria."

"Might work," said William with a smile. "Or you could put it here at O.I."

"Maybe branches in both places?" suggested Gaius.

"Don't really matter, till the library exists," said Blackie without much interest.

The animation that had appeared in his face while she was describing the Library of All Worlds had vanished, and he was back to his cold, uninterested new self. Rachel sighed and gazed out at the laboratory. Frowning, she recalled the last time she had seen Blackie.

It was her family's annual Yule party, nearly three years ago, the year that she was ten. The event had been her first after the death of her beloved grandfather, and since all her favorite Yule traditions had, up until then, involved the late duke, she had felt quite lost. The noise and cheer had suddenly become too much for her, and she fled out the back door of the manor and into the yew maze.

The maze at Gryphon Park was larger on the inside than the outside might strictly allow, but because she could see it from her bedroom window, she knew every twist and turn. She had sat on a bench near the center and watched the sun grow red in the western sky. When it dropped beneath the level of the hedge, she rose to leave.

Ahead, she heard footsteps. Blackie came strolling around a corner, humming to himself and carrying a piece of mistletoe dangling from a stick. When he saw her, he dangled the mistletoe above her head. As she squeaked in surprise, he leaned down and given her a friendly kiss on the cheek.

"Taking this home to amuse my gal," he explained.

"You have a young lady?" Rachel exclaimed with childish delight.

"Sure do. Look what I got her," he replied, his Americanisms, such as 'sure do' and 'got' with no 'have' before it, sounding exotic to her young ear.

Reaching into his pocket, Blackie pulled out a small black velvet box. Then, he squatted down and popped it open. Inside twinkled a diamond ring. Rachel's eyes bulged until they were as large as saucers.

"Are you planning to propose?"

"Sure am." Blackie's eyes twinkled as brightly as the gem on the ring.

Without another word, he stood up, snapped the box shut, and stuck it back in his pocket. The two of them walked back to the manor together.

Back in the present, Rachel glanced surreptitiously at her second cousin. Where was that twinkle now? And what had happened to that ring? Had the young lady accepted? And if so, had she left him when he lost his memory? Or had he forgotten her?

The whole thing left her feeling sick to her stomach. She wanted to rush off and help him, but there was nowhere to rush to, no target at which she could direct her wrath—other than the Raven, and that was no good. If only she knew whom to hate.

She glanced back and forth between the three young men. "Rather bizarre, isn't it, that all three of you have lost your memories."

"All three of us?" asked Blackie, looking from Gaius to William

"You have forgotten your recent life, Blackie. William and Gaius have forgotten the life they had before they came to our world."

"Quite true," Gaius nodded, "and I admit I'm now obsessed with my past. The vague hints I have gleaned from the vision of your friend the princess and from the comments of the fetch girl that inhabits Magdalene Chase's china doll have been tremendously tantalizing. 'The Destroyer of Star Yard'? 'The Doom of the Galactic Confederacy'? What deadly mistake did I made that earned me those titles? It is rather frustrating not to have some way to discover more."

"The two cases are not equivalent," Blackie crossed his arms. "Locke and Valiant have forgotten details they do not need in order to carry on the life they're living now. I, on the other hand, cannot recall stuff I knew two years ago. I can't even remember who has a claim on my affections, folks such as yourself. The effect on my life is catastrophic."

"I admit to some scientific curiosity on the subject of my previous life," William said thoughtfully. "But I am not convinced that the matter is significant. What does it mean that 'I' was someone else? In what manner am I the same person? A great deal of what I call *myself* is my thoughts, my memory, my relationships, what I know, what I chose to do. How much of this was the same before? How much changed? Was that previous person the same 'me' that I currently think of myself to be? Or was it merely a different individual with whom I share some common but unidentified qualities. Talents, perhaps?"

"But... aren't you burning to know?" asked Gaius. "Who you were, I mean?"

"That depends," William responded evenly. "Can my memories be returned? Does any of my old property still belong to me? If the answer to such questions is no, what good would such information do me?"

"I guess there's also the question of: Do we really want to know?" murmured Gaius.

"Do you mean..." Rachel glanced from one to another, "what if you used to be beastly? What if you don't like who you once were?"

All three young men fell silent.

After a time, Gaius tapped his foot impatiently against the wall he was leaning against. "I want to know, but, Rachel, you seemed to imply... I don't know how much I can say... that even just knowing could bring danger."

"I did, didn't I?" Rachel bit her lip, thinking of how it had nearly damaged the whole world when her classmate Sakura Suzuki had recalled her previous life. "Yes. My father told me that just knowing too much about Outside can cause harm. And then... well, there's what happened to Blackie."

"Why didn't the Guardian just remove the specific memories regarding what you had discovered?" asked Gaius.

"No idea," stated Blackie.

"That's the sixty-four million dollar question, isn't it?" mused William.

"I'm not sure I believe what this says," Blackie shook the folded note. "But I know myself. So I suspect I believed it when I wrote it."

"What do you deduce from that?" asked William curiously. He pushed off the wall and stood up.

Blackie shrugged his shoulders and then rolled them, stretching. "That I found out something that someone — probably the Guardian — convinced me would cause harm to people who mattered to me. So, I agreed to give up my memory — for their sake."

That was interesting. She had also offered to give up her memories to save the world. Why had the Raven rejected her offer and yet taken Blackie's memories?

Rachel gazed up at Blackie's impassive face. "It nearly happened to me, too, you know. I... can't talk about it. But... I offered."

Blackie met her gaze. This time, he did not seem blank-faced and indifferent. A kinship that had nothing to do with being second cousins bridged the distance between them. They nodded at each other.

Suddenly, William and Blackie turned their heads simultaneously, as if listening to a voice Rachel could not hear.

William nodded and said, "Understood. We'll be right there."

"Some folks waitin' to see you," grunted Blackie.

• • •

Rachel thought little of Blackie's final words, until they reached a large, wood-paneled chamber. People dressed in suits, mainly men but there were a few women among their number, stood in a semi-circle. One of the young women held a bouquet of lavender and white roses, the perfume of which scented the air. Another held a wooden plaque.

At the front of the group was her father's cousin, Iron Moth. He looked like a harsher version of Blackie carved from unyielding stone. Next to him stood an older version of William, if William were more easy-going, with heavy jowls and a ready smile. Rachel knew from the news glasses that this was Leonard Locke, William's father. These two men were the owners of Ouroboros Industries, the largest company in the World of the Wise, and one of the most powerful corporations in the Unwary world as well.

The men and women gathered in the chamber began to clap. The clapping kept rhythm with the tap of a cane against marble, somewhere down the hallway. As Rachel looked around to see for whom they were clapping, her gaze fell on William. He smiled and took a step back, gesturing for her to go forward. Startled, Rachel looked at the gathering anew.

They were clapping for her.

The athletic young woman with the plaque stepped forward and spoke. "Rachel Griffin, we would like to present you with this token of our appreciation for your bravery in facing the demon that threatened us in Tunis. Our efforts would have been for nothing without yours."

Rachel blushed. Too many people were looking at her, too many expressions to track. A familiar, crushing panic overcame her—the terror that gripped her whenever she became the center of a crowd's attention. It seized her chest like a vise. Frightened, she covered her face with her hands.

The gathering fell quiet.

"Are we sure this is the right girl?" murmured a voice toward the back. "This one doesn't seem very brave."

Behind her, she heard Gaius drawl, "Come on, Locke, you have to give. I have the cutest girlfriend ever."

"While a man must always defend his own lady," William's voice came back dryly, "you have a persuasive argument for your side."

That made Rachel blush even more, but it also made her smile.

The young woman in the business suit holding the wooden plaque tried again. "Miss Rachel Griffin...."

From behind Rachel, another voice cut across the chamber, old and dry but powerful, a voice Rachel had not heard in several years.

"That's *The Lady* Rachel Griffin to you!"

Rachel spun around, her hands still in front of her eyes. She lowered them quickly.

Great-Aunt Nimue, the sister of her beloved grandfather, stood in the doorway, her withered hand resting on the silver jackal-head of her cane. She was a tall and stately woman dressed in black and purple. White streaks marked her once-midnight hair, which came to a sharp widow's peak in the middle of her high forehead. She was nearly two hundred years old, having outlived her older brother, her younger brother, and her husband, the great American industrialist, Steel Moth—the latter two having both lost their lives during the Battle of Detroit. Her eyes were deep and keen, her expression imperious and evaluating, as she took in the shyness of her diminutive great-niece.

"Mother." Iron Moth inclined his head.

"Grandmama," acknowledged Blackie, with a tip of his hat.

Rachel raised her chin and curtsied. "Great-Aunt Nimue!"

"Child," Lady Nimue Griffin Moth walked slowly, leaning on the cane, "stand up straight. Don't hunch. If someone speaks to you, face them courteously. We are not ostriches."

Rachel straightened her posture even more.

"Better." Lady Nimue's keen gaze took in Gaius. She gestured at him with her cane. "Who's this?"

"That's my boyfriend." The words were out of Rachel's mouth before she realized that she might have chosen wiser ones.

Great-Aunt Nimue's eyebrows leapt upward. Her gaze raked over Rachel's tiny form. "You hardly look past eleven, though I know you must be older than that, since you were ten last time I saw you, at my brother's funeral. Surely, you cannot yet be eighteen?"

"No, Ma'am! I am only thirteen."

"Have things changed so much back home in England that they are now presenting young women at the tender age of thirteen?"

Rachel felt the blood coursing through her face. "No, Ma'am."

"Then this cannot be your boyfriend," Great-Aunt Nimue drew herself up, "for no Griffin would be so gauche as to form an attachment before her coming out party!"

Lady Nimue Griffin Moth's voice snapped crisply, her imposing presence commanding the entire chamber, but there was humor in her eyes. Rachel had the distinct impression that her great-aunt was more pleased with her great-niece than otherwise.

Pressing her lips together, Rachel wisely said nothing.

"Miss... Lady Rachel," the young woman tried yet again, "Will you accept your commendation?"

Encouraged by the presence of her great-aunt, Rachel bravely stepped forward and accepted the plaque. Upon it was engraved her name and *for services rendered beyond the call of duty.* Another young woman gave her the fragrant bouquet of white and lavender roses.

"Thank you." Rachel curtsied again.

Iron Moth regarded her seriously. "We regret that we cannot make this award public, Rachel. Our elite Rapid Response Team—" he gestured to the young, athletic people surrounding Mr. Locke and himself, "—are a company secret, and our presence in Tunisia was known to only a few. Our gratitude is no less for its lack of public display."

"Oh, no! This is ever so nice!" squeaked Rachel, who had no wish to be made much of in public. This crowd was more than big enough already.

"How are Devon and Falconridge?" Great-Aunt Nimue inquired, referring as always to Rachel's father and brother by their titles rather than their given names.

"Very well, thank you."

"And Laurel and Amber?"

"Sandra," Rachel prompted. Great-Aunt Nimue always misremembered the name of her eldest grand-niece.

"I won't ask after your mother," Great-Aunt Nimue announced, tapping the marble floor twice with her cane. "I abhor that woman."

"You disapprove of your brother's son marrying an Unwary? An Asian? Or is it that she was a member of the middle class?" Gaius asked boldly.

Lady Nimue turned and fixed him with her hawk-like gaze. "Nonsense, why should I care about her ancestry—so long as she is a superb sorceress and can bear strong children. But twelve centuries of Griffin men have been named after the great sorcerers of the past, particularly after those who served the Pendragon, and she names the heir of the dukedom after a *rock*!"

"Ah, yes, I see the problem." Gaius's eyes danced with mirth. Rachel knew her brother Peter was not among Gaius's favorite people.

"Cheeky young man!" Great-Aunt Nimue glared down at him. Rachel spoke up for her boyfriend. "Gaius is descended from one of the Pendragon's knights!"

"Is he?" Great-Aunt Nimue looked Gaius up and down. From the glint in her eye, Rachel guessed that the old woman admired Gaius's spunk. "Well, he might be a suitable match for a Griffin... if he could be bothered to grow a bit taller. I don't approve of short men."

"I hardly think our height is our fault," Gaius replied, clearly struggling not to laugh.

"Perhaps not," replied Great-Aunt Nimue, "but I find it suspicious."

CHAPTER FOUR:

HE BLINDED HER WITH SCIENCE!

"YOU COULD HAVE WARNED ME," RACHEL SAID SOFTLY TO GAIUS, AS they followed William deeper into the complex, "that I was about to become the center of attention."

"I had no idea," Gaius replied. "That wasn't why I brought you here."

"Oh! Why did you bring me?"

He grinned at her, an adorable grin. "You'll see. As soon as we're done with this last thing Mr. Moth and Mr. Locke wanted William to show us."

"Just a warning." William paused, as they approached a hallway that passed through a series of sliding double doors. They had parted with Blackie when they passed the lab where he was currently working. "Where we are going next, none of your magic will work."

Rachel and Gaius glanced at each other, curious.

William led them through half a dozen sliding doors. Each set of doors required a numeric code to be punched in, a card to be placed into a slot, a palm to be pressed against a plate, and an incantation to be chanted. Rachel was not sure which objects were alchemical talismans and which were mundane technology. Normally, magic and tech did not work together, but Ouroboros Industries was the exception to many rules.

The first set of sliding doors had been made of oak. On the far side, the dark maroon rug had a crimson thread running through it. Here and there, the thread had been pulled up and lay atop the rug in a tangled knot.

"Clever use of a tangled red thread," chuckled Gaius.

"And tangled red thread stops...?" William quizzed his younger friend.

Gaius tipped back his head, trying to recall his warding classes.

"Far Eastern fey and some tricksters?"

"And those?" William pointed to the daisy chains hanging along the walls.

"Um... they stop pixies, sprites, and fairies?" guessed Gaius. William gave a nod of approval. "Very good."

The next set of sliding doors was made of a pinkish-white crystal. William knocked on the hard stone. "Any idea what this one is?"

Rachel and Gaius spoke together. "Salt." William inclined an eyebrow. "Both of you! I admit, I am impressed."

"It looks like the salt licks we use for the cows on my father's farm," said Gaius.

"Salt licks," said Rachel simultaneously, adding, "We breed horses at Gryphon Park."

"Salt licks?" William's eyebrow arched ever-so-slightly upward.

"One learns something every day. Or, if the stars are in one's favor, one learns many things."

Rachel and Gaius grinned at each other in a moment of farmerly camaraderie.

On the far side of the salt doors, eyes had been painted on the walls and carved into the wainscoting. Bells dangled from the ceiling, ringing as they walked by. A horseshoe hung over the next door, which was of cedar; bunches of garlic hung over the ash door beyond.

William quizzed them on the eyes and bells, as well as on the fresh-baked bread in the following section.

"Magical beasts. They will stop to eat it. Well, if it is fresh enough," quipped Gaius, answering William's final question.

"Lavender's good for warding off magical beasts, too," murmured Rachel, gazing hungrily at the bread. Then she felt a bit foolish. Feeling tempted by magical creature bait hardly redounded to her greater glory.

"Lavender?" asked both the boys.

Rachel nodded. "No animals eat it, nor bugs either. The plant, that is. Bees and butterflies eat the flowers, of course. And unicorns, but they are hardly a problem. That's why lavender is the prime ingredient in Bogey Away."

"Bogey Away?" They both blinked at her.

Rachel shrugged. "Must be a Devonshire thing."

"Does it work?" William asked curiously. "I would be interested in examining a sample."

The next door was iron. The floor on the far side was sprinkled with round, black seeds.

"Peony seeds!" Rachel cried with delight, grabbing her boyfriend's arm. "Just like the bag you gave me on Halloween! When we were in Tunisia, we used them to stop the ravaging army of children's skeletons."

"Did you?" Gaius grinned proudly. "Glad to hear it."

"Army of skeletal children?" Locke blinked. "I hadn't heard about that."

Rachel's expression faltered. "Demons are ugly things."

William's face became grim. "Yes, they are."

Leaving the hallway, they walked through a room where powdered chalk and sawdust drifted down from the ceiling, crunching under their shoes. The scent of juniper was quite pleasant. Rachel smiled as she shook her head, shedding sweet-smelling sawdust from her hair.

In the next room, they were told to strip down and put on special jumpsuits, leaving their clothes and belongings behind. Rachel was directed to a ladies' room. The jumpsuit she changed into was far too big for her. She rolled up the sleeves and pants cuffs. Nonetheless, both boys had to struggle not to grin when she emerged. Rachel kept her face still, but inside she was tickled.

"Ordinarily, there is something we must drink," explained William. "But it has been decided not to feed unapproved liquids to Agent Griffin's daughter."

"Good grief! That's thorough!" whistled Gaius. "What does the liquid do?"

"Flushes out most alchemical elixirs," replied William. "Those who are hired to work here are required to undergo purification rituals, as well. These involve purges and having all your body hair shaved off, but it was decided to make a special exception about that, too."

"All of it?" Gaius pulled his legs together and winced.

"Leg hair. Back hair. Nose hair. The whole works," Locke replied evenly.

Gaius made a face and grabbed his nose. Rachel giggled, but her fingers wove their way through her black, shoulder-length locks, grasping her flyaway tresses protectively.

William walked up to the next door, a plate of steel, placed his palm and eye against some kind of device, and sang an incantation. "Here we go."

The door slid open, revealing a very small room. They walked into it, and William hit one of many round buttons on the wall. The door closed. A strange sensation of motion made Rachel's stomach lurch, much like the elevator that had taken her family to the top of the Empire State Building. Perhaps mundane lifting talismans, or whatever it was that made such devices run, normally produced such a sensation.

When the weird sensation stopped, William went to the far side of the small room and put his hand against another device. He also entered a code, slid his badge through a slot, pressed a series of arcane symbols, and sang an incantation.

"Whoa!" Gaius blinked. "This is... some security."

William did not smile. "When you see what is inside, you will understand."

The door opened into a semi-circular room, the curved walls of which were plated with glass. It overlooked an enormous chamber that extended both above and below this small command post. High above, in the ceiling of the outer chamber, was a giant iris, fifty-foot in diameter. Beneath, on the floor of the vast chamber, stood a huge pentagram of a hardened umber-colored substance about a hundred forty feet across. The solid pentagram was ten or fifteen feet high.

Gaius walked forward and pressed his forehead and palms against the glass.

"Ah. I see," he murmured.

Rachel moved forward until she could see, too. Inside the umber substance, caught like flies in amber, were Mortimer Egg, Serena O'Malley, and a giant bull with the face of a man—the demon Morax.

"Better not to touch the glass," warned William, "just to be sure."

Gaius took a swift step backward and wiped his hands on his jumpsuit.

Rachel came up beside him, peering down at the captive monstrosities. Gaius slipped a hand into hers. Horrifying as was the vista below, it could not stop the tiny bursts of joy that spread through her at his touch.

"So this is Blackie's work?" Rachel gestured at the window. "This material that is trapping the demons?"

William nodded. "We owe him a great deal. Without his work, there would be nothing we could do against the demons."

Rachel stared out at the three motionless forms. She vividly recalled the odor and the heat of the great furnace in Tunisia into which Morax's followers had wanted to toss her. In her memory's ear, she heard the echo of the clack of the bones of the walking childskeletons.

"How strange that demons exist." Rachel shuddered. "Creatures whose motives are to cause as much harm as possible. How could anything come to be in such a state?"

"They are more horrible than any monster we study in school," Gaius said gravely. "Dragons just want food and gold. Occasionally, a really nasty one wants maidens. Same thing with kraken and minotaurs. Even that ogre who killed the young man was defending its territory. But all those things are desires we understand. These things..." he gestured toward the pentagram. "Causing traffic accidents for fun? Sacrificing children in front of their parents? The word 'monster' doesn't even *begin* to cover it."

"They are vile beyond our ability to comprehend," William stated.

Rachel chewed on her lip as she stared at the creatures of pure malice. Gaius also seemed subdued.

"Such a beastly fate! To be trapped indefinitely!" she cried finally. "What about the good half of Serena O'Malley? Is there a way to free her, so Juma can have his mum back?"

"Not yet," William shook his head.

Mortimer Egg as well. We have tried processes that should have reversed the possession, but nothing has worked."

"What would happen to Egg, if you separated him from Azrael?" asked Gaius.

William shrugged. "We believe Egg was possessed against his will because he was in the wrong place at the wrong time. If he could be freed, he could go back to his life, such as it is."

"His wife is dead," said Gaius.

"But his son is alive," said Rachel. "Mortimer Junior must want his real father back."

"Perhaps," acknowledged William, "but we don't know how to accomplish it. We have consulted the best possession experts among the Wise—from Alaska, Bavaria, Ultima Thule, the Congo, Prester John's Kingdom, Machu Picchu, Japan, the Republic of Cathay, even Mainland China. We didn't give them all the details, of course. But, so far, they have been unable to help."

Rachel glanced sideways at Gaius, who squeezed her hand comfortingly. He stepped closer and nuzzled her cheek affectionately.

When his mouth came near her ear, he whispered, "Do you think you should tell them about what happened in Transylvania? The first time, I mean? How you renewed that spell of your Grandfather's that bound the demon into Egg? They probably won't be able to undo General Griffin's binding unless they first know about it."

Rachel murmured back, "I want to tell my father first."

"Why didn't you tell him when you saw him at Sandra's?"

"He... proved elusive." She was pleased that her voice had only the slightest wobble.

Gaius nodded solemnly. Glanced out the window again, he shivered and turned away.

"Important safety tip," he murmured in her ear. "Don't get possessed by a demon."

• • •

"And now, finally... my surprise," Gaius announced, as Rachel emerged from the ladies' room. She was back in her own clothing

"We believe she is possessed. We believe Egg is possessed.

and carrying her plaque and roses. "It comes in two parts. The first part stars William."

"Oh?" Rachel looked up at the older boy curiously.

"It will be my pleasure," William replied with a smile, bowing.

He led them to another elevator and then upward to the ninth floor, where they entered a meeting room. It had a large whiteboard on one wall and bright metal and plastic chairs. Rachel, who had hardly ever seen plastic, found them both odd and cheery—as if she had walked into a storybook about the Unwary. Gaius ushered her to a seat that had a notepad and pen resting on the table in front of it. Then he sat off to the side, one leg crossed over the other, listening.

"Miss Griffin," William Locke bowed, "I've heard that you could use a lesson in physics. I have the honor of being your teacher today."

"A lesson in..." Rachel glanced at her boyfriend.

Grinning, Gaius held his left arm straight and then pushed down on it with the finger of his right hand. He had made the same gesture a month and a half ago, while sitting in the fog-shrouded belfry discussing the jumbo jet that had nearly crashed into Roanoke Hall.

"Wait!" Rachel caught on. "Is this about Sigfried and me flying into the aeroplane?"

Locke stepped up to the blackboard and expounded upon the basics of force, acceleration, mass, and velocity. Much of this Rachel had figured out intuitively, but he drew together concepts she had not consciously connected. As his bright green pen squeaked over the white board, Rachel felt as if a door were opening in her mind, beyond which lay a new world.

William was a superb teacher. He seemed to answer her questions as soon as they occurred to her, before she could even voice them. She could not tell if this was magic, or if he was merely a natural teacher who understood his subject matter so well that he could anticipate any inquiry. She listened, utterly enthralled, her perfect memory tracking everything: her mind leapt ahead and drew conclusions; instantly made comparisons to earlier explanations; and prompted her with questions, which she immediately voiced—unless he was already answering them. As he spoke, she jotted down vector drawings for broom motions and billiard balls on the paper Gaius had given her for taking notes. She waited, eyes wide, eager to learn more.

After explaining the basics of physics, William changed the subject to sorcery. He spoke, in particular, about the *turlu* cantrip—the one that stopped a moving object in mid-air. He explained that some spells require a particular state of mind for proper casting. It helped to have a clear idea of the desired effect. Visualizing this effect could improve the outcome. It could help even more, if one understood the basic science of the effect.

"Just because sorcerers circumvent physical laws," William explained, "does not mean those laws are not there. Working with these laws can lead to a much more effective result."

The pure physics fascinated Rachel—but when he reached the part about magic, he had her complete attention. It was as if everything wonderful in the universe had converged in one place. She could memorize facts instantly, but mastering equations and complex scientific principles required significant mental effort.

Hours passed. Even Gaius started to look a bit distracted, but Locke kept going. Finally, Rachel reached a point where even she could not consciously absorb any more. She needed time to process. She was so pleased with Gaius for arranging this surprise. If she had not already loved him, she would have fallen in love with him then and there.

William put down his marker. "That is all for today. You may always come back and discuss this again, Miss Griffin."

Rachel rubbed her eyes and stretched. "Thank you very much!"

"Do not mention it. My pleasure."

"Now," Gaius jumped to his feet, "it's finally time for what I wanted to show you."

• • •

William led them to a room with a screen on the wall and a couple of comfortable couches. There was also a handsome desk. Having grown up surrounded by antiques, Rachel judged the desk to be mint condition Sixteen Hundreds, possibly from one of the French kings.

"What now?" asked Rachel.

"We're going to watch a little TV", Gaius drawled airily.

"A television?" Rachel said curiously. "I thought they looked like boxes. That looks like a sideways talking glass. Are you making them to look like glasses now?"

"Yes." Gaius looked really amused. "Yes, we are."

William winked at Rachel and left the room, shutting the door behind him.

Gaius sat on the couch and patted the seat next to him. He manipulated the controls and turned on the television. "The TV show's called *Automan*."

Rachel sat beside him and watched with great interest, examining everything.

The show was rather odd. The two main characters rode around in mundane vehicles. One character glowed blue and was immune to inertia, and the other was a normal policeman. Whenever the vehicles went from full speed to an instant stop, the first man was unaffected, but the second man was not. Seeing the policeman shoot forward and slam against the dashboard, while the other man sat perfectly helped illustrate the physics William had been describing.

"Okay," Gaius turned to her when the episode ended. Rachel was still in a daze, as if she had been part of the story and now had to wake up and remember who she really was. "Now, we're going to discuss the *turlu* cantrip."

She was instantly alert. "Oh, goody!"

"There are two ways that this cantrip can function. In one, the force in X direction might be applied in the opposite direction with no 'buffer.' If you're going slow, that's not too bad. But if you're going really, really fast, you do not want to be decelerated to zero instantly by an opposite force. You might smoosh or get badly injured.

"So there is a second way to use the cantrip. The force in X direction is not canceled. Instead, it is subtracted. This causes an instantaneous removal of inertia, like the man who glowed blue in the show we just watched. It causes the person no discomfort whatsoever. If you cast the spell this way, it's much harder. Often you get a much smaller effect or complete failure of the spell. So, normally, you could not use it against anything big or fast.

"Buuuuut, and here is the cool part that William and O.I. discovered," Gaius continued smoothly. "If you understand the math for the vectors involved, you can imagine the resulting inertia being subtracted from your target and *added somewhere else*.

"With some practice, you can not only get bigger objects to stop, you can also whomp other objects with the force you just removed. And the best part is: It's not an exact science. If you know the math perfectly, you get an amazing result. But you can still have a really brilliant result by imagining it without the actual equations."

"You mean, if I were good at this, I could have, say, taken momentum from the jumbo jet and used it to knock over trees, or move boulders, or something like that?"

"Exactly."

"Wow. That's smashing!"

"Or rather, not smashing—if we are lucky," joked Gaius.

They both laughed.

Rachel had already desired to master the *turlu* cantrip. But now, she was even more motivated. She felt as if she were falling in love with physics. She soaked up everything Gaius told her, listening and absorbing, but saying very little. The class with William and the television show had given her so much to think about that she felt dazed.

She felt doubly dazed when she remembered how early it had been, Detroit time, when she woke up in London, many, many hours ago. Giddy with fatigue, she leaned over and kissed Gaius. He kissed her back.

It was her first real kiss. It did not last longer than usual, but it was a fiercer kiss with touch of passion, not the light pecks they had previously shared. When she drew away, Gaius looked a little dreamy.

"I'd like to go home," she murmured, clutching her wooden plaque and her roses.

"Of course," Gaius said. He stood and spoke to no one in particular, "Locke, I could use transit back to school."

William Locke appeared in a flash of light. A cup of coffee steamed in his hand. He smiled at her. The odor of the rich brew made Rachel's stomach grumble. He led them outside into the cold and dark. Rachel slipped back into her red coat. They walked back along the well-lit path to the street beyond the perimeter of the wards protecting Ouroboros Industries.

"You could jump to us, when Gaius called you from the room with the telly, but you couldn't jump us home from there?" asked Rachel.

Locke smiled and nodded, "Large portions of the O.I. campus are warded. We can't have strangers jumping into our restricted areas."

The older boy took Rachel's hand and Gaius's. Another flash of light, and they were back at the docks in the darkness and the falling snow. Gaius and William put their black robes over their clothing, and the three of them walked back to school together. Rachel held Gaius's hand. She was in a daze, but not to such a degree that she forgot to curtsy to Locke and thank him.

"My pleasure, Miss Griffin." He nodded and departed.

Gaius walked her back to Dare Hall. When they reached it, he leaned forward solicitously. "Are you okay?"

Rachel nodded and smiled; however, her eyes were not entirely focused. Her thoughts raced, caught up in force and vectors. She wound her arms around his neck and looked up at him through half-closed lashes.

Without thinking, she whispered, "If I hadn't loved you already, Gaius Valiant, I would have fallen in love with you today."

He nuzzled her cheek, whispering, "Love you, too."

He kissed her a bit longer than normal. Finally, he pulled away and grinned at her. "Okay, I have returned you to your dorm. Now it's up to you to not walk into things, Miss Distracted."

He gave her a nigh bone-cracking hug and then departed. Rachel tripped up the stair to her room. No one was there, so she went next door to Joy O'Keefe's room. Grabbing the other girl, Rachel danced around with her, chanting, "He said he loved me! He said he loved me!"

Joy, a bubbly girl with mousy brown hair and a heart-shaped face, laughed as she danced. "That must be wonderful. I wish I wasn't crazy for some jerk who cares nothing for me. On the other hand, I am really glad Zoë doesn't have a boyfriend either. I've been

thinking of casting spells so she lives out her life as a crazy cat woman. Where is Zoë, anyway?"

"No idea," murmured Rachel.

Still in a daze, she returned to her room and began drawing
charts and diagrams, applying what she had just discovered to what
she instinctively understood about flying and billiards. She fell
asleep mid-chart, dreaming of math and vectors.

Chapter Five:

The Black Bracelet of Dread

THE NEXT MORNING, SHE HURRIEDLY CHANGED THE GARMENTS SHE wore under her robes and stumbled to class, still scribbling equations in her notebook. The morning went by in a blur. At lunch, Joy O'Keefe came by and asked if Rachel had seen Zoë. Rachel shook her head.

Joy pouted. "She went to bed after me and got up before me. That's really weird. Usually, she's a layabout, and I practically have to roll her out of bed to get her to class on time. Do you think she's avoiding me? I can't find the princess either. Neither of them was in Art or Math."

"Sorry, can't help you," Rachel murmured. "Haven't seen them."

A tray of food lay before her, but Rachel ignored it, concentrating on understanding the math she had been shown the previous day. A few minutes later, she overheard Sigfried Smith talking to his familiar, Lucky the Dragon. Sigfried was tall and brawny for his fourteen years. He was also superhumanly handsome with golden curls. Lucky was a red and gold *lung*, a Chinese water dragon, long and sinewy and covered with the softest fur. He did not have wings, but he could snake through the air, undulating like a sideways sine wave.

"Lucky," Siggy announced loudly, "someone has broken the brain of one of the members of my harem of cute sorceresses in schoolgirl uniforms. See? Girls are very delicate. They get broken up over anything. I would ask her what's bugging her, but the answer would probably involve emotions, or girly stuff. I know! I will ask a girl!"

Sigfried turned to his girlfriend, Valerie Hunt, who had just arrived with her tray and was taking the seat beside him. She had short golden-blond hair and a charmingly square jawline. A camera, hanging from a red strap, bounced against her side.

"Psst. Valerie. Have you noticed Miss Griffin acting oddly lately? Oddlier? More odd than normal odd, I mean?"

"Um..." said Valerie.

"Perhaps," he continued sagely, "someone with more tact than Sigfried Foot-in-Mouth-up-to-the-Kneecap Smith should investigate, or even talk to her, to find out what's what."

"What do you think it is?" asked Valerie.

Sigfried shrugged. "I assume it's child-skeleton shock, or nearly-being-sacrificed-to-Kronos shock, or maybe it's murder-of-elf-friend-from-other-dimension shock, or almost-killed-by-Headless-Horseman shock, or barely-avoided-flying-into-a-jumbo-jet shock, or couldn't-save-Mrs.-Egg shock, perhaps multiple-whole-families-killed-in-front-of-their-children-for-over-a-century shock, or math-tutor-turned-into-an-evil-dragon shock, or... maybe she read something in the sports section that upset her. I notice she's been talking to that proctor, Fuentes, about flying polo. She must really like the sport. Maybe her favorite team lost a big game."

"That's a lot of... shocks," murmured Valerie.

"Or maybe she lost money gambling," said Siggy. "Do the Wise gamble?"

"Not if they are wise Wise," Valerie quipped back. Then, she whispered, "I'll look into it. Subtle like."

Valerie rose, sat down next to Rachel, and proceeded to speak in her normal voice. "Hey, Rachel, you seem distracted or, maybe a better way to put it would be stunned. You don't seem upset, but it's kinda weird anyway. Are you okay? Do you want to talk about it?"

Rachel shoved her notebook toward Valerie and pointed at the diagrams. Without looking up, she murmured, "I'm trying to work out the forces involved with vector and mass when cornering on a broom."

Valerie nodded. Without a word, she rose and returned to her seat next to Sigfried.

"It's math. Stunned by math," Valerie whispered loudly. "I am not sure there's a cure."

• • •

As Rachel was placing her lunch tray on the conveyor belt that brought the dirty dishes downstairs to the dish room, she nearly ran into Princess Nastasia's older brother, Ivan Romanov. The tall blond college student flashed her one of his ready smiles. He had dirty blond hair and eyes of deep brown.

"Message for you, Mini Griffin," he said in his delightful Magical Australian accent. "My sister asked me to let you know that she's been called home. But she'll be back. No worries."

"Oh. That explains why she wasn't in class," Rachel said. Looking back in her memory, she realized that Joy had been right. So caught up had she been in physics that she had not noticed her best friend was missing. She felt chagrined.

"I hope you will find it in your heart to forgive her for her unexpected trip," Ivan joked.

Rachel drew herself up and spoke with a primness that rivaled Nastasia's. "Since I recently went to visit my older sister, I can hardly complain about others spending time with their families." She paused. "Do you know if Zoë went with her?"

"Don't know. Sorry." Ivan shrugged. "It's possible."

Rachel started to walk away, but she doubled back. "By the way, did you ever get a chance to speak to your mother about speaking to my father about marrying my sister Laurel?"

Ivan looked a bit flustered. "Only in passing. Mother doesn't seem to be too against the idea of me marrying beneath my station. I am thinking, though, it might be best if your sister started working for the circus and, perhaps, if she could get disowned by your parents? That way at least my father would be completely for it. He seems set on annoying my mother."

"I'll let her know," Rachel said woodenly.

Beneath his station? It took every ounce of her being to refrain from blurting out, in her most arch and British voice: *Oh? So, we Griffins are good enough for the kingdom of Bavaria—which even the Unwary have heard of—but not for the unknown and nigh-broke kingdom of Magical Australia?*

Still, as she walked away, she could not help imagining a few choice words she might share with the Queen of Magical Australia, were she to be given the chance. The Griffins might not be royalty, but they were of the highest nobility. They could trace their lineage back over two thousand years, longer than any current dynasty, and at least three Griffin daughters had become queens. Magical Australia, on the other hand, was a country of so little importance that even many of the *Wise* had not heard of it. Their currency was pink Monopoly money, and no other country accepted it. They should be so lucky as to gain a Griffin!

• • •

That night was the weekly meeting of the Knights of Walpurgis. Rachel and Sigfried arrived at the gym early. Rachel left her blood-brother with Salome Iscariot, his girlfriend's best friend, and went to sit beside Gaius near the head of the long table. It was a relief to be able to do so without worrying about disapproving looks from Nastasia—so much of a relief that Rachel was rather surprised to realize how burdensome her best friend's disapproval had become.

After the wonderful evening she spent with her boyfriend. If only she was even more eager to spend time with Gaius and William, he and the princess might become friends.

Rachel smiled at the other Knights as they entered. The first person to return her smile was Penny Royal, who had a reputation for being a detective. Rachel had noticed that Dread occasionally spoke with the sharp-eyed young woman during the second half of the Knights' meetings. Rachel found this noteworthy, as Dread almost never spoke to anyone, outside of his own people, other than to answer questions or give instructions. She was quite curious about what the prince and the detective might be saying to each other.

Others were not as friendly. Romulus Starkadder, the Crown Prince of Transylvania, was so aloof that he could not be bothered to acknowledge Rachel's existence with more than the slightest of nods. Many of the Thaumaturgy students, especially those who lived in Drake Hall, were outright hostile. Eunice Chase, a junior at the Upper School who had been the patron of Rachel's rival, Cydney Graves, glared at her in a way that made Rachel feel quite small.

Mark Williams, the young man who had knocked her off her broom during the battle with Dr. Mordeau back in early September, threw her a goofy smile as he took his seat. He did not seem to be a bad fellow, despite Gaius's poor opinion of him. He seemed to become embarrassed whenever Rachel spoke to him; however, maybe because her boyfriend had forced him to apologize to her in front of the whole dining hall.

Michael Cameron came slouching into the meeting and took a seat by himself about halfway up the table. He sneered at her as if she were an idiot, but then she had noticed that he regarded everyone that way. He did not seem to be friends with any other Knights, and he struggled when dueling. She wondered why he kept troubling to come.

Outside of the Knights, he also had few friends. He seemed to be tolerant of Joy's sister Patience, who sat with him at meals. She was obviously smitten with him, but she was so shy that Rachel wondered if he had noticed. Rachel had also spotted him joking around with another boy from Marlowe Hall, possibly his roommate. This other boy looked as if he might be of American Indian heritage. His familiar, an impressive bald eagle, often rode on his shoulder.

Rachel had been watching Michael Cameron for some time. Partly because he was kind of cute in a bad-boy way, but more because she felt grateful that he had volunteered to be Cydney Grave's second when the other girl challenged Rachel to a duel during the first Knights of Walpurgis meeting. He had shown courage, standing up with Cydney when everyone else refused to support the angry girl. Rachel had been impressed.

The entire Cydney Graves incident still made her feel uncomfortable. At first, being hated had taken her by surprise. In retrospect, however, bullies were a staple in many of the novels about schoolgirls that she had read before coming to Roanoke. She should have expected something of the sort. But the outcome of their first encounter still rankled her. What had Salome whispered to Cydney that made the other girl so angry?

After Dr. Mordeau's attack, the students from Drake had been subdued. No doubt they felt humiliated that the evil tutor had taken over their minds. Now they were beginning to show their teeth again. Rachel figured it would only be a matter of time until they recalled their animosity toward her. She was curious as to how she would handle herself this time. She felt more confident than she had two and a half months earlier. It might be exciting to have a rival.

The meeting began at seven o'clock sharp. Vladimir covered the business of the day and then turned things over to William Locke, who solemnly reported upon the death of Tommy Check, the Unwary teenager eaten by the ogre. He warned that this boy been on the far bank of the Hudson and not in the ogre's territory, like the kayakers whom the ogre had eaten two years before. However, the boy had apparently flown a mundane contraption into the ogre's cave, so perhaps the creature believed that this counted as a violation of its domain. William did not know how the drone had led the ogre to the young man or what the next step might be. Rumor had it, however, that Roanoke's Master Warder, Nighthawk, would be visiting the monster to remind it of its obligations. The boy's family believed that he had been mauled by a bear.

Rachel's heart ached with sympathy for the family of the young man. She imagined one of her friends going out for an afternoon by the river and never coming home. The thought brought unexpected tears to her eyes. She blinked them away rapidly, hoping no one had noticed.

When the formal meeting broke up, Rachel joined the other freshmen in Gaius's training class; however, her thoughts kept drifting away from what her boyfriend was saying. She wanted to think about mass and acceleration, not on cantrips and enchantments. She tried to share some of her new insights with Gaius, but he reminded her, gently yet firmly, that this was the time for dueling. There would be plenty of time for physics later.

She tried to follow his advice, but whenever she dragged her mind away from math and equations, her thoughts began revolving around the missing memory of her second cousin. The thought of his lose filled her with righteous indignation. As there was no suitable target for that wrath, however, science shock seemed preferable. Still, she did her best to heed her boyfriend's instructions and practice sorcery.

After Gaius's training session ended, Rachel looked around for a dueling partner. Nearby, Michael Cameron lounged against one of the posts separating the dueling strips, glowering at the world.

Rachel eagerly approached him. Curtsying, she asked if he would practice with her. To her dismay, he responded angrily, as if she were deliberately attempting to humiliate him. It took her a moment to realize that perhaps he *was* embarrassed. It had probably made him look bad when, during her duel with Cydney, she—a freshman who had not yet finished her first full week of school—had blown through the shield created by his *bey-athe* cantrip.

Poor guy. Rachel sighed inwardly. She seemed to have a talent for accidentally discomfiting young men. Maybe she should go embarrass Mark Williams more, too.

She stood, flat-footed, not sure how to recover. Maybe if she pretended she did not understand why he was upset? No, he looked too annoyed for that. Maybe if she lied and claimed that she, too, felt alienated here? After all, many of the Drake Hall folks were not exactly kind to her? Could she present herself as a kindred alienated soul?

"What, so you won't talk to me either?" She scowled back at him, trying this new angle. "I thought at least you conjurers would not be prejudiced against us enchanters. Marlowe Hall doesn't have anything against Dare!" Pausing, she gave him a resentful-at-the-world glare. "Or is it that, being a freshman, I'm not good enough for you to bother with?"

"Take your pick," he said with a shrug.

Turning, he stomped out of the gym.

Rachel's jaw dropped. First Freka Starkadder back in October, now Michael Cameron? Was *everyone* she spoke to at the Knights going to storm out of the meeting?

Before she could recover, she realized with a sinking heart that someone was standing directly behind her. Not just anybody, either. *The very worst possible person.*

Vladimir Von Dread loomed over her. The Prince of Bavaria was unusually tall and built like a young god. His hair was dark with red highlights. A robe of black with a golden swan embroidered on the left breast fell from his broad shoulders. He wore thick black leather dueling gloves and heavy black boots. At his waist hung a fulgurator's wand of ebony and gold tipped with sapphire.

Rachel's insides went icy cold. Had he overheard? Could he tell she was lying? What if she had accidentally violated some protocol he maintained about how students of the various Arts should get along during Knights' meetings? If the answer to any of those questions were yes, she was about to receive a serious dressing-down.

A frisson of terror crawled up her spine. *What if her offense were so terrible that he threw her out of the club?* Feeling like a mutt caught eating the Yule roast, she turned around slowly, fighting the desire to cringe.

Dread's voice rang out across the chamber. "Who has been showing you disfavor, Miss Griffin? Tell me their names, and I shall deal with them immediately."

Eunice Chase, who was standing not very far away, turned red and fidgeted nervously. Rachel, who had been expecting a severe scolding, also began to redden. The prince was coming to her defense? Of course, he did not know she was in the wrong.

She felt startled and ashamed.

"That is extremely kind of you, Vlad," she replied, dearly hoping he would not ask for the names of her imaginary persecutors. "But if I let you fight my battles for me, what will happen when you graduate and are no longer here to defend me?"

"Valiant will be here." Von Dread crossed his arms. "By the time he graduates, I expect you will be one of the greatest sorceresses at the school. Only a fool would cross you then."

Rachel gasped. That was the nicest thing anyone had ever said to her.

"If anyone is cruel to me, Vlad, I will let you know," she replied, trying to walk the tightrope between expressing gratitude and covering her tracks. "But I hardly feel it would be sporting to turn people over to your justice for such a minor crime as being less than friendly."

"Cameron is not the friendliest person," replied Dread, "but he has his uses. I suspect, in time, he will become a useful member of the Knights."

"I'm patient." Rachel glanced after the departed Michael.

As she gazed across the chamber, she pursed her lips. She was not sure she liked the idea of judging people by whether or not they "had their uses." Then her eyes widened in sudden recognition. She had years of practice in dealing with one who saw things in such terms. Even as a little girl, she had understood that this was how Blaise Griffin saw the world, but that her grandfather held himself to the same high standard by which he measured everyone else, judging himself as well by his usefulness.

Turning back, Rachel gave Dread a brisk, business-like nod, such as she might have given her grandfather. His slight nod of acknowledgement in return reminded her so much of her beloved grandfather that it made her heart ache. She bit her lip.

Von Dread dropped to one knee.

Rachel's heart stopped beating and then took off at a mad gallop. Belatedly, she realized that he had knelt to draw closer to her eye level, but that realization came too slowly. She was already breathless and struggling not to lose her composure.

"Miss Griffin," his voice was grave and deep, "I have failed you repeatedly this year. I have not protected you from harm, and, due to this, you have almost been lost. I must apologize for my... incompetence."

If a wild tiger—six hundred and fifty pounds of pure muscle forming twelve feet of precision killing machine—had padded out of the brush and lain down at her feet, accepting food from her hand, Rachel could not have been more astonished.

"More importantly," Dread continued, unaware that he had flipped her world upside-down, "I have been working to make sure I have a network set up to assist you, should I be absent. Please take this." He held out a business card with a long number on it.

Wordlessly, Rachel accepted the card. Her heart was still beating too hard for her to trust herself to speak. She gazed back at him, her eyes huge and dark, nodding.

"Do you know how to operate an Unwary telephone?" he asked.

"The card has a number you can dial from any phone on the planet. I have asked William to assign a group of people at his father's company whose sole responsibility is to assist you, in the case of an emergency. If you are off the school grounds, this may help. Nor is the card made of ordinary paper. It has been enchanted to resist damage by the elements. If you are in extreme danger, crush the card. Help should arrive within moments."

She nodded, still not trusting herself to speak. Thus, she was unable to answer his question about the use of a mundane telephone. In truth, she did not have the slightest clue. Perhaps Gaius would teach her.

Chancing a brief glance around the chamber, she quickly returned her gaze to Dread and then recalled what her eyes had just captured. From the looks of surprise—and, among the older girls, pure envy—on the faces of the other Knights, she gathered that they were as shocked by the prince's behavior as she was. Even Romulus Starkadder, who was usually so politely distant, looked avidly attentive. Rachel examined her memory of the room searching for her boyfriend, curious as to his reaction. To her disappointment, Gaius was in the midst of a duel and was not paying attention.

Rachel turned her attention back to the kneeling prince, uncertain how to respond.

Drawing close to Dread, she finally found her voice. "Thank you." She paused and then asked softly, "Since you have given me permission to call you Vlad, c-couldn't you call me Rachel?"

"I... think I should continue calling you Miss Griffin for now. Perhaps things will change in the near future." He looked into her face carefully.

Rachel nodded solemnly. She wondered if she should tell him that her mother had agreed to speak to her father on behalf of Vlad's suit to marry Sandra.

Vladimir reached forward and took her hand. Rachel stopped breathing. With strong, firm fingers, he solemnly slipped a slender black bracelet onto her left wrist. It was so much like a prince slipping a wedding ring onto a maiden's finger that Rachel felt lightheaded. She struggled furiously not to blush.

"The bracelet will tie you in to our communications," he said, still kneeling like a knight of old before his lady. "You can speak to any of us by clearly pronouncing our names. Like a calling card, the bracelet can be used one-on-one or for a group. You will hear our voices in your ear, as if we are next to you."

"Thank you!" Rachel's eyes began to tear.

Many people had told her to avoid danger or had lectured her about being careful. Until now, however, none of them had taken a single practical step to protect her. None of them had shown any understanding of the realities of her situation—that in this current supernatural battle, she and her friends were the front line. Remembering how she had wished for a protector, she felt such overwhelming gratitude she could hardly bear it.

Rachel stared at the kneeling, imperious prince as he gazed back at her, meeting her eyes steadily.

A strange joy bubbled up inside of her. For the first time in her life, she felt truly powerful—as if she need merely whisper an enemy's name, and the offender would be ripped to shreds by the razor-sharp claws of her personal tiger. The power rushed to her head. Struggling not to feel giddy, she wondered if this were what it would feel like to be crowned queen.

No wonder Sandra loved him!

The feelings inside her were so overwhelming that she could no longer bear to stand still. Tossing caution aside, she threw her arms around him, hugging him.

As her cheek brushed the black poplin covering his shoulder, terror seized her. *What if he considered her behavior too familiar and rejected her, humiliating her in front of everyone?*

She need not have feared.

Vladimir Von Dread's arms closed around her, returning her embrace. His body felt firm and warm, and he smelled good, very good—like pleasant masculine musk mixed with mountain air. She felt so safe there, within the circle of his arms. She wished she could stay there always.

She held very tightly, not letting him go. This might be her only chance to do so, ever. After his kindness to her this evening, she felt half-in-love with him. Not, she reassured herself hastily, in an imposing-on-Gaius sort of way, more the kind of devotion a little sister might feel for a heroic older brother. After all, he would be her brother, once he married Sandra.

He did not push her away but kept her in the circle of his strong arms. Eventually, she released him and took a step back, smiling gratefully. Rising smoothly to his feet, he nodded at her, a slight ghost of a smile still lingering on his lips. Rachel was aware that the two of them were drawing an audience, but, for the first time in her life, she did not care that she was the center of public scrutiny.

Right then, nothing could have dismayed her.

Chapter Six:

The Terrible Truth

About Familiars

"Do you have any questions regarding the bracelet, Miss Griffin?" asked Vladimir Von Dread.

"Yes," Rachel replied, regaining her equilibrium. "Whom can it call? How do I turn it off? Can someone else use it to spy on my conversations? When I use it, does everyone hear a voice come out of it? Or only me?"

"The bracelet will allow you to speak to myself, Gaius, William, Topher Evans, Naomi Coils, and Jennifer Dare," he replied. "I believe that Lucille Westenra will have one soon enough. As to the rest, the bracelet vibrates slightly when in use, more so when first activated. I do not believe that anyone can spy on you without it vibrating. Or, if they can, we are all being spied on. I trust that the sorcerers at O.I. have enough skill to make sure no one is eavesdropping on us. And you should be the only one who can hear the voices."

"Thank you. That's very helpful."

"While the bracelets are not a state secret, they are considered confidential by the company that created them. It's for the best if people do not know who is in our communication network. Please do not mention what I have told you to any but your closest friends."

Rachel nodded solemnly, "I don't plan to mention it, but my closest friends may find out. They're good at discovering things. If they do, I'll ask them to keep it quiet."

He nodded. "I understand your situation. I... have reservations about how well some of your people can keep secrets. But I trust that you can."

"I'll do my best." She slid the bracelet inside the sleeve of her robe. "Would these happen to be one of the prototypes O.I.'s working on in their quest to develop 'improved communiation methods for the Wise?'?"

"Indeed. Astute of you."

Rachel ducked her head shyly at his praise. She peeked up sidelong at the impassive prince. Dread gazed across the dueling strips, frowning slightly at the antics of some of the less-disciplined members. Rachel's heart began to pound. What if Gaius shared with the prince the letter she had sent from London—in which she confessed to Gaius her secret weaknesses? Vladimir was being so kind to her tonight, but he despised weaknesses. She could not bear to be the recipient of his kindness under false pretenses.

"Um, about this...." She waved her braceleted hand. "Will you want it back if I disappoint you?"

Dread gazed down at her again. "You will not disappoint me, Miss Griffin."

A wave of nausea washed over her. Lying had recently become her friend, but she felt this occasion called for truthfulness.

"But you don't like it when people are..." —she lowered her lashes, trying to hide the crumbling of her inner happiness—"...are weak. I fell apart. That's why I had to go to Sandra's. None of my friends have fallen apart, even though some of them had worse things happen to them. I'm just not as strong as they are."

She raised her eyes to his face. "I did manage to be totally unafraid while I was paralyzed by the enemy." She winced with chagrin. "Of course, I was unable to move, so nobody knew... but, inside, I was very brave."

"Bravery is not a lack of fear, but acting in the face of it." Vladimir laid his hand on her shoulder, gazing steadily down at her. "I have no doubt that you have a lion's heart, Miss Griffin. And I also do not expect you to be unaffected by the many horrible occurrences that you have witnessed. It is acceptable to feel emotion and to deal with them as you need. It is not acceptable to be overcome by them to such a degree that you are unable to accomplish your goals."

Encouraged, Rachel gave him a very slight smile.

Dread inclined his head. He felt so solid beside her, like a bulk-head against the onslaught of a strange and dangerous world.

Rachel said, "Gaius once claimed that we're not actually saving the world—though that was before I was kidnapped—twice. We are saving the world, aren't we, Vlad? We're not making things worse?"

"We are defending the world," replied Vlad, firmly. "I am not certain that all we do keeps the entire world from spinning off into chaos. But, on the other hand, I am not sure it doesn't. Why would I take the risk?"

"Very true," laughed Rachel. "Thank you."

Von Dread inclined his head again. Without another word, he took his leave, walking over to where Penny Royal dueled Ethan Warhol. Rachel watched him go, sighing. She had been calm and collected while speaking with the upperclassman. The moment she was alone, a giddy flush spread through her body, as if she had rapidly downed a large glass of champagne. When she pressed her palms against her cheeks, they felt hot.

Rachel took a deep breath, striving to compose herself. She re-fused to indulge in romantic notions about a young man who be-longed to her sister, especially when she already had the best of boyfriends. Turning her back on the Prince of Bavaria, she ran to find Gaius and show off her new bracelet.

• • •

As the evening progressed, Rachel fought several practice duels and watched others, striving to learn all she could. Around nine-thirty, Siggy and Salome got into a cheerful argument that they both in-sisted could only be settled by Valerie. They took their leave and departed the gym in search of Sigfried's girlfriend. Rachel stayed a while longer, hoping to spend more time with Gaius, but he was too busy dueling. She watched him, telling herself that this was a good opportunity to learn from an expert. He looked so cute, however, with his patched robes, his cocky grin, and the intent look in his eyes, that she kept forgetting to pay attention to the duel.

She fought another match with Salome's boyfriend, Ethan Warhol, which she lost. When it was over, she felt exhausted. As she sat down, fighting to catch her breath, footsteps approached. Looking up, she saw Freka Starkadder coming toward her. The Transylvanian princess had an almost feral beauty, with intense brown eyes and long, straight, oak-colored bangs. The older girl leaned over, her hands on her thighs, and smiled mischievously at Rachel.

"Well, aren't you the young woman of the hour!"

Rachel blinked at her, not sure what she meant.

The feral princess teased her with a big grin, "Not enough to capture the heart of one cutie of an older boy, eh? Now you must add Bavaria to your stable?"

Rachel's cheeks grew so hot, she feared that her flesh was being roasted from within. A moment later, she was unexpectedly glad of this, as the upperclassman's next words caused the blood to rush from Rachel's face. So much had suffused it, however, that Rachel had a chance to duck her head before the older girl caught her blanching.

Still leaning over and smiling, Freka was saying, "I wanted to thank you, Rachel Griffin, for your part in getting me my brother Remus's message." She raised a hand. "Oh, I know you're going to say, that it was Gaius who told me. But our gallant Mr. Valiant informed me that he would never have been in a position to speak to Remus's ghost, were it not for you. So, if there is anything I can do to express my thanks, please do not hesitate to ask."

Not trusting herself to speak, Rachel nodded wordlessly.

"I did pass Remus's message to Romulus," continued Freka. "I hope our eldest brother was able to take care of whatever Remus needed, and that Remus and Fenris are now at peace."

Rachel vividly relived the moment when the shade of Freka's handsome, blond brother was simultaneously devoured by the flames and dragged into the ground. His terrified face again hovered before her. His bloodcurdling scream echoed in her ears.

Should she tell Freka?

Rachel's heartfelt love of revealing secrets urged her to blurt out what she knew, but she balked. The princess's brother had been dragged to a horrible place of eternal punishment. Absolutely nothing could be done to help him. Might it be kinder to keep this horror to herself?

Rachel swallowed the words that fought to leap from her lips. Calling upon her mask of calm, she looked back at the other young woman, her face betraying nothing.

"What is going on with your eldest brother and Von Dread?" Rachel asked instead. "They seem… frosty."

The young woman tilted back her head, eyes twinkling. "You know boys. They're never happy unless they have rivals. But back to Remus…. I gather you're like me, then?" Freka asked merrily. "You enjoy talking to ghosts?"

Rachel nodded again. She forced herself to speak, though her voice sounded hoarse in her ears. "Do you like ghosts?"

"Oh, I do! And I'm good at talking to them, too. It's my secret talent. We Starkadders all have one. Luperca can play with fire, and Gar—that's my littlest brother, short for Wulfgar—is immune to cold. He says it's a useless power, but he has no idea how miserable cold can be."

"And Wulfgang?" Rachel inquired, curious about the elusive, brooding young prince with whom she shared all her classes.

"He can calm storms."

"Can he stop the storm goblin?" inquired Rachel.

"The Heer of Dunderberg?" Freka laughed. "No, that one is far better at raising storms that Wulf is at calming them." She flashed her bright, mischievous grin. "Poor Wulf. He objects that his gift is even more pointless than Gar's… as he can do something every Tamas, Denes, and Aris can learn to do with enchantment."

"Can Wulf calm storms without a musical instrument?" asked Rachel.

"Yes, but he says that's sorry compensation." Freka laughed, and the sound of it was so infectious that, in spite of herself, Rachel smiled. "Wulf thinks his animal talent is the worst, too. Gar can talk to squirrels, which are everywhere; while Wulf is stuck talking to wolverines, which—one must admit—are hardly as plentiful."

Animal talents!

Rachel recalled the conversation she and Sigfried had overhead between Freka and her brother Beowulf. Beowulf had said something about Freka speaking with….

Rachel leaned forward earnestly and lay a hand on the older girl's arm. "Actually, Miss Starkadder, there is a favor you could do me."

Freka accompanied Rachel to the foyer of Dare Hall, a great, high-ceilinged chamber with a sweeping staircase leading to the girls' dormitory and two sets of wide double doors—one on the far left, which led to the boys' dorm, and the other in the center, which led to the theater.

• • •

Freka waited on the black and white marble, as Rachel ran up four flights, taking the stairs two at a time. She slipped silently into her room, so as not to wake her roommates. Walking purposefully toward her bed, she navigated using the special sense granted to her by the Familiar Bonding Ceremony. It was too dark to see, but Rachel could feel Mistletoe curled up on her bed, the same way she could feel the location of her arm or foot. She crept closer, without so much as glancing in the cat's direction. It was important, when dealing with cats, to deceive them utterly about one's intention. When she was close enough, she grabbed him.

The cat was so surprised, he entirely failed to escape.

• • •

"I have him!" Rachel ran back down the vast staircase, the large cat held tight in her arms. The lithe animal struggled, but Rachel's grip was firm. When she reached the foyer, she put the black and white beast down on the marble. He *mrowed* at her reprovingly.

Freka knelt before the cat, smiling. She began to *mew* and *purr* and make cat-like noises. To Rachel's great delight, Mistletoe answered in like manner. This went on for several minutes, long enough for Rachel to begin to feel the lateness of the hour.

She struggled to stifle a yawn.

"What a sweet and feisty cat! He loves you very much!" Freka stretched as she straightened. She smiled fondly at the cat and his mistress.

"Then...." Rachel's voice caught. She hardly dared to hope.

Freka shook her head regretfully. "No, Rachel. He is truly a fine cat, but he's not a familiar."

"Yes," Rachel's voice was barely above a whisper. "I... I think I knew that."

"Familiars are to mundane cats as the Wise are to the Unwary. They have magic in their nature. Mistletoe is clever and wise, in the way of mundane cats, but he's never going to be able to do the things that familiars do for sorcerers." She pressed Rachel's hand. "I'm sorry."

Rachel nodded and swallowed painfully. "Thank you, anyway." "You're welcome. It's the least I could do, considering."

Rachel thought again of the agony on the face of Remus Starkadder, as the demons dragged him down to their fiery, subterranean lair and bit her lip.

"It's late. I should go," Freka said kindly. She gave Mistletoe one last pat, where he sat licking his paw, and departed. As the door swung shut, she called from the darkness. "Oh, and do recommend my little brother Wulf to your friend the princess, will you?"

The door closed with a bang.

Wondering about her last comment, Rachel swallowed twice. Below her, Mistletoe let out a soft *mrrow*. Seeing him there, gazing so steadily up at her, Rachel knelt and touched her nose to his moist one. As her head tilted, the single tear running down her cheek slid forward to wet the corner of her lips. She rose to her feet and brushed it away.

Together, mistress and cat made their way back up the stairs.

Chapter Seven:

The Lure of

Other Worlds

Emboldened by the favor that the Prince of Bavaria had shown her, and the continued absence of the princess, Rachel took an unprecedented step.

At lunch on Friday, instead of sitting with her friends, she brought her tray over to the central table, where Dread and his cronies gathered, and plopped it down next to Gaius's. She stood there uncertainly, the roar of the fountain only slightly louder than the thumping of her racing heart, as she hoped that her boldness would not be rebuffed by the upperclassmen. Her nervousness was made worse by the fact that her older brother Peter, with whom she still was not on speaking terms, was glaring ferociously at her from across the enormous dining hall. He was not at all pleased to see his little sister in the presence of his hated rival, Gaius Valiant.

Apparently, boys and rivals really was a thing.

Von Dread noticed her first. His regal nod drew the attention of the others.

"Rachel!" Gaius gave her a big grin and patted the bench beside him. "Come join us. We were just telling the others about our trip to Detroit—the not-restricted parts, of course."

"Tell us," asked William Locke, "what was your impression of my family's company?"

Smiling, Rachel sank down onto the bench beside her boy-friend, grateful to be welcomed into the conversation.

· · ·

Friday afternoon, Rachel's core group had Music and True History, or True Hiss, as she now thought of it, thanks to Gaius, with a free period in between. In Music, they stood in front of music stands, practicing the song for dispelling mist and clouds. True History, however, took place around one of the large rectangular tables that filled the center of the majority of classrooms, which meant that Rachel had to choose where to sit.

Usually, she sat with Siggy, Nastasia, Joy and Zoë. This time, however, the princess and Zoë were missing. She should have felt lonely. She did not.

Instead, it was as if she had been granted a reprieve.

Rachel stood in the doorway, surveying the classroom. Joy chatted animatedly with her roommate Hildy Winters, the flaxen-haired cheerleader from California. Siggy was deep in conversation with the hockey player Seth Peregrine, as they argued about possible names for their new band. The other core group from Dare was here, too, along with one from De Vere. Ian MacDannan, Oonagh's younger brother, tormented his cousin Wendy Darling by sticking paperclips into her cloud of wavy chestnut locks. Sakura Suzuki, Enoch Smithwyck, and Rachel's roommate Kitten Fabian talked with the girls from De Vere, one of whom had pink hair. The remaining crowd of boys, save one, were laughing over something under the table.

That left two people sitting alone: Freka's younger brother, Wolfgang Starkadder, and Rachel's fourth roommate, Astrid Hollywell. Wolfgang had a perpetual haughty scowl and a forbidding, brooding air about him. Astrid, on the other hand, seemed to be watching wistfully as her classmates joked and laughed. She was a shy girl with caramel skin and tight, black curls, who always wore a scarf, usually the same electric-blue one. She had seemed very sweet when she and Rachel had roasted friendship chestnuts together on All Hallows' Eve. And yet, Rachel never saw her talking to anybody. *Was Astrid always by herself?*

Rachel thought back but could not remember seeing the other girl talk to anyone else regularly. There was an empty chair next to Astrid. Impulsively, Rachel took it. Astrid looked up, startled. When Rachel smiled, the other girl gave her a grateful look. Then, she ducked her head, returning to her books, but Rachel noted that a little smile lingered on the other girl's lips.

• • •

After classes, Rachel and her classmates returned to Dare Hall. She tried to study, but Joy kept popping in every few minutes to ask if the princess had returned from Magical Australia. Finally, Rachel gave up on studying, grabbed her coat, and went outside.

Snow carpeted the campus. The cold November sun sparkled off icy crystals that topped the most recent snowfall. In the distance, the ice-covered crescent of broken stone that made up the new top of Stony Tor—ever since the demon Morax had destroyed its former rounded top when it released the imprisoned storm goblin, who had then murdered their Elf—glittered in the brilliant sunlight. Closer at hand, familiars ran back and forth through the fresh snow, while students in old-fashioned or brightly-colored parkas threw snowballs and built snowmen. One group of upperclassmen, probably alchemy students, had granted their snowman motion. They cheered and shouted as it slowly shuffled forward.

Rachel stepped over someone's familiar sleeping on the porch of Dare Hall and descended into the winter wonderland. She walked by the snow sculptures and ducked a stray snowball. Beside the reflecting lake in front of Roanoke Hall, she came upon Sigfried, his girlfriend Valerie, and Salome Iscariot. They stood by a snow-covered bench, skipping rocks or throwing them hard enough to break the thin black surface of the lake. Lucky flew over the half-frozen water, his long serpentine body undulating through the air, as he snapped at the skipping stones, blackening a few with dragon fire. Payback, Valerie's Norwegian Elkhound, ran back and forth along the shore, barking at each throw, her curly tail wagging furiously.

Valerie's cheeks were bright pink from the cold, matching her pink jacket. Salome wore a black double-breasted coat. Sigfried, however, was dressed only in his academic robes. His lips looked a little blue. With a pang, Rachel realized that he probably did not own any winter gear. She made a mental note to wangle a gold coin from Lucky—who hated to part with even a single piece of the vast hoard that Sigfried kept under and around his bed—so that she could order Siggy a proper parka and some boots.

"I'm bored. Let's go kill that ogre before he eats any more humans," suggested Sigfried. "I bet Lucky and I can take him."

"Take him out how?" asked Valerie dryly. "He has a charmed life."

"So?" Sigfried shrugged. "What's that mean?"

Salome chirped, "That he's immune to knives and arrows and spells and also guns and large ammunition." To the other girls, she said, "You always have to add that with boys, or they assume the thing can be blasted with a Howitzer."

"Aw!" The news that the ogre could not be blown away with a Howitzer, whatever that was, disappointed Sigfried, but then he perked up. "Then let's trip him into a very deep pit and bury him alive. Or dunk his feet in cement and drop him at World's End. What'd you say the water depth was there, Griffin? Over two hundred feet."

"Be serious, Siggy, how would we get to the end of the world?" asked Valerie skeptically.

Rachel pointed south. "He means the bend of the river just north of West Point. The old sailors called that area World's End, because the Heer of Dunderberg sank so many ships there. And he's right. The Hudson is over two hundred feet deep in that spot." To Sigfried, she said seriously, "It's not a bad plan, but where would we get the cement? We'd have to order it and that could take days."

"That's too long," said Siggy glumly, sending another rock skidding across the lake's black surface to plunk into the icy waters when it encountered a hole in the ice.

After watching Sigfried and Valerie slide or skip stones a bit longer, Rachel rebelliously picked up a flat piece of gravel from where someone had scuffed snow off the path and threw it, even though she knew Siggy thought she "threw like a girl." There was no shame in that, she told herself stoutly. She was a girl.

Her rock sank like a stone.

Valerie, who threw as well as any boy, snickered, but Salome, of all people, gave her a sympathetic glance. Rachel walked over to stand beside the other girl. Salome had huge luminous eyes, fair locks, and an eye-catching figure that she flaunted to its best advantage. Her black coat hung open. Underneath, she was dressed in subfusc, the most modern of the three uniforms allowed at Roanoke. Her white blouse stretched too tightly across her generous curves, and, even on this cold day, her black skirt was shorter than regulation permitted. A group of older boys pause to ogle her. With a smirk and a twinkle in her eye, Salome tossed her head and arched her back, displaying her charms. Rachel, who had trouble imagining how one might enjoy the attention of strangers, felt in awe of her cheerful, attention-seeking classmate.

Salome's red lips curled into a cupid's bow of amusement. "So. Super-aloof-but-totally-hot Vladimir Von Dread gave you a bracelet—while kneeling. That was special!"

Rachel tried vainly to stanch the tsunami of blood rushing to her cheeks. "Um... yeah."

That Vlad had acknowledged her so publicly made the whole experience headier, but she found herself wishing he had spoken to her privately. The memory was still too fresh and too precious for her to enjoy hearing it bandied about.

"Should we be expecting wedding bells?" asked Salome, mischievously.

"No!" Rachel squeaked. *Not mine, anyway.*

"Did you see Eunice's face?" Salome continued excitedly. "She looked as if she was about to wet her pants. She clearly thought she was going to be Dread Chow." Salome leaned forward confidentially, "Tell me, has she been bullying you?"

"Bullying? No." Rachel regained her aplomb. "Just less than friendly."

"Well, if Eunice does cross the line, you come to me. Von Dread will just make a mess of things. I, on the other hand, know how to get things done subtly! Look how well I did with Cydney Graves."

"Yeah," Rachel kept her voice neutral, as she still felt uncomfortable about that incident, and Salome's part in it. "Cydney has left me alone so far. Though I notice the Drake Hall girls have finally bounced back from having been ensorcelled by Dr. Mordeau. I'm expecting Miss Graves to begin oppressing me again any day now."

"Not a chance," replied Salome.

"Wha–what do you mean?"

"Cydney won't bother you, ever again," Salome confided, her luminous eyes filled with mirth. "She's totally fallen apart. She's a pariah. Doesn't talk to anyone. Even the other Drake girls won't have anything to do with her. She won't be bullying a blind kitten, much less you." Salome made a dismissing gesture with her hand. "She's done. Stick a fork in her."

Startled, Rachel searched her memory, recalling incidents from the last couple months in the dining hall, math class, and the commons, when Cydney Graves had been present. For the first time, Rachel paid attention to what Cydney was doing. Salome was right. Cydney was always sulking by herself, petulant and sullen. Even in the dining hall, she sat entirely by herself, which was unusual at Roanoke.

Rachel slid her mask of calm over her features. Underneath, she felt appalled. True, she had wanted revenge after Cydney had led a group of Drake Hall girls to cast cantrips on Rachel, leaving her on the basement stairs, paralyzed and deformed. However, her hatred had vanished during that first Knights meeting, when she had seen Cydney's face, flushed and red, after Salome had whispered in the other girl's ear. Cydney had looked so upset, so lost; Rachel's heart had gone out to her. Much as Rachel did not like being the target of nasty magic, she had not wanted some other young woman to suffer so, either.

To her surprise, she also found herself fighting off a sharp stab of disappointment. She had been looking forward to facing her persecutor. It would have given her a chance to learn about herself, whether she was the kind of person who could stand up to a bully. Having Salome solve the problem for her made her feel oddly bereft.

"What did you say to her?" Rachel asked curiously. "At the Knight's meeting, I mean, to make Cydney challenge me to a duel?"

Salome looked as smug as a cat that had caught a songbird. "Remember the time she and her friend paralyzed you? I told her that her older brother Randall was the person who set you free so quickly. She suffers from a big brother complex. She felt totally betrayed." Salome grinned. "I told you I was good at annoying people! I always know what to say. It's like a magic power!"

Rachel glanced at Salome and then out over the reflecting late, where Valerie's latest rock skidded across a patch of thin ice, Payback barking at it excitedly. In her memory, Rachel examined Salome's face carefully. The other girl's eyes had danced with glee, but Rachel saw no evidence of malice or wicked intent.

Rachel was reminded of a time when she had been visiting a tenant farm at Gryphon Park. A gangly young boarhound had come running up and dropped a dead animal at the farmer's feet. It was the family's beloved pet duck. The great pup had stood enthusiastically wagging its tail, awaiting its master's praise for its hunting prowess.

What had Salome actually done? Was Salome's glee innocent or sadistic? It made no sense that losing one duel would transform Cydney Graves from a popular girl into an outcast. Nor did it make sense that a simple lie about her brother could have upset her so much. Was Salome's "magic power" of annoyance actually something more sinister? Or was she like the boarhound, blissfully unaware of the damage she was causing?

With a sigh, Rachel returned her attention to the other girl.

"Thank you," she murmured, out of a sense of obligation.

"Anything for a friend of Valerie's!" Salome crowed cheerfully.

• • •

For her final Saturday of detention—the punishment for the time she and her friends had accidentally left campus by falling out of dreamland into Transylvania—Rachel was assigned to clean the brooms in the broom closet. She washed each bristleless, oiling the levers, polishing the shafts and the fans, testing the flight spells. Those that listed to one side or could not fly straight she put in a pile. The rest went back on the rack.

As she worked, her thoughts yo-yoed back and forth between physics equations and Gaius. How utterly sweet he was! He had gone to such trouble to help her understand both sorcery and physical laws. A girl could not ask for a better boyfriend.

She polished each fan blade in the pile beside her until she could see her reflection in the shiny wood, daydreaming, as she worked, about kisses and motion vectors. On those few occasions when her thoughts drifted too near the dangerous topic of the Prince of Bavaria, she very firmly pulled them back into line.

As she was nearing the last of the bristlelesses, Sigfried trotted into the broom closet carrying a mop and bucket. He had been instructed to clean the permanent floors in the gym. There were not many such floors, as most of the gym space was conjured anew upon request. To her surprise, the usually boisterous Siggy did his work with uncharacteristic diligence. Even Lucky helped, dusting out of reach places with the soft red puff at the end of his golden tail.

"Didn't realize boys knew how to clean," Rachel said, impressed.

"We had to scrub a lot of toilets and stuff at the orphanage." Siggy looked up from where he was scouring the flagstones with a scrub brush. "I imagine you could do it better."

"You'd be wrong," she admitted sheepishly. "I know nothing about cleaning."

"Don't girls come knowing how to clean?"

"Not those who are the daughters of dukes," replied Rachel. Rachel chuckled as she began waxing the tail fan of the next broom. "Those are *bwbach*, relatives of the *bwca*. Only *bwca* are not such bizarre dressers. Brownies do baking. *Bwca* and *bwbachs* clean. *Bean tighe* do laundry. We have *bean tighe* here at the school, too. They're taller and female. They look like hunched old ladies usually."

"When would I ever have cleaned?"

"*Bwca*? Like the brownies that clean stuff in the dorm? Those crazy little guys with loincloths and turbans?"

"Those are *bwbach*, relatives of the *bwca*. Only *bwca* are not such bizarre dressers. Brownies do baking. *Bwca* and *bwbachs* clean. *Bean tighe* do laundry. We have *bean tighe* here at the school, too. They're taller and female. They look like hunched old ladies usually."

"When would I ever have cleaned? stalls, yes... but scrub floors? Wash laundry? At Gryphon Park, we have *bwca* and *bean tighe* for that kind of work, not to mention human servants."

Siggy shook his head. "I'll never get 'em straight."

"We'll be studying domestic fey in music class in the spring. Learning to summon them."

"Ace!" Sigfried grinned. "You mean I'll be able to play my trumpet and have magic clean my room?"

Rachel laughed. "You can have *bwbachs* clean your room now —if you put milk in the bowl in front of your dorm room."

"Ooooh. Is that what that's for?"

"Oops," murmured Lucky, his golden ears and enormously long red whiskers drooping with guilt.

Rachel giggled behind her fingers.

They cleaned for a bit. Rachel found the next-to-last broom listed severely to one side. She took apart the tail fan, cleaned it carefully, and reassembled it. To her delight, it now flew straight. With a great sense of satisfaction, she hung it back on the rack.

"When does Wheels come back?" Sigfried asked presently. "Classes are boring without her there to sass the tutors."

"No idea. Ivan didn't even know if she had gone with Nastasia."

"Oh. Is Nastasia gone, too?"

Rachel sighed. "Yes, and Joy has only spoken to you about this three hundred and sixty-seven times."

Sigfried shrugged, uninterested.

Rachel paused in her work, frowning. "Not a very nice attitude to take about a friend."

"If she wants to be treated like a friend, she should act more like a friend," Sigfried scowled. "All she ever does is shoot down my ideas."

"In her defense, Siggy, your ideas are totally over the top. Everyone shoots them down."

He paused in his work and fixed her with his startlingly blue eyes. "Not you."

Rachel sighed and returned to polishing. "True."

She bit her lip, hoping he would not ask why. She did not want to explain her reasons—that she had taken a secret vow to support him, so he would not feel so alone in the world. This same vow had led to them becoming blood brother and sister. She hated the thought that he had no one who cared about him, no one whom he thought of as family (except Lucky, of course). The result was that, rather than disagree with him at the outset, she agreed with all his madcap ideas. Only once they were committed did she try to subtly introduce a note of caution.

Also, she did not wish to admit this aloud, but running full-tilt at danger helped her keep herself together. Falling in with Sigfried's crazy ideas required tremendous focus. As long as she had something important to concentrate on—such as physics, or the trip to Hoddmimir's Wood, or some other upcoming adventure—she could stave off the dark thoughts that threatened to overwhelm her whenever things were peaceful.

Sigfried, being Sigfried, did not ask. A moment later, however, she almost wished that he had. The look of black hatred that crept over his face scared her.

"Where does the princess get off telling me that I'm no longer her knight?" The words exploded from Sigfried, as if he had been laboring to keep them in. "Knights are not *employees*! Did Galahad get a paycheck? Lords cannot fire vassals! Punish them, yes. Have them flogged, killed, even. Send them to their death by ordering them to fight an ogre or a dragon, certainly! But fired? You cannot *fire a knight!*"

He looked so angry and so lost that sympathetic fury at Nastasia ignited inside Rachel. She tamped it down. It would do no good to take sides between her two dearest friends.

"I'm sorry," she said sincerely.

"I want to be a knight!" Sigfried cried, his eyes wild. "I'm no good on my own. I don't know how this crazy world works. I might not know how to make decisions but I do know how to be loyal. Kings and princesses are supposed to stay awake at night making hard decisions. Knights are supposed to serve and protect—and we sleep well."

"You could be my knight," Rachel said softly, half joking, half deadly serious.

"You're not a princess!" He scowled so darkly that Rachel quailed.

She stared down at her lap, wishing very much that she had not spoken.

"Nastasia is so annoying!" Sigfried continued. "First she tells us she has to study day and night. Then she blows off school to gallivant around Magical Australia for days. And she's never nice to you, Rachel. She treats you badly, and yet, every time you're good at something, she acts envious. Why are you even friends with her?"

There were many things Rachel could have said, but she settled for the one she thought would be most persuasive to Sigfried.

"She's going to take us to Hoddmimir's Wood," she reminded him, her voice low.

"Oh! Right!" Siggy's eyes grew huge. "Okay. When we get back from our first visit to *another world*, I'll forgive her."

"I wish I could invite Gaius," Rachel sighed wistfully. "He'd love to see another world."

"Who?"

"Good grief!"

"Oh! Your boyfriend. Sorry. I couldn't hear what you said, you were sighing so loudly."

Rachel snorted in amusement. She added, "Besides, you have to remain friends with the princess. You're both Keybearers! You are destined to do some great deed together."

"Key-wearer?" Siggy looked up from where he was scrubbing. "Like wears on a chain?"

"Bearer! Not wearer. I... don't know." Rachel waved a hand. "The Raven said the Keybearers were part of a greater working: 'Ones who have a high and weighty destiny before them—to undo a great harm.'"

"I don't want to undo a great harm! I want to *do* great harm!" Sigfried said fiercely, adding, "To a bad guy, of course. Are you one? A Key-bear, I mean?"

"No. But I get to be support crew."

"If you're not one, and she is, I'm not sure I want to play, either," stated Siggy.

Rachel frowned sadly. She could not imagine being offered the opportunity to do some great good and not jumping at the chance, no matter the cost. It baffled her that Sigfried was not overjoyed at the prospect. She returned to polishing, and they worked a little longer. Sigfried finished and tossed his rags and mop into the bucket. He leaned against the mop handle.

"Another world!" His eyes were bright and far away. "Even the sound of it's grand."

Rachel hung up the last broom and turned toward him, her eyes shining. "I cannot begin to put into words why I want so much to go. Part of it, I guess, is the newness of it. Part of it is seeing the place that was once the home of our friend, the Elf. Part is the adventure —my chance to be like my hero, Daring Northwest."

Siggy interrupted, "He's that's the Librarian Adventurer guy who disappeared through that silvery glass in Transylvania, right?"

"Yes. I should tell my father about that glass—though it's broken now," she sighed.

"Didn't he tell you to stop reporting to him?"

"Yes, and I don't know if he is even aware that I went to Transylvania," she said glumly. "Anyway, with my plan for the Library of Worlds, actually going to another world, touching truly alien soil, would be the first step of my *real life.*"

"One small step for Griffin," quipped Lucky. "One huge step for freaky, genius, dwarf girls everywhere."

Rachel and Siggy both laughed. Sigfried scratched his dragon between his ruby-colored horns. Lucky's back leg kicked repeatedly, like a dog's.

"Ooohhh yeah!" murmured Lucky. "That's the spot! That's why every dragon needs to keep a boy! It's your opposable thumbs."

Rachel chuckled. "Back to the earlier topic, though, it isn't just for fun things, like starting the Library of All Worlds, that I want to travel. There's also the search for knowledge. Dread and Gaius come from different worlds, and yet the fetch inside Magdalene Chase's doll knew of both of them. This implies that there may be worlds out there that do not have the knowledge blackout we have... where they might actually know what's going on."

"Why don't you ask the doll-thing more questions?" asked Sigfried.

"Gaius told me that Dread has tried, but it won't speak."

"Maybe we should beat the information out of it," Siggy suggested cheerfully.

"Or roast it!" offered Lucky, still kicking his hind leg.

Rachel rolled her eyes, amused at their antics but trying not to encourage them.

"Maybe there was something special about All Hallows' Eve," she said.

Sigfried turned to Rachel, his eyes burning with unexpected intensity.

"I've been trapped my whole life," he said, "in one small, stinking orphanage, in one small, stinking city, in a place that is only an island, not even properly part of the Continent. The universe is infinite, and I want to see all of it before I die." He paused. "And then I want to come back to life and see it again."

His words resonated so deeply with her that Rachel could hardly speak. She reached out and gave his arm a tight squeeze, murmuring. "Me, too, blood brother. Me, too!"

CHAPTER EIGHT:

THE ART OF FALLING

SIGFRIED PUT AWAY THE BUCKET WITH THE MOP AND DEPARTED. Her steeplechaser in her hand, Rachel went to return the key to the broom closet to Mr. Chanson's desk drawer. As she walked back through the central corridor toward the front door, she came upon Ivan Romanov stepping out of a zapball court as he headed for the boys' locker room. His blond hair was damp with sweat, a towel around his neck. With his shirt resting over one shoulder and his chest bare, he made quite an appealing picture.

Gazing up at the Crown Prince of Magical Australia, with his handsome, boyish grin, Rachel could not help smiling back. What a splendid brother-in-law he would make! She felt so flattered that he had once insinuated he might consider marrying her. That a prince had thought highly enough of her to contemplate proposing had cheered her during a number of dark times.

A momentary wistfulness that she had directed him toward Laurel rather than accepting herself assailed her, but she dismissed it. Ivan might be a great catch for her wild sister, but he struck her as too tame and boyish for her own taste. If a young man was not entirely devoted to pursuing the truth, he was not the one for her.

Still, it was would be such fun to have Nastasia as her sister-in-law, once Laurel married Ivan. When Sandra married Vladimir, both her sisters would be wedded to crown princes.

Someday, she would be the sister of two queens!

Ivan smiled down at her. "Hello, Mini-Griffin. I heard from home this morning. My sister should be back this afternoon."

"Will she! Excellent!" Rachel exclaimed. "Did they happen to mention Zoë?"

Ivan shook his head. "I didn't think to ask about her."

"I see."

An idea struck her. She stepped closer and flashed him a conspiratorial grin. "About Laurel impressing your father, Ivan. While it is true that my sister has never joined the circus, she did take two silver ribbons in equestrian vaulting. I have seen her do some amazing things on the back of a horse—splits, flips. That, combined with her conjuring light shows, might be enough to convince anybody that she was circus material. If you thought she was toying with your royal father, I could arrange for her to put on a rather splendid performance next time he's on campus. It would take a lot of work, though. I don't want to go to all that effort just to find out that you have been toying with Laurel."

"Wait, I'm sorry." Ivan rubbed his hair with the towel, "are you being serious? I can count the number of times I have spoken at length with your sister on one hand. No, I am not planning on marrying her. When did this turn into not a joke?"

"Oh. I didn't...."

Thoroughly embarrassed, Rachel turned and ran away.

• • •

CRAAACKKKK!

As Rachel emerged from the girl's locker room, where she had run to hide, cry, and wash her face, thunder rattled the windows. The front door of the gym slammed shut and locked. Rachel ran to the door and banged on it—she even put down her broom and yanked with both hands—but it would not budge.

"What's going on?" Evelyn March, an upperclassman with aquiline features and an olive complexion, stuck her head out of one of the doors. Over the older girl's shoulder, Rachel could see a zapball court and several other college girls leaping about, wide mallets in hand, trying to keep the glowing neon shuttlecocks from striking the walls or floor. Rachel recognized Kitten Fabian's older sister Panther (whose real name was Anthea); a pretty half-Japanese girl named Iolanthe Towers, who was the head of the Roanoke Bird Fanciers Club; and Minnie Forthright, a plump girl with red hair from Raleigh Hall.

"Lock down," Rachel called back. "It's thundering."

"The Heer again? Haven't they caught him yet?" Iolanthe called cheerfully. Despite her Japanese features, she spoke with a Mid-West American accent. She stuck her head out of the room sideways, her long black hair draping downward like a dark sheet. Her familiar, an Australian Shepherd—an unusual-looking canine that was part tan, part spotted black and gray—stuck its furry head out as well. "Who's in charge of doing that?"

"My father," Eve said with an expression that was half amused and half resigned.

"Ooo! The Grand Inquisitor!" Minnie's eyes widened.

"I'm not afraid of him," Iolanthe declared, tossing her head with a cheerful smile.

"You should be," murmured Panther Fabian, slamming the emerald green shuttlecock across the small court with her mallet. Even while playing zapball, she comported herself with an old-fashioned grace seldom seen in modern girls. "Fear of the Grand Inquisitor is one of the three certain signs of sanity."

Iolanthe shrugged cheerfully and popped back into the zapball court. Another bright shuttlecock, this one electric blue, shot over the girls' heads. They all jumped for it. Eve pulled the door to the court shut behind her.

All by herself, Rachel stood in the middle of the gym hall, listening to the thunder. To either side, there was nothing but a row of doors, doors that would not open into anything, unless she made a request. Had Ivan Romanov left? If he came out of the boys' locker room, and she was stuck in here with him until the thunderstorm broke, she did not think she could bear it. But it would not do to spend the time cowering in the loo. That would only make her feel worse.

Rachel approached one of the doors and tried it. It opened to reveal a blank wall, which meant that no one was using it. She shut it again and thought. *What did she want?* The Knights of Walpurgis dueling chamber? That was not much use without another person. The swimming pool? She had not brought her bathing suit. She leaned her steeplechaser against the wall as she searched for other options. The gym had a state-of-the-art conjuring system that would produce any athletic equipment a person requested, but one had to make a request.

"I know! Gym, I want a course to practice flying!" Rachel called, holding up her steeplechaser. She opened the door. "Oh, my!"

Beyond the doorway was a vast chamber that rose at least a hundred and twenty feet to a set of distant skylights. It was four times as large as the grand track, the oval chamber they used for flying class when the weather was bad. At the center stood a three-dimensional representation of the roof of Roanoke Hall made from painted foam: the six rounded bell towers with their elongated cupolas, the cylindrical turrets, the narrow chimneys, the myriad spires and gables, the external spiral staircases, the central belfry with its empty lantern housing and its bell that never rang, the triangular roof peaks surrounded by their own turrets and spires.

Only, unlike the real top of the main hall, which had glass everywhere, these windows, of many shapes and sizes, were open—to allow an intrepid broom jockey an opportunity to dart through them. Either it was all larger than life, or it was a representation of the roof of Roanoke Hall's sister castle, the Chateau de Chambord. Both castles were rumored to have been designed by the same man, the great alchemist Leonardo da Vinci.

Around this architectural wonder ran a wide track with obstacles to fly above or below, wide padded pillars to spin around, tunnels to fly through, and a rack of dummies, weights, and other apparatus that could be used to create interesting flying conditions. In the left front corner was a good-sized pit filled with chunks of foam rubber, presumably so that anyone who fell while practicing tricks could land safely on the soft foam below.

It was a steeplechaser rider's dream.

Rachel leapt onto her broom and flew the outer course. As she came to each obstacle, she turned, spun, rose, or dove as required. Parts were so easy that she literally flew them with her eyes closed. Others were so difficult that she had to go very slowly or skip an obstacle all together. When she had successfully circled the chamber several times, she turned her attention to the replica of the roof of Roanoke Hall.

Not all of the openings were big enough for her to fly through at her current skill level. Avoiding the smallest ones, she set her sights on those that she was reasonably confident she could manage. Maneuvering through narrow spaces at high speed took her entire concentration. She stopped worrying about being locked in the gym, her missing friends, or rude upperclass boys who might have misled her about their intentions toward her sister. The sheer exhilaration of flying drove all else from her mind.

She was approaching window forty-three, a diamond-shaped opening in one of the more squat rectangular towers, when a crack of thunder, like cannon fire, reverberated through the gymnasium. Startled, Rachel jerked her broom, accidentally toggling one of the levers. Her steeplechaser spun at high speed, flying erratically and nearly slamming into the tower wall.

Throwing herself forward until she was on her stomach, she kicked the fan blades. The broom jerked and twisted, spinning in the other direction. Her head slammed against a stiff foam wall. Ears ringing, she shoved her feet into the back stirrups, gripped the short brass and cast iron handles jutting from the forward portion of the shaft, and used the stirrups to maneuver the fan blades back into their proper alignment.

Her steeplechaser righted itself.

Exhausted, Rachel flew to the ground and dismounted. Her legs were trembling. The back of her head throbbed. Flopping into the foam rubber pit, she lay with her arms outstretched, staring up at the sky lights.

What a rotter Ivan Romanov was!

How dare he deceive her and Laurel in such a fashion!

Rachel closed her eyes and remembered the moment on the commons, under the giant glowing wisp sculptures illuminating the night sky, when Laurel had blushed so prettily at Ivan's request to be allowed to ask his parents to speak to hers. Wrath shook her at the notion that he had been toying with her sister's affections.

And, if she were entirely truthful, with her own.

Because if the offer to marry Laurel was false, then the hint that he might have considered proposing to her was false as well. And that was a very great let-down. Not because she had any interest in marrying him, but just because it had made her feel—well, it did not matter if she could not put the sensation into words. Whatever it had made her feel was a lie.

High above, lightning branched across the stormy sky, arching repeatedly from Storm King Mountain in the west, where the Heer of Dunderberg and his lightning imps had holed up since escaping from their prison in Stony Tor. Rachel imagined what it would be like to fly through the storm with a good charm of solid oak around her neck to protect her from the lightning—the winds buffeting her and spinning her in circles, as it had the time she and Gaius had tried to outrun the Headless Horseman. She imagined flipping on her broom, calming enchantments and sailing peacefully amidst the tempest, perhaps while standing atop her broom, like Mr. Gideon.

Standing on a broom.

The idea still amazed and appalled her. It seemed so *impossible*.

But was it?

Climbing to her feet, Rachel placed her bristleless on the ground next to the pit of foam. Even when it was lying flat on the ground, she could hardly keep her balance atop it. After a number of tries, she balanced long enough to coax the steeplechaser up an inch and....

With a shrill cry, she tumbled from the broom shaft, landing on her back in the soft foam, which folded tight around her before bouncing her up again. She lay there, bouncing, catching her breath, and gazing at the gray-black clouds that rushed by the rain-splattered skylights. Then, stiffening her resolve, she climbed out of the pit and stepped onto the broom handle again.

Fifty-seven tries later, Rachel again lay nestled amidst the cushiony foam, panting. The rain had stopped, and a single triangle of blue could be seen between the silvery clouds.

Too exhausted to move, she reached out her hand and called, "*Varenga, Vroomie*." Obeying the cantrip, the steeplechaser leapt immediately to her hand. She hugged it to her chest and lay still, her eyes half closing.

She had managed to stand on the broom for a full six and a half seconds, her best time so far. Not that it mattered. Any notion she had entertained of flying around in mid-air while standing atop a broom, as Mr. Gideon had done, were crushed. Currently, she could hardly balance on such a narrow beam, even when it was resting on the ground. She would do better to practice on a regular balance beam.

But even if she were to master the standing trick close to the ground, how would she ever learn to fly about freely? The chance of falling off was too great. It would never be safe to practice anywhere other than above this foam pit, not unless she wore a floating harness like a little child—and floating harnesses produced drag, which made many maneuvers impossible. Lying on her back, staring at the sky, her eyelids began to close. Physics and flying blurred together in her mind: flying, standing, equations, falling. *A falling object,* William's voice repeated in her memory, *accelerates at a rate of 9.8 meters per second per second.* And he'd shown her how to derive the equation for distance fallen: one-half the acceleration times the square of the falling time. Thus, she reasoned, half asleep, in the first second, a falling object would drop 4.9 meters. After two seconds, it would have fallen 4.9×4 or 19.6 meters, *roughly twenty meters in two seconds.* And two seconds was longer than the time it took to....

Rachel sat bolt upright.

Carefully, she recalled the last few minutes, exactly as they had happened. She noted the time intervals for each action she had taken. *Could it work?*

Climbing out of the pit, she put her broom on the floor and walked some distance away.

"Varenga, Vroomie."

The steeplechaser leapt immediately to her hand. Rachel recalled the memory in real time, twice. Each time, she measured how long it had taken. Without question, the broom had taken less than two seconds to come to her. In fact, it had taken less than one. It was only when she called it from across campus that it took a significant amount of time to reach her.

Very slowly, Rachel inclined her head upward toward the hundred and twenty feet of air above her.

• • •

"Siggy! Come and meet me in the gym. I've had a most superior idea! Come see!" Rachel spoke into her calling card.

"I can't. We're locked in." Sigfried sounded petulant, as if the security measures had been designed to personally stop him. "Lucky and I are burrowing through the basement floor with flaming acid. But we won't be out for another hour or two."

"Storm's let up. The doors have been unlocked for a while."

"Coming!" Sigfried announced. She heard him say, "Lucky, our brainy sister needs us. We'll have to finish this later. Cover the hole with some carpet!"

A couple of minutes later, she heard the outer door of the gymnasium banging open.

"Where are you?" Sigfried's voice came over the calling card.

"Just walk up to a door and ask for the pool."

When Sigfried arrived, Rachel was sitting on the edge of the gym's Olympic-sized pool, swinging her feet. She wore a simple black and white one-piece swimsuit with a blue racing stripe that she had discovered, after poking around the girls' locker room, in a cabinet marked "suits." When her blood brother entered the room, she jumped to her feet.

"Want to see something that is just the *craic*, as Oonagh and Ian would say?" Rachel grinned.

Sigfried put his hands in his pocket. Lucky zoomed around him, curling left and right. The serpentine dragon dived into the warm pool water and came bursting out again in a spray of droplets.

"Sure. What is it?" he asked.

"Watch this!"

The ceiling over the pool was normally the height of the gymnasium, but Rachel had asked a gym door to give her the pool but still keep the impossibly high ceiling of the flying course. To give herself as much distance as possible, she flew up nearly all of the hundred and twenty feet.

Up there, gazing down at Sigfried and Lucky, far below, a tremor of fear shot through her. At this height, the water would not give her any protection. According to an encyclopedia in the grand library of Gryphon Park that she had once read from cover to cover, a hundred feet was high enough for the speed of the descent to make hitting the water feel like striking concrete. Rachel recalled how much belly-flopping off the raft in the lake behind her parent's house had hurt, and the raft had been only a foot above the waterline.

With a snort of disdain, Rachel dismissed that fear as unworthy. She had done the math. This would work. Besides, she had tried this maneuver twice before showing it off. Taking a deep breath, Rachel pulled her feet out of the forward stirrups and dove from her broom.

She plummeted head first toward the pool. The air rushed against her face, Her hair streamed upwards. Below, she could see the look of sheer terror on the face of Sigfried. Lucky streaked toward her, as if hoping to catch her.

Rachel reached out her hand. *"Varenga, Vroomie!"*

The falling broom shot into her outstretched grip. Rachel curled her body around the steeplechaser and pulled back on the handles. The bristleless swung upward with Rachel atop it again. Grinning and waving, she flew gently down to land beside her blood brother.

"Smashing trick, eh? What did you think?"

Sigfried's face was entirely white. "I think you should warn a chap before you do that!"

Rachel's expression did not change, but inside she danced a victory dance. After all, it was not every day that she succeeded at disconcerting Sigfried the Dragonslayer.

Chapter Nine:

The Unfortunate Fate of Zoë Forrest

"Rachel! Something's happened!" Gaius's voice sounded next to her ear. "Can you talk?"

"Yes, I... oomph!" For the umpteenth time, Rachel fell off the narrow balance beam into the softness of foam rubber.

"I thought you would want to know," Gaius's voice blurted in her ear, "Your friend the princess apparently came back from dreamland without Zoë Forrest. Zoë's been lost!"

"Lost?" cried Rachel, flailing in her attempt to regain her feet.

"Lost how? Wait.—Dreamland? When?—I t-thought Nastasia had gone home for a few days!"

"That was apparently *after* she lost Miss Forrest. From what Vlad has learned, the two of them went somewhere in dreamland. While they were traveling, something snatched Zoë. Nastasia came back and contacted her family."

"W-what!" Rachel's voice grew unnecessarily shrill. "You mean she *lost* Zoë, and she didn't *tell* us? For *days*?"

Gaius sounded apologetic. "That's all Vlad knows." Rachel let out a howl of outrage.

"Look, Rach. That's all I know. Really. If I knew more, I would tell you. I swear."

Rachel gave up trying to rise. She threw herself backward into the clumps of foam and sighed glumly. "It's—not your fault."

"I—I thought you would want to know."

"Thanks. I appreciate your telling me, Gaius." She was silent a moment. "Poor Zoë. Can anything be done?"

"Vlad is doing everything he can, Rachel. If she can be found, he'll find her."

• • •

Dinner was a muted affair. Rachel had passed on the news about Zoë to Joy and Sigfried, who passed it on to Zoë's two friends from the same home town in Michigan where Zoë lived during the rare periods when she stayed with her father: Sigfried's partner-in-crime, Seth Peregrine, and Misty Lark, a sullen girl from Marlowe Hall with a head of short, straw-like hair. Rachel knew that the vile Mortimer Egg had forced Misty to watch the murder of her family.

Joy was especially distraught. She ate none of her meal but asked a thousand questions, none of which Rachel could answer. She kept crying, "First the elf lady and now Zoë?"

Siggy, on the other hand, chowed down with his usual enthusiasm. He did not seem particularly worried about Zoë, who he seemed convinced would soon reappear. His fury at the princess, however—for going adventuring in dreamland without him—knew no bounds.

• • •

"Nastasia!" Rachel raced through the slush to where her friend glided solemnly across the commons. Snow fell softly about them, illuminated by the lampposts supporting glass globes filled with fluttering will-o'-the-wisps. Nastasia Romanov wore a long blue coat with white fur trim. A golden curl or two poked out of the voluminous hood. Her face in person was far lovelier than Rachel had remembered it, a phenomenon that Rachel always found mildly disturbing.

"I have returned," the Princess of Magical Australia said gravely. Despite the golden glow of the wisp-lamps, her face seemed paler than usual. "Did Ivan give you my message?"

"Yes, he did. Are you all right?" Rachel rushed to her friend's side. "What happened to Zoë? Do you have any idea how to rescue her?"

Nastasia's face grew paler still. "How did you come to hear about Zoë?"

"Gaius told me."

The princess seemed quite agitated. "I will have to report this to the dean! We shared the information about Miss Forrest in gravest confidence. Whoever told your—friend must have been spying on the dean!"

"But.... " A terrible feeling, like nausea, gripped Rachel. Had she betrayed Vlad and Gaius without even knowing it? She took a deep breath. "What happened?"

"We managed to bring the shade of our elf friend back to her world and her husband without incident, but on the way back—"

"You *went* without *us*?" Rachel shouted.

Her voice reverberated over the reflecting lake and echoed off of Roanoke Hall. Across the commons, students returning to their dorms paused and looked their direction.

Rachel did not care. In her whole life, she had *never* been so angry.

"How could you go without Siggy and me?" she yelled. "You knew we wanted to go!"

"I am not at fault. I was taking a brief nap, a break from working on my paper, and Zoë showed up in my dream. The elf woman appeared and asked us to bring her home. Really, Rachel, what were we supposed to do?"

Rachel's face had become bright red. She fought to keep control of her mind. "You were supposed to say, *'Hold on. Rachel and Sigfried want to come, too!'*"

Her voice broke as she remembered Siggy's anger and his promise to forgive the princess—once she had taken them to visit Hoddmimir's Wood. *How would he react now?*

Nastasia held up one fair hand, her face stern. "Please, Rachel, control yourself. Such behavior is not becoming of a lady."

The Lady Rachel Griffin seethed with wrath, but her face became instantly calm. When she could keep her voice reasonably even, she replied, "Very well. Go on."

"The elf woman explained that we did not need to step down into her world, now that she was a shade. Merely bringing her back to her dreamland would be enough. So there did not seem to be any point to making a large expedition of it."

"Do you think I did not want to see that? What the dreamland of Hoddmimir's Wood looked like?" Rachel's voice was low and forlorn. "And we can't go back, can we? Without our Elf here for you to touch, so that you can find a pathway?"

"No. We certainly cannot," Nastasia replied sternly, her face ghostly pale. "But I would not return in any case. The silver ways are not safe. Miss Forrest was yanked out of my hand. One moment, we traveled the silver track together. The next, she was gone."

• • •

Saturday dragged into Sunday. They spent a dreary day inside studying quietly—except for Joy, who continued to weep loudly, mourning the loss of Zoë Forest. Rachel tried to assure Joy that Zoë would return, that everything possible was being done, but Nastasia interrupted, announcing solemnly that false hope was beneath them. After that, Joy was inconsolable.

Unable to help, Rachel fled the dorm. She spent the morning in her private hallway, practicing sorcery and experimenting with what she had learned at Ouroboros Industries. She also spent time loading into her grandmother's wand spells and cantrips she had mastered, keeping careful note of how many charges of each she stored. To her disappointment, Gaius did not come by, though he did welcome her enthusiastically when she joined him at lunch.

That afternoon, Gaius was busy studying. Rachel wangled a few coins from Lucky, enough to buy warm winter gear for Sigfried: coat, hat, mittens, scarf, and a pair of fur-lined boots, which she ordered from catalogs she kept in her trunk. Then she went for a long, quiet ride on her broom before repairing to the gym, where she continued both practicing standing on a balance beam and diving, falling, and calling her broom back to her hand. After several hours, she tripped on the balance beam and plummeted into the foam rubber pit. When, due to overwhelming exhaustion, she neglected to rise immediately, she drifted off to sleep.

She woke up after sundown, which, now that it was mid-November, came quite early. Rachel took advantage of the failing twilight and soared up to the roof of Roanoke Hall, the real one, not the copy in the gym. Flying to the hexagonal tower, she opened a window with the Word of Opening, rejoicing that she had finally mastered that cantrip. Inside was a room containing a sofa covered by a peach damask slipcover, a large cream and peach quilted comforter, two giant satiny throw pillows, creamy with bright iridescent blue and green peacocks whose tails trailed off the pillows, and, added more recently, the plushy lion with the large red bow that Sandra had bought for her in London.

Hugging the toy lion, she dropped onto the peach damask sofa, causing its old springs to creak. She lay with her feet on the armrest, turning the black bracelet on her wrist and staring up at the cracks in the ceiling. Her conversation with Sigfried weighed heavily upon her. She had hoped that the break between her friends could be repaired, but now that Nastasia had gone to Hoddmimir's Wood without them, she did not see how it could be.

If it could not, she was going to have to revise her loyalty ladder.

Ever since the first week of school, when she had been torn in so many directions, she had kept a strictly ranked list detailing the hierarchy of her relationship with each person who had laid a claim to her fealty. She was determined to avoid another mental battle over her loyalty, as her internal civil war seemed to that horrible sense that she was about to lose herself to encroaching darkness. Should an attempt be made in the future to divide her allegiances, she would need but glance at her mental ladder. A person on the higher rung automatically won out over anyone below them.

Currently, the list was as follows:

Rung One—Gaius
Rung Two—Sigfried and Nastasia
Rung Three—The Raven
Rung Four—Father
Rung Five—the rest of her family: Mummy, Sandra, Laurel, and Peter
Rung Six—other members of the Die Horribly Debate Club
Rung Seven —Agents she knew and liked, such as Darling or Standish or Bridges
Rung Eight—the dean, Mr. Badger, Mr. Chanson, Mr. Fuentes
Rung Nine—other friends and tutors she liked

In recent days, however, there had been two upsets. The first was the tension between Sigfried and Nastasia. It was bad enough that Nastasia did not want to have anything to do with Gaius or Vlad. If Rachel's two best friends stopped getting along, she would no longer be able to be equally loyal to them. If one of them should ask her to keep a secret from the other, she would have to decide which one ranked higher on the ladder.

Whom would she choose? Would she share Nastasia's private musings with Sigfried? Or would she reveal Sigfried's secrets to Nastasia? In her heart, she knew that this question had already been answered, but she did not want to face it by officially demoting one of her friends off the second rung.

The other problem was: *Vladimir Von Dread.*

Rachel ran her finger along the cool metal of her black bracelet, remembering with a tingle of secret delight how he had knelt to present it to her. Before this, Dread had merely been an adjunct to Gaius. Rachel trusted Gaius above all others, but she kept secrets from the prince. He was a dark horse, and her friends did not trust him.

But now?

Vlad was to be her future brother-in-law. Did that put him on the family rung? Rachel smiled slightly. Future Brother-In-Law had a nice ring to it. She loved giving people nicknames. She called the Raven by the name Jariel, which she had taken from a dream, and she thought of Illondria, Queen of the Lios Alfar, as the Elf, or perhaps her Elf. Maybe she would secretly call Vlad Future Brother-In-Law.

Or FB-I-L.

Or just FB for short.

But FB or not FB, the question remained: Where should she put him on her loyalty hierarchy? Should she leave him on Sandra's rung? Should she move him higher, closer to Father, now that Vlad had stepped forward to protect her personally? Should she push Gaius off the top rung and give it to the prince?

Rachel toyed with this idea. Much as she adored Gaius, the top rung of the ladder belonged to her Most-Favorite Person. This has been a good thing back when the position was held by her imperious grandfather, but she could not deny that having a sixteen-year-old-boy at the center of her universe was a bad idea. She had known this, but last week when Gaius discovered that Rachel and her friend knew one of his secrets—the content of what he had told the Agents while under the influence of the *Spell of True Recitation*—he had threatened to spill her secrets to Von Dread. That betrayal hit Rachel so hard that she had nearly lost her grip on her sanity. Only the intervention of her Elf had saved her.

It was time to take action and find a different most-favorite person. *But—who?*

Why she needed a most-favorite person in her life, Rachel did not know. Other people seemed to get by just fine without one. Or people outside her family did, at least. In her family, Sandra was Father's favorite, and Peter was Mother's favorite. She had been Grandfather's favorite, back when he lived. Poor Laurel had always been a bit on her own. Rachel wondered how her middle sister did it, or if Laurel always felt as if something was missing.

Whatever Laurel's experience, Rachel seemed unable to function without someone in whom to put her faith—a rudder to help balance the ship of her soul. More than that, though, she needed a single person with whom she could share all her secrets without fear of repercussions, a steady and reliable person, like Grandfather, or her father. Grandfather had been volatile in his moods, but he had never let his emotions affect his judgment.

Grandfather never would have threatened to betray her merely because he became upset.

Rachel had enough problems holding back the onslaught of chaotic emotions—fear, agony, sorrow—that threatened to sweep over her. Things had been better since her visit to Sandra's, but she had to be vigilant and not let down her guard. If she did, the thing that had happened to her in dreamland, after Gaius turned on her, might start again—the darkness that encroached on the edges of her vision; a buzzing noise, like a swarm of bees or perhaps distant thunder.

She did not know what caused this mental distress, but she suspected. Her mother had warned her against relying too heavily upon the family dissembling techniques. Hiding her emotions from other people was one thing. Using their secret technique to manhandle aside emotions that needed to be experienced—such as grief over a dead friend, or horror upon learning that friends had watched their families be murdered, or the terror of watching the Starkadder prince be dragged down into eternal torment—was another thing entirely.

Rachel suspected that she had destabilized the delicate balance of emotions within her mind. Only by a steady effort could she now keep herself on an even keel. Luckily, her will was strong. Pinning her faith on a boy, however, was not helping her. She needed someone calmer.

Could that person be Vladimir Von Dread?

Rachel closed her eyes. She imagined herself as a member of Vlad's group, working with William and Topher and Jenny. She could not picture Nastasia joining them, but perhaps Vlad would find a place for Sigfried. Siggy admired Dread tremendously. Maybe the Prince could make him a knight of Bavaria?

The idea of joining Vlad's group delighted her. She could be in on their secret councils, learn physics, help protect the world—and spend more time with Gaius! The problem was: Von Dread expected obedience from his people. She could not bring herself to obey her father or Dean Moth. *Could she obey Dread?*

With her eyes still closed, Rachel pictured some calamity occurring on campus. Vladimir, concerned for her safety, might instruct her to remain in a safe place. She imagined standing beside Roanoke Hall, looking off into the hemlocks, and seeing some disturbance in the distance, someone in need... and running off into the forest to help whomever needed her, without a second thought.

Opening her eyes, Rachel let out a long sad sigh. If she could not obey Vladimir, she could not join his group. And there was no way she would stand idle if someone was in need, just because Vladimir Von Dread told her to. Sighing again, she grabbed the plushy lion with its huge red bow and hugged it tightly.

By the time the bell rang for dinner, she had not come to any useful conclusion as to who should replace Gaius or where, upon her mental ladder, to place his boss.

• • •

"Marry him?" Joy was shrieking as Rachel arrived at the dinner table. "You're fourteen!"

"Please, Miss O'Keefe," —a hint of exasperation slipped through Nastasia's dulcet tones— "we are in the dining hall. Perhaps, this is not the most fitting location for drawing attention to ourselves. Especially as many members of his family are here. I would hate for the arrangement to go awry because they thought me a gossip."

"They want you to marry whom?" Rachel put down her dinner tray. Recalling Freya Starkadder's parting words, she added, "You mean Wulfgang? Who wants you to marry him?"

"My mother," Nastasia stated simply, cutting her spaghetti and meatballs with a knife and fork. "While I was at home, she informed me that the King of Transylvania had inquired about a match between our kingdoms. Mother and Queen Epona chose Wulfgang and me as the couple they thought best suited."

"But Wulfgang's so arrogant and so creepy!" exclaimed Joy.

"Would your children turn into wolves?" asked Siggy, who sat backwards on his chair, tossing meatballs into the air for Lucky to catch and swallow. "That would be wicked! But wait, aren't the Starkadders actually wolves who turn into men? Perhaps the question should be: would your pups be able to turn into babies?"

Rachel glanced at him briefly and then looked away, recalling the previous moment. She saw no sign of anger in his eyes, but there was an odd belligerence that troubled her.

"I would think your ages would be more of an issue than puppies or creepiness," Valerie said dryly. "Do people really get married at fourteen in Magical Australia?"

The notion of people in Magical Australia getting married caused Rachel to twitch. A spasm of hatred toward Ivan Romanov and his mockery constricted her throat.

"We would not be wed until we reached our majority, of course," Nastasia replied in her cultured Magical Australian accent, which differed notably from a mundane Australian accent. "It would only be an engagement at this point."

"Do you like him?" Rachel asked, sitting down.

"That is of no consequence," Nastasia replied simply. "My wish is to be useful to my family."

"Pull!" Siggy threw an entire egg salad sandwich.

The white and yellow mess tumbled through the air, shedding droplets of mayonnaisey egg. The girls threw up their arms, shrieking. Lucky proved up to the task. With a burst of red-gold fire, the entire flaming sandwich, droplets and all, disappeared down the dragon's gullet. Alas, in his enthusiasm to get the whole sandwich, the red puff of his tail knocked over Valerie's glass.

"Lucky! How could you!" Siggy chided. "You killed my G.F.'s apple juice!"

Lucky hung his head, ears drooping. "Sorry, boss. Sorry, Goldi-haired-one. Here, I'll help clean up."

His long tongue flickered out of his mouth, rapidly lapping up the spilled juice. But his method only spread the liquid around on the table.

"Huh. That's not really helping," noted Valerie.

"You want I should incinerate the mess?" Lucky opened his mouth very wide and began to breath in.

"It's okay, Lucks." Valerie patted the dragon's silky fur. "I got it." She mopped up the juice. Very quickly, it soaked through her thin napkin.

Rachel handed her own napkin to Valerie. "Here, take mine. I'll get some more."

She pushed her chair in and headed for the kitchen, where she picked up a handful of napkins and another apple juice for Valerie. As she was about to leave, the black bracelet vibrated against her arm. Gaius's voice spoke beside her ear.

"Rachel, that Maori dream expert from New Zealand—the one who made Zoë's slippers. Do you recall—?" Gaius's voice snorted with self-effacing amusement. "What am I thinking! Of course, you recall. You're Rachel Griffin! But, seriously, can you tell us his name?"

Rachel paused with her hand on the kitchen door, smiling. "Aperahama Whetu."

"Thanks, Rach. That's a big help! Vlad, the dream exp—" His voice cut off, as the black bracelet stopped vibrating.

"Move it, pipsqueak," a female voice demanded behind her. "Stop blocking traffic!"

"Oh, I'm sorry, I—" Rachel swung around and found herself face to face with a scowling Eunice Chase.

Eunice was dressed in subfusc, with a long black skirt and twin black ribbons draping from her throat. She had medium-length auburn hair and enormous hoop earrings as big as Rachel's palm. She towered over Rachel, looking down at her with a cold stare. In her hands, she held a muffin and a glass of tomato juice.

Behind Eunice, walking toward the door with their trays, were two other older girls that Rachel recognized, penny-haired Colleen MacDannan and the cool and snide Tessa Dauntless. Both girls were from Drake Hall, like Eunice. Both were Upper School Seniors in Gaius's core group, and, worst of all, both were in love with him.

Colleen, at least, had the MacDannan Irish charm. Tess was superior and haughty. With her wavy blond hair and her arresting blue eyes, she always struck Rachel as the kind of girl that boys adored but not the kind that was good for them. Rachel had heard more than one Drake girl snickering about how well the names "Dauntless" and "Valiant" sounded together. She wondered if Gaius also adored that kind of girl.

"Get out of my way," sneered Eunice, "and get out of these ladies' way. It's physically sickening to see Valiant dating a worm like you."

"I do have this to thank you for," Tess held her full tray with one hand and slipped her free arm around Colleen's waist, giving the other girl a friendly hug. "I can't think of anything else that might have made the two of us get along. Now we have a mutual foe to hate."

Colleen laughed gaily, but she looked faintly uncomfortable, as if she was not exactly sure where she stood on the matter of hating one of her cousin's friends, even if that friend were dating the boy Colleen fancied.

Tess released Colleen and sauntered forward until she stood beside Eunice. She leaned toward Rachel and drawled, "You know Valiant is only playing up to you in hopes of getting an in with your father and the Wisecraft."

Colleen burst into gales of laughter. "Fat lot of good that'll do him. My uncle says Agent Griffin is the most tight-lipped man in the Wisecraft, after Templeton Bridges, of course. They used to be partners—Agent Griffin and my uncle, I mean."

"By your uncle, you mean James Darling, Agent, right?" asked Eunice, her eye twitching.

"You don't like Agent Darling, do you?" Rachel's eyes narrowed. "Because he forced you to confess how badly you treat your little sister?"

Eunice's face grew pale. "H-how do you know that?"

Oops. Wasn't it secret that she knew this?

"Maybe Agent Griffin blabs after all," chuckled Tess.

Eunice raised her cup of tomato juice threateningly over Rachel's head. "Whatcha gonna do, baby girl? Gonna to go running to Dread?" She looked around. "Oh, wait. He's not here."

Rachel crossed her arms, careful not to spill the apple juice. "I can fight my own battles, thank you very much."

Eunice snorted derisively. "Fight? You might be able to beat First-Week Cydney but against me? You wouldn't last five seconds."

"Do pour, Eunice," purred Tess. "I so enjoy the sight of Miss Griffin covered with juice."

Rachel's face remained calm, despite her desire to clench her teeth. Tess was the girl who had been clinging to Gaius's arm the day Rachel had run by, covered with orange juice.

"Maybe I will," replied Eunice. "Or maybe I'll go pour it over my sister Magdalene."

"You wouldn't dare," Rachel replied calmly in a voice reminiscent of Dread's. She recalled Eunice's face when Vlad had first spoke in Rachel's defense at the Knight's meeting. "You might talk big here, but you *are* afraid of Von Dread. He's protecting Magdalene."

Eunice's face turned bright red. "H-how did you know that? Did Gaius blab?"

Oops again. She probably should not have mentioned that either.

"No," Rachel replied archly. "Gaius does not even know that I know."

"It's no use trying to protect him," hissed Eunice, waving the tomato juice back and forth above Rachel's head. "It has to be him.

Who else could have told you about private Drake matters? I'm going to tell on him!" she cried excitedly. "People need to know that
he's a snitch!"

No! Now she was going to get Gaius into trouble, and it was not
even his fault! Out of loyalty to her boyfriend, Rachel blurted out
the truth.

"Not so. I know because..." she paused, took a breath, and
blurted out, "I'm the person who asked Vlad to stop you from hitting
her."

An angry, high-pitched sound issued from Eunice. Her face
grew blotchy and purple. She jerked her arm, dashing her cup of
juice into Rachel's face. Bright, red, liquid tomato flew through the
air. Without hesitating, Rachel repeated the words and gestures
that Gaius had used to remove the orange juice from her robes, during the first week of school.

"*Silu varenga. Taflu!*"

The first drops spattered against her skin and robes. She
cringed, but nothing more struck her. The cantrip had worked!

Only, she had neglected to consider the glass in her own hand.
Both liquids, the tomato juice that had been in mid-flight toward
her and the apple juice in the glass for Valerie, flew away from her
and splashed across the faces and trays of the three older girls.

All three howled in outrage.

For the second time in as many days, Rachel ran.

CHAPTER TEN:

PLAYING HOOKY WITH OGRES

"PSST! SIGGY," RACHEL CALLED FROM WHERE SHE CROUCHED, HIDing, as Siggy came out of the dining hall after breakfast.

It was the next morning. The sky was cloudy and gray. A brisk, icy wind blew across the campus. Wet slush covered the ground, squelching beneath students' feet, as they tromped across the bridge that spanned the reflecting lake on their way to class or back to their dorms. Rachel squatted beside the stone wall of the bridge, clutching her broom. She was trying to stay out of sight of the dining hall, shivering despite her red wool coat and her snowman hat.

"Rachel, why are you hiding behind the bridge?" Sigfried peered over the stone wall. "Lucky, look sharp! Something is alarming our blood sister! Threats could be anywhere!"

"I see a short, humanoid, student-person in a bulky green parka and a professor-like tutor person wearing red and black robes. They are walking at five o'clock," Lucky called back from where he snaked through the air above Siggy's head. "Should I burninate them?"

"Hmm," Siggy stroked his imaginary beard. "Difficult call. Better hold off until we are sure. We just finished with detention. I would hate to have to start again, if it turned out that we burninated an innocent bystander. When would I have time to practice with Seth for our new band, the Punk Magicians—or should we go with Dragonsmiths?—if I were spending all my free periods weeding gardens and mopping floors?"

"Probably wise," nodded Lucky, but he gazed longingly after the moving targets.

"Could you possibly spare a vial of your super chameleon potion?" whispered Rachel.

Sigfried pulled out a crystal vial and handed it to her. "Whatcha want it for?"

Lucky blurted out. "You have to tell the boss, so he can be Implicated."

Rachel gestured with her broom. "I want to go into the kitchen and get some breakfast."

Siggy stared at her as if she had misplaced her head.

"Rachel," he said very slowly, "in this crazy school, the kitchens are a cornucopia of endless food. Even students are allowed to take food. You don't even have to steal it. But if you are really hungry, I saved some spaghetti from dinner last night. It's a little cold, but still good." He started to reach into his pocket.

"That's okay!" squeaked Rachel, waving her hands back and forth in the hope of not having to start the morning with a glimpse, or worse a whiff, of day-old spaghetti. "I'm hiding from some upperclassmen who are angry with me."

"And they want to hurt you?" Siggy forgot the spaghetti, suddenly alert.

"Um... they might. That's why I'm hiding."

He grinned and struck his palm with his fist. "Point me at them."

"They're girls."

"Yoooooowwwww!" Siggy threw his head back and howled in despair. "Why does it always have to be girls? Why can't it ever be a boy? King Arthur will never forgive me if I punch a girl, or smash her against a wall with an air blast, or use her to practice the one-two kidney punch and upper cut combo Seth's been teaching me, or if Lucky lit her hair on fire! Why must it always be girls?"

Rachel straightened up and smoothed her robe, leaning the steeplechaser against the wall. "I don't think it will ever be boys. The boys are smart enough to be afraid of Valiant and Dread."

"Wise on their parts." Siggy nodded sagely. "Wise."

Lucky asked, "Why aren't the girls afraid?"

Rachel shrugged. "Maybe they think they're safe because they're girls. Or maybe it is because two of them are in love with Gaius. I guess they think that if they can get him away from me, Dread won't defend me any more. So, the risk is worth it."

Siggy blinked rapidly and put his arms out, as if he were feeling around, blind. "Wha... were you saying something? Words were coming out of your mouth, but they were so excruciatingly boring that I think my ears are bleeding."

Rachel did not know whether to laugh or sigh.

"Hey," she cried excitedly, "Could you spy on them for me? Tess Dauntless and Colleen MacDannan, I mean? Find out if they're plotting to steal my boyfriend?"

Sigfried puffed out his chest and stared at Rachel as if she had asked him to commit some abomination. "Miss Griffin, I am to use my vast powers only for pranks, petty crimes, gathering gold, self-aggrandizement and/or saving the world — but not for girly stuff! I do have *some* standards. Besides, what would Valerie say, if she found out I was staring all day at the luscious yet pouty-lipped Tess Dauntless?"

"Oh." Rachel wilted. "I hadn't thought of that."

"But, if it will help," Siggy continued, "I can use my MacDannan contacts to find out if Colleen MacDannan talks about Valiant. And I am willing to give you a vial of my souped-up, Elf-Herb, Chameleon Juice Elixir, so you can sneak up and eavesdrop on them."

"No, never mind. I was just curious," Rachel said quickly, hiding her disappointment. She felt embarrassed to have voiced aloud such a petty desire. "I've already asked Ian about Colleen and Gaius. He said one of his brothers insisted they were seriously in love, and the other said they were just friends." She rolled her eyes.

Sigfried stated, "Random spying at random times on random conversations is unlikely to yield useful information. I suggest we study harder and learn how to cast the *Spell of True Recitation*. Then you can mug your rivals and force them to talk. Valiant does not seem the type to play the two-timer. If I were you, I would forget this matter and turn my vast mental prowess to a problem of greater significance, such as how to use your superior Broom Goddess talents so that Lucky and I can make money through an off-track betting ring."

"I'm not worried about Gaius!" Rachel cried, offended at the very notion. "I was just curious about the two girls: what they were like. Whether they were plotting against me."

Thunder rumbled in the distance. Siggy thrust the vial of chameleon elixir into Rachel's hand and yanked out another one.

"Quick! Drink this!" He pulled out the stopper of his vial and downed the liquid.

Rachel drank hers as well. The sweetness of it was pleasing, but the slithery aftertaste of chameleon made her shiver. She took a step toward the dining hall.

"Wait! Where are you going? If you go in there, the doors will lock, and we'll never get out. I told you, you can have my spaghetti," Sigfried sounded slightly wistful, as if parting with yesterday's dinner was difficult.

"Er... no thanks," Rachel replied politely; "But why shouldn't I go inside? It looks like it might storm and—"

"Take me up!" Siggy grabbed her arm, which was only partially visible to Rachel. She could see blotches of snow and stone where her elbow should be. However, she knew that Sigfried's superior sorcery power allowed him to see them, at least a little, even when the elixir fully took effect.

"Up?"

"I want to see the storm goblin in action."

"But he throws *lightning!*"

"I missed my chance to see another world." Sigfried scowled savagely. "She betrayed us. First, she fired a knight. Second, she made us wait instead of going right away. And then, she had the gall to go without us! That's three betrayals!"

"I'm upset, too, Siggy, but that doesn't mean I want to be fricasseed in midair."

"But how else are we going to save Wheels?"

Rachel shook her head, as if to shake away her confusion. "How does getting fried alive have anything to do with Zoë?"

"We can't get into dreamland to rescue Zoë without her sandals, right?" asked Siggy.

Rachel nodded. It was eerie knowing that Siggy, with his superior magical talents, could see her nod when she could not make him out at all.

"We need someone who can go into dreamland," Siggy continued, "like the storm goblin. If we follow him, maybe we can figure out how he goes back and forth." When Rachel stared at him, puzzled, he added, "In Art class, didn't Mrs. Heelis tell us that the fey realm and the place where humans dream are the same? One is just 'deeper in,' whatever that means."

"Sigfried!" cried Rachel. "That's brilliant!"

Siggy crowed, "See, Lucky, sometimes, even I have good ideas."

"Even a broken clock is right twice a day," Lucky replied, gazing proudly at his master. Apparently, Lucky could see them, too.

"But…" Rachel hesitated, "even if we found our way into the Heer's mountain hall—and lived—how would we find Zoë? We don't have Nastasia's magic travel power, and Nastasia didn't even tell us where she lost her. Zoë might not even be on earth. She might have fallen off one of those silvery paths of the princess's on another world."

"Lucky her," muttered Siggy.

Rachel sighed.

Lightning split the gray morning sky. The bells began to ring in a *ring-ring*, pause, *ring-ring* pattern. Wooden shutters formed out of puffs of mist that appeared in front of the windows Rachel could see: Roanoke Hall, the dorm towers, the infirmary, and the gym. Rachel wondered obscurely why no one had thought to place shutters over the skylights in the gymnasium. Or, at least, none had appeared up there the day she was locked in the gym.

"What are those? They came out of nowhere!" cried Sigfried, startled.

Rachel sighed. "That's conjuration, Siggy. Looks just like when we conjure in class."

"Oh, right," muttered Siggy, adding, "Here. Take this."

Rachel could not see him, but a hard, ridged object with a cord dangling from it was thrust into her hand.

"Put this around your neck and eat this," continued Sigfried's voice.

The hard object that felt like a key was followed by something soft and springy.

"What is this?" Rachel sniffed dubiously. The spongy substance had a lemony scent.

"Nettle cake," Siggy explained. "Protects against lightning. And the other thing is an oak amulet. Oak also protects against lighting."

"You've put a great deal of thought into this!" Rachel exclaimed.

"How did you...?"

"I've been asking around. Ian told me about these things. Apparently, his grandfather had a trick for redirecting lightning, and his father used to have to protect himself from it. Not clear on whether the grandfather and father were fighting each other—like Marvel heroes—or if the father just had to make sure he was safe when the grandfather threw lightning. Either way, I talked our Alchemy teacher into teaching me how to make them. Well, he gave me the cakes, but he taught me how to make the protective amulets."

"Really?" Rachel took a bite of the nettle cake. It tasted sweet and lemony. "That was awfully nice of him!"

Siggy coughed slightly. "He might possibly be under the false impression that the storm goblin makes me nervous."

Rachel giggled. "But he doesn't, I gather. The Heer, I mean."

"Are you kidding?" Siggy cried. "I've been after him since the day I arrived."

"Come to think of it, that's how we met, wasn't it?" Rachel mused. "You and I flew out to Stony Tor because you wanted to find the Heer's prison."

"Exactly! Let's go up now and have a look! I want to see where he lives."

"Fly across the river to Storm King Mountain?" Rachel's voice rose. "Is that wise?"

"We're protected from lightning, and we're invisible."

The last students visible on the commons ran into Roanoke Hall. As they passed through the portal, the great oak doors shut with a reverberating bang. Rachel looked up at the quickly-darkening sky and then at the rounded peak of the pyramidal Storm King Mountain, rising in the distance. She hopped on her broom, which vanished once she sat upon it, and patted the back of the long seat for Sigfried to climb on behind her.

"Mission a go, then?" ask Sigfried.

"Quite," replied Rachel with a brisk nod, as she launched into the air.

⋯

Rachel and Siggy soared across the commons and down the tree-lined path to the docks, following the same path she and Gaius had taken on their way to visit O.I. Lucky flew along beside them. He, too, was invisible, using his own natural methods. Rachel had to glance in his direction and then think back in order to have any notion of the dragon's whereabouts. Alas, that technique did not work against chameleon elixir. She could not see Sigfried at all.

"So, what about this boy-eating ogre?" asked Siggy.

"The ogre?" Rachel straightened up. "I don't know. According to *Larger Than Life: Trolls, Ogres, Jotuns, and Giants*, by my hero, Daring Northwest, ogres have a number of origins. Some were thought to be fey creatures, like pixies or trolls or leprechauns; others the offspring of giants and trolls. Still others were thought to have once been sorcerers who had practiced alchemy directly upon their own bodies. There was an ogre in the book named Mambres who had been given a charmed life by Baba Yaga, so that neither sword nor arrow could harm him. Another from France, who was turned back into a handsome prince when a girl fell in love with him, and a second French one who was eaten by an unusually clever cat. And yet another, not French this time, whose seven-league boots were stolen by a boy named Hop-o'-My-Thumb, which strikes me as a ridiculous name to call a baby."

"They probably called him Hop for short," opined Sigfried. He thought for a moment. "When Mr. Fisher warned us in Science class that bad things would happen if we put influences directly into our bodies, he didn't explain that by 'bad' he meant 'turn into an ogre.' Does that mean if I stop using elixirs for my alchemy, I can turn into an ogre? That would be wicked!"

Rachel gave the air behind her a skeptical look. "Do you think Valerie would like that?"

"I don't know. She'd get used to it."

Rachel rolled her eyes.

They burst from the tree-lined path and shot down the stairs of the ruins of Bannerman's Castle. Rain pelted their heads and slipped down the back of Rachel's neck. She shivered.

As she prepared to cross the Hudson, Siggy called out, "Eh! Before we go across, can we see the ogre?"

"What? Do you know how far that is? The ogre's cave is in Dutchman's Cove, at the northern most tip of the island. That's several miles up the coast! In the rain!"

"So," shrugged Siggy. "We're not busy, right?"

• • •

"Do you think he'll come out if I throw stones?" asked Sigfried.

The two of them hovered above the small island at the center of Dutchman's Cove, rain pelting down around them. They gazed at the dark opening in the rocky side of the curving western bluffs that Mr. Burke had once pointed out as the home of the ogre. To their left, the wooden ribs of the wreck of *The Flying Dutchman* were partially visible through the enormous branches of the fallen Roanoke Tree. The Heer of Dunderberg had blasted the great tree with the lightning bolt that slayed their friend the Elf. Farther inland, the burnt, hulking stump of the gigantic trunk still towered over the rain-soaked landscape.

Higher up the hill, beyond the towering stump, rose the rocky crescent that was all that remained of the peak of Stony Tor. Behind them, across Dutchman's Cove from the ogre's cave, lay open fields and, beyond that, out of sight, a small lake.

Rachel wiped the water from her face and glanced at the gigantic fallen trunk. She remembered back but saw no sign of the golden fire that had once danced along the limbs of the living tree.

"What if I send Lucky inside?" he asked.

"Don't send Lucky in!" Rachel screeched and grabbed for his arm, as the familiar red and gold form of the currently-visible dragon zigzagged toward the cave mouth. Only she misjudged where Sigfried was, since she could not see him, and found herself grabbing a handful of empty air. "That's how that boy was killed! He sent something into the ogre's home. It came after him. Hunted him down!"

Behind her, she heard Siggy loosen his knife. "We'll be ready for him! Won't we, Lucky!"

Rachel could not hear Lucky's answer, but Sigfried grunted with satisfaction. She could no longer see Lucky, either, unless she relied on her memory. He had faded from view.

"What if it has a charmed life, and you can't hurt it?" she asked. "Shouldn't we do some research first?"

"Charms, shmarms. What are the chances of that, anyhow?"

"Not very...." Rachel's voice trailed off. "Um, actually, the chances might be high."

"Why is that?"

"Because the person who gave that other ogre his charmed life was Baba Yaga."

"So?" Siggy asked innocently.

Why did Sigfried sound so innocent? That could not be good. Rachel glanced down and thought back. Her memory caught a glimpse of Lucky sneaking closer to the bluffs.

"She was here twenty-four years ago," she said worriedly, her eyes now tracking Lucky as he approached the cave, as his obscuration no longer fooled her eyes. "She was one of the Terrible Five."

"Baba Yaga? Did we learn that in some class? Oh! Wait! Wasn't she the gangmate of that Toast-high guy who Mr. Fisher fought?" "Yes. Koschei. Koschei the Deathless," Rachel said patiently. "Yes. They were... well, I wouldn't have chosen the term 'gangmates,' but that's close enough."

Siggy's voice suddenly became deadly serious. "But we do want to stop the ogre, don't we? Before it kills again? It isn't okay that it eats people, just because they are Unwary, is it?"

Rachel absentmindedly touched her chest above her heart as she recalled the tremendous sympathy she had felt for the family of Tommy Check during the Knights' meeting.

"No," she said softly but with great determination. "It isn't. And yes, it needs to be stopped. It must be stopped. We want to make the world a safer place—for everyone."

"Then let's vow to stop it," said Sigfried the Dragonslayer in all seriousness.

Lucky snaked through the rain and slid up to the cliffs. He disappeared into a second cave, farther to the south, and, popping out again, began sidling toward the ogre's abode. Both students fell silent. Rachel held her breath. The gold and red streamer that was Lucky zipped up to the dark mouth of the cave and disappeared from view. The silence stretched on and on.

"It's not home," Siggy scowled.

Rachel let out her pent up breath. "That's a relief?"

She wanted the ogre stopped, but rushing in half-cocked without any planning was just going to add to the ogre's larder.

"Lucky says it has some nifty treasure in its nest, though. Do you think it'd miss—"

"No!" cried Rachel, casting around for a logical reason to support her objection. "Y-you can't steal a monster's hoard unless you defeat him in combat! It wouldn't be knightly!"

"Good point." Siggy gave an exasperated sigh. Rachel could feel him securing his knife again. "How can a self-respecting person defeat a monster who isn't there?"

Lucky popped out of the cave, visible again.

"You'll just have to wait," said Rachel, much relieved.

"I hate waiting," muttered Sigfried.

The broom jerked as he suddenly leaned sideways toward the cliff. He shouted, "I'm coming for you, ogre! I hope you enjoyed munching down on that Tommy boy, because he's the last teenager you'll ever eat!"

CHAPTER ELEVEN:

STORM CHASING BY STEEPLECHASER

ONCE THEY WERE BACK AT THE SOUTHERN COAST OF ROANOKE, Rachel bent low and jetted across the Hudson at racing speeds. Keeping close to Storm King, she shot up past where a paved road had been cut into the side of the mountain, continuing up the slope. From beneath came the loud whistle of the train that wound its way around the foot of the mountain.

As they drew closer to the bowl-like, rocky peak, she slowed down. This was for the best, because she was completely unprepared for the peal of thunder that followed when a lightning bolt struck nearby. The noise was so loud that the ground trembled, and the very air itself seemed to shake. Nearly deafened, Rachel clapped her hands to her ears. The hairs on the back of her neck stood up. She could not see Siggy, but his arms let go of her waist, presumably because he was also covering his ears.

Siggy shouted, but it took three tries before she could hear him over the thunder-induced deafness and the rising winds. "Look! Over there! The Heer's fighting somebody!"

"Let's go take a look, shall we?"

She dived toward the brilliant flashes, alternating between steering the steeplechaser and covering her ears, as deafening thunderclaps shook the mountain. Below, the Heer of Dunderberg and his lightning imps fought a half a dozen Agents of the Wisecraft, who stood on the slopes in their billowing Inverness cloaks, surrounded by fog. An Agent's tricorne hat blew by, sailing on the wind. Lucky must have dashed after it invisibly, because the hat suddenly reversed direction and zipped back to the ground near the surprised Agent's feet.

The Agents shot Glepnir bonds, silver nets, and brightly-colored blue sparks from their fulgurators' staves, but the lightning imps were too quick for them. The little electric-white creatures moved in an erratic zig-zag that reminded Rachel of a skater. They threw short javelins of crackly electricity that elongated once in flight. Farther up the slope, the Heer himself stood in midair, blowing his trumpet and crying out orders to his imps and mist sprites. He resembled a young boy dressed in orange and green.

Sparks and crackling javelins crisscrossed in mid-air. A stray lightning bolt headed for the broom. Rachel and Siggy screamed, but just before the rush of brilliant blue-white electricity could strike them, it swerved away. With a ragged breath, Rachel gave thanks for Siggy's protective amulets and the nettle cakes. The Agents below must have had similar protections, because she noted that the imps' lightning javelins swerved away from them, too.

"Lucky," Siggy called during one of the quieter moments, "see if you can catch an imp!"

"Right-o, boss!"

Rachel watched, remembering back until she could see him. The dragon darted forward with river-like grace, as swift as a rushing current. The imp must also have been able to see him. Moving with the speed of lightning, it twisted and zagged, escaping before Lucky could attack. Again and again, Lucky lunged, flame erupting from his mouth. Again and again, the imp was not there.

Another imp threw a crackling lightning javelin at Lucky. Thunder ripped the sky. Siggy screamed out an inarticulate warning. Lucky dodged, twisting in mid-air but not quickly enough. The bolt struck him, electricity dancing up and down the length of his serpentine body.

"Lucky! No!" Siegfried wailed, horrified.

Rachel grabbed his arm, where it clutched her waist, and squeezed, screaming.

Lucky plummeted. Rachel dived, racing after him. Before they could reach him, Lucky shook himself and floated upward. Rachel pulled up, hovering. Lucky made his way back toward them, listing slightly to the right. His mane, the ruff along his back, his tail puff, and long koi-like whiskers were burnt and blackened. His ruby belly scales were coated in soot.

"I's okay, boss. Just—a little—tired," Lucky murmured as he reached them. Siggy grabbed him and looped the dragon's long body around himself twice. Lucky laid his head across the empty area that was presumably occupied by Sigfried's invisible lap. Rachel felt Siggy lean forward to hug his familiar with both arms. The imprint of his cheek appeared in Lucky's fluffy side, leaving tears on the singed fur when the boy pulled away.

"We should head back!" Rachel began.

The heavens opened, and hailstones rained down. Hard balls of ice struck the three of them like hammer blows. Rachel shrieked. Leaning low over the bristleless's handle, she barreled across the Hudson. From behind them came a noise like a locomotive.

A gale force wind swept down from Storm King. It picked up the broom and threw it, helter-skelter, across the river. Rachel grabbed the steeplechaser and bent low over the shaft, holding on for dear life. Siggy had one arm wrapped around her waist and the other clutching Lucky. The three of them tumbled head over heels, left over right, blown about like a bit of thistledown in the wind. Frosty waters and then trees flashed by beneath them.

Inching her thumb forward, Rachel finally reached the toggle for the becalming enchantment and struck it. The air grew calm in a bubble around them. They drifted gently, panting and shaken. Finally, she raised her head and looked around.

The wall of living trees, which made up the protective wards of the school, were almost directly beneath them.

Rachel shouted in alarm. She had purposely never flown over the wards, fearing what the anti-magical barrier might do to the enchantments on her broom. Swiftly, she jiggled the levers and jerked the steeplechaser hard to the right. The broom turned slowly, banking widely, much more like the vectors William had shown her for a plane than like a normal broom motion. With a rising sense of panic, she realized why. The becalming enchantments were dramatically increasing the drag on the bristleless. The line of trees that maintained the wards of Roanoke grew nearer and nearer.

Then, it was beneath them. The bubble of calm encircling them popped. Down they plummeted.

They crashed, Vroomie and all, into the canopy of the hemlocks. Lucky, despite his weakened state, did his best to slow their descent. Between the dragon and the brief interval with the becalming enchantment, they were not moving very fast, but they still slammed into several branches as they descended, twigs snapping in their faces. Finally, they came to rest, draped over a large branch. Short, soft hemlock needles stuck in their clothing and hair.

They could see each other again. The magic of the chameleon potion had also ended.

Frantically, Sigfried checked on Lucky, peering closely into his face. When the dragon's slender tongue flickered out and brushed his master's face, Siggy slumped back against the branch where he was wedged and breathed a huge sigh of relief. Rachel, her heart in her mouth, was busily checking Vroomie. Apart from a few jammed tail fan slats, the broom showed no sign of damage. She also breathed a sigh of relief, only to wince at the pain that jabbed at her ribs.

"Ow!" moaned Rachel, as more hailstones pelted her. Moving gingerly, she slowly checked herself, padding her arms and legs and wiggling her toes. "Ouch! Many places hurt... but I don't think anything is broken."

"Why did we fall?" asked Sigfried. "And why can't I see anything except what is in front of my face?" His voice rose querulously. "I think my amulet's broken."

Rachel pointed to their left. Through the curtain of sleet, tall trees grew so close together as to form a solid wall. This living wall stretched in both directions as far as they could see.

"What's that—" Siggy paused. "I remember this! From the first time you and I went to see the Heer, back when he was still trapped in the tor. It's some kind of... a block? A wart?"

"A ward," Rachel laughed and shook her head, an action she immediately regretted, as it was followed by a painful throbbing. "The Heer's storm winds threw us over the wards of the school. When we crossed the ward without permission, the enchantments on my broom failed, and your amulet turned off. I-I don't know if we'll be able to get them started again."

Rachel held out the broom, trying to get it to hover. It remained a dead weight. She shook it, toggled the levers, smoothed out the tail fan again. Nothing. It could have been a perfectly mundane device. Panic rose threateningly inside her, and a lump began to form in her throat.

"So we… what?" Siggy yawned, leaning back against the hemlock. "Take up residence in this tree?"

Rachel gazed down dubiously through the thickly-needled branches beneath her. "I think we can climb down.…"

The hail had stopped, but a torrent of rain fell like a curtain from the roiling sky. A noisy racket came from a nearby copse; a flock of crows rose from the branches to chase an osprey from their territory. Amidst their raucous calls rang out a single, more-familiar sound.

Caw.

A horripilation of eerie wonder passed from Rachel's toes, up her body, to the top of her head. The steeplechaser bobbed in her hand.

"Oh, look! It's working!" she cried in delight.

"I can see again!" crowed Sigfried. "Woohoo! Glad that's over! You don't know how disconcerting it was not to be able to stare at the back of my own head."

Silently, Rachel mouthed, *Thank you, Jariel.*

They mounted the bristleless. Rachel and Sigfried sat on the black leather seat, while Lucky wrapped around the two of them, his head still resting on Siggy's lap. They floated awkwardly out of the hemlock.

Rachel flew swiftly upward to gain her bearing. Ahead, through the rain, she could see a break in the line of trees making up the ward. Flying nearby, Rachel saw that the gap was about fifteen feet across. Set into the ground between the two lines of trees were large, rectangular blocks of granite that Rachel judged would come to about waist height. These blocks formed a solid line of stone between the trunks.

"What's that?" Sigfried asked, as they flew onward.

"It's a ward-lock, a place where the wards can be lifted in case of an emergency. They have one about every mile or so. I see them when I'm flying."

A large outcropping of rocks stuck up above the treetops. Rachel knew that outcropping. It was northwest of the school. Finding a clearing, she dove down and flew through the trees near the ground, where the branches were thin. Upon reaching the outcropping, she circled the rocks until she found a dry place on the lee side. There, they huddled together beneath a stone overhang, wet and shivering, and waited for the rain to let up.

"Did I just see a statue?" Sigfried asked, as he wiped rainwater from his face.

"You mean of a woman with tears made of moss?"

"Something like that, yeah."

"That statue used to have wings," Rachel stated.

"Ooo! That's the one?" asked Siggy with great interest. "The one that got changed?"

Rachel nodded grimly.

"Wicked. I wonder what else has been changed."

Rachel looked down at the steeplechaser, which had failed to work and then worked.

Aloud, she said, "I know of a few things. The farm that belongs to Gaius and his father was not there when I was young. Certain aspects of the landscape I can see from Gryphon Tor altered when I was three. Presumably, when the Raven brought Gaius here."

"You mean, you can add landscapes? Could we add new countries? New continents?"

"Beyond the existing eight, you mean?" quipped Rachel, trying not to smirk.

"There are eight continents? When do we learn that? Is the eighth one invisible to the Unwary? What's on it? Dinosaurs? Space aliens? Fairies?"

Rachel burst into laughter. "There are only seven continents. I was pulling your leg."

"Oh, right, play head games with the Unwary kid," Sigfried scowled. He crossed his arms. "I feel robbed of a whole continent."

"Other than that, I only know of two hidden things," she continued, "A page of an ancient bestiary that had an entry for *angels*—"

"What are they?"

"Like demons but not evil. Like that statue, before her wings were removed."

"Interesting. What was the other hidden thing?"

"Something really trivial and odd. A silver rattle with an—" Rachel's voice faltered. She stood with an arrested expression on her face, icy water dripping down her forehead and nose.

"A... what?" Siggy waited breathlessly.

"An A." She wiped her face. "The letter A."

"Oooh! That's scary!"

"Good thing it wasn't a B!" exclaimed Lucky, who was recovering some of his normal enthusiasm. "Might have stung somebody!"

The dragon shook himself. Burnt, blackened fur broke off, revealing perfectly normal red and gold fur beneath.

"Sorry," Rachel blinked. "It just suddenly seemed... oddly significant. But, no matter. Rain's let up. Let's head home. We're probably going to be late for class as it is."

CHAPTER TWELVE:

WAYLAYING PETER, AGAIN

"LIBRA!" THE WINDOW TO HER DORM ROOM FLEW OPEN. RACHEL had dropped Siggy and Lucky by the back door of Dare Hall and then soared up to her room. Ducking, she now shot through the open window and landed on the floor beside her bed, sopping wet.

"Miss Griffin, are you well?" Nastasia leapt up, from where she had sat before her vanity, brushing her hair. She shut the window.

"How wet you are! And what are you covered with? Moss? Pine needles?"

"Long story," Rachel's teeth were chattering too hard to speak much.

"Quick, take a hot bath," counseled the princess, handing Rachel a fluffy towel. "We'll speak after."

Nodding Rachel grabbed a towel and ran to the bathroom. She stripped out of her wet clothing with some difficulty, as they were plastered to her skin and every motion caused her pain. Once free, she stepped into the shower and enjoyed the feeling of the hot water washing away the chill. Hemlock needles accumulated at her feet. Her body was covered with bruises, and her scalp was tender to the touch where hail and branches had struck her. She found no open cuts; however, and none of her ribs seemed to be broken.

When she returned to the bedroom, Nastasia was still sitting at her vanity, reading from her old gray volume that included all the textbooks used at Roanoke. Rachel, wrapped only in a towel, moved to her own dresser and took out fresh underthings, sweat pants, and robe, which she donned, wincing repeatedly.

"I am surprised you are still here. Aren't we late for Language?" she asked.

"They postponed classes half an hour due to the inclement

weather," Nastasia replied with a sweet smile. Then her smile faltered, and her brow furrowed. "Where were you that you came home looking like a drowned kitten? The lockdown had only just ended when you arrived, and it did not end until after the rain had stopped. How could you have gotten so wet?"

Shrugging sadly, Rachel picked up her brush. "If trapped outside, what's one to do?"

Nastasia expression was unusually stern for one so young. "That is no excuse for breaking a rule! You should have banged on the doors until someone let you inside. You could have been struck by lightning! I realize that the Heer has not ventured onto campus yet, but it may be only a matter of time."

Rachel's hand clutched the little amulet that still hung around her neck. Now that it was visible, she saw that could see it, she saw that it was made of polished oak and was shaped like a key. She decided not to explain to her friend just how close she had come to the lightning.

"You know, Nastasia," she said, "Siggy was really looking forward to the trip to Hoddmimir's Wood. It mattered to him. So was I. We'd talked about nothing else for days."

"Be grateful you were not lost, too," the princess replied brusquely. "And it is not as if you haven't gone off places on your own. You were gone for several days."

Nastasia's lovely face took on an expression that looked suspiciously like a pout.

"I went to visit my sister! Because I was... ill!" cried Rachel, exasperated. "That's hardly the same as going on an adventure. And when I found something out about the demon, while I was at Sandra's, the first thing I did was tell the rest of you."

Of course, Rachel had also gone to O.I. with Gaius, but Nastasia did not know about that.

"True," the princess acknowledged. "Still, you have gone on adventures of your own. It is unladylike to complain upon the rare occasion that something happens without you."

"But—you promised us," Rachel cried. "And I'm the one who our Elf contacted."

"If Queen Illondria had wished for you and Sigfried to accompany us, she could have said so when she came to speak to Zoë and me. Had she asked you to *accompany* her? Or only to pass the message to ask me to bring her home?"

Rachel swallowed with some difficulty. Illondria had not spoken to her at all. She had sent a message through Jariel. Still, Rachel had hoped to have a chance to say goodbye. Glumly, she returned to brushing the remaining needles from her hair.

"Count your blessings, Rachel," Nastasia said sadly. "You were not lost into the darkness between worlds, as Zoë was."

"The darkness *between worlds*," Rachel gasped. "I thought she was lost in dreamland."

"I do not know where you received that impression. I never said such a thing."

"Oh." Rachel swallowed.

So much for finding a door into dreamland. Even if they found one, Zoë was not there.

"I spoke to the dean," the princess added haughtily. "She informed me that the school has an agreement with the King of Bavaria to keep his crown prince informed of certain kinds of occurrences." She sniffed. "Still, it seems inappropriate for the prince to repeat the school's private business in front of underclassmen who then go blabbing it about hither and yon."

"My boyfriend telling me something he thought was pertinent to me hardly counts as 'blabbing it about hither and yon,'" Rachel objected, hotly.

"Nevertheless," replied the princess primly.

Outside, the class bells began to toll. Silently, Rachel and Nastasia gathered their books and departed for Language.

• • •

As part of her quest to help Vladimir Von Dread convince her father that he was not "a young tyrant in the making," Rachel wrote her parents a long letter describing the recent Knight's meeting and how Von Dread had vowed to protect her. She did not mention the black bracelet, but she mentioned that he had given her a card with a number to call during emergencies. She requested her mother send something for her to carry it around in, preferably a pouch to hang around her neck.

Two days later, she received a package from home. In it was a hand-woven lanyard with a pouch the size of a small wallet and a brief cheery note from her mother. The pouch contained a space about the size of a large hand bag. The note explained that folding or squashing the little wallet would not damage the object within. This was less useful than it might have been, as Rachel could not reach up and squash the wallet to crush the card and activate the emergency measures, but she was grateful to receive it.

She put the card that Vlad had given her into the wallet and slipped the whole thing around her neck, tucking it inside her robes. Any time she felt nervous, she could tap on her chest and feel the little packet beneath the cloth of her garments.

It made her feel safer.

• • •

The next few days were a whirl of activity, as tutors gave pre-holiday quizzes and students labored to finish assignments before the four-day weekend. Over a third of the student body would be heading home for Thanksgiving—for many students, even those who lived on distant continents, home was but a few travel glasses away. Those remaining at school would be sharing a Thanksgiving feast in the dining hall.

On Wednesday evening, Rachel opened the great oak doors of Dare Hall and slipped inside, shivering from the cold. The enormous foyer, with its black and white marble floor, had two fireplaces warming it. One burned cordwood. The other had a grate of golden bars, behind which a young salamander darted back and forth across a habitat of brick and glowing bronze. Waves of warmth emanated from its red-hot body. Rachel crossed to this second hearth and warmed her cold hands before the golden bars, which she suspected were actually bronze or perhaps gilded iron. She breathed in the sweet, cinnamon scent as she watched the fiery lizard flick its black tongue in and out of its snub snout.

The doors to the boys' side opened, and her brother Peter came through, carrying his overnight bag. For the first time in weeks, he did not look away when he saw her.

"Hallo, there," said Peter.

"Hallo, yourself." Rachel dared a tiny smile.

When Peter did not immediately scowl, she darted forward and threw her arms around him. Peter hugged her back, which hurt, as not all her bruises from falling through the hemlock were gone. She did not let on though.

Peter was a slender and bookish young man whose face was an ideal mix of their mother's striking Asian features and their father's handsome good looks. Before Peter left for school, three years ago, the two of them had been the best of friends, but they had not spent much time together since. He severely disapproved of her friendship with Gaius, his personal *bête noire*, and so had not spoken to her since September, except on the occasion of their sister Sandra's visit. Now, however, he seemed to have returned to his normal brotherly self. Rachel rested her head against his chest, overjoyed that he no longer seemed angry with her.

Letting her go, he looked around. "You're not packed. Aren't you coming home?"

"Oh! I wasn't planning to," Rachel said awkwardly. "Thanksgiving isn't a holiday back home, so Father and Sandra will be working. And I just saw them and Mummy last week."

"Yes. About that—" Now, Peter did scowl, but it was a scowl of brotherly annoyance, not one of angry disdain. As they often did at home, he addressed her with the Korean diminutive for younger sibling. "*Dongsaeng*, why didn't you come and get me when you decided to go to Sandra's? I could have come with you—"

"And been kidnapped, too?" Rachel gave him her archest look.

"I might have been able to do something. I am a rather good sorcerer, you know."

"Better than Mother and Sandra?"

Peter sighed and looked away. Behind the golden bars, the ember-colored lizard dashed through its water trough, which emitted a *whoosh* of steam.

"But thank you, *oppa*," Rachel laid a hand on his arm, "for wanting to help."

"I'm just tired of my little sister being kidnapped. Most people don't get kidnapped in a whole lifetime. You've gone and done it twice in three months. Really, Rachel, you have to admit that's a bit over the top. Even Conan and Liam don't get into that much trouble."

"Very well, Peter. I did so enjoy being kidnapped, but, since it disturbs you, I'll kick the habit," Rachel drawled dryly.

Peter blinked and frowned. Then, to her delight, he laughed. She laughed, too.

"So," asked Peter, "how're your classes? Friends? Brooms?"

"Well enough," Rachel replied. "Classes are very interesting. My friends are nice. And helping Mr. Chanson teach Beginner's Broomriding is great fun. How about you?"

"I'm muddling along," replied her older brother in his extremely English way. "Heard something happened to one of your friends. Magical accident, was it?"

"Something like that," Rachel murmured.

"Sorry about that, but magical accidents are par for the course here. I'm sure it will all turn out all right. Glad you've found friends, dongsaeng. They seem a nice lot. A bit reassuring, after you demonstrated such horrid taste in boys."

Rachel stuck her tongue out at him. He returned the gesture. Then both looked around nervously, as if afraid the ghost of their stern Victorian grandmother would catch them at it.

"Who're your friends?" Rachel asked. "You haven't introduced me to a single one."

"Peter Komarek, whom I know you've met because he's visited Gryphon Park twice, and Ignatius Moth are my closest friends. We've been rooming together since our freshman year. We get along with our fourth roommate, but Romanov's, uh, a little weird. Hangs out with the vampire-hunting crowd and all that. Other than that, I spend time with the MacDannans—Oonagh, Conan, and Liam. And with Dart and Katie. And, uh, Lena...."

His face lit up when he mentioned the last girl's name. Rachel, who had heard rumors about her brother's crush on the athletic Lena Ilium, smiled secretly to herself.

"Glad you're enjoying school," added Peter. "It's important to appreciate your classes."

"Classes are fine," Rachel replied, "but I spend most of my time studying or working on this saving-the-world thing. So I may not be appreciating my classes as much as I should."

"Yeah, saving the world. How's that working out for you?"

Rachel frowned.

Peter put his hands in his pockets. "What can I do to help?"

Surprise flickered through her. She tilted her head, thinking. "Not a lot right now, though there may be something you could do to help soon. Perhaps in the body guarding department—while we do experiments in dreamland. Once we get our clubhouse set up."

She paused, temporarily silenced by jab of pain through her chest, as she remembered that Zoë was missing. "Er, never mind. We won't be doing experimenting in dreamland, in the near future anyway."

"That sounds—" he blinked dubiously. "Well, you let me know. Otherwise, carry on." He sounded so much like their grandparents that Rachel could not help smiling. She hugged him once more before bounding towards the stairs. He started for the front door, carrying his bag.

Four stairs up, Rachel paused. "Oppa! Wait."

He had opened the heavy oak door. Now he paused, letting it close. Rachel raced back down the steps and across the black and white marble squares, sliding to a stop beside him.

Arriving beside him a little out of breath, she gasped. "Peter, didn't you tell me that you knew all the graves in the family plot?"

Peter's brow drew together, but he nodded.

"Might there be... Is there a grave with the name Amber on it?"

"Amber?" He tipped back on his heels, thinking. "How long ago?"

"Older than Sandra — so more than twenty years ago. But younger than Uncle Emrys's."

"Oh, no. Nothing like that!" Peter said quickly. "The youngest graves are Grandmother and Grandfather, of course. Followed by Uncle Emrys and Uncle Cadellin. After that... well, there's our second cousin Aurie, Uncle Cadellin's son. Aurie died during World War II. And then you get to Myrddin, his four siblings, and their mother, but that was over a hundred years ago. Oh, and there is that fellow who was an MP, from the mundane side of the family."

"Owen Wyllt?" asked Rachel.

"Yes, that's the fellow. Can't recall how he's related to us."

"Great-great-grandfather Uther's sister Elaine married an Un-wary gentleman named Edgar Wyllt. Edgar was a distant cousin, descended from Ygraine, the sister of Lamorak, who was the third Duke of Devon. I believe he died during the Wars of the Roses. He was our great-great-great-great-great-great-great-grandfather."

Peter stared at her. "I've known you my whole life, and it still gives me the jitters when you do that." He patted her head. "My little walking encyclopedia of a sister."

"So, no Amber, then. She would have been a baby."

"No. Why do you ask?"

"It's just that Great-Aunt Nimue has always called Sandra by the name Amber." Rachel decided this was not the time to explain about the forgotten rattle with the $\mathcal{A}$ on it.

"And you thought," asked Peter, "having discovered only last month that we had unknown dead relatives, that you might have discovered another one? No such luck. Or unluck, as the case may be. Certainly would not have been lucky for our new unknown relative."

Peter then paused and blinked, rubbing his temples. "That's strange. You're right. She does always call Sandra by the name Amber. All this time. I could have sworn she used a different name each time."

Rachel said slowly, "You know what's strange? I would have sworn that, too. Looking back in my memory, however, it has definitely always been Amber. Why Amber?"

"Maybe she's confusing Sandra with Amber Benson," said Peter.

"Who?"

"Mum's best friend from school? The one who died in the Battle of Roanoke?"

"Oh, you mean Ambie?" Rachel cried, recalling her mother's tales of her school days. "Ambie's real name was Amber? Would Great-Aunt Nimue have met her?"

"Certainly. Ambie was going out with Uncle Emrys. That's how Mummy and Father met. And besides, Great-Aunt Nimue definitely would have met Ambie at Father's graduation."

It had never occurred to Rachel that her mother must have known her late Uncle Emrys, but of course, Father and his younger brother had been at school at the same time. It was not until after Father and Mother graduated that the Terrible Five came to Roanoke—which was why her father's younger brother had been there for the Battle of Roanoke, but her parents had not.

"But Ambie was a petite redhead," Rachel mused, "I've seen her pictures. She looked nothing like Sandra."

"No idea. Unless Mum told Great-Aunt Nimue that she was going to name her daughter after her friend and then didn't. But the old bat remembered the comment."

Rachel frowned. "I wonder why Mummy didn't name a daughter after Ambie. It does sound like something she would have done."

Peter shrugged. "Too painful, maybe? Anyway, here's Laurel. We're off."

Their older sister Laurel whooshed down the stairs in a navy parka she had outgrown since acquiring it last winter, carrying a small bag that Rachel knew was much larger on the inside and a leather case containing her long, stringed *gayageum*. With her long legs, she crossed the foyer striding like a runway model, her dark hair flowing behind her. Laurel gave Rachel a sisterly bop on the head, and she and Peter departed.

...

That night, Rachel dreamed that she stood again in Dream Carthage, watching the shade of Remus Starkadder being dragged into the ground as he burned. In the dream, she traveled down with him toward a place of torment so horrific that merely approaching it filled her with unimaginable terror. Remus became Zoë Forrest, her hair the color of blood, her forelock braid streaming upward as she fell.

The dream changed, and a hart charged across the terrible landscape. It was a titanic stag, so large that it took up most of the horizon. Its antlers were a system of thunderheads, raining wrath and lightning. Its legs dwarfed mountains. Its hooves caused earthquakes. Its eyes were burning silver stars.

The hart charged forward. In the way of dreams, Rachel knew that this was one of the four harts that ate at the World Tree. Only, this one had foresworn his old ways and become one of the Tree's defenders. Somehow, again in the way of dreams, she knew that the dead hart in the dreamland of Transylvania was an image of the fallen brother of this titan.

The dream changed once more, and the titanic hart became a man. He stood twelve feet tall, with storm-gray antlers sprouting from his head. His black armor bore feathered epaulettes at the shoulders. His storm-colored wings were enormous, spreading over a hundred feet in either direction. Up he flew, through winds, through swarms of blood-red imps, through darkness. And in his arms, he carried Zoë Forrest.

He landed on the commons, scattering the snow. Roanoke Hall was silhouetted behind him. Bending, he placed Zoë on the icy ground. Then he departed with three flaps of his enormous wings, blowing the snow away from him in every direction.

In her dream, the great antlered man turned his head, and his eyes—those burning silver stars—gazed directly into Rachel's.

"*I give you this gift, in honor of your service for my wife.*"

Surely, in reality, any such words were for Nastasia. Yet, in the way of dreams, Rachel felt as if they had been meant for her.

• • •

The ecstatic shouts of Joy O'Keefe woke Rachel from her strange and elfish dream. Zoë Forrest had returned.

Chapter Thirteen:
Training Sequence

By breakfast on Thursday morning, Thanksgiving Day, the tables in the dining hall had been pushed together in anticipation of the family-style feast to be held that evening. Rachel ate with Siggy, who had no place to go over a holiday; Nastasia, who had just been home; Zoë, whose father was away on business—despite that his daughter had just returned from being missing; and Joy, whose family had so many members attending Roanoke that her parents had decided to join the students that night for dinner, instead of asking their seven daughters to travel back to Ohio.

The Darlings and MacDannans were also present at breakfast—those who had not slept in. The whole group of them, John, Wendy, Oonagh, Conan, Liam, and Ian, would be leaving at lunch time to spend the holiday at the Darlings' place, just outside New York City. Rachel knew both families still had one additional child at home: Taliesin MacDannan would be a freshman next year, and Michael Darling would come to Roanoke the year after. These youngsters, no doubt, were waiting eagerly for their older siblings to come home.

Seeing what a large group they made, Hildy Winters, who also had not gone home, asked why the Darlings and MacDannans did not emulate the O'Keefes and join the school for their holiday meal. Liam shot back that, while it was true that their absence would deprive the other students of having the pleasure of dining with his father, Finn MacDannan, the greatest enchanter in the world and a well-known musical sensation, they would also would be able to avoid having to dine with his mother, their math teacher. As Scarlett MacDannan was among the sternest of the Roanoke tutors, Hildy let the matter drop.

⋮

After breakfast, Zoë was questioned and cross-examined, first by the dean, assistant deans, and Roanoke's head of security, Maverick Badger, and then by the Wisecraft. To the Die Horribly Debate Club and each of the others, Zoë said the same thing. After returning the shade of their dead Elf friend, Illondria, the Queen of the Lios Alfar, to her homeland, Zoë had lost hold of Nastasia while traveling between worlds on the return trip and fallen into darkness. She did not remember anything beyond that, until she awoke, standing in the middle of the commons amidst the swirling snow.

There was talk of putting her under the *Spell of True Recitation* and of a visit by the Grand Inquisitor himself, yet, nothing more came of it. According to Sigfried, who was spying on the staff's private discussions with his all-seeing amulet, it was Assistant Dean Mr. Gideon who made sure the matter went no further. Siggy, who participated in a mutual dislike club with their True Hiss tutor, suspected that Mr. Gideon was up to something sinister. But Rachel reminded them that the Lios Alfar queen, Illondria, had been a friend of their history tutor. Maybe Mr. Gideon was shielding Zoë for the Elf's sake.

The dean, however, confiscated Zoë's slippers.

This was a huge blow to Zoë. It was also a blow to Sigfried, who had set his heart on visiting dreamland and investigating Storm King, as he had not yet been able to find a door leading into the waking version of the mountain.

It was a huge blow to Rachel, too, but she did not voice her dismay.

• • •

Rachel took advantage of the general confusion over Zoë's return to slip in some time with Gaius. As they strolled through the snow-blanketed cherry trees and over the picturesque bridges of the Oriental gardens, she told him her theory about Great-Aunt Nimue and the rattle.

"So, you think this mysterious rattle with the A on it might have something to do with the fact that your great-aunt always calls your eldest sister by the wrong name?" asked Gaius. He raised a hand. "Just trying to make sure I followed what you were saying."

Rachel nodded. "The rattle is just the sort of gift Great-Aunt Nimue would have chosen. I've seen her give out other pieces with similar workmanship."

"Is the rattle still there? In your mother's jewelry box? A silver rattle doesn't sound like something your great-aunt bought at the local department store. Was it handmade? If so, it might have a trademark you could compare to other gifts from your great-aunt. If they are different, the similarity is probably accidental."

"Jolly good idea!" Rachel perked up. "I'll check on that over the Yule break."

"Let me know how it goes. Though I rather think it will not pan out."

"Oh?" asked Rachel.

Gaius gestured toward the distance, beyond the snow-covered rock garden and the pagoda. "Millions of people die every day. The Raven does nothing about it. Why would he go out of his way to hide the death of one baby girl?"

The reasonableness of his words took the wind out of her sails. Rachel kicked at the snow on the arched bridge. Seeing her dismay, Gaius tapped her lightly on the nose.

"Not everything is a mystery, Rach," he drawled, smiling.

"Maybe not," Rachel sighed, "but some power hid the rattle from my memory."

Gaius leaned forward and lowered his voice. "Vlad tells me that Zoë didn't remember anything. Is this true?"

Rachel nodded. "She doesn't remember how she came to be here. She just found herself on the commons."

"And there's nothing else. No other clues?"

It was Rachel's turn to lower her voice. "Well, there was my dream. But I haven't told anyone about it, yet."

"A dream? What happened?"

"Well, it started off as my usual nightmare—"

"Whoa! Hold on. Usual nightmare? You didn't tell me you were having nightmares!"

"Only since Carthage. I... keep dreaming about what happened to Remus Starkadder."

"Remus Starkadder? How does he figure into this? Have you seen him since the Dead Men's Ball?"

"Yes. He was in Tunis. Only…something bad happened to him."

"He deserves it. He was an ass."

Rachel gave him a mock serious frown. "Mr. Valiant, there are ladies present."

"My apologies, Lady Rachel," Gaius gave her a mock bow in return. "He was a reprobate."

"I give you that he was not a nice boy. He's the one who betrayed me, you know. He told Serena O'Malley where I was."

"Did he?" Gaius's face grew dark. "Then I doubly want him to suffer for all eternity!"

"Well, you have your wish. He was dragged off by Morax's servants. Dragged into the ground. Where he will be tortured for all eternity, I believe."

Gaius grinned. Then he stopped grinning. Then, his face turned a little green. "It's one thing to wish such a thing on someone. Another thing to have it actually happen to a guy I knew." His resolve returned. He gritted his teeth. "He betrayed my gal. He deserves it."

When Rachel did not agree, Gaius said in a low, dangerous voice. "Thanks to him, you were nearly burned to death, Rach. That would not have been a nice way to go."

Rachel sighed. "That is neither here nor there. The point is: my nightmare changed into a dream about my Elf's husband rescuing Zoë and bringing her to the commons. But I have no idea how much of the dream was real and how much was, well, a dream."

"That's rather fascinating. Do you mind if I tell Vlad?"

"No, not at all. Go right ahead. But tell me if he can make head or tail of it."

"Will do." Gaius grinned and, leaning over, kissed her on that spot, just below her ear, that always sent trills of exhilaration throughout her entire body.

Smiling, they walked back together, hand in hand.

• • •

"We're going to practice. Would you care to come?" Nastasia asked Rachel, as she came back across the brightness of the snowy commons. "I wish you would."

Rachel could not help smiling at the kind tone in the princess's voice. Ordinarily, she avoided practicing with her friends, whose sorcery was quite advanced compared to hers. But the sincerity in the princess's request touched her. She felt delighted that her friend desired her company.

"Yeah," Joy piped up. "You should come. It's pretty fun!"

"Very well," Rachel declared with cheerful resolve. "How's it done?"

"We use the dueling rules to determine what magic is safe," said Wendy Darling, who had come up beside Joy, "but we fight one another as a group. Not in formal one-on-one duels like the clubs do."

Nastasia added, "We feel it will better prepare us for real battles."

• • •

Rachel followed her friends to a field west of Roanoke Hall where the half-foot of snow was smooth and untouched. It was bitterly cold, and a brisk wind blew the branches of the hemlocks and paper birches this way and that. Siggy's new winter garments had come, and he now wore a heavy red parka, a Russian fur hat with ear flaps, thick wool mittens, and buff-colored caribou hide boots with waterproof bottoms. It made Rachel happy every time she saw him rolling in the snow while wrestling Lucky or dashing by as he threw snowballs.

A number of the other freshmen from Dare gathered on the practice field, though Rachel's other roommates, Kitten and Astrid, were not present. To Rachel's surprise, Wulfgang Starkadder joined them. She glanced at the brooding Transylvanian prince who might become her best friend's fiancé and then examined him in her memory. Wulfgang had wavy dark hair, a very straight nose, and a jutting chin. He was handsome in a wolfish, almost feral, manner, but this handsomeness was marred by his constant, superior sneer. Rachel had never seen him turn into a wolf, but she had seen his now-deceased older brother Fenris transform.

Tepes, Wulfgang's wolverine, nosed at something buried beneath the snow. Rachel found this particular familiar puzzling. Ordinarily, the shaggy brown and silver creature waddled around eating everything in sight. It almost rivaled Lucky with its voraciousness. But occasionally, Rachel would catch it, out of the corner of her eye, raising its head carefully to look around. During such moments, it had such a strange look in its eye—wise and compassionate and sad—almost as if it were a noble creature masquerading as a base one.

"All present?" Nastasia addressed the gathering of nearly two dozen students. The majority were freshmen but there were a few upperclassmen. "Very good! Everyone find your partner!"

Rachel started forward with a smile, but Joy reached the princess first and grabbed her hand, crying, "Let's do our usual maneuver. Come on!"

Immediately, the two girls in their white-trimmed coats, one blue and one yellow, ran to the center of the practice field and stood back to back. The princess lifted her violin to her chin, while Joy raised her hands in the gesture for the *taflu* cantrip. Other students paired off, as if they had done this many times. Some lifted instruments. Others raised their hands.

"We begin in three, two, one!" called Nastasia.

Mayhem ensued. Spells flew. No one was using fulgurators' wands or dueling rings, so they were limited to quick hexes and cantrips. Silver and blue sparkles glittered in the air, which now smelled like vanilla and peppermint. Familiars ran to and fro barking or yapping or growling and generally getting underfoot. Or rather, the cats watched, cool and aloof, from the sidelines, while the other familiars joined in the fray.

Rachel stood in the center of the field, all alone. Sparks flew at her from many directions. This was far more confusing than any real battle she had been part of because there were no sides. Everyone attacked everyone else. She spun about, attempting to use a *taflu* cantrip to parry incoming magic. But she could not look everywhere at once. A feeling of panic began to overwhelm her. This was almost as bad as being stared at by a large crowd

A vine, sprouting from the snow, wrapped around her leg and

yanked upwards. At the same moment, a golden Glepnir band closed around her chest, trapping her arms at her side.

Next thing she knew, she was dangling upside down, kicking her feet in mid-air, unable to see. Her robe had flopped over her face and arms. She felt grateful that she had put on sweatpants under her uniform that morning, rather than stockings. However, while her sweatpants protected her modesty, they did little to keep out the biting wind. Every time the wind gusted, Rachel's legs froze anew.

She dangled aimlessly, the blood rushing to her head. The band around her upper body put pressure on her bruised ribs. Outside the dark poplin of her robe, music and shouts rang out. Something bumped into her, hard. She cried out. It hurt, but not as much as the bruise to her heart. She had been so happy when Nastasia invited her to join their practice, but her friend had abandoned her without even finding her a partner.

Grabbing hold of her robe, she managed to gather it to her, inch by inch, until the hem was above her eyes. This took time because the black poplin kept slipping from the grip of her soft mittens. Her head was close to the ground, so when she peeked out under the hem, all she could see was legs and feet running hither and thither. Farther away, other sets of legs remained motionless, frozen by spells.

She pulled her robes up higher, temporarily grabbing them in her teeth, until she could grasp them more firmly with her mittens. Now she could see more clearly. To the left, Lucky wrestled playfully with Wulfgang's wolverine, rolling back and forth in the pristine snow. Across the field, Ian MacDannan also hung upside down, swinging slowly. However, his arms were not restrained. He struggled and cursed as he fought the tangling vine that trapped him.

The goal of the game now seemed to be: stop Nastasia and Joy. Nastasia played her violin, paralyzing Hildy Winters with a blast of blue sparks with one stroke of the strings. Then, with another stroke, she blew John Darling onto his backside amidst a shower of silver sparks. (*Hear! Hear!* Rachel cheered gleefully, grinning at the discomfort of the boy who had publicly humiliated her more than once.) Meanwhile, Joy *taflued* the incoming spells, protecting Nastasia from attacks. Their division of labor—Nastasia casting while

Joy defended—made for a winning combination.

"Get 'em!" cried Sigfried. "How are we going to beat the ogre and the storm goblin, if we can't beat two girls!"

"Right," replied Wulfgang Starkadder. "Let's go."

With a shout, Sigfried and Wulfgang broke free of the crowd and ran at the princess and Joy. Sigfried blew his trumpet, and huge blasts of silver sparkles whooshed toward Joy. She *taflued* them, sending the silvery sparks to one side or the other. Wulfgang usually played an accordion. Today, however, he held a pair of panpipes to his lips, blue sparkles rushing from the six slender reeds. The two boys rapidly closed the distance between themselves and the girls.

Joy shouted, pointing. Nastasia paused in her playing. When the boys came within twenty feet, she drew her bow across her violin, sending a ribbon of blue sparks at the oncoming boys.

Spotting the approaching danger, Wulfgang Starkadder grabbed Sigfried and swung the large blond boy in front of him. The hex struck Siggy, who froze instantly, mid-trumpet blow. Wulfgang lifted him and charged forward, using the motionless Sigfried as a shield.

The two teams traded attacks: Joy protected Nastasia; Wulfgang parried with Siggy. Beauregard, the princess's Tasmanian tiger, leapt at Wulfgang, but the young Transylvanian prince ducked behind Sigfried. Resting his frozen classmate against his shoulder, he played his panpipes with one hand, freezing the beast in place. Frowning, Nastasia played faster and faster, trying harder and harder to stop the young prince, but he continued to duck behind Sigfried.

John Darling had climbed back to his feet. He now took advantage of the distraction Wulfgang provided to cast a cantrip known as the Word of Life at Nastasia. The cantrip caused vines to grow; it was the same one that had ensnared Rachel. Joy caught sight of him at the last minute. With a shout, she *taflued* the cantrip, redirecting it toward Wulfgang.

Vines sprouted from the ground near Wulfgang's feet, wrapping around him and Sigfried. Nimble as a wolf, the Transylvanian prince back flipped free of the rapidly growing vines. In doing this, however, he left Siggy behind. Blue sparkles from Nastasia's violin struck him, dancing up and down his body.

Most of the underclassmen had been neutralized. They stood frozen or hung from vines or struggled against Glepnir bands. The battle was now Nastasia and Joy versus John Darling and his cousin Oonagh. When the two upperclassmen had been fighting alone, the freshmen girls had been able to keep them at bay. Once the upperclassmen began working together, though, Oonagh defending with cantrips, while John played his flute, the tide of battle turned. Red sparkles flew from the upperclassmen's instrument too quickly for Joy to stop them.

The two younger girls began to dance. Their feet moved uncontrollably. Joy cried out immediately, surrendering and asking to be set free. But Nastasia grimly danced on, trying to play her violin despite the wild motions of her legs. She kept this up for so long that John eventually got bored and paralyzed her.

Oonagh and John, the only people still standing, high-fived each other and declared victory. They began freeing the other students. Liam MacDannan, who was more of a gentleman than his scampish younger brothers, cut Rachel down and freed her from the band of golden light that had trapped her arms.

By this time, she was very cold indeed. Her teeth chattered, her ribs ached, and her legs were so cold, they burned. Rachel looked around in hopeful expectation, certain that her friends would come over and apologize for abandoning her. Nastasia, however, merely stood next to Joy, her brow furrowed.

"I am very disappointed in my performance," the princess said, hanging her head. "I was not able to take down all our opponents."

Joy laughed. "Are you kidding! We did great! We held our own against all comers for over seven minutes. Even Wulfgang and Siggy, who are as good as we are, couldn't take us! It took two seniors, working together! We're the greatest!"

Nastasia refused to be comforted. Her face was pale, her jaw set. She seemed unusually upset for such a small defeat. "This failure is completely unsatisfactory. I must get stronger! If I don't, I will not be able to protect my friends, and they will d...." Her voice trailed off.

"Okay, everyone!" Joy shouted cheerfully. "Regroup for Round Two."

The students immediately formed pairs. A feeling of panic returned. Rachel backed away, willing herself not to break into a run and flee.

"Rachel, aren't you going to practice with us?" called Joy.

Nastasia looked up in surprise, her bottom lip trembling slightly when she saw Rachel retreating. "Won't you stay, Miss Griffin? It is so nice when we all practice together."

"No, thanks!" Rachel called back. "I-I think that was enough for me. Must go!"

Chapter Fourteen:

Discoveries in the Snow

Rachel slipped into the woods, chafing her legs and jumping until she felt warm again. She then ran through the paper birches with their curling, parchment-like bark. Coming up behind Dare Hall, she glanced at the fourth floor window behind which lay her dorm room. The window was cracked open. Her cat, Mistletoe, sat on the sill, gazing out at the forest. He jumped out of the way when Rachel called to her broom.

"*Varenga, Vroomie!*"

The steeplechaser slipped through the opening and flew down to her hand. Rachel hopped on and sped away at high speed up over the forest. Not wanting another close call like her recent adventure with Sigfried and Lucky, she was careful to stay inside the school wards. While the wind was bitterly cold, the sky was bright and blue with only a smattering of clouds. There was no sign of the storm goblin or his lightning imps.

Rachel flew very fast for a time, until she stopped feeling quite so sorry for herself. She had known that it was a bad idea to practice with her more talented friends. She should not whine because it had turned out badly. Still, she could not help feeling a little resentful toward the princess, for not at least clueing her in and helping her find a partner.

A movement in the forest caught Rachel's attention. Slowing down, she peered through the branches. A young woman with a long golden braid and a bright blue coat stood in the snow. Beside her, an exquisite white reindeer nibbled on the bark of a young tree. Rachel could not see her face, but she knew this must be Merry Vesper, the girl from her broomriding class who worked at the menagerie with Joy's sister Hope. Rachel knew nothing about

Miss Vesper, except that she was a junior at the Upper School who lived in Marlowe Hall and who had been seriously ill during her first two years of school. She seemed very sweet and always full of bright cheer.

Rachel circled around until she found a place to land. Flying down until she was below the level of the branches, she maneuvered among the bare lower trunks. It was much warmer down here; where the wind did not blow as hard. Only now, however, did she feel how chapped her cheeks were. Darting among the trees, she drew closer to where Miss Vesper stood. As she came closer, Rachel gasped and halted.

Woodland animals were coming out of the forest and surrounding the fur-clad young lady. A yearling deer pranced toward her on slender hooves, followed by a young raccoon with bright, beady, black eyes. A squirrel leapt from a tree to her shoulder. An owl hooted sleepily on a nearby branch. Overhead, a pair of cardinals sang, adding a splash of red to the winter scene. A porcupine waddled from behind a trunk and sniffed noses with the graceful reindeer, whom Rachel recognized as Merry's familiar. Two foxes came from the underbrush and chased each other around Miss Vesper's legs.

Rachel watched spellbound. This scene would make sense to her if the young woman were playing an instrument or even singing. Enchanters could summon beasts of the forest, but Merry was standing absolutely still, smiling as if the creatures were old friends.

Rachel watched an instant longer, but it seemed a shame to disturb this pretty gathering. Much as she herself would have loved to pet a deer or chuck an opossum under its chin, she was reasonably sure that if she made her presence known, the animals would flee, and the magic of the moment would be lost. Retreating, she quietly flew away. Still, the charming mystery of it lifted her spirits, and she hummed to herself as she went.

Flying back to campus, Rachel emerged from the woods into the open area behind Roanoke Hall where, thanks to what she now knew to be the youthful adventures of Locke and Dread, only scrub grew. With its blanket of snow, it looked like a lumpy field. The tree stumps and the scars where Mr. Chanson had emerged, when thrown through the earth at high speed by the tail of Dr. Mordeau's dragon form, were all hidden beneath the fluffy whiteness.. An older student sat shivering on one of the stumps, reading a book. She was a young woman with curly black ringlets wearing a threadbare coat that looked more like a dinner jacket than a winter parka. Her familiar, a chipmunk, scampered around, poking here and there, leaving a tiny trail of footprints in the snow. Rachel nodded to her politely and continued on her way.

She flew over this treeless area and up to the roof of Roanoke Hall. Increasing her speed despite the bitter chill, she whipped around the towers and spires, racing through the icy air. Her time practicing in the gym both aided and hindered her. The larger size of the mock version nearly led to her striking her head on an arch that was higher in the gym.

She was fascinated to observe the maneuvering of her broom in light of her recent physics lesson. Her bristleless moved with nigh-inertialess grace. An airplane had to bank to turn. Rachel could bank if she wished, but she also could spin around the broom's center of gravity. This allowed her to rapidly change direction—rapidly but not instantly. As she spun, she wondered idly if she could calculate the degree of the broom's drag.

In light of her near-disaster with Sigfried and the school wards, she flew through the towers and spires with the becalming enchantments on, practicing maneuvers in this mode. This proved all but impossible, so slow and clumsy was the bristleless in this configuration. She could have gone faster on foot, and when it came to banking, her pony turned more swiftly. She had no question that *this* amount of drag could be quantifiably calculated!

After three more circuits through the roof landscape, she decided to lap the soccer field in the center of Roanoke Hall. She zoomed above the long, thin sections of roof atop the four sides of the square that made up the hall. As she sped along, dodging the corner towers, she wondered what her boyfriend was doing. Gaius had told her that he planned to spend the day studying. Was he in the library, poring over a book? Or down in the Summoning Chamber in Drake Hall, working on a practical assignment? Would she be disturbing him if she spoke to him?

She had not anticipated, when she convinced Siggy to give Gaius a calling card or when Vlad gave her the black bracelet, the enormity of the temptation involved. At any moment—in class, between classes, during meals, at work, curled up in bed—Rachel had the capacity to instantly speak to her boyfriend. And she wanted to do so all the time. The thought of it nagged at her incessantly. Some days, it seemed as if her life was nothing but the constant battle between the part of her mind that invented more and more outrageous reasons for talking to him and the part of her mind that did not want to trouble him—especially after his comment at O.I. about being interrupted by calling cards in class.

Worst of all, when she did find the courage to call to him and he was busy, no matter how nicely he explained that he was unavailable to speak, she felt crushed. Had she disturbed him? Was he annoyed? Was he actually busy? Or was he talking with friends—or other girls—and did not wish to be interrupted by the mindless chatter of his thirteen-year-old girlfriend?

She had not realized having a boyfriend would be so difficult.

In truth, she was not particularly worried about other girls, but the thought of him spending time with his friends, Vlad or William or Topher, and not inviting her along made her heart ache. If only she could be part of their group. If only the two groups, hers and his, could work together. She did not quite understand why they seemed so far apart, other than that the princess did not like Vladimir because he had brushed the back of his hand across her skin when she had told him not to touch her, causing her to disobey her father's order.

But that had happened months ago. Why couldn't the princess put that matter behind her?

Rachel thought again how the imperious prince had knelt before her and slipped the black bracelet onto her wrist. Even up here, flying into the bitterly-cold, icy winds, she felt heat rise in her cheeks. She pressed an ice-covered mitten against her face: the coldness of the scratchy wool felt good against her hot skin. If truth be told, she might have a bit of a crush on her sister's boyfriend—in a not-betraying-Gaius sort of way, of course.

If she were willing to be brutally honest, she had started to fall for Vladimir Von Dread well before she was aware he was Sandra's boyfriend. She knew the precise moment it had happened. She had been sitting, covered with a blanket, on the floor of her favorite hallway up in Roanoke Hall. It was the day after Vlad turned Gaius into a sheep (ram!). Gaius had been sitting across from her, reading a Darius Northwest book. The two of them were talking about saving the world, and Gaius had mentioned that he and William wanted to help, too.

When she had asked about Von Dread, Gaius had replied that Vladimir was different. *He thinks the world's actually under attack.*

And, of course, so did Rachel.

When it came to protecting the world, Vlad was *serious*. Rachel really admired that.

She came around Roanoke Hall and started a second lap. Below, the MacDannans and Darlings were preparing to depart for their Thanksgiving feast. A group of students stood around them with comics and pens in hand, hoping for autographs from their famous parents.

The rest of her friends were still practicing. Siggy and Wulfgang had once again squared off in front of Nastasia and Joy. Zoë Forrest was creeping around the back of Roanoke Hall, her greenstone patu in her hand, while Hildy Winters ran around in circles, waving her arms and shouting, whether on purpose or because of an enchantment, Rachel could not tell.

As she barreled along on the next leg of the square, coaxing her bristleless to higher speeds, Rachel thought back upon her friends on the ground, amused by their antics. They....

In her memory, darkness billowed around Zoë Forrest.

Rachel shouted and turned back. Below, Zoë, her Maori war club in hand, was sneaking up behind the upperclassman in the threadbare coat, who sat on her stump absorbed in her book. Zoë's face was contorted into a nasty snarl, as if she intended the hapless reader great harm.

With a shout, Rachel dived at her friend, urging her steeplechaser to even greater speeds. The freezing wind cut her face like tiny knives and blew through the weave of her mittens. Rachel whistled, and blue sparkles rushed from her lips. The enchantment struck Zoë just as she swung her war club toward the reader's head. Zoë froze, her outstretched arm a mere foot-and-a-half her would-be victim.

The young woman leapt to her feet, her eyes wide with alarm. She gaped at the frozen girl and her weapon.

"Sorry, playing a game," Rachel called cheerfully, waving from her broom.

The young woman nodded hurriedly. Closing her book, she pulled the collar of her thin coat around her ears, scooped up her chipmunk, and ran off. Rachel circled Zoë slowly. Remembering back, she could see that even though Zoë was frozen, the darkness surrounding her wavered and billowed. It leapt like flames around a burning log, only shadow-black.

Zoë was possessed!

It was not an ordinary darkness either. Merely remembering it made Rachel want to retch. She grabbed at her calling card with her mitten.

"Siggy! Nastasia! Joy! Quick! Zoë's in trouble!"

• • •

"I can see the darkness!" Lucky announced. "It's gross. Want me to breath on it? It might pop like the wraith."

Siegfried and Lucky peered closely at Zoë. Nastasia and Joy stood a little farther back. Beauregard came forward slowly, stiff-legged, sniffing and growling. Rachel, still on her broom, hovered beside them.

"Wait, Lucky! You might hurt Zoë," Joy cried. "Can we be sure you won't hurt Zoë?"

"We should not do anything hasty." Nastasia's calmness was soothing. Immediately, Joy looked less frightened, and Rachel felt heartened. "The Wisecraft have many experts on depossession. They'll have her back to normal in no time. All we need to do is go get the dean or a proctor. I suspect Mr. Badger will know what to do."

"Wish Goldilocks were here, instead of back in Maine with her dad," Siggy said glumly. "We could use some brains right now."

Rachel admired Siggy's loyalty to his girlfriend, but she couldn't see what good a girl who grew up among the Unwary would do them right now. What they needed was....

A shiver ran through her. What they needed did not exist, not on their world, anyway. If there were a way to banish a demon from a human body, O.I. would have found it—or her grandfather would have.

She had been about to call Gaius for help. Now she changed her mind. Gaius would call Dread, and Dread would order Locke to bring Zoë to O.I. where the other demons were trapped. And they had already told her that they had no way to free a host from demon possession. The image of Zoë stuck in caramel, next to Egg and Morax, filled her with horror.

And here they had all been so happy Zoë had been rescued.

Rachel's hands began to shake. "W-what do we do?"

"I told you," replied Nastasia soothingly, "we call Mr. Badger. He will know what to do."

"I... am not sure we should," Rachel's voice sounded raspy, even to her ear. "If it is a demon, there's no one on earth who can help. We must look... farther afield."

"You mean beyond the Earth? Beyond Pluto? Exactly right!" Siggy cried, "We've got to look to the Metaplutonians! One of them is sure to know what to do. Of course, this thing in Zoë is probably also Metaplutonian."

"Why assume it's a demon?" asked Nastasia, "And not a ghost or a specter or a brollachan?"

Rachel shivered. "Can't you feel the evil? Besides, she picked it up outside this world."

Rachel thought of her dream, where the storm-bearing hart had scooped up Zoë from the bowels of Hell. She shivered again.

"I think Lucky should give it a shot," said Siggy. "Lucky, pull!"

Lucky darted forward and exhales out a plume of dragon's breath well above Zoë's head, where, according to Rachel's memory, the black aura writhed. Smoke curled upward. What seemed to be the air itself issued a hair-raising scream, such as Rachel had never heard. So eerie and terrifying was the sound that her shoulder-length hair lifted off her scalp. Her friends also drew back, alarmed.

Zoë began to move. Joy's cheer of delight died stillborn as they watched the awkward, jerky motions of Zoë's body. A sharp crack rang out with each movement. Beauregard let out his yippish growl, baring his teeth and running back and forth, guarding his mistress.

"It's forcing Zoë to move!" Rachel cried. "Even though she's still paralyzed."

Nastasia's face had gone entirely bloodless. "Will that hurt her?"

"Yes! Yes!" Joy cried. "Unparalyze her! Quickly!"

"But then it might do worse things! She was about to... hurt somebody when I froze her," Rachel cried. "Which do we do? Keep her this way, or let her go?"

"Attack it again, Lucky," cried Siggy. "It's weakening."

"Pathetic worm," a harsh voice spoke from Zoë's mouth. "Harm me again, and I shall kill this weak mortal. As it is, she shall suffer for my pain."

"Oré!" Siggy used the Word of Ending—which had freed the ensorcelled pilots of the jumbo jet—to no avail. All it did was free Zoë from the paralysis.

Zoë was still paralyzed Each motion of her body caused a painful cracking noise. She began to writhe, and a low, horrible, slurred moan issued from her mouth.

Immediately, Rachel whistled again. Zoë froze in the act of kicking Siggy in the head. Sigfried shouted the other cantrips he knew, but none had a useful result.

"Do something! Call a tutor! Maybe James Darling and Scarlett MacDannan are still on campus. I'll... go get help!" cried Nastasia.

"Take my broom," Rachel jumped off and locked the levers for simpler flying.

The princess met Rachel's eyes and nodded once, a silent vow to protect Rachel's beloved bristleless. Then she grabbed Vroomie and climbed on. Nastasia zoomed off around the building with Beauregard running beneath her. Rachel could hear her shouting, "Help! Someone! Help! Emergency!"

"Wha—" Rachel's head felt cloudy, full of uncertainty. Her normal decisiveness had fled. She considered over and over the same fruitless options. "W-what do we do? Keep her frozen or let her go?"

"I don't know! Zoë!" Joy grabbed her head and started crying.

Siggy pulled out his knife and stabbed the frozen, snow-covered ground repeatedly, howling in frustration. "Why can't we ever fight something I can hurt!"

"Maybe a god could help," suggested Lucky. "Or some really, really big dragon."

Rachel turned back to Zoë. Again and again, her mind ran over the list of things she could do, none of which were helpful under this circumstance. She began to wonder if she should call William and ask him to send a team from O.I. after all. Surely, Zoë would be better off frozen in the stuff Blackie had invented than—

"Zoë!" Joy screamed again. "Somebody! Help her!"

There had to be someone who could help! But who? Nobody from Earth knew what to do. She would wait another minute. If they could not think of something better, she would call William over the bracelet.

"Jariel!" Rachel shouted. "Help us!"

She heard no answering *caw*.

Her whole body began to shake.

"Somebody," she screamed at the sky. "Zeus? Athena? Won't someone help us?"

"Isis? Osiris? Hermes?" Joy shouted. "Isn't anyone out there?"

"Thor?" cried Rachel.

"Amaterasu!" cried Joy.

"King Arthur!" shouted Sigfried.

He lunged at Zoë and tried to wrestle her contorting body, to keep her limbs from moving. With horrible popping-sounds accompanying her every movement, the paralyzed girl picked him up and threw him. He landed on his back across a snow-covered stump. There was a painful *cracking* noise.

Terror gripped Rachel.

Throwing her head back, she screamed the name of the only other supernatural being who had helped her in the past.

"*Leander!*"

CHAPTER FIFTEEN:

THIS TIME I COME AS A LION

A TINY LION PADDED AROUND THE CORNER OF ROANOKE HALL. Only, with each step, he grew larger. First he was the size of a small dog.

Step.

Then, he was as big as a fox. *Step.* Then he was the size of Wulfgang's wolverine. *Step.* Then he was as big as Valerie's elkhound. He paused and tossed his bright mane. His eyes were huge and golden and wise.

Step.

Then he was as big as a wolf. *Step.* Then he was the size of a deer. *Step.* Then he was as large as a bear.

Step.

Rachel glanced over her shoulder toward her friends. To her wonder, they were entirely motionless. Siggy lay upon a stump, his face contorted in agony. His hand grabbed his back, as if reaching for the source of the pain. Joy's arms were raised in supplication. Even Zoë, now collapsed upon the ground, was still and silent. And they were not simply holding still. The hair on their head and the wrinkles of their clothing were not moving either. Snow swept off the ground by Lucky's tail hung motionless in the air. Even the biting wind had died away.

The Lion came inexorably forward. He was now as big as a Clydesdale.

Caw!

A giant red-eyed Raven flew out of the trees and landed between the Lion and Zoë. It hopped around, pecking twice at the ground. Then it transformed into an eight-foot-tall man with huge black wings. He was shirtless, even in the snow, with black pants and bare feet. Reaching up, he plucked the golden hoop from over his head and held it in his hand.

His eyes were red as blood.

"You are not welcome here," the Raven spoke hoarsely.

"Where I am called, I come," said the Lion.

"Who called you?"

The Lion turned his huge golden head until his gaze rested upon Rachel. The Raven, scowling, turned as well.

"Ah." The Raven stopped scowling. "It is you."

"Have I..." Rachel swallowed, feeling very small. "Have I done something wrong?"

"No, Rachel Griffin." A slight smile touched the perfect lips of the winged man. "You have done something very, very right."

He cupped his black wings, like a bird of prey catching an up-draft. Immediately, his body was drawn upward and away, dwindling as he receded, until a huge black Raven flew off into the distance *cawing*.

Time started again. The bit of tossed snow plopped to the ground. Siggy groaned and rubbed his back. Joy shouted out the names of more gods and then froze, staring at the Lion with her jaw hanging open. Zoë, who lay sprawled across the snow, began to twitch and moan. The wind picked up, blowing little balls of ice across the white expanse and causing evergreen branches to sway.

Where Rachel stood, however, the air remained as calm and balmy as an April day. It was as if she stood in a tiny oasis of spring amidst the wastelands of winter.

Step.

The Lion was now the size of an elephant. Joy screamed. Siggy tried to scramble backwards but stopped, gasping in pain. Lucky rushed forward and stood between them, his mouth open, ready to breathe fire to protect his boy.

"Who is that?" cried Joy.

"Lion god, I guess," Lucky opened his mouth wider, preparing to strike.

"Did we call it?" Joy cried. "Oh, I hope it's not Sekhmet! Did I call her by mistake?"

Sigfried lunged to his feet, even though he could not straighten his spine. He was bent double with obvious pain. Yet, he staggered forward, supporting his back with one hand. His other hand held his knife, threatening the elephant-sized Lion.

"I won't let you hurt her!"

The Lion's eyes twinkled with kind amusement, but his voice was rich and regal. "*I come that she may have life and that she may have it more abundantly*."

Joy took a trembling step back, staring up at the massive beast. "C-can you help her?"

"I can," replied the Lion.

Joy's face lit up.

"Don't you two recognize him?" Rachel cried joyfully. "This is the Comfort Lion."

"Wait, you mean the one that lives in your room? Kitten's familiar?" Joy stared at Rachel as if she were crazy. "Griffin, that one's tiny. In case you haven't noticed, this one is *huge*!"

"He's quite the same," Rachel laughed with delight. "Just bigger."

Only, he did not look the same. The golden hair of his mane rippled like living flames. Its edges seemed to stretch out into the vast distance. Those lights caught in it—Rachel peered closer, awed —were they *stars*?

The Lion opened his mouth and breathed, the misty plume spreading outward, enveloping them all. Like morning frost vanishing from a window in the sunlight, the feeling of panic that had held Rachel in its grip since she first became aware of the shadow around Zoë, melted away. She could breathe freely again.

"Huh?" Siggy said suddenly.

Straightening up, he rolled his shoulders to the left and then to the right. A huge grin spread across his face.

"Hey, my back stopped hurting! Ace!"

Throwing his hands in the air and whooping, he shook his hips back and forth to emphasize his freedom of motion.

The Lion strode past Sigfried and Lucky. He raised his huge paw and pressed down on Zoë's chest. Her body spasmed. She began to cough. Her head jerked forward, and she vomited up a black mist.

The dark writhing cloud hung in mid-air, two red eyes glaring from it. Again, the terrible sense of wrongness, of something twisted and rotten began to creep over Rachel.

"I know you," it rasped. "Your shape does not deceive me. You are the Lamb Who Was Slain. I fear you not." It cackled. "Who would fear a lamb?"

The Lion growled, a tremendously ominous sound. All the students took a step back, even Rachel, who swallowed nervously. The demon, too, shrank away. It did not seem as menacing as it once had. The sense of wrongness was fading.

The Lion spoke with a voice that rang like a thousand trumpets. "Little fiend, bring this message to your fellow denizens in the fiery pit: *Our Father is beautiful in his mercy and terrible in his justice. Tell them that I said: Last time, I came as a lamb and went meekly to my slaughter. This time, I come as a Lion.*"

Then, it *roared.*

The sound was earthshaking. It shook Rachel to her very bones. And yet, somehow, the roar seemed more real than the world around her, more real than the cold and the stumps and the snow. Hearing it, she felt as if she were about to wake from a dream and remember her real life, a life far more glorious than this present nightmare.

Silence fell. This strange sensation slowly faded. The snowy field surrounded by the castle wall on one side and hemlock forests on the other, with the Watch Tower overlooking it in the distance, again seemed like the only reality. When Rachel thought back, she could remember the roar, and she could remember what she had experienced, but the strange feeling, as if she were about to wake to a better place, was not repeated.

From the writhing cloud of darkness came a wail both horrible and petrifying. Raising one great paw, the Lion swatted. A single moan issued from the air, and the darkness fled away.

⁘

Lowering his head, the Lion nudged Zoë with his moist, pink triangle of a nose. His great rough tongue licked her face. Zoë's body trembled. Then her chest heaved with indrawn breath, and she sat up, blinking. Rachel, Joy, Siggy, and Lucky all cheered.

Joy squealed into her calling card. "It's okay, princess! Zoë's all right!"

Zoë moved to a sitting position. She did not seem injured, despite the demon's treatment of her paralyzed body. She gazed thoughtfully up at the great Lion, who stood over her. His mane rippled like golden fire, reminding Rachel of the glorious light that had blazed around the branches of the Roanoke Tree.

"I know you," Zoë whispered hoarsely. "I read about you in a book, though you had a different name."

The Lion's great head nodded. "In the place you came from, there are many stories about me. The one of which you speak is a favorite of mine. It was partially to honor my servant Jack that I chose this form."

"You can take other shapes?" asked Joy.

"I can," said the Lion. "But if I came in another, those who know me would still recognize me."

"I don't understand what you mean," said Joy.

The Lion regarded her with calm wisdom. "Do you not? If I came in the shape of a bear,"—the Lion was gone, and in its place stood a huge golden bear with thick shaggy fur and gleaming claws. It towered over the students in the midst of the snowy field—"those who recognize me would cry: *Lo, there goes the Lion of Judah in the shape of a bear.* Or if I came in the shape of a hart,"—the bear vanished. In its place stood an enormous stag of dark golden hue with huge branching antlers of ivory. It looked so fierce and so regal that Rachel felt like crying, though she could not have said why—"they who know me would say: *Lo, here is the Lion of Judah in the shape of a hart.*"

"And Kitten?" Zoë pressed. "Is she also from that book?"

The Lion shook his great head. "She appears in a different story, though she, too, bears a new nickname—her former one having been painted with the taint of iniquity." At it spoke those last words, the Lion growled again, a dangerous, menacing sound.

"What does it all mean?" Rachel cried. "Tell us more!"

"I cannot." There was sorrow in his voice and compassion. "The time for that is not yet."

"But... why not?" cried Rachel. "Why can't anyone just tell us what is going on?"

The Lion padded toward her and lowered his enormous head until his mouth was beside her ear. His breath was warm and sweet, like the first flowers of spring, newly washed with fresh rain.

"Child, we are behind enemy lines." His voice was powerful yet soft. "We must be patient."

"Behind enemy lines?" mouthed Rachel.

The Lion nodded, "But, *fear not*. A time will come in the end when you shall know all."

"*Know all?*" whispered Rachel, her eyes as large as lanterns. Without another word, the Lion turned and began walking back the way he had come. With each step, he grew smaller, just as he had grown larger during his approach.

"Wait!" Sigfried ran forward.

Sprinting until he was in front of the beast, who was now merely the size of a large dog, Siggy knelt and laid his knife at the Lion's feet. The girls were too far away to hear Sigfried's words, but his expression was unusually serious. Rachel longed to know what the boy and the Lion said to each other, but Zoë was rising to her feet.

"What am I doing here?" Zoë said. "Griffin? O'Keefe? What happened to Nastasia?"

"You're all right! You're all right!" Joy grabbed Zoë and hugged her and then danced her in a circle. "I'm so glad! I'm so glad!"

Rachel joined them in their dance, her heart light with relief. The worldly burdens that had oppressed her for months felt light, as if they were far away. She could feel that they would return. Now, however, she felt carefree, as if the yoke she had carried was suddenly as light as snowflakes.

Over the calling card clutched in Joy's hand, Nastasia's voice called, "Is she well? Are you sure? Should I bring the dean or a proctor anyway?"

"No!" Joy shouted back. "She's fine. All taken care of."

The three girls held hands and danced in a circle. Nastasia came zooming around the corner. She hopped off the bristleless and politely returned it to Rachel.

"I am glad to see that you are well, Miss Forrest." The princess inclined her head toward Zoë. "I was… quite concerned upon your behalf."

"Sorry to have worried you," Zoë shrugged. "I'm fine."

"Most glad to hear it." The princess's smile was like the sun coming out from behind a cloud. She seemed tremendously relieved.

Zoë looked around. "How did we get here? I thought we were on another world. No. We had left that place and were coming home, right? What happened next?" Glancing down, Zoë suddenly gasped. "My feather! It's gone!"

They all looked at her hair. Both the short, pixy-cut part and her long, slender forelock braid were the same dark auburn as her eyebrows and eyelashes. The mottled feather that usually stuck out of the braid was gone.

"Was it important?" asked Joy.

Zoë made a little sad noise in her throat. "Not in the grand scheme of things."

"We can find you another one." The princess spoke firmly, giving Zoë a kindly pat on the shoulder. "Just let me know what kind of feather you want, and I am sure my father can commission someone to find one for you."

"That one was the last thing my mother gave me before she died," Zoë said flatly.

"Oh." The princess wilted.

"I'm so sorry," whispered Rachel.

"Yeah, so am I," muttered Zoë.

"Any idea where the feather might be?" asked Joy. "Do you remember what happened while you were lost?"

Zoë was quiet for a moment. Her shoulders twitched, as if she were shivering. "I remember I was holding the princess's hand, and then everything was dark. We were on a silver path. Then, something yanked on me, and I was falling. Then I remember waking up with a whale of a Lion breathing on me."

"Lion?" Nastasia asked. She looked across the snowy field to where Sigfried and the dog-sized Lion were speaking intently together. Sigfried was on his feet again.

"That's Kitten's Lion," said Rachel.

The princess blinked. "He looks so big. Why is he here?"

"Big?" snorted Zoë. "You should have seen him a few minutes ago."

"He kicked the demon out of Zoë," said Rachel proudly.

"He truly is the Comfort Lion," laughed Joy.

Nastasia's eyes narrowed. "I spoke to him when I came back without Zoë, as I must admit," she paused briefly, "I felt in some need of comfort. All his advice was military in nature. Something about 'did I expect that, as a general, I would never lose any men?' I did not find it comforting in the least."

"Our general, the princess!" exclaimed Joy.

Rachel, however, frowned, disappointed to hear that the princess had not found comfort in the Lion's counsel.

"I am not sure I trust that lion," Nastasia said calmly.

Rachel's jaw dropped. "On what grounds?"

"He has not made his loyalties known. I am not convinced that he has the interests of Magical Australia at heart," said the princess. She turned to the other girls. "It is growing cold. Shall we go in? It is almost lunch time, I believe."

As the other three girls began to walk around Roanoke Hall towards the warmth of the dining room, Rachel paused and looked over at the Lion, who stood regally before Sigfried. She remembered the peace it had brought. With a shiver, she remembered when he had *roared*.

Softly, she repeated an idea that she had first voiced the day she met her Elf: "Whatever side *he* is on, that's the side I want to join."

Chapter Sixteen:
The Mysteries of
Roanoke Island

After lunch, the remaining students gathered in the theater in Dare Hall to watch a magic lantern show. The theater was a cavernous chamber with red velvet chairs, the bottoms of which folded up to allow people to file through the aisles. A curtain of gold velvet hid the stage. In front of the curtain hung a huge white screen. Next to it sat a chair.

The narrator for the event was Rachel's language tutor, Hieronymus Tuck, a heavyset man with brown hair and beard. He walked ponderously onto the stage, his customary green and black robes swishing about his legs. With him were his two tiny children, a boy and a girl of about two and four respectively. Mr. Tuck crossed the stage to the seat beside the screen. For every step he took, the little ones took three running steps to keep up with their giant of a father. They gazed up at him with such adoring looks that Rachel had no doubt why Mr. Tuck had allowed them to accompany him.

"Good afternoon, all," Mr. Tuck rumbled, upon reaching the side of the screen. The enchantments woven into the theater amplified his voice. Behind him, his children climbed into the chair that had, presumably, been meant for him. "And welcome to our yearly Thanksgiving Day magic lantern extravaganza. In honor of this holiday, celebrating one group of persecuted settlers who came to the shores of America, we shall present the story of a different group of persecuted settlers, one whose journey touches more closely upon all of you than does that of the Pilgrims. Even if the Pilgrims are responsible, albeit indirectly, for the delicious, delicious tradition we shall enact later this afternoon of stuffing ourselves on turkey and pumpkin pie.

"The official name of this presentation is the History of Roanoke Island," Mr. Tuck continued, "But I like to call it the Mysteries of Roanoke Island. Mysteries are so much more interesting than histories, are they not?

"Now, you may wonder why I, a canticler, am narrating this presentation instead of a tutor from the History Department. This is the first of the mysteries. It shall be answered anon."

Without further ado, Mr. Tuck launched into the magic lantern show. A black and gold box in the middle of the chamber issued a light that projected hand-painted slides onto the screen. Some of the slides were colorful. Others were simple silhouettes.

"Our story," announced Mr. Tuck, in his deep booming voice, "begins when the sorceress queen herself, Elizabeth the First, granted Sir Walter Raleigh—after whom Raleigh Hall is named—a charter to found a colony in the newly discovered lands that were, at that time, called Virginia, in honor of Elizabeth, the Virgin Queen.

"Actually, Queen Elizabeth originally gave the charter to Sir Humphrey Gilbert, Raleigh's half-brother. But Sir Humphrey drowned in an ill-fated attempt to found a settlement in what is now Canada. So, Sir Walter took up the cause.

"Raleigh organized an expedition that arrived on Roanoke Island—which was at that time a normal island off the coast of what we now call North Carolina—on July fourth, fifteen eighty-five. The expedition established a small settlement and built a real wooden fortress. Raleigh himself, incidentally, did not accompany the expedition. He was the queen's ambassador to the City of the Wise known as El Dorado. But I digress.

"Incidentally, their new home was originally called Rune Oak Island. Only later did the story spread that the name came from the Algonquin word for 'money.'

"Two years later, on August eighteenth of fifteen eighty-seven, the colonists witnessed the arrival of the first English child to be born in America, our founder and benefactress, Virginia Dare—after whom this dormitory was named?" Mr. Tuck gestured encouragingly toward the audience with both hands.

The crowd roared back, "Dare Hall!"

Mr. Tuck smiled and nodded. Stroking his beard with his hand, he gestured for the next slide, which showed a ship at sea.

"A year later," he continued, "the next ship from England found the settlement abandoned. To this day, the fate of these settlers remains a mystery to the Unwary.

"We of the Wise know what became of them. But we have a different mystery in relation to these settlers, as we shall soon see. What we do know, that the Unwary do not, is that many of those who volunteered for the journey were members of the Wise, who were fleeing persecution, and in fifteen eighty-eight, news arrived that their persecutors were about to catch up with them.

"But, to continue my narrative: In fifteen eighty-five, the *Tiger*, a ship coming from England, was separated from the rest of its fleet by a severe storm and ended up in Puerto Rico. There, they came in contact with the Spanish before continuing on to Roanoke Island. In fifteen eighty-six, another great sorcerer, Sir Francis Drake—after whom was named...." He cupped one hand to his ear and gestured toward the crowd with the other.

The students shouted: "Drake Hall!"

"Sir Francis," Mr. Tuck continued, gesturing at the screen, which now showed the acclaimed sea captain and sorcerer with his high, stiff, white lace, Elizabethan collar, "stopped by Roanoke after a successful raid in the Caribbean. He warned the settlers he had received word that the Spanish in Puerto Rico had alerted their enemies to their position. Rumor had it that a fleet had been dispatched to destroy them.

"The settlers were quite dismayed. They had fled to a new continent, leaving behind house and home, and now their persecutors had found them again. One member, however, Ananias Dare, befriended a medicine man of the Croatan peoples named Achakahanu or Spirit Who Laughs. Laughing Spirit, as he came to be called, taught the newcomers the secret of uprooting an island. This was something that his people did occasionally, so as to move an island to better fishing grounds.

"Our settlers worked together with Laughing Spirit to weave a great enchantment. They uprooted Roanoke Island permanently, making it into a floating island. Before they left, they built a ramshackle version of their settlement on a nearby island; however, they did not bother to rebuild the fortress.

"This is why, when John White, the governor of Roanoke and the grandfather of Virginia Dare, returned from England in fifteen eighty-eight, he found the town but not the fortress, which he reported had been dismantled. The ruins of the fortress, by the way, are still visible on our island, just north of the Lower School, to the south of our current position.

"But to continue, Laughing Spirit went on to marry our heroine, Virginia Dare, and to aid her, in sixteen twenty-four, in the founding of what today we call Roanoke Academy, though originally it was just known as the College at Roanoke. He took the last name of Dare, which is why Virginia's descendants are still Dares today—including our own Jenny Dare. Is she here?"

Jenny Dare, a huge smile on her face, rose from her chair and waved. Her exuberance caused her straight brown hair to bounce around her head and shoulders.

Mr. Tuck gestured toward her. "Including Jenny and her brother Thomas, whom some of you may remember. He graduated—three years ago, I believe?

"To continue, Roanoke was now a floating island. But I promised you a mystery. What we of the Wise still do not know today is: from whom were these settlers fleeing? This should be a simple historical matter. These events were not so very long ago, as the Wise count years... and yet, we can find no definitive record as to who was doing the persecuting.

"Some records suggest that the goddess Hecate was offended that these folks strayed into areas of magic she had forbidden to mortals. Others claim that they were secretly worshippers of Orpheus, who made many enemies among the immortals. Still others say that it was Dionysus whom they had offended.

"Based on a few symbols the persecutors left behind, some historians of the Wise believe the settlers were pursued by the followers of Thor or of Indra. These claims, however, are not confirmed by any of the known activities of these peoples at the time.

"And so, students, we have a mystery," Mr. Tuck spread his hands. "How it could be that the Wise, who keep such scrupulous records—going back to the Age of Stone, when humans lived in caves and still drew pictures on walls—could have lost this crucial piece of information?" He shrugged his large shoulders. "No one knows."

"Pressing on." He gestured. The next slide showed the leaning tower of Pisa. "Leaving the Americas, the floating island began to travel with the current. But this is a different matter for the Wise, to whom winds and currents bow, than it is for the Unwary. So our ancestors had some control over where Roanoke wandered.

"Within a quarter of a century, the island had reached the Italian peninsula. There, Virginia Dare commissioned Leonardo da Vinci to design Roanoke Hall, which was then called Roanoke Castle. Mundane records claim Mr. da Vinci died over a hundred years before Roanoke's arrival. But we of the Wise know that the venerable alchemist lived to the ripe old age of two hundred and three.

"After that, the island traveled around the world, often taking a few decades to complete each circuit. Enchanters used their mastery of weather to influence which way the island drifted and to keep it from growing too warm or cold. Originally, the college at Roanoke only taught Enchantment and basic Enochian warding. They relied on mist and fog to keep them hidden in those days, not yet having the advantage of Obscuration. As they traveled and made new contacts, however, new branches of study were opened."

The screen displayed a black-and-white etching of an island surrounded by mist with a huge tree with seven branches rising from the center of the island, the same tree that Rachel and Sigfried had so recently seen laying fallen at Dutchman's Cove.

"In sixteen thirty-seven, the island traveled to England, where John White was reunited with his daughter, Eleanor White Dare and where he met for the first time his now-grown granddaughter, Virginia. While there, the island was visited by the aged sorcerer extraordinaire, John Dee, who had retired from public life years before—upon a day that the Unwary still take to be the date of his death. Mr. Dee bequeathed his books to the college, and Dee Hall was built to house them. Does anyone know what Art was originally the focus of Dee Hall?"

Students raised their hands, calling out answers as Mr. Tuck pointed at them.

"Divination?"

"Scholarly pursuit of pure wisdom?"

"Omen readings?"

"No, those are the modern studies associated with Dee Hall, but what was the original purpose? Hmm? Anyone?"

Rachel raised her hand. During the period of her life when she had kept a picture of Dee Hall hidden under her bed and dreamed of living in the dorm whose hallways were lined with books, she had read everything she could about the fascinating building. The memory of her love for Dee Hall and how the opportunity to live there had been denied to her still caused a lump in her throat.

Alas, Mr. Tuck did not call on her.

"Augustus Dee, I see you in the crowd," boomed her language tutor. "You are an actual descendant of the great John Dee. Are you not?"

The young man, a round-faced college student wearing glasses, rose to his feet.

"I am!" he yelled back cheerfully, "for all the good it does me."

That earned him a laugh.

"What was the Art originally studied at the hall named for your illustrious ancestor?"

"Theurgy," Augustus Dee answered smartly.

"Which means—?" Mr. Tuck pressed.

"The practice of rituals intended for the purpose of invoking the gods."

"And why, pray tell, Mr. Dee, is that Art no longer the center-piece of Dee Hall today?"

Augustus Dee stood straighter, "Because the gods no longer come. Elves come. Star fairies sometimes come. Chthonic monstrosities still come. But gods? Even demi-gods? No one has seen one in generations, not counting Rory Wednesday, of course."

The crowd burst out laughing. Rachel looked around the theater but saw no sign of the extraordinarily beautiful upperclassman who was rumored to be descended from Odin.

"I mean no disrespect to the priests and monks and all," added Augustus Dee. "I am sure that the gods still watch over us and come among us in secret. But, in the old days, they used to appear to us in the open quite regularly."

"And when, Mr. Dee, was the last verified sighting of a god or goddess by mortal eyes?" asked Mr. Tuck.

Augustus replied with a big grin, "At the groundbreaking ceremony of Dee Hall. Athena walked upon the earth of this island and gave the hall her blessing. She has not been seen since."

Mr. Tuck gestured toward the screen, which showed a silhouette of the goddess of wisdom with an owl sitting on her shoulder. "Very good. Does anyone here know why that is?"

No hands rose.

"Anyone?" Mr. Tuck looked around hopefully. "Me, neither. And in that, we have yet another mystery. Why have the gods abandoned us? Or at least, no longer visit us openly?"

Rachel did not raise her hand, but she recalled a cryptic comment made by Cassandra March, the wife of the Grand Inquisitor, when they had met her in dreamland: *No real gods or angels are allowed on this world.* Why was that? Was it because of this rule that the Raven had tried to keep them from speaking to the Lion? If so, who had made the rule? The Raven? If that were the case, why had he then declared that she had done something *very, very right?*

It was almost as if she had been disobeying an ordinance that he was honor-bound to enforce but with which he disagreed. But, if the Raven had not established the rule, who could have done so? *Whom did the Raven obey?*

Upon the stage, Mr. Tuck continued, "After that, Roanoke visited many distant lands. Our sorcerers would meet with their sorcerers. Occasionally, for different reasons, some foreign practitioners of the Sorcerous Arts would ask or agree to move to the island and teach.

"From China came our first alchemists in the early seventeen hundreds. From India came the Art of Obscuration, hypnotism, and a whole Pandora's Box of similar disturbing powers. From Prester John's Kingdom, deep in Abyssinia, came wise men who recalled the Original Language once spoken in Sumeria, before the curse of tongues robbed men of the Gift of Moira.

"From Prussia came thaumaturges, those who could weave together the powers of the other Arts into potent spells. From Australia and New Zealand, shamans who knew the ways of the Long-Ago Dreamtime and could draw gifts from the sky—what we call Conjuring. From many tribesmen on various continents came taboos that have been added to the Enochian Arts—the Art of Warding said to have been established by an ancient sage named Enoch. Enoch is said to have built the first city. Or perhaps it was the first city wall. Accounts differ."

Slides went by showing ornate Mandarins surrounded by Chinese water dragons—who looked much like Lucky; elegant Rajas atop war elephants; silhouetted Ethiopians holding conversation with the brooks and trees; German scholars bent over great tomes; and Aborigines pulling balls and snakes from mid-air.

Rachel wondered if the aborigines were from Australia or Magical Australia. Did Magical Australia have aborigines? She knew they had emus and wombats and kookaburras, but Nastasia had not said much about the people her father ruled.

"As Roanoke Island traveled from place to place," Mr. Tuck continued, "sorcerers from different countries, different continents even, began to meet, to speak, to swap knowledge and expertise. The idea began to germinate that perhaps there should be some kind of community, a council that could handle problems and decide disagreements.

"Thus was born the Parliament of the Wise. It was not a parliament at first. That came about fifty years later, in the seventeen forties. Though the Charter was revised again in seventeen ninety-two to reflect some of the wisdom of the American experiment—as it was known at the time.

"Oh, and Roanoke was right here in America during the Revolution, fighting side by side with their fellow colonists, despite our strong ties to England. Several of the founding fathers were educated here on the island. Most notably, the great alchemist Benjamin Franklin, whose works we continue to study today. Other members of the founding fathers who studied...." Mr. Tuck waved a hand. "But I digress again.

"As time went on, members of the Wise began to chafe at having a government seat whose location could not be predicted. So, in eighteen twenty-four the government left Roanoke Island. First it met in London. Then, for several decades, it moved every few years, from Vienna to Johannesburg to Verhängnisburg to Kyoto to Thulhavn and finally Machu Picchu, where it resided for over a decade. But it was eventually agreed that this inland, mountainous location was too remote—travel glasses not being as prevalent as they are now. So, in eighteen fifty-two, the Parliament of the Wise settled permanently in its current location, in the Republic of Cathay—which, as the Wise-born among you know, is south of China but north of Vietnam.

"After the Parliament of the Wise departed the island, those who stayed behind reorganized, forming Roanoke Academy for the Sorcerous Arts. The College at Roanoke was divided into the current college and the Upper School. The Lower School was built four decades later, in eighteen sixty-four, before that older and younger children had been educated together."

Mr. Tuck gestured to the screen. Images flashed by showing Roanoke Hall, the seven dormitories and the Tudor-style castle of the Lower School, with its tall round spires.

"Now, finally, we come to the very first mystery I mentioned: why I, and not Mr. Gideon or Mr. Sanchez or one of the other Scholars, am speaking to you today. For the two hundredth and fiftieth anniversary of the founding of the college at Roanoke, the island returned to England. During this visit a very important event occurred. Can you guess what it was?" Mr. Tuck leaned forward, his eyes twinkling. "Anybody?" He looked back and forth, squinting at an arm that was raised in the dark auditorium. "No comments from those of you who have heard me give this speech before.

"No? I shall tell you. It was in this year, eighteen sixty-four, that my great-grandfather, Onesimus Tuck, joined the staff at Roanoke Academy." He bowed toward the audience then gestured toward the screen. The slide showed a portrait of a portly bearded man dressed in the style of the early nineteenth century. "Yes, it is true. I am that rare bird, the native Roanokean."

Applause briefly drowned him out. When it grew quiet again, Mr. Tuck continued, "My father taught here, as did his father, and his father before him—Onesimus Tuck himself. I grew up in the same cottage in the Staff Village where my children live today."

He gestured at his little ones. The girl hid her face shyly, but the little boy leapt to his feet and stuck out his tongue at the audience, sparking laughter.

Mr. Tuck continued, "You may have heard that when the Terrible Five first came to Roanoke, they slew the school's seven most potent sorcerers, hoping to scare the rest. My father was one of those seven. I was away that year, having already graduated. I was doing advanced studies in Mesopotamia. When I heard the news, I returned. I was one of only five people who came back to Roanoke, when so many were fleeing. I was here, twenty-five years ago, come May, for the Battle of Roanoke. I fought. I was wounded. I lived.

"A great many of my friends and two of my siblings were not so lucky."

Mr. Tuck took off his mortarboard hat with its green tassel and held it against his chest, bowing his head out of respect for the deceased. There was a moment of silence. Rachel bowed her head, too, and silently repeated one of the traditional rhymes to quiet the uneasy dead.

Replacing his hat, Mr. Tuck boomed, "And now you know why it is that I like to be the one to give this talk—even though I am not a member of the History Department. This story, the story of Roanoke, is also my story.

"But this is not the end of our tale. One part remains: Coming to the Hudson Highlands. It is here that a name that many of you have heard of late, perhaps more than you might like, enters our narrative: the Heer of Dunderberg.

"Does anyone here know the origins of the Heer?" He looked back and forth across the crowd. "Anyone? Anyone?"

Rachel checked the many memorized books in her mental library. To her surprise, she did know the answer. She raised her hand.

"Ah. We have a hand. Miss…" Mr. Tuck shaded his eyes, as he stared into the dark auditorium, perhaps to block the glare of the magic lantern. "Miss Griffin?"

Rachel stood up and called, "The first Dutchman murdered in North America was John Colman, a sailor from Henry Hudson's *Half Moon*. Colman was shot in the throat by a native arrow. Some believe that his uneasy spirit made a compact with dark powers, transforming him into the Heer. He was said to destroy ships because he was trying to scare the Europeans away, so they would stop coming to these lands, where he believed they will die."

"Very good!" Mr. Tuck looked impressed. "And how did you acquire this bit of arcane knowledge?"

"It was in *Legends and Lore of Sleepy Hollow and the Hudson Valley* by Jonathan Kruk," explained Rachel. "One of the books on display in the library before All Hallows' Eve."

"I am impressed, Miss Griffin. I shall inform our librarian, Mr. Poole, that, occasionally, his library manages to trickle a bit of knowledge into the head of an actual student," said Mr. Tuck. "Yes. Some believe that the Heer was once a man. Others believe he has always been a goblin, but Colman's dying curse drew him here, which is why he dresses in the Dutch style."

The next slide showed a fanciful depiction of the Heer, dressed in his green and gold Dutch doublets. He looked more like a wizened goblin than the young Dutch boy Rachel had seen.

"Either way, the Heer is a menace," boomed Mr. Tuck. "And he has been a menace for centuries. Thanks to him, many ships were sunk at World's End." Mr. Tuck pointed to the south. The screen showed an image of an area of river south of Roanoke, just north of West Point. "Among them, a ship belonging to the notorious Captain Kidd.

"Eventually, the Heer got to be such a bother that locals appealed to the Parliament of the Wise for help. This was in the early twentieth century. The Parliament chose Roanoke to solve the problem. So, the island headed up the Hudson and moored itself to a small lump of land in the middle of the river known as Pollepel Island.

"Now, you may ask, why did they send Roanoke? While the Parliament of the Wise had departed just over seventy-five years earlier, the Wisecraft still had offices on the island. They were housed in a

Scottish-style castle that their leader Frances Bannerman, the Grand Inquisitor of the day—Is Molly here? Molly Bannerman? No? Well, no matter—had built on the southwest tip. The castle, incidentally, was constructed to guard the only permanent opening in the formidable wards of Roanoke Academy.

"If any of you had wondered why you must walk up the stairs and pass through the ruins of Bannerman's Castle to reach the campus from the docks, yet another mystery has been solved for you today.

"The Island arrived in its current position, and the battle against the Heer ensued. The Heer is a dangerous and potent enemy. He had many allies and more than one domicile. He had halls in both Storm King and in Dunderberg—Thunder Mountain—some twenty miles south. This battle raged, on and off with interruptions, for almost two decades, culminating in the death of Grand Inquisitor Bannerman, when Bannerman's Castle exploded under the onslaught of the Heer and his lightning imps. But thanks to Ben Franklin's great-granddaughter, the Heer was snared.

"To this day, the Unwary believe that the castle was a weapons arsenal, and that this is why it exploded. Mundane history books claim that Francis Bannerman was an arms dealer. That much was true. He did own a mighty arsenal of weapons both mundane and arcane—but this is not why his castle exploded.

"In the midst of all this, however, something else happened in nineteen oh-seven. As many of you know, Roanoke Island and Brendan's Island—which is actually situated on the back of an unusually large and sluggish whale—were the only earthly places where the crew of the *Flying Dutchman* could step. At a ball on All Hallows' Eve, the captain of that cursed vessel fell in love with a young Roanokean girl. When she was still loyal to him seven years later, it broke the curse that had caused his ship to eternally wander.

"Alas, the spell that kept Roanoke afloat also ended. When the tutors and Wisecraft gathered to recast the spell to move the island, they found that the original settlers had not recorded what Laughing Spirit taught them. Nor could they find any remaining Croatan Indians able to tell them how the island-moving spell was accomplished.

"So Roanoke found itself stranded in a rather dangerous area. Many brutes and beasties live in the Hudson Highlands, including the Heer, whom they had not yet trapped. There were also the lightning imps; the mist sprites; the storm witch Mother Kronk; the *Mexaxkuk*, a native horned serpent that supped on human flesh, which dwelt on the old Pollepel Island against which Roanoke had moored; and a family of water panthers living in the river. Not to mention the Headless Horseman, who rides up from the south on All Hallows' Eve.

"On top of that, Roanoke has gathered its own collection of supernatural nasties over the years, the price of visiting so many foreign lands. There are the water leapers who now live on the small islands just beyond the east cove; the woodwose in the southern forest outside the wards; the wight by the standing stones; the Each-Uisge and Wilis in the marshes. Redcaps in the forest. Trow in the valley north of the tor, and a phooka in the meadow beyond that. Spruce trolls on the tor's slopes, not to mention dozens of mischievous fey who make their home on the island. Oh, and, of course, in the cave in the cliffs by Dutchman's Cove, the ogre who has caused such grief of late."

Mr. Tuck leaned forward and wagged a finger at the audience. "This is why we emphasize that students should stay inside the wards. The outside island can be very dangerous."

For a moment, Rachel thought he was looking directly at her. Her heart skipped a beat. But he was not, and she breathed more easily. The lawyerly portion of her brain noted, with relief, that he had said "should stay," not "must stay."

Beside her, Siggy murmured to Lucky and Seth, "Ace! Let's go out after this and see if we can find some of those woses and eek-uglies!"

"Once we captured the Heer, we discovered that, so long as we kept him locked up here, all the rest of the supernatural baddies left us alone—because they were afraid of the Heer. Thus, an agreement was arranged between the island and the local supernatural beings, which we call the Roanoke Covenant." Mr. Tuck paused and puffed out his cheeks. "Unfortunately, this agreement is only good for a year and a day once the Heer escapes. Last time, we caught him within the allotted time. Fortune willing, we will do so again."

"In orchestrating this agreement, known as the Roanoke Compact, we were aided by one who knew the local native spirits. You may have noticed all the parkland near us: Storm King State Park to our west, the Hudson Highlands to our east, Fahnestock State Park beyond that, and the Shawangunks farther north. Even today, unknown to the Unwary, there is a Lenni Lenape tribe of the Wise living in these areas. Their medicine man came to help with the negotiations between the fey and Roanoke Island, and he stayed. In fact, he is still here to this day."

An image of Nighthawk, Roanoke's Master Warder, appeared on the screen. The Lenni Lenape man looked younger than he had when Rachel met him, but he had the same hawklike nose and formidable bearing.

"Three of Nighthawk's grandchildren attend our school today, I believe. Dirk, Glaive, and Kris Wright? Have I forgotten anyone?"

Three students stood up. To Rachel's surprise, one of them was the pink-haired girl from De Vere. All three had Asian features. They looked more like Laurel and Peter than like their American Indian grandfather.

Kris Serenity Wright, the outspoken, pink-haired De Vere girl, stepped forward. She waved to the audience in the quick, graceful way that she did everything. "Hi! We're the Wrights. Our father is Master Warder Nighthawk's son. Our mother is Katana the Kitsune. We're honored to be here at this school that still continues to exist, despite all odds, because of how awesome our granda is. He's the one you have to thank for the fact that we don't all get skewered in our beds by red caps or eaten by the ogre!"

Mr. Tuck nodded pleasantly. "And that concludes our little trip down memory lane. Some mysteries have been solved. Others remain a mystery. Before we depart to prepare for feasting, so that we may eat until we are so stuffed that they will be required to roll us back to our beds, are there any questions? Problems? Major dilemmas?"

Students raised their hands, asking for clarifications about various points. One student asked about the other three sorcerers who gave their names to Roanoke dormitories. Mr. Tuck explained that when the island went to England in eighteen twenty-four, Raleigh, De Vere, Drake and Spenser, who were all still alive, visited the island and bequeathed libraries to the school—though that was the last public appearance Drake ever made, as he vanished two months later, en route to Russia while carrying an important missive. Only Kit Marlowe never actually set foot here, having been killed in a tavern brawl in fifteen ninety-three. Marlowe Hall was named for him as a memorial.

Another student called out, "If some of these fey creatures are so terrible—like the woodwose, the ogre, and the wight—why don't we kill them?"

Mr. Tuck shook his head. "Can't. That's part of the compact. So long as we don't kill them—except when directly attacked—they agree not to kill us, except when we stray into their territory. And since, when they feel unconstrained, they often begin with the hapless Unwary, who know nothing of them and cannot defend themselves, it is our responsibility to see that compacts such as this one do not get broken. That is why it is imperative that we recapture the Heer. The Wisecraft is hard at work on that matter. Yes, next? Miss Wright?"

Kris Serenity Wright jumped to her feet again, her pink hair bobbing. "Also, charmed life! Some of the baddies, like the ogre and the woodwose have charmed lives. That's why they weren't already killed long, long ago. And—before you who grew up among the Unwary start bragging about your big weapons—" She turned and stuck her tongue out at her Unwary-born roommate. "It's been tried. As Mr. Tuck said, Grand Inquisitor Bannerman was an arms dealer. He shot the ogre with a machine gun, a flame thrower, and an anti-aircraft weapon. Oh, and he tried a landmine. Back then, no one had better ordnance than Bannerman."

"Thank you, Miss Wright. Anyone else?"

When Mr. Tuck first asked for questions, Siggy's hand had shot up, waving back and forth. Each time Mr. Tuck did not pick him, he waved it more vigorously. Eventually, his was the only hand still waving.

Mr. Tuck looked left and right and then sighed. "Courtesy requires that I call upon you, Mr. Smith, but experience suggests that such a course of action is a chancy venture at best. Please, surprise me."

"What did the Terrible Five want with Roanoke?" Sigfried called, rising to his feet.

Mr. Tuck looked pleasantly surprised and mildly relieved. "That is another mystery, Mr. Smith, that we can add to our collection. No one knows.

"One reason may have been that, other than the Scryory at Casan—the capital of Prester John's kingdom—and the Academy on Mount Hua, in China, Roanoke was the last bastion of truly powerful sorcerers. The Terrible Years had begun with the slaying of the entire staff of the Wisecraft, including Herodotus Powers, the Grand Inquisitor of that era, Bannerman's successor. The great sorcerers of India had fallen at Mohenjo Daro. Those of Europe had been slain at the Battle of Ittoqqortoormiit, in Ultima Thule, and those of America at the Battle of Detroit.

"So part of the purpose of the Terrible Five was to complete the defeat their opposition. But if that had been their only goal, however, they would not have bothered to hold the school—which required keeping order among over two thousand student hostages. And yes, the school was much bigger in those days.

"No, all five of them and their crony, Aaron Marley, were clearly searching for something. They left gouges all over the island, where they had dug up the ground. You may have noticed how some portions of the memorial gardens are new? The Terrible Five dug up the former shrine garden.

"And they released the Heer, of course—some of you know about the historic battle between the storm goblin and our head of security, Maverick Badger? But the Terrible Five kept searching after that, so the Heer was not their ultimate target, either.

"What they were looking for, however, we never did determine. Perhaps, they found it. Perhaps not. Most likely, we shall never know. Some mysteries remain mysterious."

CHAPTER SEVENTEEN:

GRIPING AND GIVING THANKS

THE LIGHTS CAME ON IN THE AUDITORIUM. RACHEL AND HER friends rose and stretched. Moving closer to the others, Joy whispered, "It's that Raven, isn't it? Hiding all these things?"

"Probably," murmured Nastasia, from where she had leaned over to pet Beauregard, who was sniffing under Siggy's seat. "I do not trust that odious creature."

"Possibly," Rachel frowned, "but why? He said he was changing memories to help the newcomers settle in. Were there already newcomers back then?" She lowered her voice. "I bet I know what the Terrible Five wanted on Roanoke, though."

"Oh?" The princess asked. "What might that be?"

Rachel lowered her voice even more. "I bet they were looking for the demon, the one they were trying to summon in Tunis."

"Moloch!" Nastasia straightened up. "What makes you think so?"

Rachel flinched at the sound of the fiend's proper name. The other students were filing out of the auditorium, which had been cold when they arrived but which now felt stuffy. Rachel's friends dawdled, waiting to hear her answer.

"I thought they were looking for the Heart of Dreams," said Joy.

"The what?" asked Nastasia.

Rachel checked her mental library. "You mean that object Mr. Fisher mentioned—from an unfulfilled prophecy?"

Joy nodded

"Clever, O'Keefe," said Zoë. She had fallen asleep during the presentation and was now rolling her neck and yawning. "Very clever."

Joy looked both embarrassed and pleased. "I pay attention to prophecies. Since I'm part of one—the one the princess and I are both mentioned in, about a seventh daughter of a seventh daughter and one who was born early morning on the winter solstice who together stop a great evil?—I think about prophecies a lot. The one about the Terrible Years that was never fulfilled—or if it was, no one found out—was that the Terrible Five were going to acquire a powerful talisman called the Heart of Dreams. I would think that's what they were looking for."

"Oh. That could be," Rachel said, feeling a bit deflated.

"Does that happen a lot?" asked Sigfried.

"Does what happen?" asked Joy.

"That prophecies don't get fulfilled?"

"Of course," shrugged Joy, "Otherwise, no one would ever try to stop them. But the really good seers are correct the majority of the time."

"Rather like the princess," said Rachel. "Her visions, I mean. How we stopped the one about Fuentes and the one where Gaius, Dread, and Locke ended up dead, but not the one about Mrs. Egg."

"But they all started to come about," Nastasia stated. "I wonder what halted the Heart of Dream's prophesy."

"Why did you think they were looking for the demon?" Zoë asked Rachel.

"Or that he's here on campus! That would be excellent! Maybe we could find him and blast him before he wakes up!" declared Siggy, from where he sat on the narrow ridge of a chair back, his feet resting on a folding seat—pushing it, letting it spring back, and pushing it again.

"Yeah," drawled Zoë, "because we have about as much chance of 'blasting' a demon as an ant has of eating the Taj Mahal."

Rachel said, "When I was in Carthage, about to be sacrificed in the burning furnace—"

"You say that so matter-of-factly," Zoë yawned, covering her mouth with one hand and stretching with the other. "I think I would have been more upset, had it been me. You know... about almost being *burned to death*!"

"No point in fretting about it now," Rachel shrugged. "While they were preparing the furnace, the demon Morax said something that I've been thinking about. He said of Moloch: *When first I spied it, I did not recognize his prison. Now that I know where he is, it will be a simple matter to rouse him during Saturnalia.*"

She shivered unexpectedly, even remembering Morax was disturbing.

"What about it?" asked Nastasia.

"It is just that I recall seeing Morax standing on Stony Tor, staring at where the Heer had been imprisoned, right before Vladimir Von Dread appeared and distracted him. I wondered if Moloch, too, might be imprisoned in the tor?"

"Surely, no one would imprison something so a dangerous being so near to children!" exclaimed Nastasia.

"They imprisoned the Heer here," said Joy.

"Hear, hear," drawled Zoë.

"I don't think 'they' imprisoned him at all—Moloch, I mean," murmured Rachel, who did not add that she was rather sure it must have been the Raven or some supernatural being who locked up the dread demon. She shivered again. *Moloch must be kept asleep, at any cost.*

Nastasia frowned thoughtfully. "We have no evidence that Morax was speaking of Stony Tor. He could have visited any number of places on Earth."

"True." Rachel faltered. "But when the Elf spoke of Moloch waking, she turned and looked off into the distance. I couldn't tell exactly where she was looking, as we were inside, but I think she was facing toward of the tor."

Sigfried leaned forward. "The Elf thought Mr. Big and Bad was sleeping in the tor?"

"She looked in that direction. Maybe she was looking at the tor. Or maybe she was glancing off toward Ireland, for all I know... it was the kind of look one gets when one is thinking of a place beyond where you can see—which, at that particular moment, was the inside of the Roanoke Tree. Maybe it had nothing to do with the tor at all, but...."

"I've looked at the tor with my amulet for any buried gold the Heer of Dunderberg might have had," said Sigfried, "but I can't see more than about a hundred yards into the dirt. If the demon is down deeper than that, I wouldn't be able to see him."

"But we know for certain, then, that within the top hundred yards, there is no buried demon, right?" asked Nastasia.

Siggy nodded. "Unless he's disguised as dirt."

Zoë sank down in her seat with her knees resting on the chair back in front of her. "How could the Terrible Five know about Mol-face?"

"Azrael was a demon, too," replied Rachel.

"Oh. Right."

Rachel continued, "Gaius and I have been talking about the spell Egg cast...."

"You mean the spell used on my friend Misty's family?" Zoë spat, from where she slouched on the red velvet chair, knees above her head. "That spell? What did that do again? Brought us all from other worlds? And by us, I mean Seth, Misty, and me—not you natives."

Rachel nodded. "Gaius and I wondered: who was the first person this spell ever brought to our world—back in the eighteen nineties, when Azrael killed my Grandfather's family? Was it one of the Terrible Five? Were they, or some of them at least, from Outside? Or could it have been Moloch? Could Azrael have been here looking for him? Could that be why Moloch is here to begin with? Because the Raven caught him and put him to sleep when Azrael's spell brought him here, the same way he caught the Terrible Five and turned them to stone—which, come to think of it, could be why they were statues when Aaron Morley found them."

"This is all conjecture on your part," said Nastasia.

"True," Rachel sighed, struggling to put her conviction into words. "I just had a feeling that Azrael—might have been looking for the demon. But Joy has a good point. We should find out more about the Heart of Dreams, too. Does anyone even know what it is?"

No one did.

• • •

As they filed out of the dimly-lit auditorium, Wulfgang Starkadder stepped from the shadows beside the doorway.

"Princess Nastasia, I would speak with you."

The princess nodded and gestured for the others to continue without her. Rachel peered closely, but she saw no sign of blushing or nervousness on her friend's tranquil face. Once the rest of them reached the foyer, Zoë announced that she was exhausted and headed upstairs to take a nap, along with Joy, who had not slept much of late out of concern first for the princess and then for Zoë. That left Rachel alone with Sigfried and Lucky.

Rachel grabbed Siggy's arm. "Quick, what are Nastasia and Wulfgang saying?"

"What, them?" Siggy yawned. "Why, is it important?"

"Yes!"

"Okay. Okay. Look at your card. I'll make it show what I am seeing through my amulet," said Siggy, adding, "I'll stop at the surfaces of objects, so as not to freak you out. Unless you want to see Wulfgang's liver and the princess's spleen."

Rachel pulled out her calling card and peered into it. The green color of the glass cleared, revealing the dim auditorium. Nastasia and Wulfgang stood in an aisle near where Rachel had left them, speaking softly to one another. Nastasia looked like a vision of loveliness. Her golden curls seemed to float above her black poplin robes. Wulfgang was out of uniform and instead wore black leather pants and a black shirt with traditional Transylvanian embroidery on the collar and front piece: blue, black, and white. With his thick hair hanging low over his dark, brooding eyes, he looked unexpectedly distinguished and handsome.

Wulfgang spoke graciously rather than in his customary laconic manner. "—in keeping with our parents' desires, we might endeavor to know each other better, do you not agree?"

He attempted what Rachel suspected was supposed to be a congenial smile, though he looked as if he had had little practice.

"I see no particular need for us to fraternize," the princess replied solemnly. "If we are wed, there will be time enough to come to know each other. Should it be decided that our union will not forward our families' purposes, forming any kind of bond of affection ahead of time will merely prove inconvenient."

"But—" Wulfgang spoke courteously, although his voice was slightly gruff. "Would it not make sense for us to find out whether we are suited? While we still have plenty of time?"

"I do not see how our being suited is pertinent. If our families determine that a match is in the best interest of both our countries, we will do our duty and comply."

"But—" Wulfgang's face started to fall into his perennial scowl. He rearranged it into a look of polite inquiry. "Would it not make sense for us to become friends?"

"I have quite enough friends at the moment, Mr. Starkadder. Or, should I perhaps call you, 'Your Highness,' considering the subject of our conversation. More friends than I can safely protect. Circumstances constrain me from adding more friends to my personal circle at this time, as I would not be at liberty to speak openly to any newcomers."

"O-kay." Wulfgang blinked, stymied. "Um—" He pushed his hair out of his eyes. "How about—acquaintances? Might we at least become acquaintances and occasionally speak to each other. Unless that would be too—er—taxing for you?"

"Acquaintances would be acceptable."

Nastasia inclined her head and gracefully exited the auditorium. The last thing Rachel saw, before quickly stuffing her calling card in her pocket, was Wulfgang, who had smiled politely until the door shut behind the princess, throwing his arms up toward the ceiling and exclaiming in a language that Rachel could not speak. From his expression, she suspected his words meant something like: *By the gods, what was up with her?*

• • •

The princess came gliding out of the auditorium and across the black and white marble. Rachel ran to meet her.

"What happened?" she cried. "What did he have to say?"

Nastasia shrugged. "He wanted to talk about our families' plan to have us marry."

"And are you friends now?" Rachel asked, feigning ignorance.

A look of sorrow and bewilderment appeared on the princess's face. Immediately, it vanished behind her well-bred smile. Yet, while it lasted, it was so heart-wrenching that Rachel would have hugged her had she not known that the princess was not comfortable with familiarity. Instead, Rachel lunged forward and grabbed her friend's hands. Nastasia squeezed Rachel's fingers in return. Her face was calm, but her eyes were still filled with sadness.

In a small voice, the princess said, "Rachel, I am not skilled at dissembling. I know how to parley politely with mere acquaintances; how to conceal state secrets from strangers. But once someone is my friend, I have no talent for recalling what I am supposed to say to whom and what I am not. I cannot at this time be friends with one with whom I cannot discuss the secrets we know. There is too much at stake. The danger is too grave."

"Oh," Rachel whispered, feeling very sorry for Nastasia. "Yes. I see how that could be a problem."

Nastasia lowered her head and squeezed Rachel's fingers again. Rachel squeezed back. The two girls stood together like this for just a moment. Then, raising her head and adjusting her smile back to its customary regal calm, Nastasia took her leave of Rachel and Sigfried and glided across the foyer to speak with her siblings.

Rachel watched her go. Alexander Romanov and his twin sister Alexis stood near the hearth with the salamander. Alex threw pennies through the grate to the fiery lizard and then watched them melt. Alexis, who lived in Dee Hall, was examining the Dare foyer with interest.

Nearby stood their eldest brother Ivan, laughing with a group of admiring girls. Among these, Rachel recognized Mr. Fisher's daughter Marta, two of the Hirvela sisters with their long, Scandinavian blond hair, and Lena Ilium. Rachel's hands curled into fists. It made her angry enough to see Ivan cavorting about with young women other than Laurel, but to see him charming her brother's heartthrob, Lena Ilium, filled Rachel with righteous hatred.

She *hated* Ivan Romanov.

• • •

"I hate him!" screamed Rachel.

By herself in her room, she jumped up and down on the princess's Persian rug, bursting with fury. *How dare he steal the affections of the girl Peter adored! How dare he mock Laurel!* Shouting in frustration, she stomped across the room and kicked one of the wardrobes.

Pain exploded through her leg.

"Yoowwwww!"

Rachel sat down on her bed, holding her throbbing foot and whimpering. The surge of wrath ebbed, leaving her feeling shaken and ill. A noise in the hall startled her.

"Please, don't be Nastasia! Please don't be Nastasia," she prayed, not feeling up to looking upon Ivan's sister.

Then she felt even worse. The whole point of wanting Ivan to marry Laurel had been to draw Rachel's family closer to Nastasia's, not to drive a wedge between them. She hung her head, feeling miserable.

A noise caused her to glance up. Two felines stared back at her. Mistletoe sat on the windowsill, his black and white form almost a silhouette against the cherry light of the setting sun. Leander lay curled upon Kitten's bed, gazing at her with his huge golden eyes. Looking at them, a feeling of peace touched her heart. Rising, Rachel petted and kissed the head of both the cat and the tiny lion, momentarily burying her nose in the latter's sweet smelling-mane.

Feeling lighter of heart, she pulled off her robes and donned a favorite blue and white dress for the fancy dinner, adding a matching bow in an attempt to contain her flyaway hair. With a last word of goodbye to the familiars, she ran down the stairs to join her friends for Thanksgiving dinner.

• • •

Outside, Rachel nearly tripped over the wolf familiar that had taken to sleeping on the porch of Dare Hall now that the weather had grown cold. Some familiars were flourishing in the change of weather. Others were thoroughly miserable. Rachel hoped they would all get something special to eat for Thanksgiving.

Nearby, her friends walked down the snow-covered path through the woods that led to Roanoke Hall. The sun was setting, painting the sky in vibrant reds and deep purples.

As they walked toward the dining hall, Rachel asked, "What did the Lion say to you, Sigfried? When you talked to each other after he saved Zoë."

"I asked to be his knight," he replied. "But he talked about his father. I think he meant I should be his father's knight? Not exactly sure. Lions are sneaky. They only talk in parables."

"The Lion has a father?" murmured Rachel in surprise.

"Wake up, Griffin," Zoë said snidely. "Everyone has a father."

"Not me," muttered Siggy. Then, his eyes lit up. "You'll never guess what else the Comfort Lion said!"

"They'll never guess," said Lucky.

"They might!"

"They won't."

"Won't guess what?" asked Joy. "The sky is up? Roses are red? You read in bed?"

"Nothing stupid!" Siggy scowled, kicking a large piece of gravel down the path. Joy, whose face always grew a little pink when she talked to Sigfried, looked crushed.

"Any other guesses? No?" He looked from face to face.

The girls shook their heads.

"I'm a robot!"

"What?" Rachel exclaimed.

Joy laughed as if he had said something funny.

"No. For real," said Sigfried. "The Lion told me that I was a robot."

Lucky added, "It explains a lot."

"Like why I heal so quickly and why I am so much stronger than most boys my age."

"And so impossibly handsome?" sighed Joy.

"That, too, most likely," Sigfried replied, not missing a beat.

"He said... what?" Rachel exclaimed again. "The Lion said the words, '*Sigfried, you are a robot*'?"

"Not those particular words in that particular order, no. But he said it."

"What words *did* he use?" pressed Rachel.

"He said that his father made me."

"He *made* you?" gawked Joy. "You mean you're an automaton?"

"Or maybe you were conjured," the princess stated. "Similar to Mrs. March."

Sigfried dismissed this idea, as if brushing off a fly. "He did not say 'conjured.' He said, 'made.' That means I am an exquisitely crafted, finely-made machine." He flexed his arm to form a muscle and pointed at it with his finger, wiggling his eyebrows for emphasis.

"You're such a ham," Zoë snorted. "Really, Siggy. You can be relied on to say something totally incoherent."

Siggy frowned slightly. "What I'm saying is coherent. You just can't understand the workings of my finely-crafted robot brain."

"Did he mention the name of this father?" asked the princess.

"Yes," Sigfried said with some importance. "He's called the Emperor of All Things Seen and Unseen."

"An emperor?" The princess nodded serenely. "Interesting. That makes the Lion at least a prince. Perhaps, he is of rank to advise a Princess of Magical Australia after all."

Rachel whispered the name several times. "That's a nice name. Kind of eerie. Is that like Seelie and Unseelie?"

"Don't know."

"Did he say anything else?" asked Rachel. "The Lion, I mean."

"Nothing important." Sigfried scowled. "He breathed on me, and I saw a vision."

"I didn't see a vision!" Lucky said, astonished. "I thought we shared everything!"

"Sorry, bro. I'll imagine it, and you can see it. Though you might wish you hadn't." Siggy leaned toward his dragon and confided. "It was all about how girls have emotions and stuff, and, from time to time, this causes them to malfunction. They must be treated gently. There are ripples, ripples I say! Ripples, I tell you! They flicker outward from our every insignificant act and hurt the feelings of girls."

"The Comfort Lion showed you a vision about ripples?" Lucky asked curiously, as he undulated through the air beside his boy.

"Ripples, and girls," Siggy said sagely. "He showed me a vision about how my actions inadvertently caused girls to cry. There were no boys in that vision. I assume from this that boys are immune from the ripple effect. We don't need to care about them."

"Them, ripples? Or them, boys?" Zoë asked, as they walked over the icy bridge and into the dining hall. She ran her hand over her dark hair. Nothing happened.

Zoë stopped walking. She tried again and then again, running her hands over both her head and her braid, her expression growing more alarmed.

Her hair stayed dark auburn.

"I didn't just lose my mother's feather," Her voice sounded unnaturally wooden. "My gift. My ability to change my hair color? It's gone, too."

· · ·

Dinner was held around long tables and served family style with platters passed up and down. Before the feast, one of the Scholars, a dark-skinned tutor dressed in black and yellow, gave the opening benediction and poured the wine for Hestia. Prayers and sacrifices of honey cakes and fresh herbs were also offered to Demeter and several of the other earth goddesses. Next, baskets were passed up and down the tables. Students threw in offerings of money, jewelry, talismans from charm bracelets. These would be given to the Order of Hestia in New York City to be sold, the proceeds to be distributed to the poor.

Then came the food: plates of carved turkey; steaming bowls of wild rice; freshly baked bread with newly-churned butter; candied sweet potatoes; green bean casseroles; jellied cranberry sauce; buttery squash; roasted venison; warm corn pudding made in Lenni Lenape style; and hot pumpkin pie. Cups overflowed with mulled cider, hot wassail, cold sparkling pear juice, and eggnog. A heavenly aroma filled the chamber, and the feasters commented to one another that even nectar and ambrosia could not smell more delectable.

The gods of luck must have been smiling upon Rachel, for by some quirk of good fortune, she arrived at exactly the right moment to sit at the long table with Sigfried and her friends and the entire O'Keefe family to her left and Gaius and a few of his friends to her right. A more fortuitous position could not even be imagined.

If only it could be like this every day.

Maybe, together, the two groups of friends could solve the many mysteries: sleeping demons, forgotten persecutors, missing talismans, unfulfilled prophecies. As she sat sandwiched between her blood-brother and her boyfriend—the two young men at Roanoke who were dearest to her—listening to the laughter of friends, including one who had been lost and was now found—Rachel Griffin acknowledged that she had much for which to be thankful.

Chapter Eighteen:

The Case of the

Burnt Homework

The rest of the long weekend passed without event. Rachel and her friends spent much of their time studying. To Rachel's delight, she was able to spend a whole lazy Saturday afternoon in the library with Gaius, reading and talking quietly about physics.

Rachel discovered that she could follow conversations between Gaius and William about physics—up to the point where the talk turned to math. Without trigonometry and calculus, she was quickly left behind. Gaius gallantly offered to teach her these more advanced mathematics. They chose Wednesday nights, while everyone else was at the YSL meeting, as the time to devote to this study. Rachel could not have been more delighted. Finally, she had a regular appointment she could look forward to when she could spend time alone with her boyfriend.

Life was finally as it should be.

Classes resumed Monday, and things went back to normal. Word soon spread across campus of the fight between the Heer and the Agents that Rachel and Sigfried had glimpsed. Apparently, the Agents had caught several lightning imps but had failed to capture their leader. The storm goblin had taken enough damage, however, that he had withdrawn, leaving Storm King Mountain and retreating to his other stronghold in Dunderberg, some twenty miles away.

Rachel began spending her extra time, when the tutor was reviewing lessons she already heard, drawing Yule cards for friends. Her drawings were still wobbly, but she was making progress. She sat in Science, or Language, or True History, with her eyes resting on the tutor, while she read from memory the drawing book she had borrowed from Mrs. Heelis. She would learn about perspective or shading and then tried out what she had just learned on the paper.

In Language, they were studying Shakespeare's *A Midsummer Night's Dream*. On Fridays, for the Original Language portion of their class, they learned a few new words: *ah* – one/being/person, *nothor* – to swerve away, *lu* – go or move, *luathe* – foot. Since in October they had learned *athe* – place, Rachel could now confirm for herself what Gaius had told her during the first week of school —that her favorite cantrip, *ti-athe-lu*, meant: *up-place-go*.

In the interest of protecting themselves from the depredations of the Heer, they also learned *ahura*, a cantrip meant to calm men, beasts, and storms. However, it proved too advanced. Even the Top Four, as the class had started calling the quartet of Nastasia, Sigfried, Joy, and Wulfgang, could not achieve much of an effect. Mr. Tuck noted that experienced canticlers often struggled with this one.

In Art, they had moved from conjuring hoops to rectangles, triangles, or even pentagons. In Music, they were still on dispelling fog, though some of the more advanced students, such as the princess and Joy, were learning how to dispel rain showers. In Math, they had reached *Book Two* of Euclid and were also reviewing the many uses of running water as a ward. Nearly any sort of undead or spirit creature was unable to cross running water. Some could not cross it at all. Others could cross bridges. Still others could only cross specially-constructed bridges, consecrated with blood. Wilis, vampires, and specters fell into this last category.

In True History, they were still studying Frazer's *The Golden Bough*. Rachel found the study of primitive spells and taboos fascinating. She had not realized that accomplished thaumaturges could stick a pin in a person's shadow and curse them, or that the fur of a black cat could be used to make one invisible. In Science, they had begun making their own rudimentary shadowcloaks—the garments the Wise wore to hide themselves when traveling amidst the Unwary. To Rachel's delight, "hair from a black cat" was one of the main ingredients.

Partway through the week, however, Mr. Fisher had them put their unfinished cloaks aside in favor of making lightning-bane talismans, such as the key that Sigfried had given her. This way, Mr. Fisher assured them, if the Heer were to return to Roanoke and get through the wards to attack the school, they would all be protected from the lightning imps.

Rachel's hard work was finally paying off. The spells and cantrips she had singled out and practiced diligently were improving. In addition to practicing in her private hallway, she went down to the gym and asked for a ball thrower, the kind used to practice baseball or tennis. She used this to practice the *turlu* cantrip, concentrating on the principles of physics William and Gaius had taught her. If she set up two devices, she could knock the inertia from one ball into another, so that the first ball stopped in mid-air and plopped to the floor, while the second crashed into the padded walls at a considerably faster speed.

The three-dimensional quality of her perfect memory that helped her so much when she was flying made it easy for her to track the trajectories of the balls. This exercise was a lot like playing billiards, a game she rather liked—partially because she used to play it with her grandfather and partially because the locals in Gryphon-on-Dart were so amused by watching her hustle visitors. In the past, however, her success at hustling had depended mainly on the fact that she was significantly better at billiards than a stranger expected a tiny girl to be. Now, as she figured out the forces involved with *turlu*, she felt that, if she played again, she might actually become very good indeed.

All the while, the Lion's promise that someday she would *know all* quietly reverberated through her thoughts. Rachel wondered what he had meant by that and whether *all* would include the name of the Raven, the location of Moloch, and how to restore Blackie's memory.

As the week continued, she found herself dreading the beginning and ending of Science class. The source of annoyance came from Ameka Okeke, the go-getter girl from Raleigh Hall, who excelled at every sport the school offered: soccer, track and broom, crew, flying polo, basketball, gymnastics, bow and arrow, swimming, fencing, and zapball. From her Orkoiyot (a supreme chieftain of the Nandi people of Kenya) father and Chinese mother, Ameka had inherited a bone-structure and dark bronze skin color that was both unique and lovely. This, combined with her athletic prowess, had made her a huge hit among the jocks and sports fans on campus. Rachel found this classmate as charming as everyone else and looked forward to her witty repartees with their tutor.

However, the usually stylish young woman had recently begun boasting loudly about her interactions with Dash Darling down on the sports field. Only the way she pronounced his nickname, it sounded like "*Dash, darling,*" as if she and he were sweethearts, which was clearly what she had in mind. At first, this did not trouble Rachel. Seeing John Darling laid out on the ground back in October, after having been doused in flaming skunk spray, had gone a long way to mollifying any anger she felt toward him. Tuesday morning, however, all this changed.

Rachel had put her hair in pigtails that morning. She loved the way the short braids stuck out, wiggling when she shook her head, and Gaius had chuckled at how sweet she looked. When she went back into the lunch line, to get a slice of the apple pie that the cooking brownies had just brought up, piping hot, from the kitchen, Claus Andrews, the class clown of the college freshmen, grabbed her braids from behind and made *clck-clck* noises, as if he were encouraging a horse. Rachel thought he was funny—until she saw John Darling smirking.

All her wrath and indignation returned. It horrified her that she had wasted three years crushing after this detestable young man. He had seemed so gentlemanly at her family's Yule parties. It must have been an act he put on to impress the adults.

At first, Rachel had assumed that Ameka and "Dash" Darling were dating, but going back to the dorm that night, she had heard him make a crude comment to Claus and Conan MacDannan on the subject of the physical desirability of Merry Vespers, the sweet girl with the reindeer Rachel had glimpsed surrounded by animals, and what his plans were for "nailing" her. Rachel gritted her teeth. Merry was too good for him—Ameka, too, for that matter.

After hearing Darling's bawdy talk about a different girl, Ameka's confident comments about her "Dash, darling" made Rachel's skin crawl. She felt so bad for her classmate, caught in the grip of an identical crush to the one that had enslaved her.

It did not help that, everywhere she went—Dare Hall, the dining room, hallways, the gym—Rachel ran into Ivan Romanov. He was always smiling, always surrounded by young women, always looking so cocky and suave. Each time she saw him, her stomach clenched. She averted her eyes and hurried by, unwilling to so much as look at the blackguard. Between Darling and Romanov, Rachel found herself out of sorts with smug young men. She was grateful that lunch allowed her a chance to sit with young men of another sort.

• • •

At least her job at the gym was going well. The students were learning quickly, and several graduated to the intermediate class. Hildy Winters even approached Rachel about private lessons, as she wanted to participate in the broom-based sports. She and Rachel worked out a plan to meet on Tuesdays and Saturdays.

After assisting Mr. Chanson on the Wednesday following Thanksgiving, Rachel remembered to ask him about the flying course in the gym, hoping that he might shed some light on who had designed it. The gym tutor had never seen that particular configuration of the gymnasium before. He agreed that the course must have been intended for steeplechasers, but he did not know of anyone else at Roanoke who rode one. When Rachel mentioned that Agent Darling had told her that he had once known a girl who rode a steeplechaser, Mr. Chanson suggested that the Agent might have been referring to someone who was a student before the Terrible Years. As Mr. Chanson had not been at Roanoke during that period, he could not help her decipher this mystery.

Rachel longed to ask him other questions, like: Why had the King of Magical Australia called him by the last name St. Michael? And why had the princess seen him in a vision on another world dressed in armor and wearing a golden helmet? But she dared not. What if her words brought his memories back, and something terrible happened, the way it had when Sakura Suzuki remembered her past? So Rachel bit her tongue and kept her many questions to herself.

• • •

At dinner that night, Rachel's favorite proctor, Mr. Fuentes, was on duty. She went by to commiserate with the handsome young man over the losing streak of their favorite flying polo team, the Lake Michigan Falcons. As they spoke, Mr. Fuentes's boss, the head of security at Roanoke Academy, came by, accompanied by his familiar, a great brown bear with silver paws.

"Mr. Badger!" Rachel curtsied.

Maverick Badger, a short man with broad shoulders and a shaggy head of steely-gray hair, paused and scowled when he heard his name called. His expression softened slightly when he saw her. "Well, if it isn't Pint-Sized Griffin. What can I do for you today?" An idea struck her. "You've been here a long time, haven't you, sir?"

Mr. Badger shrugged. "Compared to some."

"Would you happen to have been here when they built the gym?"

The older man snorted with amusement. "I should say not! The gym had been working for almost two centuries before my student days. Course, it was updated in the Forties."

"But you know how it works?" Rachel pressed. When he nodded, she asked, "Can it—I don't know—See? Read minds?"

"Nope. Just follows verbal commands."

"But then... how did it know that I had a steeplechaser?"

"It didn't. It couldn't."

"But it gave me a steeplechaser course."

"What did you ask for?"

"I said: 'I want a place to practice flying.'"

He shrugged. "The last person who asked for a flying course must have given specific instructions. So the spell reproduced the previous request. The same way it always produces the same pool or basketball court, unless someone gives specific instructions to the contrary. If Mr. Chanson wanted an indoor area for Track and Broom, he'd have asked for the grand track, not for 'a flying course.'"

"So someone else at Roanoke has a steeplechaser?" asked Rachel, curiously.

"Not in years," replied Mr. Badger, looking unusually grim.

• • •

Rachel returned to her seat. Behind her, Mr. Badger and Mr. Fuentes were still speaking. On the spur of the moment, she turned to Sigfried and asked him to let her eavesdrop on the proctors' conversation. Siggy yawned and rolled his eyes, but he must have agreed, because an image of the head of security and the proctor appeared on her calling card.

Mr. Badger was saying, "—you here, Carlos? The time the Freverchild raced the storm goblin through Roanoke Hall, trying to save her sister?" He whistled in admiration. "Man, could that girl fly!"

"Um. No, sir," responded Mr. Fuentes. "I don't think I even know what a freverchile is."

"Oh, right. You would hardly have been born yet." A strange look crossed Mr. Badger's face. Rachel could not quite identify it, but if she had been hard pressed, she would have guessed sadness. "Better not to talk about those times." He stuck his hands in his pockets. "But I tell you true," his face broke into a craggy smile, "There's no one who can outfly a little girl on a steeplechaser!"

Rachel turned to Sigfried. "I wonder who—or what—that was? The freverchile? Foreverchile? Freverchild? I couldn't quite make out the word they were saying."

"Have you heard even a similar word before?" asked Siggy.

Rachel thought back and then shook her head. "No. Never."

Across the dining hall, a motion caught Rachel's attention. Near the back door, the young woman in the threadbare coat was approaching Mr. Burke, the gardener.

"Hey!" Rachel grabbed Sigfried's shoulder and pointed, "What are they saying?"

"They... who?" Siggy asked, leaning his chair back on two legs.

"That's Mr. Burke, the gardener—he took us to gather herbs the time we met the Elf?"

"Sorry, don't remember." Sigfried shrugged, "Who's the girl?"

"I don't know. Some upperclassman from Marlowe—but she's the one that Zoë tried to kill back when she was possessed."

Siggy's chair hit the floor with a *bang*. "Zoë tried to *kill* somebody?"

"The demon possessing her did. That's why I paralyzed her."

"Sweet!"

Rachel blinked.

" — that you paralyzed her in time," Siggy said innocently.

"Here. Okay, look."

Rachel's card cleared again to show the face of the gardener, a young man with curly brown hair, and the long black ringlets of the back of the girl in the threadbare coat.

"—so much extra work," The young woman was saying, "I know you could use some help. Would it be possible?"

Ulysses Burke shook his head sadly, "I'm sorry, Miss Druess. I know you would do a fine job, but our student positions can only be offered to students in need of financial aid."

"That's what the assistant dean's office told me, but it's not true! I've talked to a number of people who have jobs on campus due to their abilities, rather than financial need—such as nearly every tutor's assistant. I'm good with plants! You know I am. Not as good as Evirene Ev or Iolanthe Towers, but nearly."

Mr. Burke sighed and wiped his glasses. Putting them on again, he said, "The circumstance is not the same."

"But... I..." the young woman began, clearly in distress.

"You know the situation, I am confident, Miss Druess. Your parents have made enormous donations to Roanoke," Mr. Burke said sadly, "and they have specified as a stipulation for their generosity that we are not to offer you a position here... that you must go to them, if you need anything."

"But... I can't do that!" she cried. "I... cannot!"

"I am sorry. Your knowledge of plants is excellent, but there's nothing I can do." Mr. Burke gave her a regretful smile. "My hands are tied."

The young woman gave a tiny nod and walked away quickly, heading for the back door. Siggy's vantage point switched to in front of her. Tears streamed down her cheeks as she left Roanoke Hall.

Rachel felt a stab of sympathy for the young woman. "What do you make of that?"

Siggy attacked his food angrily with his fork. "I think she's despicable. Anyone lucky enough to have a family should be grateful for them!"

Rachel glanced at the door through which Miss Druess had departed and sighed.

• • •

The next morning, Rachel came out of Dare Hall to find Siggy and her girlfriends gathered on the wide slate stoop at the top of the stairs outside Dare Hall. Zoë Forest stood on the top stair, laughing and running her hands over her hair, half of which was hot pink and half of which was forest green.

Zoë cried out loudly, "Thank you, Nastasia! I will never forget this!"

The princess shook her head. "I would have been glad to help repair your power, were I capable of such a thing, but I regret it is not within my abilities. I did nothing."

Confusion clouded Zoë's face. Then, her eyes widened and she nodded, "Ohhh. Riiight. Okay."

She winked at Siggy and Joy. Siggy nodded knowingly.

"Very cunning! Of course, the princess cannot admit the true depth of her *awesome yet dread-inspiring powers in public!*" Siggy gave the princess a wink.

Then he winked several more times.

Nastasia peered at Sigfried, first puzzled and then with some concern. "Mr. Smith, are you well? Did you get something in your eye?"

Leaning toward Rachel, Sigfried whispered, "I never expected the princess to be so subtle. She just went up a notch in my estimation."

"What happened?" asked Rachel. "What is all this about?"

"Princess Nastasia fixed my hair power," announced Zoë.

Joy cried out, "The princess saved Zoë! She can do anything!"

"How did this happen?" Rachel looked from Zoë to Nastasia and back.

Zoë grinned, "While I was napping, I had a dream that the princess came and played her violin. After that, she said my powers would work again. She also said something about how light refracts and how the 'depth' of a material, off of which the light is reflecting, can change how it appears. When I woke up, my power was back! Now it works even better."

"Better?" asked Rachel.

"How so?" asked Nastasia.

"Look!" Zoë cried. "Now I can do this!"

She ran her hand over her hair. It turned to burnished gold, as if each strand were made of the precious metal.

"Gold!" Siggy gurgled. He rubbed his blond curls as if trying to transform them.

"Luscious gold," Lucky murmured, dreamily.

"How I love its weight and luster!" Sigfried spoke in the same dreamy tone. The boy and his dragon inclined their heads together and gazed longingly at Zoë's hair.

"I am not responsible. I did not do anything," Nastasia sent Rachel an anguished look, begging for help to make this clear to the other girls.

"I don't think Nastasia did it," murmured Rachel.

But Zoë continued to babble on, praising her princess savior.

• • •

The gods of favorable seating, who had smiled on Rachel at Thanksgiving dinner, were not so kind to her during the week that followed. As each new class dawned, she found herself trapped in a dilemma. If she timed her arrival perfectly, she could arrange matters so as to position herself between the princess and Astrid and thus sit next to both girls. But if she arrived too late, they were already sitting separately, and she was forced to choose.

Principle required that Rachel sit with Nastasia, by virtue of the princess's higher rung on the loyalty ladder. To her shame, however, Rachel was more influenced by the fact that, if not picked, Astrid did not chide her and make her feel bad. This was partially because Astrid was so shy but also because she was so good-natured. If left alone, she never seemed dismayed; yet she always seemed so pleased when Rachel did sit beside her. The two of them would talk earnestly about homework and Astrid's concerns about doing well in class—when not giggling about the manly charms of Rachel's boss, the handsome P.E. teacher, upon whom Astrid had a crush.

Nastasia, on the other hand, seemed quite distressed if Rachel sat elsewhere. She pouted and frowned, even if Rachel's absence was because she "accidentally" arrived too late to find a free seat beside her friend. So every time it came down to a choice, Rachel picked Nastasia, and then had to sit and endure the sycophantic idol-worshiping of Joy and Zoë, who—since regaining her hair-changing talent—had taken up Joy's habit of doting on the princess. Rachel kept up a cheerful demeanor, but she could not help feeling a little sad.

Zoë had originally been her friend.

By Thursday morning, Rachel decided to start arriving at class very early, though this sometimes proved difficult, as it meant she had to shake Nastasia and the others in order to arrive before them. But she managed to reach the classroom for Math before anyone else got there. She chose a seat, put her books prominently atop the table, and ran off for a quick dash to the loo.

When she returned, Nastasia and her entourage were all seated at one end of the table. Astrid sat by herself at another. Zenobia Jones—the dark-skinned Drake Hall girl from Chicago who always referred to Rachel as "training broom," or, worse, "training bra"—was seated in the chair Rachel had originally picked, chatting with the plump and ostentatious Charybdis Nutt and with ringleader Belladonna Marley—the granddaughter of Aaron Marley, associate of the Terrible Five, and descendant of Ebenezer Scrooge's ghostly partner—who as always, had drowned her eyes in eyeliner. Rachel's books were nowhere to be seen.

Looking around, she saw Napoleon Powers, the grandson of the Grand Inquisitor who had been killed at the start of the Terrible Years, and the ever-sneering Arcturus Steele tossing her copy of Euclid back and forth across the table. Her notebook was sticking out of the trash, and, upon closer inspection, she realized that Zenobia, Belladonna, and Charybdis were doodling in her math manual. When they saw her, they began whispering feverishly. Rachel could not hear them, but she made out the word "Eunice."

Rachel did not let on that she had heard, but, underneath, she seethed. Colleen and Tess seemed to have forgotten the incident with the juice in the kitchen, but Eunice still scowled at her or, worse, tried to trip her, at every opportunity. Apparently, Eunice was now engaging little helpers to do her dirty work.

Rachel snatched her manual away from the mocking girls and retrieved her notebook from the trashcan, amidst snickering — some from her fellow Dare students, who did not realize how the book came to be there. The boys, however, just tossed her Euclid higher.

"Sigfried," Rachel walked over to her blood brother, where he was recounting the story of his fight against the dragon in the London Underground to Seth Peregrine, who was apparently laboring to turn the event into a song. She pointed at Napoleon and Arcturus. "That flying copy of Euclid? That's my book."

A happy grin spread slowly over the handsome boy's face. He rolled up his sleeves. By the time Mrs. MacDannan arrived, Powers had a black eye, and Steele's nose bled steadily. As the tutor took her seat, Lucky burped loudly, having just swallowed the ashes of what had once been Steele's homework.

Chapter Nineteen:
Stealth Boyfriends

"Nice work back there," Seth slapped Siggy on the back as they left class, heading down the marble staircase. "I credit my leet teaching skills."

"The upper cut worked great, but I think I need more work on my left cross," Sigfried replied, still grinning the huge grin he had kept up all through math class. He swung his fist once or twice, demonstrating one of the moves he just named. Rachel had no idea which one.

"You were so brave!" squealed Joy.

"You know they're going to try to get back at you," drawled Zoë. Siggy snorted with infinite disdain. "I fight dragons. And demons. They can take a number and stand in line. But I don't mind beating them up again, if they want to come at me," he added. "I can use the practice."

He paused and tried another two or three punches at some imaginary opponent, still bobbing and weaving his head.

Seth stepped beside him and demonstrated a stance and punch. "Try it more like this."

Joy paused to gawk at the two boys and their display of prime masculine flesh in action. Zoë stayed with her, leaning casually against the wall and smirking, more at Joy's expense than because of the boys. The princess gave the two young men a royal nod of approval and glided onward, in keeping with the opinion she had voiced on previous occasions that fisticuffs was a fine activity for young men but not one that ladies cared to watch.

When Rachel fell in beside her, Nastasia sighed. "I wish Zoë and Joy would not make such a fuss over me. It is most undignified."

Rachel nodded, "I guess Zoë's grateful."

"But I did nothing!" The princess's voice wobbled slightly. "All I did was *lose* her!"

Rachel nodded sympathetically, and the two girls exchanged looks of kindred dismay.

• • •

They reached the lunch room. Rachel was waiting for an opportunity to discreetly peel away from Nastasia, so she could sit with Gaius, when her older sister Laurel grabbed her wrist.

"*Dongsaeng*," — Laurel peered down at her through long, straight hair — "did you actually talk to Ivan Romanov about him marrying me?"

Laurel was tall and sprouting ever taller. Over the last few years, she had developed long, long legs that drove the local farm boys at home wild when she strolled casually down the dusty lanes in skirts that were way too short. While not as absurdly curvaceous as their tiny mother, Rachel's middle sister turned heads wherever she went. Rachel had once seen an experienced aristocratic horseman, three times their age, so stunned by her sister's prodigious bust line and coltish charms that he rode smack into a branch and knocked himself senseless.

Unlike Rachel and Peter, Laurel preferred the subfusc style uniform. Her dark, knee-length skirt stuck out from beneath her old parka that was now too short for her. Around her neck, she had wound a bright red scarf.

"He said he was going to, but now it's just a joke," Rachel replied, downcast. "Though he also told me that his mother said that marrying you would be marrying beneath him. Why he would ask his mother, if he was just joking, I don't know."

She did not know what was worse, having been tricked by Ivan Romanov or having Laurel discover that her little sister had been duped.

"Sweetie, he was probably being nice. Could you come with me? I should have done this a while ago."

Laurel took Rachel's hand. The two of them walked out of the dining hall and across campus to Dee Hall, a great granite edifice with four domed towers and statues of famous sorcerers and philosophers gazing down from pedestals set around the roof. On the high steps, before the imposing great oak door of the hall, Laurel asked a student who was heading inside to please grab Charlie. The student nodded and went into the dorm.

Laurel and Rachel waited. The day was balmy. Puffy white clouds sailed through a brilliant blue sky. Rachel and her sister stood on the landing, looking out over the snowman-dotted campus. Watching students skating on the lily pond, Rachel wondered what happened to the sea fairies who lived in the pond during the winter. Did they hibernate, like fish?

A tall, brown-haired young man emerged. He wore glasses and had a bookish look to him. Yet, he was quite physically fit. From the shape of his features and his expression, Rachel guessed that when he spoke he would sound British. He had a look that reminded her of several distant cousins.

"Hello, Laurel," he exclaimed in a crisp upper-class English accent.

He leaned over and kissed Rachel's sister on her mouth. Laurel looked a little flushed. Rachel blinked at the tall young man in puzzlement. *Who was he? Why was he kissing her sister?*

"You're Rachel, correct?" the young man asked cheerfully. "It's a pleasure to finally be introduced. I am assuming I am finally being introduced, that is...."

He glanced at Laurel who smiled and nodded. He straightened.

"The Lady Rachel Griffin, I am Charles Fairweather." He spoke with great formality. "I believe you have heard of my family. We've produced a long line of Agents, and my grandfather fought under yours, before Granddad retired to our country seat. Also, my mother is an Abney-Hastings, as is your grandmother. It is a pleasure."

He offered his hand. Rachel stared at it suspiciously.

Laurel rolled her eyes. "Charlie, could you turn off the pompous? It gets old rather fast."

"This is our first meeting," he objected. "It should be proper, should it not?"

A loud *whomp* came from behind Laurel. Laurel's eyes became very wide, and she squeaked. Then her face turned bright red. She was still smiling, but her "Laurel is about to do something bad" look had begun creeping over her face.

Rachel took in the ramifications of the cheerful, smiling beanpole, the kiss, and the swat on her sister's behind. Her cheeks began to turn redder and redder, until she was the same color as her sister's scarf.

Laurel had a *boyfriend*.

The other two smiled down at Rachel. A terrible shyness stole over her. Suddenly, she could not bear to be the center of their attention. Ducking around Laurel, she hid her head behind her sister's shoulder. The other two watched her antics without comment.

As she head there, questions ran through her head. How long had Laurel been dating? Why hadn't she told anyone? Had they just started seeing each other? Rachel could not bear it any longer.

"*Unni!*" The words burst out of her. "Why didn't you mention you had a *boyfriend!* Why didn't you say 'No,' when Ivan spoke to you in September? Oh! The princess would have been my sister!"

"I thought he was teasing," Laurel shrugged. "I thought he knew about Charlie."

"What's this about Ivan?" Charlie looked from one to the other.

"Nothing," Laurel gave him a sweet smile.

A group of athletes returning from the gym came clomping up the stairs. With a gracious gesture, Charlie opened the door for them. They passed by, stamping on the doormat to shake the wet snow from their boots. As Charlie let the door close after them, Rachel pulled herself together and bravely came out from behind her sister. Walking up to the tall young man, she extended her hand.

"Please excuse me, Mr. Fairweather. I was taken by surprise. How do you do?"

He accepted, and the two solemnly shook hands.

Looking the young man directly in the eye, she demanded coolly, "What are your intentions toward my sister, and what are your prospects?"

She had hoped to embarrass Laurel by flustering her beau, but Charlie was not the least bit flustered.

"I have been dating your sister for some time," he replied cheerfully, "and my intention is to marry her, should I receive the permission of her father and mine. If not, I fully intend to kidnap her, roll her up in a flying carpet, and elope. I apologize to you in advance, if that should come to pass."

Rachel narrowed her eyes and stared at him, trying to take his measure. He seemed enthusiastic, a bit goofy, and sincere. She did not sense any dissembling or devious intent.

Leaning forward, she whispered to Lauren, "Do you like him, *unni*? Should I offer to help with the kidnapping?"

Laurel blinked. "Yeah, he's okay. I really don't think he'll need help kidnapping me...."

"Oh... he's just 'ooo-kaaay'." Rachel drew out the word as long as she could. She turned back to Charlie, tossing her head imperiously. "You'll have to elicit a stronger endorsement from my sister than '*okay*' before I help you. Besides," she sighed with dramatic sadness, "I had so hoped both my sisters would be queens. You wouldn't happen to be a prince of anything, would you? Some hidden kingdom of which you could make Laurel the queen?"

He sighed in return. "Sadly, no. My family is rather well off, though, and I promise I shall treat her like a princess."

"I suppose that will have to do." Rachel gave a curt nod of approval. "Do keep me in mind, should the need to kidnap arise. You will find me surprisingly resourceful."

"I certainly shall," Charlie promised solemnly.

Rachel concluded with a wicked twinkle in her eye, "After all, there's no better bonding for future brothers and sisters-in-law than committing some outrageous crime together."

He looked around and then whispered, "Of what kind of crime are we speaking? A heist perhaps? I've heard good things about them. Terribly exciting and all that."

"I had meant the crime of kidnapping my sister," — Rachel glanced sidelong at Laurel and then leaned toward Charlie in a conspiratorial manner—"but if you are up for some other crime, I'm in! So is Sigfried!"

He interlaced his fingers and stretched, as if limbering them up. "Being a rebel who plays by his own rules means I am *always* up for some type of terribly illicit deed."

Laurel rolled her eyes. "No, he is not! For some reason, he got it in his mind that I want him to be a ne'er-do-well. Or a rotter. But

I like him because he's nice! If I wanted a cad, I'd go date Almeida or some other idiot. Also, Charlie's terribly smart. I think smart is sexy."

Rachel shivered and blinked rapidly. She could not imagine any member of the Griffin family dating a bully like Seymour Almeida. But then the latter part of Laurel's comment dawned on her, and her head nodded up and down very rapidly.

"Oh, I do, too!" cried Rachel. "Smart is the best!"

The funny thing was, if Rachel had been asked to pick what kind of man her sister Laurel would most likely date, she would have chosen someone like the very kind of ne'er-do-well that Charlie Fairweather was pretending to be. It amazed her that Laurel would pick someone so bookish and goofy. It made her think much better of her sister.

Eager to establish a rapport with this young man who might someday be her brother-in-law, Rachel turned and gave Charlie an evaluating glance. "Smart... eh? Would you be up for joining the Library of All Worlds project?"

"What now? The Library of All Worlds?" he asked curiously.

"Sounds terribly fascinating. Where's it located?" Glancing surreptitiously at Laurel out of the corner of his eye, he puffed out his chest. "Cause, you know, I wanna smoke in its parking lot."

Laurel pursed her lips and tried to look annoyed. At this, she utterly failed. Giggles escaped from her like bubbles from champagne. She rested her head on his shoulder and looked extremely pleased. He put his arm around her and looked very pleased as well.

Rachel smiled at them both. "It isn't located anywhere yet. I haven't started it. But it's been prophesied, so I'm looking for good people. As to where? I don't know? Bavaria maybe? The Lesser Realm of Dreams? We'll find a good spot."

"Von Dread's kingdom? A bit barbaric, is it not?" Charlie's eyebrows shot up. "As for the lesser realm of dreams, aren't books notorious for being unreadable in dreams?"

"I haven't worked out the details yet," Rachel said, "but it sounds like a really wonderful idea. A library bigger than any other library."

"I'm in!" declared Charlie.

Rachel looked from Charlie to Laurel and back to Charlie.

"Excuse me a moment," she said to him.

She walked around until she stood on her tiptoes by Laurel's ear, her hand beside her mouth, as if she wished to speak privately to her sister, but she did not bother to whisper.

"Umm, *unni*... hallo? What is it about our family and *Stealth Boyfriends*? Is the Stealth Boyfriend a family tradition? If so, why didn't you and Sandra tell me? I could have kept Gaius a secret, so as to be part of the club. Does Peter have a Stealth Girlfriend? And do you all know about each other's Stealth Significant Others? Am I only I kept out of the loop? Or do you keep them secret from each other, too? Does Sandra know about your Stealth Boyfriend? Do you know about her Stealth Boyfriend?"

"Sandra has a boyfriend?" Laurel practically shouted. "*Who is it?*"

"Didn't... she have a boyfriend last year?" Rachel asked, puzzled.

"Sandra? The Vestal Virgin? No way! I mean, she had lots of friends who were boys, but I didn't think she was dating any of them. I thought she was waiting for Daddy to say it was okay for her to date or something. You know how protective Dad can be. *Who is it?* Oh my gosh it's not William Locke, is it?"

Rachel felt extremely puzzled — though inside, she gleefully crowed at how secretive her oldest sister was: *No wonder the Wise-craft picked Sandra for spy work.* Aloud, she asked, "But... how come Seymour Almeida knows who Sandra's dating, and you don't?"

Laurel glared at her. "*Dongsaeng*, tell me now! Is it Locke? Locke's richer than Midas. I think he'd be a suitable brother-in-law."

"Can't be Locke," Rachel replied. "He's dating Naomi Coil."

"Finally got over Cousin Blackie, did she?" smirked Laurel.

Rachel's jaw dropped. She stared at her sister, bug-eyed for a full half of a minute before blurting out, "Naomi Coil is the girl Blackie wanted to marry?"

"I don't think he wanted to marry her," Laurel scoffed. "They were just dating."

"He did so want to marry her! He showed me the ring—at a Yule party, before he lost his memory."

"Really? No wonder she was bummed," said Laurel. She wagged her finger at Rachel. "But you are changing the subject. Who is

"Sandra dating?"

The gods would descend from Mount Olympus and roll up the sky before Rachel would betray Sandra. She crossed her arms and said nothing.

Stepping back to where she could see Charlie again, Rachel asked, "So, what do you do—beside smoke in library parking lots. Was that smoke as in a pipe? Or smokes as in you know a spell that makes a person smolder?"

Laurel stamped her foot. "Gah! My thirteen-year-old sister is holding out on me!"

She pouted.

Charlie replied, "When I am not spending time with your lovely and fascinating sister, I like to read a good book, or study the stars. Astronomy is fascinating."

"What are you planning to do when you graduate?" asked Rachel.

"I'm thinking of going to divinatory school."

"What kind of career did you have in mind?"

"Temple work, most likely. I'm leaning toward Athena or Apollo or maybe Orunmila."

"I don't think I've ever heard of Orunmila."

"He is the god of divination of the Orisha."

Rachel rifled through several encyclopedias in her mental library before she came upon Orisha. "Orisha — emissary gods. Orunmila is worshipped in Nigeria?"

Charlie added, "And in Prester John's Kingdom."

"Do you think you might have trouble finding a flock back in England?" asked Rachel.

"Perhaps. Or perhaps I'll engage in a grand adventure and take your sister to Africa! Fancy living in Prester John's Kingdom, my love? They say the streets are paved with precious gems, and legendary animals meander through the parks."

Laurel rolled her eyes. "I hardly think that Prester John's people are going to want a skinny Englishman for their spiritual councilor."

"Maybe not," replied Charlie, his cheerfulness unperturbed. "What I would really like is a pastorship. I think I would prefer being a local pastor to working a big city temple. Might even take up the abandoned living on my parents' estate; a lovely little cottage down by the river. Locals could use a bit of divinatory insight."

"That would make you a real embryo parson," giggled Laurel.

"Right-o!" Charlie grinned broadly. Leaning his head toward his girlfriend's, he whispered to Rachel, "Just like a character in one of our favorite books."

Rachel, who had read the same book, asked innocently, batting her eyelashes. "Isn't that story about the poor relations of the Transylvanian royal family?"

Charles blinked and then chuckled. "Oh! Yes. I see what you are doing there. Very droll. Except the name of the family that owns Cold Comfort Farm is pronounced Stark-adder. While the royal Transylvanians are Star-kadders, as they take their name from the Kadder Star. The priceless heirloom of eldritch power which that prig Romulus is always waving about."

"Speaking of books," Rachel asked suddenly. "Are you related to Lloyd Lord Fairweather, the great Thriomancer who wrote numerous books on the sorcery of horse breeding and other fascinating topics? I've always admired his work, though my boyfriend says he's a bit confusing to the Unwary-born."

"I am!" Charlie replied. "My father is his nephew. Marvelous chap. I met him when I was very young, and he was in his dotage." Smiling, he concluded, "So it is a parsonage for me. Unless I decide to join the Wisecraft, as every other able-bodied male member of my family has, stretching back to the nth generation."

Laurel smiled, looking very proud of her multi-talented boyfriend. "He's very brave."

"You know me," Charlie ducked his head at Laurel's praise. "*Never show fear*, and all that. Oh. And, of course, I play rugby and flying polo for the Spartans."

"He's actually very good," Laurel said. "He's the Captain of the Spartans. And he's on the student council, like Sandra was. He's the boys' delegate for Dee Hall."

"I heard, through a source surprisingly close to me," said Charlie, "that you are not going out for Track and Broom, even though you're such a good flyer that they call you the Broom Goddess. I have to say it's a smart move—even though I am sure your team is disappointed. Takes time to adjust to school and all. Lots of things to study."

"Broom Goddess," Laurel snorted. "Who started that anyway?"

Charlie chuckled, "Rather a mouthful of a nickname for one so young."

Rachel cocked her head. "Are you two busy? Come with me." She led them to the gym, where she stopped at the broom closet and picked up a red Flycycle. She chose it because, from her work cleaning and polishing and testing them, she knew this one was in the best shape. Then, she walked up to a door and asked for the high-ceilinged pool.

As she climbed on the bristleless, she turned back to Laurel and Charlie, "Siggy said I must warn people not to be frightened. So, don't be afraid."

Rachel flew up to near the top of the hundred and twenty foot chamber. Once there, she dived off the broom, stretched out her hand, and called out, "Varenga, broom!"

She plummeted.

The broom raced to her hand. She grabbed it and swung herself over the seat, zooming up again. The maneuver had proved both easier and harder with the borrowed broom. The longer handle made it easier to grasp, but the Flycycle took a lot longer to engage after she mounted it than the steeplechaser did. (The first time she tried it on the borrowed broom, she had feared, for a long moment, that it was going to continue to fall.)

Below, she could see Laurel and her boyfriend gawking. They looked obviously impressed.

Rachel landed and raised her arms like a gymnast, "Ta-da!"

"Rachel!" Laurel ran over to her and grabbed her shoulders, shaking them. "Dongsaeng! Gah, I was so scared! You can't tell me not to be scared. It doesn't work like that!"

Charlie said, "That is very impressive. I see the Broom Goddess moniker is well deserved. How long have you been practicing that move?"

"It came to me last week. I had to figure out how to make sure that if I fell off, I wouldn't get into trouble, and I'm sure to fall, since what I'm really trying is this."

She put the broom down and stepped onto it, so that she was standing on the broom as it wobbled back and forth, trying to balance with her arms outstretched like a wire-walker's.

"Maybe you should get a pole," Charlie suggested, "like in a circus, to help with your balance."

Rachel started to ask Laurel if she wanted to join the circus, but then sadly remembered that Laurel no longer needed to impress the King of Magical Australia.

"Well, be careful," Laurel ordered. "Don't break your neck. You need it for stuff."

Charlie was gazing down at her Flycycle. "Have you tried supporting the broom from two ropes? So it is not completely stationary? More like being in the air. For practicing, I mean."

"Good idea!" Rachel cried. "Thanks."

"No wonder there's so much talk about you going out for the team," stated Charles.

Rachel, who had not known there was such talk, blinked. "I have a lot going on, what with having to save the world and all, so I thought I'd wait a few years. Also, I don't want to play while Gaius is here. I don't want to have to choose between practicing and spending time with my boyfriend."

"Don't make lame excuses," said Laurel. "It's okay you don't want to play."

"It's not a lame excuse," Rachel objected hotly. "I spend hours and hours practicing spells. Then, I have saving-the-world experiments, then there's broom practice, and homework, and learning to draw. And now there's physics! As it is, it's hard to find time to see Gaius, outside the Knights. Can you imagine if I had Track and Broom practice, too?"

Laurel said, "You do too much. Cut half of it. I suggest True History be the first to go."

"Now, now, that's not a good idea," objected Charlie. "History is very important. Yes, it's a little dry, but those who forget the past and all that...."

Laurel blinked up at him with feigned innocence. "Those who forget the past? Was that the end of that sentence?"

Charlie rolled his eyes. "You realize I know you're not an airhead, right?"

Laurel retorted, "You can prove nothing!"

"You pretend to be shallow, and she pretends to be dim?" giggled Rachel.

"Listen, Little Miss Snippy—" said Laurel.

"I'm not snippy," Rachel replied, surprised at the claim. "Just... enthusiastic."

"You're snippy," Laurel insisted. "And rebellious. That's supposed to be my job! You and Sandra are the goody-goodies, Peter's the dork, and I am the wild child. No muscling in on my territory! You can be Dork Number Two, if you want."

"I'm not rebellious," Rachel protested, truly shocked. "I'm completely and utterly devoted. I never so much as waver. How can that be called rebellion?"

"You're dating Gaius Valiant. Daddy told you not to. That's not rebelling?"

"No he didn't," Rachel said slowly. "You told me that Daddy wanted to see me. I ran away. Then Peter told me that I should not date Gaius. Daddy's... Daddy's never told me anything! He never wrote to me about it. He never said a word on the topic. Neither Father nor Mummy has ever uttered a single word to me about Gaius."

Laurel said, "That's odd, since they both mentioned to me that you *shouldn't be dating*. You're too young. Stop being evasive. You know Daddy doesn't want us dating. Which is why I didn't tell him about Charlie and probably why Sandra didn't tell him about William."

"They haven't told me, no matter what they said to you," replied Rachel firmly, deliberately ignoring Laurel's comment about William. "Which is good... because I don't think I could survive without Gaius. He's sane. All calm and cheerful. He makes all these crazy horrible things seem... bearable. Besides, why would they object to Sandra dating? She's twenty."

Laurel scowled, "Well, whatever. Sandra will do what Sandra does, and Mummy and Daddy will gush and say she's perfect. Yay." Charlie stared at the pool, as if the bluish waters were suddenly extremely interesting.

Rachel thought about Sandra, Sandra's boyfriend, and the campaign to convince Ambrose Griffin that his daughter's beloved was not a 'young tyrant in the making.' She wondered if life might not be much harder for Sandra than Laurel realized.

"Why shouldn't I be dating?" Rachel asked. "What's wrong with it? Sandra told Gaius he could date me, so long as we didn't do anything we wouldn't do if she was in the room."

Laurel shouted, "*SANDRA IS NOT YOUR MOTHER!*"

Charlie jumped. Laurel stamped her foot, turned, and stomped out of the gym. Rachel stared after her, shocked and hurt.

Charlie leaned down. "I'm sorry, Rachel. She's been very agitated for the past week or so. I really think she's been worried about, well, you. She was truly scared when she heard you had been kidnapped, even though it was after the fact. She's not been dealing with the stress very effectively. I hope you will forgive her for her outburst. I'll go speak to her."

Rachel nodded numbly. Then, she shook herself and smiled. "I understand... probably better than you might believe. I've been through a lot lately, too. I didn't... I didn't know she was upset. She doesn't talk to me a whole lot."

"I'll see what I can do to help you two patch things up," said Charlie. "I think you being safe helps her a great deal."

With an apologetic smile, he hurried off in the direction that Laurel had stomped. Rachel watched him go, but what she was thinking was: *Why hadn't her parents said a word to her about Gaius?*

Chapter Twenty:

Forgotten Gifts at Yuletide

The remaining time before school let out for Yule Break was a blur of activity. Rachel and her friends worked hard to finish their assignments in time for their upcoming vacation. Occasionally, Rachel had free time, while others were struggling to memorize material for upcoming tests, but there was no one with whom she could spend it.

Even Siggy actually studied, chewing a pencil as he pored over his books.

Rachel spent the extra time filling her grandmother's wand. She now had quite a collection of paralyzing hexes, wind blasts, *ti-athelu*, and her new favorite, since her visit to O.I., *turlu.* Having a collection of spells instantly available dramatically improved her performance during the second half of the Knights of Walpurgis meetings. Gaius even told her she had the makings of a good duelist.

High praise indeed from the best duelist in the school!

The week before the Yule holiday was Don Rag week, during which, in the tradition of great schools such as Oxford and Cambridge, every student was required to appear before a panel of their tutors and sit uncomfortably while their teachers discussed them in the third person, as if the person was not present. Rachel's first Don Rag went very well. Her tutors were delighted with her progress. The only sour note was when Miss Cyrene, her Music tutor, expressed a desire to see how her flute playing would progress over the next few months. Since Rachel never practiced her flute outside of class, she feared Miss Cyrene was ultimately going to be disappointed.

Then, before she knew it, with a flurry of snow and goodbyes, she and Peter and Laurel (who spoke to her only grudgingly) and their familiars were heading home to Gryphon Park, their family's estate in Devon, England. Rachel was grateful to return to the enormous, sprawling manor house, every stone of which was like an old friend.

Once home, however, the week leading up to Yule was even more heavily scheduled. There were shopping trips to London, visits to friends and family, holiday cards to be sent, and skating parties on the lake. Even a day trip to their village of Gryphon-on-Dart was a whirl of shops and boutiques and calling on old friends, with highlights that included a reunion with her favorite librarian and a visit to the Gryphon's Nest Pub—where she beat all the locals at billiards and lost horribly to them all at darts.

The busy trip to Gryphon-on-Dart, however, seemed lazy compared to those that followed, days filled with preparing for Yule, decorating with pines and holly the manor house and the stone statue of a giant carrying a child, which stood at the base of the Old Castle just beneath Rachel's bedroom window. Next followed the festivities of Saturnalia—though this year, Rachel begged off with a fake headache. She could not bear the thought of praising the Titan of Time, whom she now knew to be the horrible demon Moloch, who had compelled so many parents to sacrifice their children.

It was rather lonely to be missing the games and merriment, especially when she could hear the sounds of celebration from the windows of her room. Yet she would rather be lonely than praise a fiend. She had tried twice to convince her family not to hold the Saturnalia festivities, but her father had insisted that the tenant farmers and villagers looked forward to it all year. He did not wish to disappoint them.

Rachel did not think he quite believed her when she explained that Saturn was the same entity to whom she had almost been sacrificed.

After that, an entire day was spent wrapping presents and addressing cards. Rachel posted the Yule cards she had drawn, along with hand-picked presents for her closest friends. For those she knew less well, such as Astrid, Kitten, Sakura, Wendy, and Hildy, she included perfume, soap, or candles from the Gryphon Park Lavender Farm, the only farm that was overseen directly by the family, rather than by tenant farmers. While at the farm's lavender shop, she also picked up a handful of bottles of the Bogey Away spray she had described at Ouroboros Industries, sending one each to Gaius and William along with her gifts for them.

For Astrid, who always wore something around her neck, Rachel searched high and low for a new scarf, but nothing seemed quite right. She finally found what she wanted at a Korean store in London. The shop was full of brightly-colored silk *hanbok* and dark wood furniture, lacquered tables and folding screens, inset with mother-of-pearl flowers and butterflies. The back room, however, included K-pop posters and the latest fashions from Korea—including a cute purple scarf, bristling with more tassels than a hedgehog had quills, that she chose for her roommate.

She realized that she did not know where Sigfried was spending the holiday. She had asked him several times, but in typical Siggy fashion, he had somehow never given her an answer. She sent his present to Valerie, figuring that if he was not with his girlfriend, she was the person most likely to know where he had gone.

During her one free afternoon, Rachel took Vroomie for a flight over the moors. On her way back, she flew up to Gryphon Tor, which rose high over her family's estate, just north of the lake behind the enormous manor house. From the top, she could see the rolling hills of Dartmoor National Park stretching out around her. Gryphon-on-Dart lay beneath her. Smoke curled above the chimneys of the town.

Floating above the ruins of the Saxon castle atop the tor, she stared out to the west, where she knew Gaius's farm to be. It seemed unfair that her boyfriend was so close, and, yet she could not visit him. Her parents insisted their schedule was too full, and Gaius reported that his days were crammed to overflowing with chores his father needed him to do around the farm. Rachel was grateful to Vladimir, however, for her black bracelet, as it allowed her and Gaius to speak to each other regularly.

She also found a few minutes to steal away to her grandfather's library, the round, tower-top room that was her favorite place in the house—and also the mansion's highest chamber. It was a sorcerer's library, cared for by an elusive book bogel, so that the books occasionally rearranged themselves. Sometimes, Rachel came upon volumes she had never seen before on shelves she had examined a thousand times.

She read an old volume about ogres and looked up the subject in several bestiaries. She also searched for mentions of the Heart of Dreams but found none. Eventually, she curled up in one of the huge leather chairs with a new novel and divided her time between reading and daydreaming—mainly about the dream she had dreamt in September in which she leapt from some high place to save her friends and called the Raven, who dived down and possessed her, so that instead of falling to her doom, black wings sprouted from her shoulders and she flew—and wondering what the Comfort Lion had meant by: *A time will come in the end when you shall know all.*

Her one real disappointment was that her father was too busy to sit down with her for any length of time. Several times, she asked him if he could please make time to speak with her. Each time, he assured her that he would try but explained that certain matters at work were taking all his concentration. He begged her to be patient with him.

She longed to tell him what had actually happened at Beaumont, the time she had saved the world—and him—from the demon Azrael. On the holy days, however, Saturnalia, Yule Eve, Yule, etc., his time was occupied with duties required of his rank and there was no time to speak privately. The rest of her stay, he was so busy she hardly saw him. He and Sandra left for Scotland Yard, where their offices were, before she rose in the morning and came back only after she had retired for the night.

Yule Eve brought their yearly journey into the forest behind Gryphon Park Manor to find next year's Yule Log. This was followed by smearing butter on the outer lintels for the returning sun to melt —so the sun would have the sustenance it needed to burn more brightly again—and the moonlit Yule Buck procession, as Rachel and the other children from Gryphon-on-Dart paraded from house to house carrying the last wheat stalk of the harvest. They sang songs that honored the returning sun and the god Thor; while the houses they visited rewarded them with candied fruit and mulled cider.

Upon coming home, the duke and duchess threw three burning coals into a barrel of water, and nobles and servants alike washed hands and feet there. Then, they all donned new garments, never before worn—ensuring that neither troll nor trow would trouble them during the year to follow. And, of course, they played snapdragon and, as always, Rachel singed her fingers trying to steal raisins from the blue flames of the burning brandy. She recalled Gaius scoffing that no one ever burnt their fingers at snapdragon and smiled sadly.

Then deep into the night came Candle Dark, when every light in the mansion must be extinguished. This period of darkness was one of Rachel's favorite times all year. After the hour of Candle Dark, the winter lamps were lit and placed in windows, where they would keep burning until the spring equinox. Candle Dark was the one hour all year when the Vestal Virgins extinguished their fires.

Rachel and her siblings woke up early on Yule Day amidst mistletoe and piles of presents. Nibbling her slice of Yule cake— all spongy and creamy—she watched with happiness as her family and their servants opened the gifts she had chosen for them and exclaimed with delight over gifts they had picked for her. Her favorite came from Peter, a pretty aquamarine on a silver chain, an amulet of protection against the paralysis hex! Laurel received a beautiful red parka with white trim. She gleefully deposited her old navy one in the arms of their butler, Tennyson, instructing him to give it to the needy.

As the butler left the green drawing room, where the family exchanged their gifts, Rachel ran after him.

"Tennyson, that coat. Might I have it?"

"It is far too big for you, Lady Rachel."

"Oh, not for me. It's just... I know someone who has need of a coat."

"Ah. In that case." Tennyson bestowed the navy parka upon Rachel, who ran upstairs and put it with her things to go back to school.

After the gifts came the boar sacrifice to Lord Freyr. Rachel held her ears during the actual sacrifice; she hated to hear the beast squealing. The sacrifice was followed by feasting and the burning of this year's Yule Log.

During the afternoon, The Duke of Devon and his family set out on their yearly pilgrimage to the tenant farms and the village, giving out gifts and coins to all. Rachel loved this procession, throwing Yule feed to the pigs and ducks of her family's tenants and eating the freshly-baked cookies and pies that the farmwives had prepared just for them. That night, the duke lit the great Yule bonfire upon Gryphon Tor, illuminating the entire sky above the town. Down in the village square, dancing and singing and free-pouring spirits were provided for one and all, by the grace of the duke and his family.

Yule was followed in quick succession by the Twelve Days of Yuletide, including Boxing Day, Winter Cleaning Day, Dartmoor Fey Day, New Year's Day, and Twelfth Night, where girls dressed as boys, masters waited on servants, and everything was topsy-turvy. For New Year's this year, the Griffins visited Rachel's mother's family: her Aunt Melissa, Uncle Frederick, and her two younger cousins, Ferdinand and Orlando. Grandpa Kim was there as well. During a break in the festivities, Rachel knelt beside the taciturn old Korean gentleman, as he rocked in his rocking chair, and asked him about his mother.

Grandpa Kim had a wrinkled face and a salt and pepper goatee. He was advanced in years and seldom spoke. This time, however, he chose to answer her question.

Gruffly, he replied, "I was six when she died. We had just moved here from the old homeland. My step-mother, she did not like my father remembering his first wife. But I kept mother's portrait under my bed. You want to come and see?"

Rising and moving slowly, with the help of a black and gold crane-headed cane, Grandpa Kim led her into another room. He took from a closed cabinet a framed portrait of a lovely young Korean woman dressed in a traditional white and lavender *hanbok*, a high-waisted, A-shaped garment. Rachel stared at the portrait. Her great-grandmother had an ethereal beauty so haunting that it caused an odd lump to form in her chest.

"What was her name?" Rachel asked softly.

"Sun Li," said her son.

Sun Li. It was a beautiful name.

"How did she die?" Rachel dragged herself away from the painting and turned to her grandfather. "Was there an accident?"

He shook his head and grunted. "One day. She went to sleep. Never woke up."

"I'm so sorry."

Grandpa Kim squinted down at Rachel. Then he extended his arm, holding the portrait. "Here, Granddaughter, I give you Mother's painting. You care for it."

Awed and honored, Rachel hugged the picture to her chest. "Thank you. I will keep it under my bed, too."

That earned her a gap-toothed smile from the normally-taciturn Grandpa Kim.

. . .

This year, the famous Griffin Family Yule Party was on Twelfth Night. As with Saturnalia, Rachel feigned illness and begged off, partially because she had no desire to come face to face with John Darling, but mainly because it was her only opportunity to slip into her parents' room without fear of discovery. She would miss spending time with her friend Benjamin Bridges, but maybe she could make it up to him over the summer.

In the week leading up to the party, Rachel had sought out some of the silver pieces that her Great-Aunt Nimue had given the family. In one room, she found an antique candle snuffer that looked like a griffin, a Vesta case to hold friction matches—it had been Grandmother's, but the imperious late duchess had once mentioned to Rachel that it had been given to her by her sister-in-law, Nimue—and a small silver muffineer for sprinkling sugar or cinnamon. She also snuck a good look at the griffin-headed chatelaine her mother often wore at her hip, upon which hung some of her mother's favorite alchemical charms: a thimble imbued with protection cantrips; a whistle that summoned the household fey; a tiny key that opened any unwarded locks; an acorn-shaped vinaigrette containing a healing elixir for cuts and scrapes; a watch set with jasper; and a pincushion holding a needle that sewed on its own.

The silver pieces all bore the same series of hallmarks, except that next to last mark in each series differed. None of the encyclopedias Rachel had memorized explained these marks, so she had to search in the house's main library until she found a book specifically on British hallmarks. Apparently, the lion *passant* indicated the piece was sterling silver. The three towers meant it had been made in the nearby town of Exeter.

The next stamp was a date stamp, but date stamps were issued in a strange way. A new letter was assigned each May, but every twenty years the font changed to distinguish one set of letters from another. There was no way to figure out which font corresponded to which dates without a legend, which Rachel did not have. It was this stamp that differed from piece to piece.

The final stamp, the maker's mark, was two letters, JA. According to the book, this would be the initials of the silversmith. Rachel checked two or three dozen other pieces of the household silver, pieces that did not come from Great-Aunt Nimue. A few were from Exeter, but not a single one bore the initials JA.

The next day her friend Taddy, the cook's grandson, came to visit. Rachel was excused from preparing for the party to spend the day in the kitchens with him. The two had a wonderful time together, reminiscing, swapping tales, and sampling Cook's pies. When Cook headed out on a shopping trip, Rachel convinced her to take the two of them to Exeter, where they visited the boutiques, went skating, and saw a pantomime. While there, Rachel stopped at Johannes Ashley's Silversmith Shoppe and asked the clerk about the stamps on their wares. Sure enough, he confirmed that silverwork from this shop was marked with the initials JA. The clerk also showed her a chart on the wall that displayed the date stamps for the last four hundred years.

The night of the Yule Party, she slipped out of bed, where she was pretending to be sick with an all-too-real stomachache, brought on most likely by nerves. She tiptoed down to the floor below, to her parents' bedroom. Her mother's jewelry case sat upon the vanity. It was a black-lacquered Oriental antique inlaid with mother-of-pearl in the shape of roses and butterflies.

Rachel crept over and opened the jewelry box. The top of the case lifted, revealing three little drawers. The first two drawers contained fine pieces of jewelry. Odds and ends filled the bottom drawer: charm bracelets, long dangly earrings, old medals, and commemorative coins. Gently, disturbing as little as possible, she felt her way to the back of the bottom drawer and found what she had been seeking, a silver baby's rattle engraved with an $\mathcal{A}$. Turning it over, she checked the hallmark. Sure enough, three of the four marks were familiar: the sterling mark, the Exeter mark, and the *JA*.

Rachel stared at the rattle. The *JA* confirmed that the piece was most likely a gift from her great-aunt, whom the clerk at Johannes Ashley's claimed as a long time client. However, this alone did not tell Rachel when the piece had been commissioned. Perhaps her great-aunt had bought it over a hundred years ago, for the birth of one of Myrddin's siblings—her father's dead brothers and sisters—three of whose names Rachel did not even know, and it had only been given to Rachel's mother more recently.

Rachel listened, but she could hear no noise in this wing of the house. Closing her eyes, she recalled in perfect photographic detail the chart on the silversmith's wall. She compared the third mark on the silver rattle with the date stamp letters and fonts on the chart. A cold shiver ran up her spine. According to the silversmith's chart, the hallmark on the delicate silver rattle had been stamped two years before Sandra's birth.

Shutting the jewelry box with a snap, Rachel ran upstairs and crawled back into bed; however, even the warmth of her blankets could not stop her shivering. Safe under her pink and white quilt, inside the curtains of her pale rose canopy bed, she called Gaius on the bracelet and told him all that she had found.

. . .

Like all wonderful things, the three weeks of Yule Break came to an end all too quickly. Arriving back at school on Monday, January 8th, Rachel discovered that Sigfried had spent the break at Roanoke, even though the school was closed. For the first week, he had managed to stay in his room, eating his stored food and what Lucky could catch in the forest. Sometime during the second week, however, a proctor had caught sight of him, when Siggy had accidentally crossed a ward near De Vere Hall, and his chameleon elixir failed. Sigfried and Lucky had spent the rest of the holiday as the guests of Maverick Badger and his wife Maggie at their cottage in the Staff Village along Roanoke Creek.

Recalling the vastness of her family's mansion, with its hundreds of empty rooms, Rachel resolved to write to her parents about inviting Sigfried to Gryphon Park for Spring Break.

As Monday continued, Rachel kept her eye out for the upperclassman from Marlowe with the threadbare coat. Catching sight of her long curling locks as the older girl was rushing across the commons on her way to lunch, Rachel ran up to her and presented her with Laurel's old navy blue parka.

"Hallo. Um… I thought you might want this."

It was snowing again. When she saw the coat, the shivering young woman's eyes grew wide with longing. But then she took a step back.

"Did my family send you?"

"Your family? No. I… don't know who they are."

Her expression was wary. "I'm Chalandra Druess of Druess Confectionaries and Druess Cosmetics?" Her voice rose at the end, as if posing the question, "Do you recognize me?"

Rachel had heard of the Druess family holdings. Laurel had received a gift of expensive Druess perfume just this Yule.

Chalandra cupped her chipmunk protectively in one hand. "If my family has put you up to this, I cannot accept. If you don't get paid unless you trick me into taking the coat… I'm sorry."

Very properly, Rachel replied, "I am The Lady Rachel Griffin, daughter of The Duke of Devon. I have never met your family and am certainly not in their pay. My sister outgrew her coat this year. I couldn't help noticing, the time my friend nearly hit you with her war club, that you looked cold. So, I kept it for you." She thrust the navy parka at the shivering girl.

Chalandra looked from the coat to Rachel and back. "You mean, you're giving this to me of your own free will. Out of kindness?"

Rachel nodded.

The young woman's eyes filled with tears. "Th-thank you."

"You're welcome." Rachel smiled back. She held out the coat again.

Chalandra grabbed the warm garment and, shrugging off her old dinner jacket, snuggled into the navy parka. She was shorter and slenderer than Laurel. It fit her well.

With a smile and a wave, Rachel said goodbye and sped back to her dorm.

Chapter Twenty-One:

Unhealed Scars

"Listen," Joy whispered, as she steadied the ladder upon which Rachel stood. "Did you know that Zoë has scars all over her body?"

"What?" Rachel paused on the ladder, tape in hand, trying to fasten a giant poster of Sigfried's head to the wall.

It was Saturday, the 13th of January, a week after they returned from Yule break. The Die Horribly Debate Club had spent the afternoon decorating their clubhouse, Room 321, which currently consisted of a large rectangular table surrounded by chairs. It was on the third floor of the back leg of Roanoke Hall, where many of the school clubs met.

Some of the bigger clubs met elsewhere. The school paper—the *Roanoke Glass*, the Photography Club, and the yearbook had offices on the floor below. Music groups like the Ginger Snaps, the Madrigal Singers, and the Geometric Quartet, met in the basement of Dare Hall. The botany club met in the greenhouse, which was between the Staff Village and the Oriental gardens. The Fencing Club met in the gym, along with the Knights of Walpurgis and the Young Sorcerers' League.

The majority of the rest of the clubs, however, met on this floor. Until this year, Room 321 had been the home of the Saturday Night Probabilities Study Group, which was a fancy name for a poker club that had been started by Blackie's younger brother, Granite Moth. That club had become so big that it had moved to a larger meeting area, vacating 321.

The Roanoke Seers met in Room 319 and the Bird Watching Club met in 323. Across the hall in 324 was the Treasure Hunters' Club, a gathering of alchemy enthusiasts who searched for new and interesting items for use in elixir recipes. They were right next door to 326, which housed the Hudson Highland War Gamers, a club that studied the military uses of sorcery. Farther down the hall was a chess club and the haunts of the Vampire Hunters' Club led by Abraham Van Helsing. In the other direction, Room 318 belonged to the Sacred Days Club, devoted to celebrating the many holidays and sacred festivals throughout the year.

A wonderful aroma wafted down from Room 311, the home of Cooks' Broth. Upon hearing that today was their official move-in day, the president of this cooking club, Joy's eldest sister Temperance, had brought the Die Horribly Debate Club a plate of maple-glazed apple crisp cookies as a housewarming gift.

Only two remained on the plate.

Rachel and her friends had been granted the room a couple of months earlier, but they had not been able to agree on décor. Zoë had recommended plastering the walls with posters of punk bands. The princess had voted for Magical Australia's stunning natural vistas. Valerie, the rock hound, had wanted photographs of smoky quartz and red chalcedony. Sigfried suggested decorating the walls with the heads of their enemies. When the others pointed out that they had no heads to post, Valerie offered to make some from paper mache.

It did not help that matters between Sigfried and the princess were growing worse. Ever since Nastasia had failed to take him along on her trip to bring the Elf home, Sigfried had declared a private vendetta against her. Since she was a girl, he could not solve the problem in his preferred fashion, punching her in the face. So he was forced to express his outrage more subtly. What he did instead was both utterly effective and infinitely worse for Rachel.

Had he acted like Zoë, who needled her target with sarcastic comments, or like the Drake Hall girls, who specialized in petty, mocking snipes, he would have failed to achieve his purpose. The princess graciously ignored all attempts to provoke her, declaring such behavior to be beneath her notice. But such was not Sigfried's style.

Instead, no matter what subject was broached by the Die Horribly Debate Club, Sigfried proposed a response that required ever increasingly dangerous and illegal activities. Since Nastasia had no notion that his responses were directed at her, she took him seriously. So if the subject was how to acquire heads to mount on the walls, Sigfried would suggest leaving campus to raid a zoo of the Wise and bring back the head of a chimera or cockatrice. Then the princess would immediately bristle and remind him in no uncertain terms that they were absolutely not allowed to leave campus, much less to kill a beast belonging to someone else. Or if the discussion turned to what their next activity should be, Siggy would recommend sneaking into the dean's office to steal back Zoë's shoes. To which the princess would reply coolly, despite her growing indignation, that the dean was her friend and stealing was wrong, under all circumstances.

The more outrageous Sigfried's suggestions, the more severe and disapproving the princess's reaction. And the more disturbed Nastasia became, the more over-the-top was Siggy next suggestion. It might have been funny had Rachel not been stuck in the middle.

Watching Sigfried effortlessly infuriate Nastasia, Rachel could not help wondering if this was how his younger self had handled the nuns of the Order of Hestia. She could imagine him, a skinny little orphan boy, bright-eyed and tousle-haired, too small to fight his cruel caretakers directly, cheerfully exasperating them at every turn.

Finally, after hours of debate—during which Zoë fell asleep; Salome claimed to have died from the horrible boredom; Siggy continued to infuriate an increasingly disgruntled Nastasia; both of whom called upon Rachel to mediate; and Xandra Black dropped in to wish them well, claiming that the voices that spoke through her had clued her in to the presence of excellent cookies—it was decided that each of them could have a section of wall and decorate it however they pleased. Salome had simplified things by declaring herself an auxiliary member and, thus, did not need a wall space of her own.

So, now, Maori punk rockers and Canadian hockey players were splattered on one wall, along with a giant image of Red Ryder, the lead singer of the band Bogus (and father of Oonagh and Ian). He sang into a microphone with his back arched, his red hair spiked, and his signature golden safety pins stuck through his ears. On the opposite wall hung posters of the jungles, orchards, and scrublands of Magical Australia.

Sigfried had ceded his space to his girlfriend but had reserved the right to mount an enemy head, should he acquire one. He had already picked out a spot for the ogre's head and that of the Jabberwocky, which, for some reason, he insisted would be one of the first monsters he defeated.

Valerie had eventually decided to decorate her double section with blow-ups of her photographs. Some were of precious stones, some of her hometown of Kennebunkport, Maine, and others had been taken during their ill-fated trek through the dreamland. These included shots of Beaumont Castle in Transylvania and of the dream hippocrene and amphitheater where they had met the dream muses and Mrs. March.

Valerie had offered to blow up the photo of Gaius wrapped in a pink blanket, which she had taken just after he returned from being a sheep (ram!), but Rachel thought that that would not be seemly. She had, however, accepted a copy for herself, which she stashed in the pocket in one of her voluminous sleeves, so she could pull it out and stare at it dreamily any time she pleased.

The last section of wall was split between Rachel and Joy. Rachel had plastered hers with drawings of magical beasts she had cut from a coffee table book of Daring Northwest's larger bestiaries that she had picked up in London over Yule Break. She had deliberately chosen illustrations of the creatures Mr. Tuck had mentioned during his History of Roanoke lecture. She figured that it might prove useful someday, if the other members of the club were also able to recognize a water leaper or tell a spruce troll from a trow.

After much giggling, Joy had plastered her span of wall with posters and news clippings of the most famous boy of the Wise: Sigfried Smith the Dragonslayer. It was these that Rachel had stayed behind to help Joy with, after the others had left for dinner. Joy was running behind because she had spent the afternoon hanging Zoë's posters. After dumping her choices on the table, Zoë had lost interest in the project and had spent the rest of the afternoon goofing off, making sardonic quips, and chatting with Siggy and Salome about music.

Now, as she held the bottom of the ladder upon which Rachel stood, Joy's eyes filled with alarm. "I knew she got yanked off the road and stuff, but I didn't realize she got cut up. She's been wearing long sleeves ever since. Even to bed. I thought it was a style thing… until I accidentally glimpsed her changing. She thought I was asleep. Then, I started paying attention. She's even wearing makeup to cover scars on her face."

Shock jolted Rachel, followed by guilt. "And here I was just looking at Valerie's photos and thinking that we shouldn't be afraid to travel to other worlds, just because one of us had been yanked off the road."

Joy bit her lip. "I was hoping you might know someone who could help cure her."

"Did you ask Xandra Black?" inquired Rachel.

Joy nodded. "Indirectly. She doesn't know how to cure scars."

"My mother can cure cuts, bruises, and broken bones," Rachel said slowly, thinking. She taped the next corner of the poster. "But if Xandra can't do it, Mum probably can't either. Her knowledge is pretty basic. Should we tell a tutor? Insist that Zoë go to the infirmary?"

"I'm pretty sure Zoë doesn't want anyone to know," Joy replied. "I think she's embarrassed—which is why I haven't talked to her. I was asking you because, well, you have better information and contacts. Can you ask one of your many peons? But don't tell them what it's for! And don't tell Zoë! Or anyone!"

"Peons?" Rachel blinked, wondering to whom Joy might possibly be referring.

"You know. Your boyfriend and his scary friends."

It took all Rachel's expert control to keep from bursting into loud peal of laughter. Gaius, William, and Vladimir Von Dread were *her peons?*

"Yes. Yes, I can."

She went back to taping the huge poster. A blown-up photo from a news glass that showed Sigfried standing with his hands on his hips and grinning, like a modern-day Peter Pan. She finished the last two corners and came down the ladder.

Joy looked relieved. She taped another magazine clipping to the wall. This one read: *Orphan Boy Slays Dragon, Makes Good.* "I would have asked our princess, but she doesn't like Dread or his evil minions. You, on the other hand, are dating one."

That made Rachel giggle. Though, to herself, she added: *She's a princess, not our princess! Or not mine, anyway.*

Pleased as she was to have Nastasia as a friend, the idea of having to kowtow to her, to serve her as royalty, was extraordinarily distasteful. Rachel felt suddenly very grateful that she was English, and that Magical Australia was such an insignificant place. Nastasia and her family would never be Rachel's superiors.

Aloud, she said, "Should I ask my evil minion boyfriend? Or should I go directly to the dark lord of villainy himself?" She paused and then grinned. "I'll ask Gaius. He can call upon his resources." Not wanting to reveal the black bracelet, she pulled out her calling card. "Gaius?"

The green glass in her hand cleared to show his face.

"Hi there, Gaius!" she waved. "Do you have a minute? Could you...?" She mouthed to Joy, "Do you want to be there?" When Joy nodded, Rachel addressed the card again. "Joy and I have a question for you. Can you meet us at our clubhouse? It's a delicate matter."

"Sure," Gaius replied. "I'll be there in five minutes."

• • •

Gaius arrived about ten minutes later. Rachel ran to meet him. Just seeing him made the matter less disturbing. She stopped when she was standing very close to him, her eyes shining with happiness, but she felt too shy to kiss him in front of Joy. Gaius smiled down at her, grinning his lazy, amused-at-the-world grin.

He stepped into Room 321 and took one of the two remaining cookies from the plate, trying a bite. He made a noise of pleased surprise and quickly ate the rest of it. Then, he looked around, his eyes resting on the incongruent wall hangings.

"This is...." Gaius pursed his lips.

"Totally schizophrenic?" asked Joy.

"I was going to go more with modern-baroque-stream-of-consciousness?" Gaius offered, gesturing expansively at the varied content. He stopped before the bestiary pages and nodded at Rachel. "Nice choice."

Rachel ducked her head, beaming at her boyfriend's praise.

Joy frowned, "How did you know which stuff was Rachel's?"

Rachel smirked and quoted Laurel's Charlie. "We read the same books."

She and Gaius exchanged secret smiles. A happy blush spread across her cheeks. Suddenly shy, she lowered her eyes demurely. Gaius chuckled in delight.

Recalling the seriousness of the matter, Rachel assumed a more somber demeanor. "Gaius, would you know anything about healing scars?"

"What kind of scars?" asked Gaius, still staring up at the drawings of the horse-like Each-Uisge and the hairy woodwose with its crown and loin-covering of leaves. "Normal? Caused by curses? Magical diseases? If they were incurred in the mist between the waking world and the dreamland, no magic could cure them... but mundane technology might help." Turning, he looked from Rachel to Joy, as if searching for scars. "What's this about?"

Rachel ran to the door. Sticking her head out, she looked both ways and confirmed that no one was listening in the hall. Then, shutting the door, she returned to where Gaius was now leaning against the dark polished wood of the central table.

"First, um... promise not to tell," Rachel began. "She's hiding the scars, so she must not want anyone to know."

"Whoa Nellie!" Gaius raised his hands. "Back up. Who doesn't know... what?"

"Zoë," Rachel clarified. "Joy says Zoë has scars all over her body."

Gaius looked grim. "Do we know what caused them? Considering she was pulled off the path into some dark place between worlds, it may have been something rather... awful. I am guessing, though. It could be something simple like she fell through trees and was cut by their branches. Joy, has she tell you anything about the cause?"

Joy shook her head. "She didn't tell me at all. I woke up while she was changing."

"It was probably something pretty bad," said Rachel. "Dream demons. Something like that... Does Vlad's group have a medic or someone with healing talents?”

“Jenny—but she's only a college student.” Gaius looked concerned. “She's not nearly as talented as the school nurse. She's fine with broken bones and even punctured organs, but healing magical injuries is another matter. That can get tricky.”

“So... what do we do?” Rachel looked to the older boy for guidance.

It was such a relief to be able to turn to someone more experienced. This was one of the perks of having an older boyfriend. She gazed at him enraptured. Joy crossed to stand beside Rachel. She, too, gazed hopefully at the older boy.

Gaius's ears turned a bit red. He muttered under his breath.

“Okay, on-the-spot much?” Aloud, he said seriously, “I want to be able to say, ‘She can take this pill, and she'll be fine.’ But, honestly, she needs to tell us how the scars were acquired. It's been, what, two months since it happened? How healed are they, if at all?”

“I've only seen them clearly the once. She's being really careful,” Joy sat on the table, hugging her arms and looking miserable. “She wasn't like that before she disappeared. Also, she's even lazier than before. Now, she doesn't seem to care about anything.”

“And she hasn't said anything about what happened after she fell?” asked Gaius. “Oh, that's right. You told me she doesn't remember.”

“We need to do something, but... what?” cried Rachel. She cast her thoughts about, trying to think of some option, some avenue they had not yet exhausted. “Our Elf's gone, and we already tried the Comfort Lion, right? He stepped on her and pushed a shadow out of her.”

“Maybe we should ask the Comfort Lion again,” urged Joy. “He could at least make her feel better about the scars, right? He got that smoky thing out of her.”

“We could ask the Lion again.”

“That sounds like a good idea.” Joy nodded eagerly. She lifted herself on her hands, preparing to slide off the table. “Let's go ask Kitten.”

Rachel ran toward the door and froze. In the doorway was a tiny tawny Lion.

Chapter Twenty-Two:

Defying the Wolf Spider

The Comfort Lion padded across Room 321 and rubbed against Rachel's leg.

Immediately, she saw a vision: Zoë lying on the snow behind Roanoke Hall and the giant lion with its paw on her chest. This was followed immediately by a second vision: She was standing on a silver line and, in the distance, was a sphere of colored lights. It reminded her of the object that the Guardian pulled from Sakura Suzuki's chest. It had many different colors running through it, but it was large. Very large—as large as a world. The sphere hung above a boiling pit of darkness. Above the sphere danced something that looked look like the Northern Lights. Beholding them, Rachel was gripped by longing and hope, such as she had never felt. Down below, however, the darkness made her feel lonely and afraid.

A brilliant light flashed above. The darkness below receded from it, until it seemed a great distance away. From the brightness, a ray of pure white light shone down upon the multi-colored sphere. Again, she saw the image of Zoë on the ground, and the Lion swatting at the darkness coming from her.

Then the beam from above dimmed and faded. The darkness below rose back up to where it had been. The darkness below, and everything seemed darker. A ray of darkness climbed up from below and struck the glowing world-sphere.

A third vision impressed itself on Rachel: a man with long pale silver-blue hair stood atop one of the stones at Stonehenge. His face was handsome, but his features were twisted by a scowl of impatience. He was dressed in thorns. His eyes, which were like chips of ice, momentarily turned red. He hopped off the thirteen-foot-tall stone and started walking.

Suddenly, Rachel was back in the clubroom. Gaius and Joy also looked disoriented. Gaius raised a hand to his temple, and Joy clutched the table.

Gaius rubbed his eyes. "I think I just had a vision."

"Oh!" Rachel pressed her fingertips against her lips. "Oh."

"Oh my. Oh no!" cried Joy. "That thorny guy. He didn't appear because of some disaster that Egg created, right? He's new, isn't he?"

The tiny Lion growled menacingly, though not, Rachel felt, at Joy.

Then, turning, it departed.

"What was that thorny guy?" Joy cried excitedly. "Is he like the Guardian? Like the Elf? What does it mean?"

"Beats me," muttered Gaius. "I didn't understand any of it."

"I think I understand what the Lion was trying to tell us," Rachel struggled to put her thoughts into words. "When the Lion acts, the other side is allowed to act, too. He told me, when he saved Zoë, that we are behind enemy lines. I think this has something to do with that."

"Enemy lines?" Gaius asked. "Who is fighting whom?"

"So, Thorny is something horrible?" Joy shuddered.

Rachel nodded. "We have to find a way to help Zoë ourselves."

"Okay," Gaius ran a hand over his chestnut hair. "Plan One, call the Lion, crashed and burned. What's Plan Two? If the nurse or Halls of Healing cannot assist, then Ouroboros Industries is the place to go. They have an advanced lab with magical and technological systems, specifically to diagnose new diseases and hexes and figure out the cures. Is she getting worse?"

"I don't know," Joy shuddered. She turned to Rachel. "Would your dad know someone who might help?"

"He might," Rachel replied slowly. "He's got connections all over the place. He might know someone who would be gentle and competent. Someone Zoë could talk to without anyone else having to know about it."

"Can you ask him?" asked Joy.

Rachel considered this. She was still disappointed that her father had not taken time over Yule Break to hear the important things she wished to tell him. But ever since she had seen the memorial at

O.I. to the man who died at Tunis, her previous anger had begun to fade. Her father had a very dangerous job. He worked so very hard. There were many deadly things in the world. Maybe she should not be angry at him because his job was so important.

In the back of her mind, a tiny voice whispered urgently that involving her father would end badly. She pushed it aside. He was her father. Of course, he would want to help her.

"Very good," said Gaius. "I'll hold off until I hear more. But call me if you want William's help, and I'll arrange it."

Rachel nodded. Sitting at the table, she wrote a letter asking her father if he could recommend an expert on magical ailments. She explained that a friend needed help but would not ask for it and that she would like someone on hand when she and her friends confronted the girl. Then, waving goodbye to Joy, she and Gaius set out for the mailroom to post it.

• • •

Sunday passed quietly. On Monday, she and her friends had a free period in the afternoon. Joy went back to her room to keep an eye on the brooding Zoë. Rachel, Nastasia, and Valerie headed for the practice lab on the second floor of Roanoke Hall, where Sigfried was trying out a recipe for a new elixir. Nastasia and Valerie pulled out their school books and sat down by an unused lab station to study. Rachel tagged along, following Sigfried as he gathered his equipment and supplies.

The practice lab was designed to allow students to perform al-chemical experiments outside of class time, so long as they had a tutor or lab assistant present. Sigfried had befriended their tutor's lab assistant, a Russian college student named Varo Varovitch, by giving the lab assistant a few samples of the plants from the Elf's garden that Sigfried had managed to save. Varo had been impressed. He now opened the practice lab any time Sigfried wished.

Today, he was showing Sigfried how to create the Achilles elixir, which temporarily protected the drinker from a single type of damage. Sigfried was tremendously excited about this—until he learned that he could not just uncork the elixir and shout out the name of the danger from which he wished to be protected. The threat to be resisted had to be chosen at the time the elixir was created. Also, this particular elixir was extremely specific. It could only protect against a single type of creature or spell or weapon.

Attached to the practice lab was an enormous specimen closet that was the size of a classroom and smelled of formaldehyde. Rows of shelves held large glass jars containing specimens of every kind. Siggy pored through it, looking for something dangerous that he could make himself immune to. Finally, after some nudging from Varo, he grudgingly settled upon concocting an elixir that would protect him from the bite of a wolf spider.

"Wolf spider!" Sigfried exclaimed. "How often am I going to have to face off against wolf spiders? Are there even wolf spiders here? Giant wolf spiders? Werewolf spiders? Now those would be worth being immune to!"

"Nyet," stated Varo. "No giant volf spiders."

"What good is this, then?" exclaimed Sigfried. "Why can't I make an elixir to protect me against something important? Like a dragon or the ogre?"

"You bring me hair from ogre," said Varo, "I teach you make ogre-proof Achilles elixir."

"Okay, Lucky, let's...." Siggy began heading for the door.

"Oh no, you don't, big boy!" Valerie jumped from where she had been sitting at a lab station, reading a Shakespeare assignment for Language class, and hooked her arm through Sigfried's. Turning to the lab assistant, she raised her other hand. "Hey, I have a question."

"Yes, Miss Hunt?"

"Why don't the Agents carry Achilles elixirs to protect them from everything?"

"First, this elixir not as effective against sorcery as bey-athe can-trip. Good bey-athe stop all enchantment and cantrips. Achilles elixir stop only one spell. Second, unless they know ahead of time vhat enemy they face, not help—unless they carry huge bandolier of million elixirs."

"Bandolier of elixirs!" exclaimed Sigfried.

He nodded knowingly. Valerie kept her arm locked through Sigfried's and shook her head at Lucky when he tried to sneak out the door. Lucky drooped and slunk back.

"Can't, boss," whispered Lucky. "Goldilocks nixed the plan, and her hair is the same color as treasure!"

"She is the brains of this operation," Siggy whispered back.

"Then," Valerie said, still addressing Varo, "if this elixir is so specific, who uses it?"

With great solemnity, the Russian lab assistant pronounced, "Gardeners."

"Gardeners?" asked Sigfried, bug-eyed.

"*Da*. Who else know ahead of time what bad things they face? Gardeners know. Today, work near poisonous snake. Tomorrow, near bee hive. Next day, poison ivy. Day after that, dig near home of volf spider. Wery useful for gardening."

"Achilles elixir, you have betrayed me!" Sigfried held up an empty crystal vial at arm's length. "And I thought you were going to be this great achievement. I thought you would make me invulnerable, invincible, impenetrable, and every other word starting with im!"

"Immiscible?" inquired Valerie innocently.

"Yeah," nodded Siggy. "That, too."

"You know vat you are, Mr. Smith? Too impatient," said Varo, as they carried several large jars back to the lab. Placing the jars on the lab station, he stroked his forked, black beard. He had a youthful face, despite his beard, and at over seven feet, he towered over the freshmen, even Sigfried. "This elixir is first step. Baby step. You master it. Next step, you make stronger elixir. Keep going, someday, you will be as good as Baba Yaga at protecting from harm."

"The witch?" Siggy asked. "Was she good at making elixirs like this?"

"Baba Yaga!" He pronounced it *Baba YaGAH!*. "She could put charmed life on frog, so that even being run over by Mack truck would cause not one smidgen of harm."

"How was this terrible witch ultimately defeated?" asked Nastasia.

"Oh! Oh! Me, I know! I asked about that," cried Siggy, raising his hand. "They used *Nothung*, the Free Sword—whatever that means. It was said to have been forged in dragon fire! But it's gone now. Ian said it didn't exist any more."

"*Nothung* is the Great Talisman that Mr. Fisher created that they forgot to put out in the light of the full moon one month," Rachel said sadly. "It lost its enchantment."

"That's 'cause I didn't make it," Sigfried pointed his thumb at his chest. "Everyone knows Nothung has to be re-forged by Sigfried!"

Valerie blinked at him, confused.

The princess said kindly, "He is referring to the *Ring Cycle*, Miss Hunt, in which a hero named Sigfried re-forges his father's sword."

"Oh! You mean Wagner! Sigfried. The sword *Nothung*. Right," Valerie smacked herself on the temple. "I should have gotten that. I did some research into the name Sigfried when I was back home in October. Of course, I hadn't pronounced it aloud. Guess I was reading *Nothung* as something else."

Rachel turned to Varo, "But I thought that Ellyllon MacDannan defeated Baba Yaga. She's a conjurer. Did she hit the witch with a sword?"

"Vell," Varo took a deep breath. "Mrs. Darling is a friend to mermaids. I am told that she and her siren companions danced and put all Baba Yaga's servants to sleep. Even the valking hut with its chicken legs. Vhen the old vitch had no one left to help her, Miss Ellyllon stabbed her vith the sword. Baba Yaga did not believe she could be hurt by it, so she just laughed and did not raise her vand to defend herself. But the sword cut through all her magic charms. Though I think it vas Miss Ellyllon's brother Finn who ultimately cut off the vitch's head."

"Why didn't Ellyllon cut off Baba Yaga's head herself?" challenged Valerie.

Varo raised a bushy black eyebrow. "Have you ever tried to cut the head off a vitch? It is hard vork."

"Charmed lives aren't all that impressive," boasted Siggy. "The dragon in the sewers had a charmed life. Where's he now? Dead!"

"You mean the dragon in London? The one you killed to get your fortune?" asked Valerie, surprised. "You never mentioned that."

Siggy shrugged nonchalantly. "He said he did, but Lucky and I attacked him anyway, together. I grabbed a sword from his hoard and went at him. The first blow bounced off, but the second one cut! Some charmed life."

Siggy stomped over to the lab station, grabbed a tricorne mirror, and went to work. Rachel waited to see if he was going to explain that the fight with the dragon had not been ended by a sword, but he did not mention it. She smiled and kept his secret.

"Excuse me, Mr. Varovitch," Rachel asked politely, suddenly curious, "but did Baba Yaga put a charm on the ogre that lives here on the island?"

"Our ogre? One who eats high school students and pleasure-boaters? That I do not know. But I heard, as boy in Russia, that she vunce put charm on famous ogre named Mambres, in return for him vhispering in her ear certain spell he knew. Mambres said to be brother of Ogre of Smeeth."

"The Ogre of Smeeth!" cried Rachel, delighted. "I know about that one! It was slain by Tom Hickathrift, who was said to be a gi-ant…." Her voice trailed off because Varo Varovitch was gazing at her oddly.

"Hmph." He rubbed the back of his neck and his shoulders slumped, as if this might make him shorter. "How could human be also giant?" He spread his hands. "Absurd."

Rachel craned her neck to gaze up at the towering young man. "You don't think he was a giant?"

"Probably part titan," muttered the Russian, under his breath. He returned to Sigfried's side to comment on his progress.

Later, after Sigfried had finished, as they left Roanoke Hall, Rachel whispered to the princess, "You haven't happened to touch him, have you? Mr. Fisher's lab assistant, I mean."

Nastasia whispered back, "Actually, I did once, by accident, while he was helping me to cut ingredients for an elixir."

"Did you have a vision? What did you see?"

"I saw him in the woods, hunting. He had a young woman with him. I think she was his wife. She looked a bit like Wendy Darling, but… it wasn't her. The girl looked daft, moonstruck, but very sweet and cheerful. Varo looked almost exactly the same but even bigger. He was stalking a deer, and when it came running out of the thicket, he threw a spear at it and hit it straight in the mouth, which is quite extraordinary, when you think about it."

"Moonstruck?" Rachel's brows drew together. "Do you think she could have been Wendy MacDannan? She's daft, and they say she looked like her niece when she was young."

The princess shook her head, "I doubt it. First, I have touched all the Darlings and MacDannans on campus, and they are all native, as is their mother, Mrs. Scarlet MacDannan. So it is likely that Wendy MacDannan is a native, too. And secondly, were she not, this vision would have to have taken place before she came to Roanoke—in other words before she was cursed by the Terrible Five—so she would not have been crazy yet."

"Oh. You're right."

• • •

Outside, the air was brisk. As Rachel and her friends walked back toward their dorm, they noticed a group of students gathering on the commons. Drawing closer, they found a crowd was circling around a new freshman girl, who had only just arrived on campus. She had walked all the way from her home forest in the Pacific Northwest.

"No one told her about travel glasses," Salome whispered to them, gleefully, as they walked up beside where she and Joy and Zoë were standing in the snow.

"Such a shame," Nastasia replied softly. "She's missed so much of the school year."

"You would worry about *that*," smirked Salome. "I'm more worried about her feet."

Ahead of them, the pink-haired Kris Serenity Wright called for attention. With quick, purposeful motions, she leapt atop a large mound of snow, left from shoveling the walkways, and sat cross-legged, her face alight with amusement. As she leaned forward to address the crowd, Rachel thought she resembled a kettle of mirth in constant danger of boiling over into giggles.

"Hey, everybody, this is my new roommate!" she declared, gesturing with both arms toward the new girl.

"Mine, too!" cried her roommate, Rhiannon Cosgrove, a young woman with a head of long brown curls. She jumped up and down with excitement. Her familiar, a house cat-sized pony, cantered back and forth across the commons, trampling the snow and neighing.

Rhiannon climbed onto the snow mound beside Kris. Leaning down, she offered a hand to the new girl, who climbed up on Kris's other side, eyeing the snow as if doubting whether it would support her weight. A little mouse sat on her shoulder, its nose a-wiggling.

"Right, Rhiannon's and mine," continued Kris, putting a sisterly arm around the shoulder of the new girl. "Her name is Hekpa Tenatyee."

Hekpa waved at everyone with a wry, alert smile. She was tall and gangly with prominent cheekbones. Her hair, which stood up from her scalp like bushy slender twigs, was russet and brown, with hints of green here and there.

"Hekpa and I have something in common," continued Kris, addressing the crowd. "We are both fey-born!"

"What's that mean?" asked Rhiannon, who had grown up among the Unwary. "We didn't have fey-born in Hoboken, New Jersey. Or at least I didn't know about them. Of course, I didn't know anything about magic until the day I kicked over a toadstool and got stuck in a fairy circle. You should have seen how angry my mother was when I didn't make it home in time for my piano lesson that she had already paid for. Somehow, 'stuck in a fairy circle' didn't cut it."

"Fey-born's an old term for anyone with a parent who was a supernatural creature," replied Kris. "As opposed to most of the Wise, who are distantly descended from some fairy or god. My mom is a kitsune. Hekpa's mother is a dryad."

"Does that make you better than us?" Rhiannon gave a mock-pout.

Kris reached over and ruffled her friend's long curly hair, laughing. "Nope! We can sometimes do things no one else can; we tend to have splendid talents. But fey-born often find that their magic is unpredictable and sometimes goes haywire. Oh, but during the summer, we do get to go to Camp Half-Blood, with Percy Jackson. He's a hunk. I'm totally going to gouge out Annabeth's eyes and take him for myself."

Rhiannon laughed heartily, but Rachel blinked, not sure who they were talking about. Siggy cocked his head, also staring blankly.

Valerie moved forward and began taking pictures of the new girl and her roommates atop the pile of snow.

"Um… who? Where? And can I watch?" he asked. "Girls fight dirty. At least, that's what I learned from the older girls at Sister Rahab's Home For Unwanted Tramps, the sister-institution to the orphanage where I grew up. When those girls fought over boys, heads were slammed and ears were burned by cigarettes!"

"My money's on Annabeth," quipped Rhiannon. "She's tough!"

"Kris is talking about characters from a book," Hekpa, the dryad's daughter, gave Sigfried an apologetic smile. "It's just a joke."

"Oh." Siggy instantly lost interest.

Despite the brisk cold, the throng of curious onlookers grew larger. Hekpa, though embarrassed by all the attention, addressed the gathered crowd, answering questions about her long trek and her happy life growing up in the forest with her mother, the dryad of a Douglas fir, and her father, a canticler who farmed and trapped for their living. According to her stories, she had spent much of her time alone, but she spoke glowingly of her visits to the ice cream parlor in her local town. Far from the shy, retiring person Rachel might have expected from her circumstances, the skinny young woman proved quick-witted, and, from her stories, quite resourceful. When Hekpa Tenatyee finally bowed and sat back down with her roommates, the crowd clapped. The dryad's daughter blushed, but she nodded her head in acknowledgment.

As the crowd began to disperse, Siggy, who had wandered off, suddenly reappeared.

"Hey," he called to Kris, "Aren't you the one whose grandfather knows about fairies and other girly stuff? Has he done anything about that ogre yet? What is an ogre anyway? Are they giants whose growth was stunted by too much coffee and cigarettes at a young age? Or oversized dwarves? Really oversized?"

"No one really knows where most fey things come from," Kris replied. "Or rather no one knows for sure. Everyone has theories." She turned to her new friend. "Hekpa, you're the daughter of a dryad. Did she ever share any enlightening thoughts about their origins?"

Hekpa pulled her knees up and leaned back into the snow. "No. Not really. She used to talk about the council of old trees and the tree-telegraph network. But if she said anything about the origins of things, I don't remember it. If you want, I can ask her when I go home."

"Grandfather tells many stories about where creatures like ogres come from," Kris turned back to Siggy, "but they all contradict each other. Like the Storm Goblin who lives over yonder. In some stories, he's the ghost of a dead Dutchman. In others, he's a spirit of nature; yet in still others, he's a reduced god."

"A reduced god?" asked Rachel, intrigued. "What does that mean?"

Kris turned to her, "It's a god who isn't worshipped much anymore, so there's not much meat on him, so to speak. He turns into... something like a hungry ghost. Hangs around looking for a new gig. I think Grandda thinks Dwerg is an old god who acquired a new gig from the dead Dutchman. Not sure what he thinks about the ogre. He said the ogre came from far away and didn't fit in well with the local spirits. They hate each other—Grandda and the ogre." She turned to Sigfried. "Like mortal enemies!"

Sigfried scowled. "He's going to have to move over. I'm the ogre's mortal enemy now."

Zoë rolled her eyes. "Let's hope it doesn't end Sigfried-zero, ogre-one."

"It won't," Sigfried assured them, patting his knife. "Did your grandfather mention whether ogres were good to eat?"

Chapter Twenty-Three:

Busted

Monday evening, Rachel received a reply from her father. She contacted Joy and Gaius during lunch and asked them to meet her at the clubhouse again.

"My father has offered to send Templeton Bridges, his second-in-command," she told the other two. Holding up the letter, she waved it back and forth. "He says that Templeton has access to Shadow Agency talismans not available to Halls of Healing or even the regular Wisecraft."

"I don't know." Joy worried the ends of her hair with her teeth. "Do you know this person?"

"Oh yes," Rachel nodded decisively. "He's a close friend of my father's. I've known him my whole life. The Bridges have two children, Benjamin and Yasmin, who's seven. Benjamin was probably my best friend, before I came to school." Inwardly, she cringed, recalling how she had slipped off to invade her parents' room and investigate the rattle, rather than spend time with Ben at the Yule Party. She vowed to make it up to him.

"Um—" Joy looked torn.

"We don't have to say a word about scars," Rachel assured her. "We can just tell Zoë that Mr. Bridges is a family friend who is visiting Roanoke because Benjamin will be a student here next year. That way he can get an informal look at Zoë—before we do anything more drastic.

"If he thinks he needs to examine her more carefully," she continued, "we can tell Zoë that he's my father's physician-sorcerer friend, and that the Wisecraft thought she should have a check-up—just to make sure that getting pulled off the path had not harmed her." Rachel recalled Colleen MacDannan's comments in the kitchen about the tight-lipped Agent Bridges. "My father's friend is known for his discretion. He won't tell the nurse or the dean or anyone."

Joy wavered, unsure. "I feel like we're plotting. But I'm only doing it because I'm worried about her. But what if she's really self-conscious about the scars? She'll be so embarrassed we know! On the other hand, she might say no, because she doesn't know we know. But we do know!"

Gaius laid a gentle hand on Joy's shoulder. "Joy, you need to relax. I honestly do not think Zoë is in any immediate danger. Has she been sickly or tired or depressed? We have time to figure something out."

"How do you know?" Joy shouted. "You don't know what happened to her! None of us do!"

Rachel jerked back, as shocked by Joy's words as by the volume of her voice.

"That's true, Joy," replied Gaius, patiently, "but it doesn't mean we should panic. It doesn't help Zoë if we lose our heads. Really, Joy, we'll figure something out."

Joy burst into tears. Gaius took a step back, uncertain. A look of resolve came over his face. He moved forward and pulled her into a hug. Joy cried on his shoulder. Touched by her boyfriend's gesture, Rachel, too, hurried over and hugged Joy.

"You didn't see the scars," Joy choked out, weeping against the older boy's shoulder. "They look terrible! What if... what if having them examined makes her remember what happened? It must have been so horrible!"

"Don't cry, Joy," begged Rachel. "You are doing exactly the right thing."

"Am I?" Joy bawled. "Sometimes our best isn't enough. Look what happened to the elf lady! She was *murdered*! Because of us! That's what Siggy's vision was about, you know! The one the Comfort Lion showed him? How his blabbing about her got her killed and made Zoë and me cry. And Valerie. She's even more upset—since she's the one we told." She paused, wiping her eyes. "Maybe I should have asked the princess about Zoë."

"If you asked Nastasia," Rachel said sadly, "she'd go right to the Dean or Nurse Moth. That's how she does things. We're trying to give Zoë more control over what happens."

"T-true," hiccupped Joy.

"We'll introduce Agent Bridges to Zoë and tell her who he is," Rachel resolved. "Then we can take her aside and tell her that she should let him examine her."

She spoke calmly, but inside, she grew more and more alarmed. What if her whole dream about her Elf's husband were true? What if Zoë had fallen into the same place to which Remus had been dragged? She felt certain, as certain as she had ever been of anything, that it was a place of horror and madness.

She had been so relieved that her friend had not been conscious during the period when she was lost, but what if Joy were right, and Zoë had suffered some horrible fate that she merely did not currently remember. What if she did remember? Rachel shivered. Forgetting was terrible, but could there conceivably be a situation where remembering was even worse?

"A-and if s-she objects?" asked Joy.

Rachel blinked and pulled herself back from the yawning brink of emotional chaos.

"We'll have Gaius talk sense into her." She patted her boyfriend's upper arm. "He owes her one, after the time she yelled at him when he got upset at me. The time I… well, never mind that. I think Mr. Bridges can help her. If not, you can tell Nastasia, and she'll tell the dean."

Gaius blinked. "Um, yes, I'll speak to her, if she doesn't listen to reason. I hope she does, though, without my getting involved. The fewer people whom she has to find out have learned about her situation, the better. Of course, I could try to convince her without mentioning her scars. There are a number of ways to approach this to minimize embarrassment to her."

Releasing Joy, he held her at arm's length, looking her straight in the eye. "But we will do this, Joy. If Zoë's in danger, we will help her! No matter what. I'd rather have her dislike me for embarrassing her and be safe, than like me and be injured or ill. I'll make sure she gets examined. I promise."

Joy gaped at Gaius, as if he had shocked her out of being so upset.

"Okay." She swallowed and nodded, sniffing once. "Okay."

"Good." Rachel folded her father's letter. "I'll write and ask Father to send Templeton."

• • •

Templeton Bridges arrived the next afternoon. Mr. Fuentes pulled Rachel from class, causing a stir among the other students. The handsome proctor led her to a side room on the ground floor of Roanoke Hall where her father's second-in-command waited. Agent Bridges was a tall, dark-skinned man with severe features. Like all Agents, he wore a tricorne hat, an Inverness cloak, and a medallion showing a lantern surrounded by stars. He carried a fulgurator's staff that had a fist-sized emerald set into the top. A white silk pilot's scarf circled his throat.

Upon seeing her, he gave her a stiff nod with just a hint of a smile. Rachel smiled back, tremendously glad that he had come. Just seeing him, looking so familiarly severe, helped lift the weight that had oppressed her since Joy first told her about Zoë's scars. She suddenly felt very glad that she had written to her father.

Mr. Fuentes departed, leaving the two of them in a small, triangular room under the eastern spiral staircase, near the library, one wall of which was the curving, creamy marble of the stairs. Agent Bridges took off his tricorne hat and hung it on the back of a chair. His deep brown head was shaved close to the skin. He did not, however, remove his Inverness cloak. Shivering next to the cold stone wall, Rachel slipped into her own red coat.

Agent Bridges moved directly to the business at hand.

"Hello, Rachel." Bridges spoke in a deep voice with a crisp British accent. "Your father asked me to speak to you about an incident. One of your friends has been injured? Possibly while outside the borders of the world? Can you fill me in on what has happened?"

Rachel took a deep breath. "My friend Zoë has a pair of sandals that let her walk into dreams." She did not bother keeping anything back. The princess had told the dean anyway, and the dean had told the American branch of the Wisecraft. "My friend Nastasia can move between worlds, if she is in dreamland. They were walking down one of the silver tracks that stretch between worlds, and Zoë was pulled off the path." Her voice wavered slightly. She took another deep breath. "Zoë was returned, but she had some kind of dark shadow possessing her. When it left, she did not remember what had happened—between when she fell off and when she woke up without the shadow in her.

"Now," Rachel continued, "she has scars all over her body—but she is hiding this. We haven't told her you're coming. I'm not sure how best to tell her. Maybe," She shrugged, uncertain. "Could we have her brought to see you, without telling her that we're involved? Say you were here to follow up on her previous conversation with the Wisecraft, maybe?"

Agent Bridges regarded her seriously. "Rachel, if those sandals truly 'go between worlds,' you should turn them over to people who are older and more skilled than you and your friends. Our department—your father says you are cleared to know—deals with the activity of beings from outside of our own world. Our efforts are crippled, though, as most Outsiders are masked. They befuddle those around them. Or, worse, the entire world changes to pretend that they are a part of it. Who knows who is from Outside, and who is not?"

Rachel thought: *Nastasia can tell if she touches them.* She did not say this aloud, but, she was reasonably sure that the Wisecraft knew, since the princess had told the dean and the Grand Inquisitor.

Templeton Bridges pulled up a seat. Rachel expected him to sit down, but he lifted her up and planted her in it, as if she were a small child. She squirmed. She hated when people did that. Then he drew up a chair of his own.

"What you have done so far is amazing. But—and I want you to listen to me carefully—the world needs you alive, Rachel. I fully believe you and your friends will play a part in saving the world in the future, as you have in the recent past. But, you can't do that, if you are dead.

"So I am giving you an order. As of now, you are to act in an observational capacity *only*, until you are older and more skilled. Observe and report. We will try and respond in a timely manner. Your father and I and our fellows at the Shadow Agency are stretched extremely thin. We are traveling the world, looking into disturbances and trying to resolve incidents with minimal damage to civilians. The work is dangerous. What you are doing is even more so. The negligence and inexperience of your friend nearly led to her death. She was lucky."

Rachel nodded seriously, but inside her heart was dancing. She had loved reporting to her father. Doing so had brought her a sense of purpose and made her feel useful. Being told she could report again was like being told, after hiding under cold water for months, that she was being allowed up for air.

She ignored the "observe only" part of the order.

"Now, back to the matter at hand," Agent Bridges continued. "Who returned your friend? You're leaving out information, and I need to know everything before I can treat her. If I can treat her. You say she had a shadow in her? Was it like a black, inky smoke? Did it come out of her mouth and nose as though she was vomiting? After it came out, did you see where it went? Did it touch anyone?"

He sat back. "I should add, if the Guardian of the world has told you not to repeat something specifically, I do not expect you to disobey. I know you have interacted with it. It most likely knows what is best for the world as a whole, and for now, we are following its lead, what little it shows. But I do expect you to report anything pertinent which has not been forbidden by that power."

The Guardian? Rachel's world reeled. Her father and his people knew the Raven was the Guardian? Why had her father told her to avoid the Raven, as if it were a wicked thing?

"These things are difficult to talk about," she replied slowly. "We know who the Outsiders are. At least, we have a way of finding them. But even talking about the fact that they are from Outside can cause harm. If too many people find out, the Walls that protect our world will fall down, and the whole world will be lost to the kind of things that hurt my friend.

"As to my friend, I'm afraid I don't know very much. I was not there. Only the Princess of Magical Australia knows the whole story, which she told to the dean and the New York Agents. Darling and Standish, I believe.

"But I can tell you that an elf brought her back. My dead Elf's husband."

"I know people are coming from Outside", said Bridges. "You can tell me who they are."

Rachel frowned, not certain whether he meant he wanted to know who at the school had come from Outside, or whether he was asking about people who might have recently come from Outside, such as her Elf's husband—who, so far as Rachel knew, had immediately left again.

"I can't tell you who they are," she said. "That... that would be bad. It's bad to know. It's bad to tell. Bad things can happen. It's best to pretend that everyone has always been here."

"Very well," he stated. "Now—"

A note in his voice set alarm bells ringing in Rachel's head.

Agent Bridges leaned back and crossed his arms. "Rachel, please say: 'Mr. Bridges, I will act only in an observational capacity unless my life or another's is directly in peril.'"

When Rachel did not answer immediately, he added, "I don't expect you not to save someone, if you get the chance. But your father is concerned that you are actively seeking out threats to confront." Agent Bridges leaned forward, his elbow resting on his knee. "I am giving you an order that is not as restrictive as you might think. Our Agents are given more precise and restrictive orders than what I have asked of you. Keep that in mind, when you're considering whether you're going to listen or not."

Rachel stared at him attentively, saying nothing. By a Herculean effort of will, she did not so much as nod her head. She just looked at him, silently willing him to take her lack of comment as acquiescence and move on. So far, this had worked. Everyone else had taken her silence for agreement. Of course, they had not asked her to repeat something in particular.

Agent Bridges sat there, waiting, piercing her with his keen, dark gaze. He did not move or waver. Deep inside, Rachel began to quake, but her many years of practicing her dissembling arts helped her keep calm. She felt oddly dizzy, though, as if the room was spinning.

He was not going to fall for her innocent stare.

"Please give me your word, Rachel. I am not going to assume your assent from your silence."

Busted!

Chapter Twenty-Four:

Dread versus

The Agents of

The Wisecraft

Devastated, Rachel opened her mouth to repeat the words and paused.

In her mind's eye, Siggy's face stared back at her. He had the same crazy-eager look as when he asked her to take him to see the ogre and the storm goblin. She imagined his expression would if she had told him no. She imagined the long dull hours, sitting in classes listening to repetition of material she already remembered—with no hope of trips into dreamland or journeys to another world to look forward to. No adventures would mean no new secrets with which to dazzle Gaius and Vlad, no reason to talk to Jariel, or even see him again.

It would mean going back to being an ordinary girl.

She had tried the ordinary girl path once. It had not worked. She could not keep this promise, even if she were willing to try. Maybe once she could have, before she discovered the atrocities that Azrael had committed; before she saw Remus Starkadder dragged down; before she learned about Moloch, the demon who created the very concept of sacrifice; before her diligence in pursuing these matters stopped Azrael and saved the world—and her father. Now that she knew these things, however, she could no more stop doing everything in her power to find out more than she could halt the progress of the sun.

She did not mind lying. She had been doing more and more of it of late—ever since lying to Mortimer Egg had saved Valerie's life. But lying was not the same as breaking her word. When she gave her word, she intended to keep it. So she could not tell her father or Agent Bridges what they wanted to hear. She was not capable of it.

"Rachel?" Templeton Bridges waited patiently.

She bit her lip. What could she say? Sadly, she shook her head. Agent Bridges shut his eyes and ran a hand across his shiny dark pate. Opening his eyes again, he said, "Very well. Come with me. We need to go speak with Dean Moth."

Rachel took a step backward. "W-wait. Why?"

"We are going to see your father. He will ask you to make the same promise. If you do not, he will, most likely, pull you from Roanoke and have you tutored at home."

What?

No!

Agent Bridges stood and retrieved his hat. "I think at this point, you should verify that I am who I say I am. Ask questions only I would know, and make sure they are random."

Rachel struggled to wet her extremely dry lips. "Okay, um, why were Ben and I dripping wet the time you came for dinner last summer? What are the marks on Ben and Yasmin's necks? Why was Yasmin crying after we exchanged presents at the previous Yule party?" And several more questions in the same vein.

Bridges answered reasonably well. One or two details, he did not remember. Not remembering always mystified Rachel, and she was not sure how to judge whether these particular lapses of memory were ordinary or suspicious. But, as the particulars he could not recall seemed similar to the kind of details other people forget, she gave him a pass.

Agent Bridges departed the room. Rachel followed, feeling particularly small and sad.

• • •

"Mr. Bridges, Miss Griffin," Dean Moth straightened behind her desk. "How can I help you today?"

The dean was a short, stocky woman with a page bob of white hair and an air of brisk authority. She sat behind a large cherry-wood desk covered with an old-fashioned black blotter. Shelves filled with arcane tomes and jars of specimens for alchemy lined the walls. In one corner, a large golden eagle with silvery talons perched on a stand made out of a young tree. The office smelled like leather and sandalwood, with just a whiff of bird.

"Greetings, Dean Moth. I am taking Miss Griffin to the Wise-craft Offices in London to speak to her father," said Bridges, in his deep, deep voice. "I have a letter here with his permission to remove her from school grounds. Her father has let the Agents know, so you can verify the request with Scarlet MacDannan. You may, if you wish, send an escort with her."

He handed the dean a letter, which she read, frowning.

"Very well," she said. "Let's go speak with Mrs. MacDannan."

Rachel stood before the large desk of the woman who was, still today, a heroine among the Wise for her courage and perseverance during the Terrible Years. When all the other tutors and staff fled Roanoke, when the Terrible Five seized the school almost twenty-five years ago, only Maverick Badger and then-Art tutor Jacinda Moth had stayed to protect the captive students. Furthermore, the dean was a friend of the princess's family and already knew almost all the secrets Rachel knew—all the ones Nastasia knew, anyway.

Gazing at the dean's careworn face, Rachel made a difficult decision. She would ask the dean for help. She would tell her everything and would beg her not to let the Agent take her off school grounds. Maybe, by some extraordinary miracle, the dean would understand and help her.

Rachel stepped forward and put both hands on the black blotter atop the desk. The thought of not having all these weighty issues on her own slender shoulders was a tremendous relief. Her spirits lifted.

"Um, Dean, could I talk to you privately?"

Dean Moth glanced at Bridges, who nodded and stepped outside and partially closed the door. "Yes, Miss Griffin?" asked Dean Moth.

"I... I don't want to go see my father."

"Why not?"

"I-It'll g-go badly." Rachel bit her lip. "May I sit down? This may... take a while."

"Miss Griffin," the dean said severely, "you have been summoned by your own father. An Agent of the Wisecraft is here to escort you. Do you believe he is not who he claims he is? Do you believe you are being led into a trap?"

"No. I believe him," Rachel began eagerly. "But—"

The dean held up her hand. "Miss Griffin, if you believe that going with this man is going to put you in danger, you must tell me now."

"No." Rachel's voice sounded flat in her ears. "I don't think Agent Bridges will put me into danger."

Rising to her feet, the dean came around the desk and put her hand on Rachel's arm. "Then we must let him take you to your father."

"If my father doesn't let me return," she said in a small voice, "thank you. For everything."

"Excuse me?" Dean Moth's eyebrows leapt upward.

On his perch, the golden eagle shifted its weight and cocked its head, regarding Rachel.

Rachel attempted to swallow, but her throat was too dry. "Agent Bridges says that my father may pull me from school and have me tutored at home."

The dean was short, but she was still taller than Rachel. She stooped over and fixed Rachel with her hawk-like gaze. "Miss Griffin, if your father says you cannot return, I will personally go speak to him. Your father is a reasonable man and would not pull you from this school, unless he thought something terrible was going to occur. Were that the case, he would have warned me first, I would think."

A spark of hope attempted to rekindle inside of Rachel, but it sputtered in the emptiness of her despair. She nodded, not quite looking up.

"Thank you, Dean."

Rachel blinked in shock. She had finally decided to confess everything, and her chosen adult would not even listen? The animation drained from her, leaving a Rachel-shaped husk.

"thank you. For everything."

"Speaking of gratitude, I wanted to say thank you, Rachel. I know that you must have your reasons for not wanting people to know about your part in saving the school from that aeroplane." The dean pronounced the word carefully.

Rachel's pupils expanded into black pools. It took her a moment to find her voice again. "How did you...?"

"I learned about your part from Mr. Chanson, who can see very well. He could tell you and Sigfried were both on the broom, defending the school. I hope that you understand just how important that was. How many people you saved. And how your hard work and obvious practice with the sorcery you are learning made it possible," she added dryly, "And I will be sure to tell your father how much you are learning here and what good you are doing with it, if he persists in attempting to remove you."

"I didn't want anyone to know about the plane," Rachel's voice dropped to a whisper. She glanced toward where Bridges stood in the hallway. He had pulled out papers from an interior pocket of his cloak and was reviewing them. He could have been faking, but he looked as if he were not paying attention to her conversation. "Because, among other things, I was hoping my father wouldn't find out. But you are welcome. I am so glad that I could help the school."

Dean Moth nodded.

"And glad that Siggy was able to take the credit. It makes him happy, and he really did his part. More...." Her voice broke, as she remembered how bravely Sigfried had supported her foolish plan that would have killed them both. "More than you know."

Dean Moth frowned but did not ask.

The dean gestured and her golden eagle glided silently from the perch to her shoulder. Leading the way, she brought Rachel back to Agent Bridges. The three of them walked down the hall, past the library, and up the stairs to Mrs. MacDannan's classroom. Rachel hurried to keep up with them, but her heart was so heavy that she found it hard to lift her feet. A terrible foreboding settled over her. She wished bitterly that she had heeded the little inner voice that had warned her not to involve her father in the matter of helping Zoë.

The bell rang as they went up the stairs, announcing the end of the previous period. Suddenly, the hallways were full of students rushing to and from classes. As they rounded a corner, a sudden clatter startled Rachel. Glancing down the hall, she saw an embarrassed Astrid Hollywell stooping to pick up her school books, which had tumbled to the ground. Had someone knocked into Astrid? Was it the same mean kids from Drake who often picked on Rachel? She looked around but could not see anyone who might have been at fault. Embarrassed, Astrid ducked her head and hurried off.

By the time they reached Mrs. MacDannan's classroom, the previous period's students had departed and the next period had not yet arrived. Scarlett MacDannan and Templeton Bridges whispered to each other in the corner of the empty classroom. The math teacher's rat ran and hid under his mistress's hair to avoid the sharp-eyed gaze of the eagle. Some type of exchange took place, as if Mrs. MacDannan had passed the Agent something, and he handed it back to her. They came back over to where Rachel and the dean waited.

"He has verified that he is who he says he is," said Scarlett Mac-Dannan. "I will join them and escort Miss Griffin to Scotland Yard, if you don't mind, Jacinda."

Dean Moth nodded. "I will personally oversee your classes until you get back, Scarlett."

Scarlett MacDannan handed her an extremely detailed lesson plan, drawn up in three colors. Dean Moth blinked at it as she accepted it.

The dean turned to Rachel. "We are trying to protect you, Miss Griffin, but, unfortunately, we are only human. We can only do what we think best with the information we have. Remember that when speaking to your father. And remind your father, for me, that he got into plenty of trouble his freshman year as well."

"Did he?" Rachel's voice squeaked, surprised.

Dean Moth smiled a tight, wry smile. "I expect you back for classes tomorrow, or I will come looking for you myself."

The dean wished them well. Rachel, Bridges, and MacDannan began walking back toward the front door of Roanoke Hall. Rachel's footsteps rang on the marble floor, her gaze taking in the familiar hallways, the great oak doors, the cheerful noise of the dining room behind them. *Would this be the last time she ever walked these halls?*

No, that was foolish. Even if her father did not allow her to come back now, she would come back at some point, for college, if nothing else. Still, she wished she could grab her broom.

They stepped out into the biting cold of the January afternoon, crossing the bridge over the reflecting lake. Skaters twirled to their left, and three hockey players slammed a puck around to her right. Rachel gazed longingly at the icy lake, the snowy commons, the lampposts, and benches. Everything seemed so beautiful, so familiar. She loved the school so much, yet, once again, grown-ups had let her down. She felt as if she were being ripped away from a dear friend.

Friends! Rachel nonchalantly brushed her fingers against her black bracelet and casually sighed aloud, "I wish I could have told my friends, *Gaius* and *Vladimir*, that I was leaving school grounds to go to London and see my father."

She carefully pronounced the names of both boys clearly, intending to call them. The bracelet vibrated. Both Gaius and Vlad responded instantly.

"Are you okay, Rach?"

"Do you need assistance?"

Vlad's voice spoke again in her ear, "If you are able, you can subvocalize. Unfortunately, you will have to speak at least slightly. The bracelets will pick up soft sounds but not thoughts, other than your intention to activate or deactivate them."

There was a pause. William Locke's voice sounded in her ear, "I've asked them to be ready to rescue Miss Griffin from the Wisecraft. They're ready."

Jenny Dare's cheerful voice sounded next. "Rachel, sweetie, we've got your back. Don't be scared. Just be careful with the Wisecraft. If this is something like before—when they were all crazy—we have people in there who we know are not corrupted. They'll get you out safely."

Bridges and MacDannan continued escorting Rachel across the snowy campus toward the path that led toward the docks. As they passed the gymnasium, before they reached the frozen lily pond,

Gaius and Von Dread came strolling around the corner of the gym. Seeing her, Gaius crossed the snow with a big smile and gave her a hug.

"Hi, Rachel." Gaius looked up at Bridges. "Who's your friend?"

Rachel hugged him back, hard.

"This is my father's friend, Templeton Bridges," she murmured, still hugging him. The look she gave Gaius said: *I've been betrayed by adults once again.* Or that was what she wished it to convey. She acknowledged to herself that the chances Gaius would be able to decipher her exact meaning were slim. "The one I told you about. He says my father wants to talk to me. Could... could you tell Siggy and my girlfriends?"

"Definitely." Gaius squeezed her one more time. Then he stepped back and addressed the Agent. "Um, Mr. Bridges, I had thought you were here to speak to someone else—about an issue we wanted addressed. Are you leaving now, before talking to the person you came to see?"

As Gaius addressed the adults, Rachel threw Vlad a wan smile. To her surprise, Dread no longer stood by the gym. He had moved forward, until he was directly on the path before her. He stood with his hands at his side, one black dueling glove quite close to where his teak and gold wand, with its sapphire tip, hung at his side. He looked deadly serious.

Rachel glanced around at the snowy campus. Jenny Dare and Topher approached near the icy lily pond, skates in hand. To her right, over near the Memorial Gardens, William Locke leaned casually against the shrine of Mars, speaking with Naomi Coils.

Such a feeling of joy suffused Rachel that she felt as if she were too light to stay on the ground. These friends of Gaius's—these people she barely knew—they had come to protect her.

Agent Bridges was saying, "I'll be back to speak to Miss Forrest. This matter shouldn't take long, but it took precedence over the original issue."

Bridges seemed relaxed, but Scarlett MacDannan was glancing back and forth between Dread and Locke. She looked puzzled and the slightest bit nervous.

Rachel stepped forward and squeezed Gaius one more time. She spoke very softly, knowing her voice would be carried over the bracelets. "The Dean has promised to come get me, if I'm not back by tomorrow. If that doesn't work... well, you can write me at home."

Gaius smiled confidently down at her. "I will see you soon."

He hugged her one last time and then stepped back.

Vladimir Von Dread was still standing directly in their path. Dread looked at Agent Bridges. Bridges looked back at him. Bridges was exceptionally tall, but Dread, though more slender, matched him inch for inch. The two stared eye to eye. To her right, she saw William grow alert and move to the balls of his feet. His hand casually rested in his sleeve, where Rachel knew he kept his wand in a spring-loaded sheath.

Rachel's lips parted in awe. Templeton Bridges was a member of the Shadow Agency, the most elite Agents of the whole Wisecraft, and, not only had Scarlet MacDannan been one of the Six Musketeers who defeated the Terrible Five, but she also had served as an Agent of the Wisecraft for many years, before recently joining the staff of Roanoke Academy. These were two of the most dangerous people alive upon the earth.

And yet...

Vladimir Von Dread and his people were offering to fight them, for *her.*

Rachel looked at Gaius and his friends, gazing from one to another. They were all so much bigger than she and so confident. It made her feel both safe and strangely beautiful—as if she were a precious child, safe in their care. It struck her that it should have annoyed her to feel this way, but it did not. It was a surprisingly happy feeling.

Dread glanced at Rachel. Rachel gazed back at him, her lips still parted. He arched an eyebrow a quarter of an inch, inquiringly.

Rachel felt so tempted to accept his offer and let him fight the Agents for her. The feeling of betrayal, the fear of her upcoming interview with her father, was so great that she almost felt that whatever came next would be worth it. But that was foolishness. Even if Von Dread and his group won, what would they all do next? Go on the run? She could imagine how well that would go over with the young prince's father, King Ludwig IV of Bavaria.

Meeting his gaze evenly, Rachel gave the barest perceivable shake of her head.

Dread gave a nigh imperceptive nod in return and stepped aside, slowly. Mrs. MacDannan and Agent Bridges briskly walked Rachel past him, and past William and Naomi, and then around the lily pond, where Jenny waved gaily.

Only after Dread and his group fell far behind did the tension drain from the shoulders of the two Agents.

Chapter Twenty-Five:

A Difficult Interview

with the Duke

Agent Bridges and Mrs. MacDannan led Rachel down the tree-lined path and through the ruins of Bannerman's Castle to the docks. A solemn foreboding still held Rachel in its grip, whispering in her mind that this trip was a bad idea; however, there was now a tiny bounce to her step. The support of Gaius and his friends had lifted her spirits.

At the docks, the *Pollepel II*, the school's gold and green ferry, was waiting. As they boarded, Captain Zephyr, known to all as Zephy, doffed his captain's cap to the ladies. He was a white-bearded old man dressed in a black and gold uniform. Rachel, who had met him on her first crossing, back in September, returned his greeting with a smile.

The good captain took them to the shore near the base of Storm King, just south of a small marina. The Roanoke Glass Hall was nestled in a copse of trees that stood between the river and the train tracks. The inside of the small stone cottage was much larger than it appeared from the outside. Agent Bridges led them past several blue travel glasses to the same large glass through which Rachel had first arrived last September. The three of them stepped through into a much larger room, handsomely appointed with wood paneling and a red velvet carpet. This, Rachel knew, was the Glass Hall in New York City. Crossing a corridor to a blue-carpeted room, they stepped through another travel glass into a similar hall in Victoria Station, London.

Agent Bridges led them down the hall to a locked door, which he opened with a key. Inside was a small room containing a single walking glass. This one came out in another small, well-appointed locked room. A second key opened that door from the inside, and they stepped into the busy foyer of the Wisecraft's offices in Great Scotland Yard.

Once in the reception area, Mrs. MacDannan nodded to the receptionist and turned to take her leave. The receptionist glanced wide-eyed from the short, red-headed tutor to the wall of the main hall, where Scarlett MacDannan's bushy-haired younger self gazed down from a huge portrait of the Six Musketeers, commemorating the victory of the six Roanoke students over the Terrible Five. The starry-eyed young receptionist asked in a hushed voice whether she might get Agent MacDannan's autograph. Scarlett snapped back that she was retired but then relented and, with a sigh, signed the young lady's comic book.

Agent Bridges took Rachel down a hallway she had not previously visited. He led her to a liftwell. His deep voice echoed in the cylindrical opening before them.

"Shadow Agency."

Taking her hand, he stepped off the platform into the open air. Rachel jumped into the well beside him. Normally, when she visited her father's office, this liftwell wafted them upward. This time, they plunged down, rather quickly, causing her stomach to flip-flop.

They passed four parcels traveling upward, accompanied by a bored-looking bellhop. Then there was no one else in the well. Still giddy from the exhilaration of Gaius and his friends coming out to protect her, Rachel tucked her legs and turned somersaults in mid-air.

Spreading her limbs, she slowed until she was floating on her back. Descending in a liftwell always felt a bit like wearing a flying harness. There was the same odd, floating sensation toward the bottom, as one slowed until merely drifting. As they continued downward, an idea occurred to the slowly twirling Rachel that altered her entire outlook.

She was going to see *her father!* Finally, she could tell him about how she saved him, and the world, from the demon Azrael.

Humming, she spun again, until her feet were beneath her, ready to land. As she neared the bottom of the well, it occurred to her that the spells that created the lifting effect must work similarly to *tiathelu*. She could even picture a number of ways that a lift-creating talisman could be made. She felt obscurely pleased that she had learned enough in her four months at school to figure out the basic principles of a liftwell.

They landed on the very lowest level of Great Scotland Yard and set off on foot. After passing through a series of locked gates and magical protections, similar to some of those she had seen at Ouroboros Industries, Rachel found herself in a hallway full of identical, unmarked doors. Bridges stopped at the fifth door on the right and knocked.

"Come in," called the voice of Ambrose Griffin, The Duke of Devon.

Bridges opened the door and motioned her inside. Rachel's father sat behind a large desk. He raised an eyebrow at Bridges, who shrugged and said, "She wouldn't say it."

Agent Griffin frowned. "Thank you, Templeton. If you could leave us for a bit."

Bridges nodded and started to depart. Then, he paused and crossed the office to lean over beside where the duke sat at his desk. Bridges spoke quietly, but Rachel, who inched closer, was able to make out most of his words.

"About the other matter," whispered Bridges, "the King of Transylvania denied us entrance. Again."

"Did he?" Ambrose Griffin's eyes narrowed. "I will speak to him. He will change his mind. Have the team ready to leave in the morning."

Bridges nodded and departed, closing the door behind him.

Rachel walked into the center of the room and turned slowly in a circle. The office of the head of the Shadow Agency was a large chamber with exposed brick walls and polished rosewood furniture including a large main desk, roll-topped filing cabinet, china cabinets, bookshelves, desks at which secretaries could take dictation —though no one was seated there now—and a leather couch. The shelves held an unusual mix of sorcerous equipment—astrolabe, *cinqfoil*, magnifying glass, an essence glass in an oak casing—and mundane devices, many of which Rachel did not recognize. There were also things that she could not make heads or tails of: a cone of shiny gold, a squat black rock that glowed with points of starlight. Knowing that the Shadow Agency dealt with magic from Outside, she wondered if any of the unfamiliar items might be from other worlds.

The large office had her father's stamp upon it. The pitted iron sword that King Alfred the Great had given to Athelward Griffin, in thanks for his defeat of the Danish wizard Hjorvart, hung on the wall behind his desk. Next to it was a photograph of her family, taken when her grandfather was still alive. Three or four photos of her mother, showing off Ellen Kim Griffin's lovely charms and impish smile, also graced the walls. A rug that had once been in her grandfather's study covered the center of the wooden floor. On a shelf, to his right, rested an antique, two-hundred-year-old tea service from Gryphon Park. Rachel recognized the lopsided green and pink tea cozy that covered the teapot as something her sister Sandra had knitted for him at the age of five.

The Duke of Devon came around his desk and sat on the edge of it, scrutinizing his daughter with keen interest. He was an extraordinarily handsome man, with dark hair, steady hazel eyes, and an air of implacable calmness. He was dressed in an expensive gray plaid suit; his Inverness cloak and tricorne hat hung from a coat rack in the corner.

"Hello, Rachel."

"Hallo," she replied with a curtsey.

"Have a seat." He gestured to the couch. "Let's talk."

Rachel sat down. The leather couch was low, and, as her father was tall, she found herself staring up at him. She felt awkward and at a disadvantage. Still, she bounced happily on the cushions. Finally, she would be able to tell him all that she had been longing to say.

Before she could begin, her father leaned forward, his palms resting on his knees.

"So here is my dilemma," said the duke. "I need to protect my thirteen-year-old daughter. She has somehow made friends with people who have abilities that make this extremely difficult. She thinks she is specifically required to save the world from danger, and that this needs to be done immediately. Please stop me when I say something incorrect, okay?"

Rachel sat ramrod straight, as her grandparents had taught her. "If you were the only person in position to solve a problem, wouldn't you feel that it was your job to solve it?"

"Perhaps, were it true," replied her father, in a tone that made it clear he believed otherwise. "Your memory, the power you received, thanks to your mother and, to a lesser degree, because of me, is a great power. There are those who treasure it tremendously." A shadow passed across his face, like a cloud racing across the silvery visage of the moon. Then it was gone again. "It allows you to remember things that most people cannot even see. On top of this, you've spoken to a being of great power, and it has explained that there are certain dangers facing the world—which you have decided are your responsibility to correct, correct?"

Rachel struggled not to giggle at "correct, correct?"

"And do not tell me," he continued, when she did not answer immediately, "that just because my father, your hero, was sent down from Roanoke freshman year, that you feel you must follow in his footsteps."

Rachel's jaw dropped. "Grandfather was expelled from Roanoke?"

"His first year. Yes. Eventually, my grandfather talked the school into giving him a second chance. But let's not change the subject, shall we? Explain to me why fighting these supposed threats requires the personal participation of my thirteen-year-old daughter?"

"Because I was the one who was there. On the front line," Rachel said humbly. "I already stopped the first threat. And the second. That one took a bit of research, but I figured it out, with help from friends."

"And that is it? Or is there more?"

"I wouldn't say anything needs doing immediately. There are things to be done."

He cocked his head attentively. "What things need to be done?"

Rachel spread her arms. "Whatever is needed. Such as stopping the next demon: the silver-haired one dressed in thorns that appeared at Stonehenge on Thanksgiving."

Her father blinked. Striding around his desk, he picked up a notepad and jotted something down. To Rachel's disappointment, he did not ask any follow up questions on that subject.

"And this 'whatever is needed' requires—what?" he asked, looking up from where he was writing. "Traveling in the land of dreams?"

"Sometimes," Rachel said haltingly.

"And you need to be there—why?" He came around the desk again and crossed to stand beside her. Resting one foot on the couch, he gazed steadily into her eyes. "Help me here. I am trying to understand."

It took some effort to put into words a truth that she had not previously acknowledged, especially as she found it unexpectedly difficult to praise herself.

"I-I h-have to go because my friends don't remember what they see. They don't remember what questions to ask. They don't even remember what they should be looking for," she explained. "Valerie is very good at putting clues together, but she grew up as an Unwary. So, she doesn't always recognize what's significant. I am the one who remembers the important points and who tries to make sense of the things we are seeing."

That had been surprisingly hard to say.

Her father nodded. "You're very smart, Rachel. You get that from your mother. She has always been extremely clever and observant. Now that you're at Roanoke, she was hoping to take up some kind of work. She won't be able to do that, if I pull you from school, and she has to tutor you at home. You don't want me to pull you, right?"

"No," whispered Rachel. "I-I don't."

The buoyant confidence that Von Dread's support had lent her was fast fading. Maybe this interview was not going to be as easy as she had hoped.

"And you do understand my point of view, right?" Ambrose Griffin continued in his same calm, stern manner. "At least somewhat? You understand why I would pull you from school? Today? This very moment?"

She bit her lip again and smoothed out her robes. "I s-said good-bye to a few people, just in case."

"That's not an answer to my question," her father pressed. "Knowing *what* I might do isn't the same as acknowledging *why* I might do it. Do you understand why I would do this?"

"Of course." Rachel rolled her eyes. "But being at home isn't going to protect me. I am perfectly capable of getting into danger there, too. Look what happened at Sandra's."

His jaw twitched, but he remained calm. "Sandra's apartment is not our home. I think you underestimate the wards at Gryphon Park, built by generations of our family."

He closed his eyes and rubbed the bridge of his nose. Rachel fidgeted nervously, tracing her finger around the buttons set into the warm brown leather of the couch. She imagined life at home, studying by herself again, lonely and far away from everyone who had come to matter to her. How bleak such existence would be.

"But let's not change the subject," stated her father. "I need you to promise me you will not rush into danger."

Rachel decided that the truth was the best response. "I... can't do that."

"Oh? And why not?"

"Because I couldn't keep such a promise."

"And why is this?"

Rachel swallowed, tongue-tied. She did not want to say the wrong thing, as she had so many times of late. Finally, she choked out, "Terrible things would have happened this fall, if I had not rushed into danger. The Walls that maintain the world would have fallen down. Veltdammerung would have woken Moloch—who is much, much worse than Azrael ever was!" She gazed up at him. "Aren't stopping these horrors more important than safety?"

"Rachel, you are thirteen. It is not *your* responsibility to save the world."

"But it is!" insisted Rachel, jumping to her feet. "Who else is going to do it? *You?* You would be *dead* if I had not been at Beaumont Castle that night!"

"Rachel," her father frowned, concerned. "You did not save me at Beaumont. Finn MacDannan did that."

"No he didn't! That's what I have been trying to tell you! I've been trying and trying to tell you! At Sandra's, over Yule break! But you've been too busy to listen!"

"Is that why you are angry?" The duke's steady hazel eyes searched her face. "Because I did not come speak to you after the raid on Veltdämmerung? Rachel, honey, I was busy hunting down a demon that someone released at Beaumont the next day. The thing kept trying to sacrifice children, and it took everything the Wise-craft could do to stop it."

Oops. He had been hunting Morax.

"Um... about that...."

"Rachel, please stop changing the subject." Her father's jaw twitched again, but that was the only sign that he might be annoyed. "Do you really think that young girls should be left to their own devices? That parents should not look out for their children?"

"No, but...."

"Okay, Rachel." The Duke of Devon held up a hand. "Tell me what it is you think I have done wrong. I know you're upset with me. Over the course of the last few months, you have decided I am not to be trusted. I think I understand some of the reasons for this, but, please, explain them to me."

It all came flooding back—the moment when her soul had shattered into a thousand pieces. Her perfect memory presented it exactly as it had first occurred—her beloved father rejecting her attempts to report all the unusual occurrences to him, even though doing so had been her only way of coming to grips with the strange and horrifying events occurring around her. He had told her to ignore the Raven, to be an ordinary girl. Much as she had longed to please him, those instructions had proved impossible. Unable to do the impossible, she....

The memory proved too painful, her mind shied away from it. To her extreme embarrassment, tears began spilling over her lashes.

Sniffing helplessly, Rachel spoke in a very small voice. "I told you everything. I thought you would be proud of me. But you never once said: 'Good job.' All you did was tell me to pretend that nothing had happened." Her voice rose plaintively. "I'm not capable of doing that."

"I did say that." He knelt before her, so that their eyes were of a height. "I needed time to investigate everything you told me. And I had to keep it quiet, because I was not sure if I was being watched. We knew there was a leak, but we could not pin down who was doing the leaking. Your information about the new geas helped us immensely. But if the post was being watched, and students had been taken over, how could I keep the enemy from knowing what we had figured out?"

"Why didn't you tell me this?" Hot tears streamed down Rachel's cheeks.

"I did not know who might hear," said her father, gazing steadily at her. "You really thought I was just ignoring you? When have I ever been untrustworthy? When have I ever not listened?"

"Right now!" Rachel wept, beating his shoulder with her closed fists. "You're not listening right now!"

"Very well." Her father rocked back on his calves. "Talk."

Finally!

Rachel took a deep breath. Words rushed out of her mouth at breakneck speeds. "Finn didn't save you at Beaumont, I did. If I hadn't been there, you'd be dead. Smashed against the wall. Sandra, too. Egg tried to compel me to kill you all—you and Sandra and Sigfried and Nastasia. Only I was immu—"

"Stop!" The Duke of Devon's hazel eyes were filling with concern. "Rachel, didn't I teach my children never to lie."

Rachel flinched. "Wha... what?"

"You remember the trouble Laurel got into when she thought she could lie to us?" His words rang in her ears like cannon fire.

She nodded, her head bobbing up and down several times.

"Is there anything you wish to say to me?" His voice was deceptively calm. "Instead of what you just said?"

"No!" Rachel wiped her eyes angrily. "I'm telling the truth. I've been *waiting and waiting* to tell you!"

He cut her off. "Then choose your words carefully, because I already know all about what happened to you at Beaumont."

"But... how?" cried Rachel, terrified and suddenly uncertain.

"I asked Scarlett." He replied. "She gave me access to the transcript of what you said under the effects of the *Spell of True Recitation*."

Hoisted on her own petard. Of course, her father had not come to hear her side of the story. He had not known that she was capable of lying under the influence of the *Spell of True Recitation*.

"I-I did lie," Rachel chewed on her lip.

"Yes. But it is your motive that puzzles me. Why claim you saved me? Did you think that would make me more malleable? Affect my decision?"

"Not to you!" Rachel cried, scandalized. "I lied to Mrs. MacDannan!"

"To Scarlett?" Her father gave her a strange look. "That's impossible, Rachel."

"You would know it was not impossible if you would just stop and actually listen!" Rachel shouted, angrily wiping her eyes. "Besides, you lie, too!"

The duke became entirely calm. "When have I lied to the family, Rachel?"

"How about when you didn't tell me that you had *five* siblings I had never heard of?"

"Ah. That was not a lie. We... just did not speak of them. Not even when I was young. The subject brought grief to Father and upset Mother."

Oh. That made sense, but Rachel was too angry to stop now.

She cried, "Then how about every time you say that you have only four children?"

"I... beg your pardon?"

"Why do you never mention my sister who died as a baby? A sister named Amber?"

The moment the words left her mouth, she regretted them. If she was wrong about the rattle, she was about to feel very foolish indeed.

Ambrose Griffin blinked rapidly. He did not blink once or twice like most people do, but six or nine times.

"I am sorry," Her father rubbed his left temple, puzzled, "What were we talking about?"

CHAPTER TWENTY~SIX:

FAREWELL, SWEET RAVEN

LIKE THUNDER OVER STORM KING, RACHEL'S HEARTBEAT POUNDED in her ears. She repeated her question. "Do I have a dead sister named Amber?"

Ambrose Griffin blinked again, repeatedly. He rubbed both temples, grimacing.

"I'm sorry." He winced and ran his hand over his face, "I... seem to be developing a headache. What were we talking about? Ah, yes. Why my daughter will not obey me."

Other than the hiss of the heating system behind the brass grate, the office seemed unnaturally silent.

What had just happened? Rachel did not bother repeating her question. Whatever had hid the rattle from her memory was hiding the knowledge of this matter from Ambrose Griffin.

"I don't—"

"Why aren't you answering me?" Her father's voice grew more concerned. "Is something wrong, Rachel?"

"I—can't." She spread her hands helplessly.

Her body was trembling, but she forced herself to marshal her thoughts. Memory loss terrified her. She felt nauseous. The room swam before her eyes. She grabbed the arm of the couch. More terrifying was the realization that the matter of the rattle was not just a crazy pet theory. She must *really* have had another sister.

"Rachel," the duke said sternly, "my patience is wearing thin. Answer my questions."

Rachel was quiet for a long time. She had been trying to answer him. She did not know what else to say.

Finally, in a very small voice, she squeaked out, "I thought we were a team, but you never listen to me anymore."

283

Kneeling before her, the duke took her small, cold hands in his large, warm ones. His hazel eyes were filled with concern. She could smell the spicy musk of his familiar cologne.

"We are a team." He squeezed her fingers. "I am the field agent. You are support. You are not supposed to take risks in the field. That's my job."

"But...." Her voice rose, breaking. "I am in the field. I am on the front lines. Like with the Raven. You told me not to talk to the Raven. But it was right there! It was looking at me! H-how... how could I ignore it?"

Her father looked up, suddenly alert. "What did the Guardian ask of you?"

"He doesn't ask me to do anything," Rachel sniffed sadly, wiping her eyes. "I wish he would."

"If it did not ask you to do anything, then why didn't you listen to me?" he frowned. "What does it have to do with anything?"

Rachel stared blankly at him. His question seemed strange, until she realized that her father had no notion of the enormous place the Raven now held in her life. And yet, what could she say about Jariel? That he had brought Enoch Smithwyck back from the dead? That he had saved her from the Headless Horseman? That he seldom spoke to human beings, and yet he had chosen to speak to her? That the brightest memory in her perfect collection—the best moment of her short life—was the look of pride and admiration upon Jariel's face, as he gazed down at her, after she had chosen to sacrifice herself to protect the world?

She had been told not to speak about that incident. She could not tell her father this dangerous secret without endangering the Wall. Even if she could have, however, she hardly wanted to. It seemed too private to share.

"Are you afraid of the Guardian?" the duke demanded. "I'm your father. Your first loyalty belongs to me. You may tell me everything. Has he threatened you? I will deal with him."

His words reverberated in her ear: *Your first loyalty belongs to me. You may tell me everything.* Joy leapt in her breast. Was not *this* what she had wanted? An invitation to return to the happy times when her father had been the center of her world? No more would she have to worry about her world revolving around a sixteen-year-old boy. Could she go back to the way things had been?

No.

The days when her father had been on the top rung of her loyalty ladder were long gone. Currently, he was on Rung Four, and Jariel was on Rung Three. She would not violate her promise to the Raven to please her father. Alas, this invitation came too late. Still, he was her father, and she loved him.

Rachel dropped back to the couch and briefly closed her eyes. She sought out happy memories of the time the two of them had spent together. The recollections came in a rush, one following another: riding in front of him as a toddler atop his tall horse, his arms wrapped around her waist, as they paraded down the dusty road that stretched from Gryphon Park through the sheep-dotted tenant farms to town; walking hand in hand between the rows of blooming plants, as they inspected the family's lavender farm, the flowers' sweet fragrance perfuming the air; sitting across from him in the Oak Drawing Room as he taught her to play chess, while her grandfather watched from his throne-like chair, making wry observations and calling them "Falconridge" and "Lady Rachel".

More recent experiences followed: cantering together across the moors, her riding her trusty little Shetland pony, Widdershins, her father on his huge, black, long-maned Friesian, Passelande; dancing together on the town commons last year on Mid-Summer's Day, he in his ducal finery, she in a lovely green and white dress with a huge bow in the back; picking wildflowers together by the Dart River the day before she left for Roanoke, bringing the blooms back to lay on Grandmother's and Grandfather's graves.

After her grandfather died, her father had become the center of her life. Had so much changed? Staring into his puzzled face, so familiar and dear, Rachel resolved that she would tell him anything she could about the Raven and what had happened to her at school, without directly violating the promise she had made to Jariel. She had been willing to tell the dean. Should she not be willing to tell her own father? She would tell him the truth.

He deserved the truth. Then, maybe, he would let her tell him about Beaumont.

She did not dissemble. Instead, she pushed aside her normal caution and strived to put into words what was truly in her heart.

"The w-world was in danger," she said hoarsely. "Saving it required that I... not be me any more. But that would be better than letting it get destroyed, right? Better me than the world, don't you think? Only... he would not accept my sacrifice. He gave my life back to me. But everything is different now. As if I have been granted extra time. As if everything beyond the moment of my sacrifice is an unexpected gift.

"So, now I am devoted to protecting the Earth." The words flowed more joyfully from her lips. "You and Mr. Bridges say I need to concentrate on growing up. But if the Earth is destroyed, I don't get a chance to grow up."

She gazed at him hopefully, willing him to understand her.

Her father stared at her, dismay growing more evident upon his features. The muscle in the side of his jaw ticked. A cold chill crawled up Rachel's spine. She had the distinct impression that he was not hearing her. Her hopes began to sink. Not being understood when daring to share her innmost secrets made his lack of comprehension so much more painful.

"What sacrifice?" Ambrose Griffin voice was clipped. "Of what are you speaking?"

Her body grew clammy. She had promised the Raven never to tell anyone, except Gaius, about the time he had changed her friend's memories. Had she already said too much? It would break her heart to accidentally betray the Raven. *Please let it not be so.*

"Please tell me exactly what happened," he said slowly.

"I can't," whispered Rachel, forcing words from her throat. "I gave my word."

Her father's voice was as stern as she had ever heard it, "I excuse you from your vow. You are underage and are not legally allowed to make binding promises."

Wordlessly, she shook her head.

"Rachel, you have known me your whole life. You know I am looking out for you. Why would you trust someone you just met, someone outside our family, over me? That monster is not even human."

Rachel's heart, which seemed to be stopping up her throat, constricted in pain. She opened her mouth but no voice came out.

Her father stood. "Give me your grandmother's wand."

Icy cold fingers of fear crept up the back of her neck. She could hardly draw breath. Clutching the slender length of silver hanging at her side, she thought of the hours she had spent filling it with spells, of the look of pride in Gaius's eyes when she had used it to beat Ethan Warhol in a duel at a recent Knight's meeting. Was her father going to take back the silver wand? Or, worse, destroy it, as Vlad had destroyed Gaius's old wand after their duel?

"Wh—why?" She backed away from her father, scooting down the couch.

Ambrose Griffin put out his hand. "Don't question me. Hand me your wand. Now."

She felt meek and humbled. She had no desire to rebel, no matter what Laurel might have said. However, she also felt no desire to hand the wand to him, none at all.

She did nothing.

"What part of 'Don't question me' do you not understand?" Her father voice's snapped like a captain addressing his troops, his hand extended toward her. "Has the school addled your mind? Hand me your wand, young lady. I am not going to ask again!"

Rachel's shoulders slumped. Slowly, she picked up the wand and forced her hand to extend it towards her father. She had to push her elbow with her other hand.

Ambrose Griffin took the silver wand and hefted it, his face grim. Turning, he pointed it at the corner of his office. A beam of white flame tinged with gold shot across the room, striking the brick wall. Rachel gasped. The wand only had two charges of Eternal Flame left, with no chance of her ever getting another. *Her father had just used one of them!*

"*Endro!*" he commanded in a loud voice.

The white flame flared. The bricks it struck distorted. They seemed to elongate and warp, as if the fabric of reality were stretching. Looking at it gave Rachel an odd, dreamy sensation. In spite of her despair, curiosity impelled her to lean forward. *What was he doing?*

Red lines appeared around the distortion. Rachel recognized them, though she had never seen them. Nastasia had described seeing similar lines during her visions. Illondria had later told the princess that these lines had appeared because the Raven was trying to keep Nastasia from falling into another world.

The red lines grew thicker. The corner of the office warped in a way that was hard for her eyes to follow. Then, everything snapped back to normal. The brick corner was just a brick corner again.

A giant red-eyed Raven hopped on the rosewood desk. Her father turned and looked right at it, as if he had been expecting it. Rachel's heart frozen in her chest, mid-beat.

What had her father done?

Even worse, what had she done?

The Raven flew off the desk and landed on her grandfather's rug. Then, he stood up, an eight-foot-tall winged man of inhuman beauty. A ring of brilliant light hovered above him. It shed *diligence* throughout the brick chamber the way a lamp sheds light. For a split second, Rachel felt entirely resolute, as if she would continue to do her duty with care and without shirking, no matter what. The moment the Raven reached up and pulled the circle from over his head, the outside emotional influence stopped.

The glowing circle turned into a hoop of gold in his hand. The great black wings folded into his back and disappeared. He stood before them, shirtless and shoeless, dressed in a pair of dark poplin slacks, his feathery black hair falling about his head and shoulders.

The Raven scowled, his voice gruff. "That was an inappropriate way to call me."

Ambrose Griffin glared. "I do not care. Guardian, you have been interfering with my daughter's life!"

Rachel grabbed onto the couch arm again, suddenly dizzy. Her father had *summoned* the Raven? After all she had done to protect the world, her father had deliberately damaged it—because she now felt certain that was what he had just done—to draw the Raven's attention. To question him about what she had said? Because he thought that the Raven had hurt *her?*

No!

The color ran out of her world. It was as if everything were drawn in pencil. In some distant part of her mind, she knew that only her perceptions were affected, that nothing had physically changed, and yet, she felt as if she had fallen into a nightmare.

The Raven croaked, "I did not act to interfere with her."

"You threatened her life?"

"I did not threaten her life."

The duke looked at Rachel, who nodded. Again, her head bobbed up and down rapidly. She wanted to cry out, to explain, but the thought that Jariel might think that she had made accusations against him—that she had complained to her father—struck her dumb.

"We had an arrangement." Ambrose Griffin spoke calmly, but Rachel could tell he was extraordinarily angry. "I do not believe you are abiding by it."

"I have not broken our arrangement," replied the Raven. "My dealings with her were because of her. I did not seek her out."

That made Rachel feel even smaller. The Raven had not even wanted to speak to her.

Rachel felt utterly mortified. It was as if she were a peasant who, by some astonishing good fortune, had gained the good will of a king, a sovereign who had treated her with kindness far above her station, only to be dragged in chains before this same monarch under an accusation of treason, forfeiting what little trust she might once have earned.

Would he speak to her again, now that his once-in-the-history-of-all-humanity act of kindness—befriending a lonely little girl—had been rebuffed with such ingratitude?

Most likely, not.

"He hasn't hurt me!" she cried, finally finding her tongue. "He's looked out for me. He hasn't done anything!"

She noted, obscurely, that color had returned to her environment, but she still felt as if she were viewing the events from far away.

Her father asked sharply, "How much does she know?"

"She has discovered many things on her own," said the Raven. "I have not done anything to alter her memory."

"If she learns too much, won't she draw Outside forces to herself? She needs time to grow into her power," the duke insisted. "Her being in danger now does not help us. It does not help you. It does not help anyone."

"She is just one person," replied Jariel. "I can shield her."

That brought a ghost of a smile to Rachel's lips. Jariel turned and regarded Rachel. "You may speak to him of anything I have told you. He knows more than you do."

If the Raven had taken a red-hot iron spear and shoved it through her abdomen, Rachel could not have been more shocked. Her father *knew*? More than *she* knew? Why hadn't Jariel told her? Why had he said that she could only speak to one person?

"Guardian, you know why I am here, and you know why my wife is here." Ambrose Griffin spoke very sternly. "We cannot raise our family, if you are interfering with them."

Here? As in on earth?

Did her family come from Outside?

"I cannot control fate," replied the Raven. "That is not within my power. A convergence of random chances has occurred that was obviously not random."

"Guardian, I cannot command you," her father said hoarsely. "I'm not Romanov. But I do not think you would lie to me."

"I would not lie," replied the Raven.

Her father sat down on the edge of his desk and rubbed his temples.

"I have broken no agreement". The Raven grew taller as he spoke. His perfect face was stern, forbidding. "But the same cannot be said for you, Ambrose Griffin. Your disobedience comes with a high price."

Price? Rachel head jerked up. *What price?*

Ambrose Griffin nodded slowly, his face grim.

No! A shudder ran through Rachel's entire body. Something bad was about to happen. She could feel it. She had to do something to stop it, anything!

Like a prisoner on death row begging for her life, Rachel dashed across the room and threw her arms around the Raven's legs. He was so tall now that she could not reach his waist. Her head came only to his hip. She pressed her cheek against his thigh and hugged his leg as tightly as her arms could squeeze.

"I'm sorry!" The words felt as if they were ripped from her. "I'm so sorry!"

Jariel rested his hand on her shoulder. His fingers felt warm, like the unexpected touch of the sun on a long cold day.

"Child, you have done nothing wrong. I did not ask anything of you."

"I wish you would ask more," she whispered, tears stinging her eyes.

He bent down over her, his voice gentle. "You do not yet know what will be asked of you in the future, Rachel Griffin."

Behind her, she heard a strangled sound. Peeking from under her hair, she saw her father staring at her, his expression odd.

Jariel gently pushed Rachel away. Immediately, she released him and jumped back, her eyes lowered. She felt even more mortified at the thought of staying where she was not wanted. The chill where the Raven's warmth had just been felt as icy as a glacier. Her body seemed too frozen and stiff to move. Then, the room was empty, except for herself and her father.

He was gone.

If everything of value had been ripped from her life in one violent motion, leaving her an empty husk, it could not have felt worse.

The dam in her mind that held back the swirl of chaotic emotions and buzzing darkness gave way. Grief swept over her. Sorrow —for the death of her Elf, for the horrors that Zoë had suffered, and for a hundred other things, big and small, that she had thrust aside with her dissembling skills—now returned and battered her. She struggled, striving to gain control of the tide of unleashed emotions. Alas, the misery was too great, and her humble skills too meager.

Rachel's knees buckled. She collapsed to the floor. Curled in a ball on her grandfather's rug, she wailed.

Squatting down beside his daughter, The Duke of Devon tried to return the silver wand. Rachel wept, too distraught to pay attention to his actions.

"Rachel, you must stop crying!" her father spoke urgently. "There are things I must say."

Rachel merely wailed louder.

The duke lifted her off the floor and put her on the couch, sliding the slender length of silver back into her hand. She clutched it to her chest, still weeping piteously.

"Rachel, daughter." Ambrose Griffin knelt again, until they were eye to eye. He grabbed her by the shoulders. "You need to listen to me. I know that you are upset, although I.... You have to look at me and listen. You have to stop crying. Or cry a little more quietly, because I might not have a chance to tell you later."

That broke through her misery. She tried to stop crying. She really tried. All she achieved was some ragged gulping. This abysmal failure, in comparison to her normal mastery of her emotions, only made her wail more loudly.

Ambrose Griffin sat down beside his daughter and lifted her onto his lap. Pulling her against him, he hugged her, rocking her back and forth. She sank against his chest, her head resting on his shoulder. A calming warmth emanated from his body, bringing with it a peace that pushed back against the chaos inside her mind. Her gulping quieted down to soft sniffles.

"Forces Outside are trying to destroy us," her father said urgently. "A difficult balance is maintained—which I have now disrupted."

Turning her head, she looked up at him. To her relief, she found that she could focus on what he had been saying. While she felt shaky and miserable, her inner landscape was slowly returning to normal. Pain and agony still swirled deep inside, but the dam that restrained them was reforming.

Her father spoke rapidly, "I broke an agreement just now, when I unveiled the Walls of the world—to get the Guardian's attention. This did not endanger the world. It did not endanger you. It just endangered me. If I talk about it more now—I'm digging a deeper hole."

Rachel blurted out hopefully, "Then don't talk about it!"

His arms squeezed her more tightly. "As to why the Guardian speaks to you...."

"He talks to me because I like him," whispered Rachel softly.

He frowned at that and smoothed her hair. "You are much more mature, Rachel, than I could imagine someone your age could be. You are very special. You are not a normal thirteen-year-old. Even Sandra is not like you."

Despite her sorrow, a little smile touched Rachel's lips. It her whole life, it was the first time that someone had told her she did something better than Sandra.

"I'm not really sure why," her father continued, "I have my suspicions. But in this case, maturity does not matter. There are things I cannot tell you until you are older. If you don't believe me, you can ask the Guardian. It will confirm or deny what I have said."

"Him," murmured Rachel. "The Raven is a him."

"*It*," clarified her father. "The creature is a spiritual entity, neither male nor female."

Rachel nodded thoughtfully. That made sense. It explained why, even though Jariel was so handsome, he did not seem—well, like a boy.

"I will not be able to remember this conversation next time we speak," Ambrose Griffin spoke calmly, but Rachel heard a note of sadness in his voice. "And I do not want the same thing to happen to you. Next time you speak to your friend the princess, please ask her to put in a good word to her father for me."

What did the princess's father have to do with anything?

"Can't you do something to keep remembering?" asked Rachel, urgently.

He shook his head sadly. "Your mother will remember. I think."

"You're going to lose your *memory*?" she gasped. "Because you called the Raven? Because I didn't answer your questions the way you wanted me to? But! But...."

He nodded, chagrined.

Terror swirled around outrage, catching her in their whirlpool. She clung to the outrage, willing herself not to succumb to the tempest within again. Using her anger to keep herself from weeping, she thrust the pain aside. She could deal with it later.

"Why couldn't you just have trusted me?" she raged, pulling away from him enough to see his face. "Instead of dragging me here today? I didn't want to come! I knew something would go terribly wrong! I didn't want to tell you anything! If you forget, it will be exactly the same as if I had said nothing—only you won't remember other things, too. Important things. At least, if it is anything like what happened to Cousin Blackie!

"I could have said nothing," she wailed, "and we would have ended up with exactly the same result. Only better!"

Rachel recalled Illondria's dead body, charred upon the ground. She recalled Michael Cameron storming out of the Knight's meeting; the look on Eunice Chase's face, right after Rachel mentioned James Darling; or on Gaius's, the time she let on that she had overheard his interview with the Agents. She remembered Sakura Suzuki suddenly growing into an adult.

A low moan started deep inside her and rose until she practically howled, "Everything that goes truly wrong is because of something I say!"

Ambrose Griffin sighed and hung his head. "Well, because I am going to win the Worst Father of the Year award, anyway: If I forget, and then I start asking you questions anew, I'm giving you permission to lie to me."

Rachel whimpered and said nothing.
She had nothing left to say.

CHAPTER TWENTY-SEVEN:

THE MASTER OF THE WORLD

"I'M GOING TO HAVE TEMPLETON SEND YOU BACK TO SCHOOL." Ambrose Griffin pulled out a calling card and spoke Bridges's name. Slipping it back into his pocket, he said to Rachel. "If your friends ask, tell them that I complained about you having a boyfriend. I've been thinking about that for a while, so I'll probably bring it up again."

"My boyfriend takes very good care of me," murmured Rachel, her head still resting on her father's shoulder.

"That's not the point. That's never the point."

"Yes, it is precisely the point!" Rachel declared fiercely, sitting up again. "Nobody else takes good care of me, except for him and his friends!"

Ambrose Griffin opened his mouth and then shut it again, shaking his head sadly. He rubbed his forehead and sighed. There was a knock on the door. Gently sliding her to one side, he rose to his feet and let Agent Bridges into the room.

"Could you take her back to school, Templeton?" asked Ambrose Griffin, looking unusually weary. "And please see to her friend."

Agent Bridges looked back and forth between the two Griffins, curiosity writ upon his features, but he did not ask any questions. Rachel followed him, as he escorted her through the same series of glass houses and across the Hudson by ferry, back to Roanoke.

"Family issues can be trying." The tall man spoke softly, as they took their leave of each other on the snowy Commons. "But it will get better. Your father's a good man. He loves you very much. He is only trying to look out for you."

Agent Bridges shook her hand. Then, he left to seek out Zoë

Forrest, promising not to let on to Miss Forrest that her friends knew about her troubles.

• • •

Rachel did not say much for the rest of the day. Gaius came to find her and asked how the visit had gone. Rachel merely shook her head. She was too worn out to say more. Gaius nodded, saying that he understood. He gave her a warm hug, and they spent the rest of the evening studying quietly together in the library.

That night, she woke up to find her dorm room aglow with a silvery light. The Raven stood in her room in his human form. With him was a man who resembled Nastasia's father, only more severe. This second individual was dressed in strange flowing garments that reminded Rachel of styles from yesteryear but not of any particular style she had seen in a book or painting. The two of them stood on a silver road, a wider version of the princess's slender, track-like path. It was this that lit the dorm room with its moon-like glow.

Jariel was dressed in a dark robe. His black wings were folded behind him. In one hand, he held the gold coronet that sometimes hovered like a bright circle over his head.

He gestured to her: *be still.*

Rachel kept her eyes almost-closed, peering through her lashes. The man who looked like the King of Magical Australia, but older and sterner with gray at his temples, stared at Rachel as she supposedly slept. He turned to the Raven and gestured curtly.

"Do it."

The Raven waved his hand. Rachel saw nothing, but when she thought back, her memory showed her a rainbow light that spread from Jariel's feet to ripple over her. A complex, second layer of memories settled into her mind. This new intrusion did not disturb her original set.

"I have created the false memories in her mind," said the Raven.

The stern, older man nodded. Turning, he strode down the silver path. His body seemed to move away from her in a direction that Rachel could not ordinarily see. After a few steps, he vanished. The Raven remained and counted to ten.

The silvery light winked out.

Jariel crossed the room and knelt down beside Rachel's bed. Other than the pad of his bare feet against the floorboards, the room was utterly silent. Her roommates made no sound. Mistletoe was suspended, motionless, in mid-air, halfway between the windowsill and the throw rug. Beauregard had frozen half-risen from his bed at the foot of Nastasia and Rachel's bunk. Astrid's red-winged black-bird, Faraday, still sat upon its perch, its head tucked under its red and black wing. The Lion, however, opened one golden eye, where he slept upon Kitten's bed.

"Who was that?" Rachel whispered, afire with curiosity. She pointed toward where the silver path had been.

"I… may not say." The Raven paused. "You must be careful what you tell your friend, the Romanov girl."

"Father wanted me to recommend him to her father—"

"It is too late for that."

"Oh." Rachel fought back tears. "Then, I won't tell her anything."

"That would be for the best."

She swallowed, feeling suddenly shaky. "Poor father!"

"I do try to protect the individuals of this world as much as I can," said the Raven, "but in the end, the protection of the world itself takes precedence. Your father picked protecting you over protecting the world."

Rachel bit her lip, feeling miserable. She had tried so hard to help. To have her be the one whom someone chose over the world seemed painfully ironic.

"That was the princess's grandfather, wasn't it?" A shiver ran down Rachel's spine. "The one she had seen as a child but had been made to forget?"

He bowed his head but said nothing.

"And he's in charge here?" she asked. A tightness seized her chest. She found it hard to swallow. "You have to do what he says?"

The Raven did not answer.

Rachel's mouth went dry, her worst fears confirmed. The princess's grandfather controlled the Earth but not just the Earth. He did not merely have the power to arbitrarily take away the memories of people she loved. He also controlled Jariel. He could compel the

Guardian to do these terrible things. The idea that Nastasia's family, and maybe Nastasia herself, had such power over the Guardian made Rachel feel physically ill. The relief she had felt, when she dismissed Magical Australia as unimportant, now mocked her.

Then, another thought struck her.

Finally, she had found someone to hate.

She scowled and practically spat. "This monster who robbed my father of his memory, I have to call him something. If you won't tell me his name, I'll pick one for him." She recalled a Jules Verne novel she had read the previous year. The villain had borne an appropriate moniker. "Let's call him the Master of the World."

The Raven inclined his head. "Very well."

"So, now I have fake memories." She paused. "Am I supposed to pretend they're true?"

"That would be wise."

"May I tell Gaius?" Rachel asked. "The truth, I mean? Does the protection that covered one person, so I could tell him the other secret, cover all matters, or only that one?"

"You may tell him. I can continue to guard him indefinitely."

She let out a breath she hadn't realized she was holding.

"I am so sorry!" Her eyes filled with hot tears. "I'm trying to make things easier for you. I want so much to help! To do something useful. And, here I'm making things harder."

Jariel gave her a bittersweet smile. "You did not make things harder for me. I've seen many different problems. I will see many more before my task is done."

Rachel nodded and wiped her eyes, sniffing.

The Raven lifted the coronet of gold in his hand. "Take my halo. I wish to show you something that you may come to value."

He extended his hand, but he did not give the gold circlet to her. Instead, he put it over her head. Brilliant light shone from above her. A feeling of diligence coursed through her so fierce and firm that she felt she would never cease until she had done everything that could possibly be needed. The feeling was so familiar, so much like *her*, that it filled her with a quiet, inexplicable joy.

Images flashed through her mind. She saw herself from her father's point of view, so tiny and quick and bright. Emotions came with the images, worry and love and a ridiculously fierce protective-ness. The scene in her father's office replayed in her memory, but this time, she felt the emotions her father had felt: his confusion, his frustration, his tender love for her.

The flickering memories came to the moment when Rachel had run and hugged Jariel's leg. The instant the arms of the little her wrapped around the winged being, she felt a pain so sharp that she cried out. It was her father's pain. To him, it looked as if his dar-ling little daughter preferred this monster—Rachel could feel her father's distrust and hatred of the Guardian—to him, her own fa-ther.

"Poor Father!" Rachel cried again, chagrined. "Oh! I never meant to hurt him!"

With the pain, however, she also felt his love for her. Rachel's eyes widened. Her lips parted in awe. She had no idea that her father loved her so much. He loved her with the same pure, abiding love that she loved the world—the world she was willing to give her life to protect. If he loved her that much....

Rachel imagined what it would feel like to love something that much and lose it. No wonder he was so concerned about her safety! In that instant, she swore to herself that she would be more careful, that she would try harder not to rush headlong into danger.

Jariel pulled the halo away. It turned back into a gold hoop. He smiled at her, his eyes dark and kind, and patted her hand comfort-ingly. "I know you did not intend to cause him pain, but I thought that, perhaps, it would help heal the wounds between the two of you, if you knew."

"Of course," the winged man frowned, "next time you see him, he will not remember."

"I will get his memory back!" Rachel declared fiercely. "I am going to find a way!"

He nodded at her, as if he was pleased by her resolve.

Rachel regarded the Raven as he stood beside her. She wished so much that she could help him. "If there is something I can do to make it easier for you, you will tell me, won't you?"

Jariel nodded. "In the fullness of time, I will, I believe, have need of you."

Those simple words went far towards lifting the pall of guilt that this day's events had cast over her.

"I'll grow stronger!" Rachel vowed. "Until I am strong enough to help you!"

Perhaps the Raven replied, but Rachel recalled no more when she awoke in the morning.

• • •

The next morning dawned bright and clear. Rachel might have thought that the whole incident was a dream, except that, upon waking, she found that she still had a false set of memories—false memories, she realized with dawning dismay, that made no sense.

According to the fake memories, she had gone to see her father, and they had argued about her boyfriend. He had said that her mother did not object in principle to her dating Gaius, but *he* did. Rachel had cried and yelled and fussed—displaying much more emotion than she ever would in real life. Her father had insisted that Gaius was not the right kind of boy, that he did not have the right background. Rachel had shouted at him, listing Gaius's Arthurian lineage. Her father had finally agreed to look into the matter at more length and had insisted that they would speak about this again.

It would not have been a problem if the new memories had stopped there, but they did not. They covered the entire period that she had been at Roanoke, except all knowledge of the Metaplutonians had been removed. It was as if she had come to school and everything had gone well: no priests summoning Moloch, no Morax among the bones of Carthage, no Azrael, not even Dr. Mordeau turning into a dragon.

Everyone at Roanoke knew that Mordeau had turned into a dragon. How was she going to pretend that these new memories were true, without alerting her friends instantly that something was wrong? And yet, if she spoke of the real events, would the World know?

• • •

The next two days passed in a daze. She had hoped to speak to Gaius at the Knights' meeting, but, as often happened, he was so busy, between teaching and dueling, that there was no opportunity for anything except a few public comments and squeezing hands as they passed each other on their way to their next dueling strip. Friday evening, he was busy again with Vlad and his crew.

Saturday morning, Rachel received a message that Sandra was on campus and wished to see her and Peter and Laurel. The siblings met in the purple common room in Dare Hall. Rachel had never seen her oldest sister in her working clothes. Sandra looked quite dashing in the Inverness cloak and tricorne hat of an Agent, her medallion with its lantern surrounded by stars swinging in front of her chest. Or, rather, she would have, had her eyes not been red from crying. Sandra swept off her hat and hugged Rachel very tightly. Rachel hugged her back. Then she sat down on the purple cushions and waited.

"I need to let you all know, Daddy is sick," said Sandra. "It's bad enough that they are transferring him out of his current department, back to being a plain Agent of the Wisecraft. And they are putting him on holiday for a few weeks. He... had an accident with a memory spell.

"It's okay, *uri dongsaengdeul*," Sandra assured her younger siblings quickly. "He's all right. He knows who he is. But he's lost some time, going back a year. Maybe more. He's being checked by one of the foremost experts on memory magic. So, just hope he gets better soon."

Knowing it was coming was bad enough. Hearing it had actually happened was too much. Rachel put her face in her hands and began to cry, silent tears streaming down her cheeks.

Peter leaned over and hugged her. "Don't cry, *dongsaeng*. Dad's tough. He'll get better."

"Yeah," Laurel patted her head. "Nothing'll take Daddy down for long. He's awesome."

Sandra nodded. "Yes, he is getting the best care possible. Pearl Moth is checking him over. She's doing it especially for our family. We should be happy Daddy has so many friends. His second, Templeton, is temporarily in charge of Daddy's department. He'll keep things going until he is better."

Rachel wiped her face and nodded. Pearl Moth was Blackie's mother. She was a famous nun in the Order of Asclepius. (Unlike some orders, nuns of Asclepius were not forbidden from marrying.) Since her son's accident, she had specialized in restoring memories.

Wiping her face did not stop the tears. Sandra hugged her once more and departed with Laurel. Peter stayed behind a little longer, patting Rachel's shoulder. Rachel longed to confess to her brother, but she dared not, lest he be robbed of his memory, too.

"Listen, it will all work out," he said. "You'll see!"

Due to the cruel nature of the universe, she could not share with her sibling her hatred for the man who had harmed their father. Nor could she cry out, "It's my fault."

• • •

Rachel wrote her father a short letter, saying that she had heard the news and hoped that he would be feeling better soon. She included an origami griffin she made from lined paper. It looked more like a sick pig, but she hoped he would like it. After posting the letter, she wandered over to Room 321 to see what her friends were doing. She felt calm when she started up the stairs, but by the time she arrived at the third floor, she was crying again.

The others looked up in surprise. Nastasia sat at the table doing homework. Joy was attempting to make Zoë waltz around the room. Zoë's expression was a cross between extreme boredom and sarcastic amusement. Valerie was fitting a new brass and leather bandolier around Sigfried, who had taken off his robes. Over his extremely well-toned body, he wore a black sleeveless shirt with gold letters spelling: *I flexed and my sleeves exploded.*

Rachel averted her eyes. While her affections for her blood-brother were entirely sisterly, even she could not help but notice, even in her tear-sodden state, that his shoulders and biceps looked as if they had been personally-crafted by an emperor of all things seen or unseen—and, right now, they were too much in the seen category. Out of the corner of her eye, however, she noted that instead of bullets, the loops of the bandolier held elixir vials.

Rachel noticed that while Joy was pretending to dance Zoë around the room, she was mainly staring at the half-naked Siggy. Salome, who was lying on her back on the table, painting her nails, was also surreptitiously watching her best friend's hunky boyfriend and smirking. The room smelled strongly of nail polish.

"Rachel, did you hear?" Joy shouted excitedly, the moment Rachel stepped in the door. "There's going to be a ball for Lunar New Year. A masquerade ball! It's the Year of the Dragon! Lucky will be the star of the.... Wait. Are you crying?"

Then everyone was staring.

Rachel sat down hard next to Nastasia on a straight-backed wicker chair that put her facing Zoë's punk rock bands. This was too much for her current state of mind. She turned her chair until she was facing Daring Northwest's sketches and the large pictures of Siggy's head. Under other circumstances, she might have preferred to stare at the pretty Magical Australian vistas, but at the moment the very thought of Magical Australia made her feel ill.

The princess's eyes filled with concern. She laid a comforting hand on Rachel's shoulder. Rachel gave her friend a little smile and, reaching up, squeezed her hand in appreciation.

"Rachel, what's wrong?" asked the princess solicitously.

"My father suffered an accident. He has I-lost a portion of his memory. He's forgotten so much that he's been transferred out of the Shadow Agency and back to being an Agent. Or he will be after some weeks of holiday."

Weeping openly, she added, "The one silver lining is that I-I think he forgot his argument with me, too."

Joy ran over and hugged her. Nastasia held her hand in her own. She also drew a pale yellow handkerchief from her house-containing purse and handed it to Rachel, who wiped her eyes and blew her nose. Lucky snaked over to join them, wrapping around Rachel's shoulders, so that his soft, furry body rubbed comfortingly against her wet cheek. Even Salome rolled off the table and sauntered over, looking concerned.

Zoë, released from the torments devised by Joy, lounged against the large central table scratching Lucky behind the ears. Rachel noted that Zoë looked more cheerful than she had before Agent Bridges's visit.

"It's okay, Griffin," Zoë said. "We have crazy power girls and Siggy. We can get him fixed, right?"

"D-did he... did he get attacked at the Wisecraft?" Valerie had stopped trying to buckle the bandolier. Her hands were shaking too much to continue. Leaving it hanging half-buckled, she, too, crossed to where Nastasia and Joy were comforting Rachel and joined in hugging her. At this, Salome joined in, too.

"One big girlfriend hug. Can't fail to make you feel better." Salome gave her a surprisingly compassionate smile.

Rachel, surrounded by girls, blew her nose again. Very carefully, she said, "According to my sister, Sandra, he wasn't attacked. He was doing an experiment and messed up."

"What happened when you were at Scotland Yard?" asked Valerie, still worried. "Did your father mention any memory experiments?"

Rachel hated having to use her new false memories. She waved her hand vaguely. "Apparently, we had a huge argument."

Joy asked, "What did you argue about?"

Valerie's voice rose, panicky, "Apparently? Do you not remember it?"

The usually-calm girl reporter's face seemed unnaturally pale. Salome moved over and stood beside her, a comforting presence. Lucky, too, shifted to Valerie, wrapping around her like a stole.

With a start, Rachel realized that Valerie was recalling her own trip to the Wisecraft in New York, during which she had been put under a geas that allowed Dr. Mordeau to control her—and worse. Rachel felt great sympathy, and yet, it seemed unfair that everyone else could get away with not remembering details all the time, and she was not allowed to pull it off even once. No wonder her mother had warned her not to tell anyone about her memory. She should have prepared a more convincing lie.

"Argument about what?" asked Siggy, who was fiddling with his new bandolier and not looking up. "And what was it really, if it was not an argument?"

Rachel said, "I hardly know what we argued about.... You know what parents are like."

"No. No idea," muttered Sigfried.

"Oh... sorry." Rachel grimaced. "As to our arguing—mainly about Gaius—I'm finally talking to Peter again and, now, in the last month, I've argued with both Laurel and my dad."

Zoë shrugged. "You've changed. Your family is trying to adjust. My dad and I used to get along pretty well, until a few years ago. Then suddenly, he had no time at all for me." She shrugged and then added, "You get used to it."

"I'm sorry about your dad," whispered Rachel. "Do you really get used to it? Or does it just kind of fade to a dull numbness? What kind of things did you do when you were little?"

Zoë said, "You know, things girls do with their fathers. Get attention. Get spoken to. Not be told you're a mess or embarrassing the family. That sort of stuff."

Valerie's voice trembled. "Wait, are you sure you're okay, Rachel? What if someone grabbed you in the Wisecraft? Should we have you checked out?"

"I am all right," Rachel said, hiccupping as she began crying again. "I-if they had messed with me, I'd know. Thanks to our Elf. Arguments with one's family are... just weird."

Valerie's blue eyes were still round with concern. Still wearing Lucky like an overlong scarf, she crossed over to Siggy and held on tightly to his arm. He gave her hand a comforting pat. Salome watched this with a little smile. Then she joined Joy in hugging Rachel one last time, before returning to the table and her nails.

Choosing a vial from his new bandolier, Sigfried held it up, as if he were about to pull out the stopper and down the contents. "This is obviously an attack by an enemy with memory-eraso powers. I suggest we divide the world into quadrants and start searching. Wheels and the princess can examine dreamland, and Lucky can look in that area behind Drake Hall, where they keep the snacks... I mean sacrificial animals.

"Kidding," he sighed. "Actually, I have no idea what to do. Or even how to prove this was not an accident."

Joy pulled up a chair and sat down on Rachel's other side. "We have to try something. He's your father! Maybe... maybe the princess's father could help?"

Rachel felt like a deer that discovered that what it had taken for a bicycle headlamp was actually the forward lights of a battle cruiser. As Nastasia was sitting right beside her, gazing at her with kindly concern, Rachel fought to school her expression.

"That is an... interesting idea," she choked.

"I am certain my father can help," offered Nastasia. "We have many useful resources in Magical Australia."

I bet you do, thought Rachel.

Aloud, she murmured, "That... might not be a good idea."

"I know what we need to do," announced Siggy, his face bearing the beneficent look Rachel knew meant that whatever came out of his mouth next was guaranteed to alarm Nastasia. "Using my trusty, Elf-enhanced invisibility elixir, we need to break into the Wisecraft offices! First, they turned my G.F.'s father into a duck...."

"Goose," said Lucky.

"Moose," agreed Siggy. "Then, they messed with Goldilocks herself. Now, they've knocked Rachel's father on the noggin so hard that the last couple of years fell out of his ears. Clearly, the offices themselves must be evil! So, in the interest of goodness, lollipops, sparkly rainbows, dancing unicorns, not to mention lonely magic items yearning for new owners, we've got to break in there, search the place, and relieve them of cool enchanted talismans and secrets."

"Mr. Smith." The princess looked up from where she comforted Rachel. "The Wisecraft is a law-abiding agency that works for my family's friend, Mr. March. I am sure if there are evil elements among the Agents, the Grand Inquisitor will see to their arrest."

"Unless *he's* the evil element!" Siggy cried gleefully. He pulled out his wand and flourished it wildly. "I think we can take him! I'll put his head on the wall over there!" He gestured in the general direction of Valerie's photos. "Right next to spots I have picked out for the ogre and the Jabberwocky. Do you think that the school will mind if I affix shelves to this wall? I don't think double-sided tape will do. Maybe we could install huge hooks in the ceiling, so that the heads can dangle from them and drip blood and gristle onto the ground."

"Thank you, Sigfried," mouthed Rachel. "You are making me feel so much better."

"We are certainly not going to 'take him'," the princess insisted. She spoke graciously, but Rachel could hear the strain in her voice. "We could not, if we wished to."

"Sure we could!" continued Siggy.

"He would stop us in an instant," she said coolly.

"Great, then he can come after us... while Lucky slips by and raids the magic items, er... I mean looks for the baddy who hurt Rachel's father. It'll be a win-win!"

"I don't see how getting our hinnies kicked by the Grand Inquisitor is a win," admonished Valerie, as she returned to buckling Siggy's bandolier. "Besides, I got attacked in New York, but Agent Griffin works in the London office. Which one would we raid?"

Sigfried did not miss a beat. "Both of them, of course."

"Mr. Smith, you are suggesting behaviors improper in a knight." A furrow marred the princess's perfect brow. "This is unbecoming."

A dangerous gleam came into Sigfried's eye. Rachel sighed. If she did not interfere, things were quickly going to get much worse.

"I appreciate your loyalty, Sigfried," Rachel looked up and smiled at him warmly. "But I'm not sure it would help my father. I... don't think anyone in the Wisecraft hurt him."

"Too bad," Sigfried glowered, disappointed, whether at not raiding the Wisecraft or not getting his chance to needle the princess, Rachel could not say.

"Did you know that next year is the Year of the Dragon?" Valerie asked quickly, attempting to change the subject. "On the Lunar calendar, I mean."

"As it should be," said Siggy. He and Lucky nodded at each other. "In fact, every year should be Year of the Dragon."

"I could eat the other animals: the rat, the monkey, the cow," said Lucky, who was still wrapped around Valerie. "Then all twelve years would be mine."

"All dragon, all the time!" declared Siggy.

"The Sacred Days Club thought Lucky's appearance here at school was so propitious, they chose Lunar New Year as one of the holidays to celebrate this school year." Salome's luminous eyes sparkled. "That's why they're throwing the masquerade ball!"

Valerie finished buckling Siggy's belt. "When will it be?"

From where she lay on the table, applying polish, Salome waved her sparkling bronze fingernails. "Whenever Lunar New Year is."

Rachel wiped her eyes and consulted an almanac in her mental library. "February Tenth."

"That's something to look forward to," said Valerie. "What's the Sacred Days Club?"

"Wanna-be priests and nuns, mainly, but also people who like to party." Salome waved her painted fingernails, perhaps helping them to dry. "They hold celebrations for some of the many, many, many holidays and sacred days of the many, many, many gods and goddesses. Each September they meet with the Oracular Department to decide which of the hundreds of greater and lesser holidays it would be auspicious to celebrate on campus that year. For this year, they've picked Lunar New Year and May Day—since May Day is also the twenty-fifth anniversary of the Battle of Roanoke. Of course, Roanoke usually has some kind of party on May Day, even when it's not one of the ones the club picks."

"What about Halloween?" asked Rachel. "We celebrated that." Salome rolls her eyes. "This is the Hudson Highlands, honey. Home of the Headless Horseman? We celebrate Halloween every year."

Rachel nodded solemnly, thinking about what Salome had said for a bit. Then, the weight of her problems hit her anew, and her shoulders slumped again. Joy looked at her with concern.

"We can get him fixed, right?" insisted Joy. "Your father, I mean. Er, I guess we can't ask Agent Bridges, though, since he probably would have fixed him already, if he could, right?"

Zoë threw Joy a quick, odd look.

"I... I don't think he's going to be fixed," muttered Rachel, "not any time soon."

"No one is having me fixed!" announced Sigfried. "That's the trouble with girls, always trying to have boys fixed! But I do think we need more crazy girl powers. We might want seriously to consider bringing Miss Winters, Miss Ilium, Miss Dibble, Miss Fabian, Miss Darling, Miss Black, and Miss Wednesday into the outer circle. And that girl who wears bells in her hair. No one who did not have crazy girl powers would wear hair bells and make brooms rocket off campus. And what about Astrid, whose last name I can't remember?"

"Hollywell," murmured Rachel.

"Dibble?" Valerie looked up at her boyfriend. "Who is that?"

Joy objected, "Miss Ilium isn't our year. You can't trust people who aren't freshmen! They'll tell us not to do stuff! Or worse, tell on us!"

Sigfried replied, "Miss Dibble is on the Track and Broom team. She is the only person as good on a broom, who I have ever seen in my *entire life as a sorcerer*—which, come to think of it, covers only a period of time of about five months—as Miss Griffin, our Broom Goddess. Miss Ilium is not a freshman, but, then again, neither is Mr. Valiant, who is in the inner circle, nor Mr. Chanson, who is at least an ally—even if not officially part of the Dark Lord Hunting and Demon Irking Association."

"I am pretty sure her name is Laura Diggle, not Dibble," said Joy. "And I don't know Lena Ilium. Has anyone ever spoken to her? If Mr. Chanson wants to join our club, though, I am all for it." She sighed with a dreamy look on her face.

"Mr. Valiant is not a member of our club," Nastasia stated firmly.

Rachel, who had finally stopped sniffling, began weeping all over again.

CHAPTER TWENTY-EIGHT:

THE WAR OF CREAM AND JAM

LEAVING HER FRIENDS, RACHEL CALLED GAIUS ON THE BRACELET. She wanted to confess that this fiasco had all been her fault, to tell someone what really happened, and, most importantly, to share the burden she currently carried alone. Gaius was the only person it was safe to tell, now that her father—who had apparently also known all along—no longer remembered. However, it was not just guilt that pressed upon her. The part of her that loved sharing secrets longed to see his face when she revealed the startling things she had discovered. In particular, the most shocking secret of all: The existence of the Master of the World and the role the Romanov family played in maintaining the secrecy of the Metaplutonians.

Gaius met her on the commons, shivering in his drab green parka with its fraying sleeves.

"Sandra came to talk to Vlad," he blurted out.

"Then you know," replied Rachel.

"Rather strange, don't you think, that this accident happened so soon after your visit?"

"Nothing strange about it."

"It wasn't an accident?"

"No. The M...." Rachel looked right and left. The day was so cold that few students were out, but the commons was not empty. Two girls were adding flourishes to a snowman, and a group of others passed by on their way to the gym.

"Come on," she said. "I know a private place we can talk."

"Is it warmer?" asked Gaius, through chattering teeth.

"Much."

"I'm in."

Seated on Vroomie, Gaius's arms tight around her waist, Rachel headed for the hexagonal tower. The day was bitingly cold. Flying through the January air felt like having one's cheeks caressed by icy sandpaper. Midway, however, an idea struck her.

She swerved and flew over Roanoke Hall and on to the tall, round, stone tower that rose above the hemlocks just north of De Vere. The Watch Tower had four faux arches and four real ones. The real windows contained no glass. She flew through the south-facing arch into the round, top chamber and landed on the frozen straw. Next to her was a gigantic brass device, as large as a lighthouse lamp, with an enormous cut-crystal bulb that was much taller than she. Above it hung huge, tubular chimes.

"So this is the top of the Watch Tower!" Gaius looked around with interest. "I've never been up here. Hey, is that an obscuration lantern? Is it the one that protects the school?"

Rachel nodded. "Don't touch it. That goes... badly."

"Don't turn off the school's protective obscurations, so that we suddenly become visible to the Unwary world? Right-o."

The wind roared through the open arches. Rachel shivered, drawing her red wool coat tight around her.

Gaius, whose coat was much thinner than hers, chafed his arms. "I thought you said it would be warmer. We're several stories up. I think it's definitely colder!"

"Sorry. Brief detour," said Rachel. "I had a thought."

Here inside the belfry, the four faux windows were filled with mirrored glasses, the same size and shape as the open arches. Each glass had a colored hue, one green, one blue, one purple, and one gold. Her stomach lurched as she turned to examine the golden mirror. She had suddenly remembered that, last time she was here, it had broken when, upon discovering the horrible things that Mordeau's teacher's assistant had done to Valerie, Sigfried had punched it. To her relief, the thinking glass had been repaired.

Rachel took off her mitten and walked over to the golden glass, placing her bare hand on its surface. It was so cold that she cried out in pain. She tried remembering, but nothing appeared in the thinking glass. Rachel sighed.

"Trying to use that, are you?" Gaius asked. "Here."

He pointed his wand. The sapphire tip glinted. Suddenly an image of the belfry, from Rachel's point of view, appeared in the glass. Rachel jumped.

"Oh!" She took a step back, and then stepped forward boldly, "Thank you. Here goes!"

Rather than tell Gaius what had happened, she showed him. With her perfect memory, she recalled the entire event of her trip to London, from the moment she and Agent Bridges walked into her father's office until the Raven vanished. It was painful to recall all this, but it was a great relief as well. She had felt so weighed down, so alone, when she was the only one who knew these terrible things. Sharing them with someone else, particularly with Gaius, was a big relief. Just knowing that he was entirely on her side made everything in her life better.

She stopped at the point where the Raven left because, while she wanted to be honest and straightforward with her boyfriend, she did not think that had to include sharing her most embarrassing moments. As she considered where to pick up, Gaius laid a hand on her arm.

"R-rac-ch. T-too. C-co-ol-ld!" he stammered over the chattering of his teeth. His lips were blue.

"Right." Rachel inclined her head briskly. "Let's go!"

•••

This time, she did fly to the hexagonal tower. It took a bit of maneuvering to get them both in through the window. Upon entering the room, the difference in temperature from outside made her suddenly feel the chill. Her whole body shivered violently. As she shut the window, however, she began to enjoy the heat and sighed in delight.

Dismounting, Gaius made a beeline for the sofa and wrapped himself in the peach and cream comforter. Rachel propped Vroomie against the wall and then turned toward her boyfriend. He lifted the quilt and gestured for her to climb under it with him. Rachel did not need to be asked twice. Throwing off her red wool coat, she ran to the sofa and scooted up beside him. He pulled her onto his lap, his arms wrapping tightly around her waist.

"It's important to be under here—for the body heat. Because it's so cold," said Gaius. Leaning forward, he whispered in her ear, "It has nothing to do with my wanting to snuggle up to my ridiculously cute girlfriend."

Rachel giggled happily. She curled up against him, her head on his shoulder. It felt so warm, so pleasant, to be in his arms, surrounded by his warmth and a faint scent of lavender from the quilt. There was something illicit about breaking into a closed room she technically had no right to be in and snuggling under a blanket with an older boy. It made their closeness all the more deliciously intimate.

Gaius kissed her cheek, his lips brushing across that spot, close to her ear, that caused tingling tremors to tremble throughout her body. Rachel drew in a breath. It was the most sweet and marvelous sensation, but it scared her, too. There were things that she was not ready for yet, and this strange, grown-up tingly sensation teetered dangerously close to being one of them. And yet, at the same time, she could not help wondering why he never tried to take things further, snogging her properly, or even running his hand down her back. Why he did not at least try? In the back of her mind, she was still haunted by Claus Andrew's mocking words, suggesting that she was too young and too flat-chested to be attractive to an older boy like Gaius.

"That was cold! Brrr!" Gaius shivered once more time, still hugging her tightly. "Okay. So.... Um. That... went rather badly, didn't it? With your father, I mean."

Rachel nodded her head against his shoulder, her eyes half closed. "Yes. He got in trouble for doing whatever he did to the bricks. That's why he lost his memory."

"Yeah. That was weird. What... was that?"

"I don't know, but the princess has seen those red lines. Our Elf told her that the Raven put them there to bring her home or something. Maybe... the lines were trying to keep Father from piercing the Wall?"

"Could that be what the Wall looks like?"

"Oh!" Rachel was silent a moment. "Maybe. I always assumed the Wall was black."

"Hmm." His hand came to rest on her shoulder. "Something to look into."

His fingers gently stroked her upper arm. Rachel caught her breath. With a sigh, she leaned against his shoulder.

"So, tell me what happened," he said.

"You saw."

"I did." He frowned, still stroking her arm. "But… there are things I don't understand."

"Like what?"

"Well…" He paused, as if choosing his words carefully. "Rachel, why didn't you just do what your father asked?"

Rachel's head jerked up from his shoulder. "What?"

"He wanted you to promise to be careful, right? Why didn't you just agree?"

"I-I can't do that."

"Why not?"

"Because…." Rachel drew away from him, to clear her head. This was not the way that she had envisioned this conversation going. Sliding farther away, she waved one hand outside the comforter, as if gesturing all around her. "I could not do any of the things I do, if I agreed."

"But did you ever think, maybe you shouldn't?"

"What do you mean?" she cried.

"You're thirteen, Rachel. Not rushing into danger seems like a perfectly reasonable thing for a father to ask of his young daughter, doesn't it?"

That stung like a stubbed toe. *If she did nothing, how would she be able to impress him and Vlad? If she were the kind of person who could do what he suggested, Gaius would ever have even come to know her.*

Gaius pushed the blanket off and rose. Wandering around the hexagonal room, he tugged at the curtains and stomped on the rug a few times, making a hollow *thud.*

"When did you find this place?" he asked.

"While flying around."

"It's nice. Out of the way. I like it."

"Thanks." She brightened up a bit at that.

She had been looking forward to sharing her secret place with him. She did feel a slight qualm that another human being now knew the location of her most secret room, but he was her boyfriend. She was supposed to share her secrets with him.

Crossing back to where she sat, he fingered the peach damask slipcover. "This is rather fine quality for an abandoned school attic. It's much nicer than even our best sofa at the farm."

"I brought that from home," Rachel admitted. "The sofa underneath was rather worn."

She bounced up and down, so he could hear the rusty twang of the old springs. Gaius grinned at her and mussed her already flyaway hair. Dark strands went everywhere. This made him smile. She ducked her head, embarrassed but happy.

The sting of the mental toe-stubbing was fading. She should not be angry with him for asking questions. Wasn't that what boyfriends and girlfriends did—help each other examine and analyze their experiences?

He tapped the low coffee table with his toe. "Looks like the kind of table where ladies drink tea. Maybe with scones and clotted cream with jam on top."

"Jam on top?" Rachel straightened up. Her voice sounded particularly British, even to her ear. "Jam comes first. The Double Devon Cream goes on top."

"Ah, the age old rivalry between Cornwall and Devon," drawled Gaius. "Double Devon or Cornish Clotted? Jam on the bottom or jam on top?"

Rachel's back was now ramrod straight. Her Victorian grandmother would have been proud. "I'll have you know that milk from cows from our tenant farmers goes to make Double Devon Cream."

"Well, I will have you know," Gaius leaned against the wall next to Vroomie, "that the best clotted cream of all is made by Trewithen Dairy. They only use the milk of Cornish cows—from a twenty-five mile radius around their facility, to make sure that the milk stays fresh. And," he gestured at himself, "we are one of their suppliers. Trewithen Dairy is family owned," he drawled. "The wife's name happens to be Rachel."

That made Rachel laugh.

"I've heard of Trewithen Dairy," she said, "but I've never tried their clotted cream."

"You're in for a treat!"

Rachel smiled at him. "You've convinced me to give it a shot... but," she crossed her arms, "on the matter of where the jam goes, I shall not be budged."

Gaius came over and sat on the arm of the sofa, gesturing airily, "On that, we shall have to agree to disagree."

As they sat there, grinning at each other, Rachel's mind wandered, daydreaming. She pictured herself and Gaius married and surrounded by their six children—five great wizards and a librarian —still arguing over where the jam goes. She imagined their disagreements over tea and crumpets, with the whole family taking sides, ending with jam everywhere and cream on the tip of her nose. She imagined Gaius leaning over to wipe it off, or... kiss it off. Rachel smiled up at him, and then the smile slipped from her face.

"Gaius... I don't know what to do?" she whispered, a note of fear creeping into her voice.

He crossed and squatted before her, taking her hands. "Don't lose heart, Rach. We'll figure it out."

She swallowed, unconvinced. It must have shown on her face.

"Hey, there," he said comfortingly. "It'll be all right, sweetie. We'll find a way to get your father's memory back. Vlad has amazing resources. And, as for William, O.I.'s already working on memory issues—to help Blackie. They are sure to have a breakthrough soon. Was just your father's memory changed? What about your mother?"

"Sandra thought Father had suffered an accident. That would suggest that Mummy wasn't affected, but I don't know what she knew to begin with." Rachel sighed.

"Look, I know you feel hanging about the whole thing—"

"Hanging?" asked Rachel.

"Bad," he waved a hand. "Exhausted."

"Oh, you mean like the farmers say." Rachel nodded. She knew West Country farmers who spoke that way.

Gaius's face grew red.

When he spoke again, his whole accent had changed, returning to the crisp English sounds he normally made. Rachel realized that ever since they had spoken about farms and cream, a West Country lilt had been creeping into his voice.

"I realize you had a rather bad day, Rachel, I do."

"Don't you like sounding Cornish?" she asked.

Thinking back, she could think of other times that his Cornish accent had snuck in. She wondered why she had never realized before that he was deliberately hiding it.

"Nobody wants to be taken for a farmer," Gaius spat bitterly.

"Oh," murmured Rachel, who thought farmers were quite romantic.

They were both quiet for almost a minute.

"Rachel, you know..." Gaius began.   Then he shook his head.

"It's not my place to criticize."

At the word 'criticize' her whole system went on alert. She looked up at him, eager to show how open she was to his counsel. What might he feel she had done wrong? She was very curious.

"No. Please!" she insisted. "I want to know what you think."

"It's just that," Gaius looked very serious, "Vlad's always lecturing us about being loyal to our fathers. How that's the most important thing. Are you sure that showing preference for the Guardian over your own father was a good idea? I think it might have really hurt him—seeing you hug that... whatever that thing is. It was inconsiderate of you, Rachel. I'm rather surprised at you, really."

Rachel sucked in her breath, exactly the way she might have had she been punched in the solar plexus. Why had he picked that, of all things? The Raven had already shown her how her father felt. She already felt bad about that mistake. She had hoped that Gaius, of all people, would understand why the Raven was so important to her. She wanted to explain how lost she had felt, how terribly her father had embarrassed her, but she found herself tongue tied.

As to why she felt the way she felt toward the Raven and her father, it really did not seem like any of Gaius's business, anyway.

"You rather brought all this on yourself, Rachel," Gaius added. "If you'd shared more information with him—if you had answered him more quickly—this would not have happened."

"Oh." Rachel sat on the couch feeling unusually small for a mouse.

Gaius rose again and began pacing around the six-sided room. "I'll be totally honest, Rach, it was in part because Vlad thought that a contact in the Shadow Agency would be valuable to us that I spoke to you in the first place. Do you remember, the first few times we talked... I wanted to get a message to your father? About the new geas? And now, that connection... is lost."

"Oh," she mouthed again.

She and her friends had joked about the idea that Gaius's main interest in her had been her father. She had worried about it for a time, but then she had dismissed this concern as foolish. The revelation that there had been a grain of truth to it was disorienting.

And painful. His disapproval hurt much more than she could explain. Of course, she had asked him to speak, so she could not complain. She had been so certain that whatever he said would not bother her. But then, he had never been anything but supportive before, so how could she have foreseen how much his words would hurt her?

"But... wait," objected Rachel, haltingly. "What about Vlad and Sandra? Isn't Sandra all the connection you need to Father? She even works for the Wisecraft."

Gaius made a wide airy gesture. "Sandra is a riddle smothered in the clotted cream of enigma and slathered with the jam of mystery."

Rachel laughed in spite of herself. Her heart ached as if Gaius had taken a hacksaw to it, but she refused to let her boyfriend see that his words had cruelly pierced her. With grim determination, she swept these latest lacerations to her heart beneath her mask of calm, along with the rest of her emotional injuries.

She gave him her most arch look. "Sandra, being from Devonshire, would most definitely put her enigma cream on top of her mysterious jam!"

He leaned back, stroking his chin. "You make a good point."

They grinned at each other, a happy moment of camaraderie. Then Rachel's expression faltered. She looked down, smoothing the blanket across her lap.

"The whole thing is quite disturbing," she whispered. "I wish I was a real Griffin and not from some other world."

"From another world?" Gaius frowned thoughtfully, as if straining to remember what he had seen in the Watch Tower. "You were born here, right? Or the princess would have seen a vision of you when she first touched you. Did your father say you were not from this world? Or are you assuming it is the case, because he knew what the Guardian was?"

Rachel matched her father's intonation: "He said, 'You know why I am here, and you know why my wife is here. We cannot raise our family if you are interfering with them.' I think that means that I am from here. But I don't think we're actually from the Griffin family of England—the one that goes back sixty-four generations. I don't even know," her voice caught, "if Grandfather was my real grandfather."

Gaius frowned.

"You don't understand." She wet her suddenly dry lips. "I was given false memories, too. Only, I don't know what I'm supposed to do about them! In my new memories, nothing strange happened this fall—nothing! Not even the attack of Dr. Mordeau, which everyone else remembers! If I comment on these fake memories, my friends will know something is wrong. But what if something bad happens if I let on that I remember the real version?"

"Wait." Gaius ran a hand over his chestnut hair, ending by smoothing back his short ponytail. "Let me make sure I understand. You have fake memories, but, because of your secret—you still remember the real version, too?"

"Yes."

"Huh." He blinked. "That is...."

"Yeah," murmured Rachel.

"Wait. You said something bad... if who finds out? Is it the Raven who is attacking you? Can't you trust your secret to your friends?"

"No!" Rachel squeaked. "I mean the Raven is not my enemy. But Nastasia never puts me before her other contacts. I can't trust her with something I don't want all a whole parcel of adults to know."

"Can't you ask her to keep your secret?"

"I'll say not!" Rachel said angrily. "She's betrayed me repeatedly, Gaius. She has no loyalty to me. If I told her, she'd run home and report. And it's her family we need to hide from."

"From Magical Australia?" Gaius gave her a skeptical look. "Are emus out to get you?"

Rachel almost laughed, but the truth was too awful. "The Romanov family is in charge. Of the Earth. They can order the Guardian around."

Gaius stared, as if he were having trouble comprehending what she was saying.

"They're in charge? Why? Wait, but they're in Australia!" He seemed stuck on repeat.

Sitting down beside her, he hugged her tightly.

"Do you think Vlad knows?" Rachel asked intently. "About the Romanovs? I doubt it, or he would not have touched the princess and angered her family. Should we tell him?"

Gaius shook his head. "I am not going to tell him. It might get him mind blanked. We can't afford to lose him. Also, we only know the rather convoluted things your father said—some random comment to the Guardian about him not being Romanov. I am not sure it made sense. There's definitely information missing. Maybe left out on purpose."

"No! We know a lot more than that," Rachel said slowly. "*He* came in my room… the other Romanov. The one the princess had forgotten, until she was under the influence of the *Spell of True Recitation*. I don't know his name, but I call him the Master of the World. He…." Her voice dropped to a whisper. "The Raven had to pretend to change my memories. That's why I have a fake set. Jariel did promise to keep protecting you, though, so I could talk to you."

Rachel watched his face hopefully, waiting for the significance of all this sank in, for him to be impressed with the magnitude of what she had discovered, but Gaius just looked stunned.

"That's good. I think," he murmured, blinking. "I hope he can keep his word. Otherwise, we'll all end up without our memories. We'll probably forget about magic entirely and take up knitting those crazy jumpers for chickens."

"Is knitting chicken jumpers something that's done?"

"In Cornwall. I used to think the idea was bonkers. After our flight to the Watch Tower, though.... Well, if I was a chicken, I think I might want a jumper on a day like today!"

Rachel pictured a chicken yard, such as those kept by her family's tenant farmers, but with a dozen hens in brightly-colored sweaters.

"Are you going to knit jumpers for your chickens?" she asked.

"I live on a commercial farm," drawled Gaius. "We raise ninety-six thousand chicks at a time."

"Oh. That would take a lot of yarn!"

"Yes. Yes, it would."

Rachel gave him a wan smile. "There is one good thing. I don't think Father remembers the fake argument from the fake memory chain. That means that he and I still haven't argued about you. We spoke about me having a boyfriend very briefly, but not long enough for it to be considered an argument."

"There is that positive side," said Gaius, but she could tell he was not paying attention.

Rachel hugged him, looking up at him, searching for comfort and encouragement. He hugged her back, but his expression remained distracted, as if his mind could not quite comprehend all that she had revealed. Sighing, Rachel closed her eyes. She felt even more as if she were facing these terrible things alone than she had before she had told her boyfriend.

CHAPTER TWENTY-NINE:

MOVING DAY

GAIUS REMAINED DISTRACTED FOR SEVERAL DAYS.

Rachel tried to make herself available to him, in case he wanted to talk, but she did not pry. Unfortunately, he did not seem to wish to talk. After she had been so eager to discuss with him all that occurred, it made her sad that he did not share his distress with her. She would have felt bad about having distressed him, except that she had so needed help bearing the burdens weighing upon her that she did not regret telling him. His facing these hard things with her was a bit like him taking a blow for her. She resolved to feel grateful rather than guilty.

As the week went on, Gaius recovered his normal good spirits, but Rachel found herself slipping deeper and deeper into gloom. The more she thought about her father losing his memory, the more upset she became. The very thought of not remembering something was enough to make her feel ill. To be the cause of such a calamity, and to have the victim be someone she loved so much—her father, the dashing and capable Agent Griffin, The Duke of Devon upon whom so many depended—left her completely devastated.

She tried to regain her composure and cheer. Each time she noticed herself faltering, she bucked up and attempted to push her fears aside. However, for the first time in her life, it just did not work. Every time she raised her chin and straightened her back, she would suddenly find herself slumping and close to tears again.

As time passed, she felt more and more dazed by the burden of her own fake memories. She was afraid to talk to her friends, afraid to say the wrong thing, afraid of the Master of the World. It was not for herself that she was afraid. What was the worst that could be done to her? She might somehow be made to forget for real, too? A horrible fate, but no worse than her father's. No, her fear was all for the Raven. *What would the Master of the World do if he discovered that Jariel had tricked him?*

For the next two weeks, she went about her daily routine in a daze. She did not smile. She did not chat with her friends. She was even late for class. Once, she did not show up at all. Everywhere she went, except classes, she carried the plushy lion Sandra had bought her with its bright red bow, clutching it tightly.

At breakfast and dinner, which she spent with her dorm mates, she filled her plate, but she ate no more than a few bites. Instead, she sat pushing her food around with her fork and pretending that she had eaten it. At first, she feared her friends would notice and question her, but they showed no sign of noticing.

No one noticed.

Siggy was as loud and as boisterous as ever, but he had never been very observant when it came to the behavior of girls—except, of course, that if food was not being eaten, he and Lucky were always there to finish it off. Rachel suspected that the concept of someone not eating, when food was available, was not one that ever occurred to Sigfried Smith.

The princess had been withdrawn since the trip during which she had lost Zoë, becoming even quieter than before. Rachel felt she should be doing something to help her friend, such as gently pushing to find out what troubled Nastasia. But that would require her to gather the energy to open her mouth and speak, which she found herself unable to do.

Valerie only came around to hang out with Sigfried. Thinking back, Rachel realized with a sinking heart that this was always the case. She had tried a number of times in the early part of the school year to reach out to the other girl, hoping they would become friends, but somehow it had never quite worked. Valerie treated Rachel kindly, but if Sigfried was not around, she hung out with Salome or other girls from Dee Hall. She certainly did not respond to the fact that Rachel was unusually silent. In fact, even the time when Rachel had been absorbed in vectors and physics, Valerie had come to investigate only because she had been prompted by Sigfried.

As for her other friends, Joy had eyes only for Siggy and Nastasia. Zoë was more cheerful than she had been before Agent Bridges's visit, but she, too, now doted on the princess. Also, she had become meaner and more caustic than she had been before her disappearance. Maybe she needed help, too, but Rachel could not gather the energy needed to inquire.

Rachel excused the princess and Zoë's behavior, telling herself that they, too, had suffered terrible things; however, this did not make her feel any less lonely. Worse, she realized that, even if she found the strength of will to do so, she could not choose to put her own woes aside and comfort them — because that would have required that she talk about events she was supposed to have forgotten.

Gaius might have noticed her distress, once he recovered his aplomb. He was wiser in the ways of girls than Sigfried and more solicitous of her well-being; however, he never had the chance — because one time that she routinely felt cheerful was in his company. She now spent all her lunches at Vlad's table. She would feel just as bad when she arrived for lunch as she did at breakfast and dinner. But when she sat down with Gaius and his friends, she found herself talking and laughing normally. By the time the midday meal was over each day, she had emptied her plate. A couple of times, she even went back for seconds.

So Gaius had no opportunity to detect that anything was wrong. The rest of the time, however, it was as if she traveled beneath her own personal black cloud. The darkness encroaching upon the edges of her thoughts grew worse, as did the buzzing — like the beating wings of a thousand locusts. As this strange distant noise grew louder, Rachel began to feel quite frightened. She had never heard tell of anything like this before. *What was happening to her?*

The strangest thing was: she could not bring herself to eat, or talk — except during lunch — but neither could she bring herself to slack off. No matter how dark her days became, Rachel diligently did all that was required of her. Every day, like clockwork, she rose, went to class, did her homework, and practiced — practiced her sorcery, practiced her flying, practiced balancing on a balance beam. Even the one time she could not rouse herself from bed and missed a class, she spent the period reading the textbook. An inner voice kept whispering to her that eventually things would get so bad that she would stop doing what was required of her. To date, that little voice had been wrong.

There was something pathetic, almost frightening, about the fact that, even in such misery, she could not seem to break her routine and stop studying.

• • •

Wednesday morning, Rachel stood in the kitchen, trying to find something that looked appealing. She did not feel up to eating pancakes, but the cinnamon-swirled bread dotted with raisins actually smelled good. She watched her piece warm above the toasting grill, carefully choosing cream cheese and honey to go with it. When it was done, browned and crispy, it smelled so good that she spread on the toppings and ate a few bites on the spot.

As she turned to go back to her table, she heard a throaty laugh. Eunice Chase leaned against a wall and waved a hand in her direction. "Get her, girls!"

Rachel spun around. Belladonna Marley stood with her posse of friends, Charybdis Nutt, Zenobia Jones, sophomore Lola Spong, who bore an uncanny resemblance to a dark toad, and another sophomore from Drake, slender and leggy with short hair, whom Rachel did not know.

The girls all held cups and bowls. They converged on Rachel and dumped the contents of everything they held over her head. Tomato juice, jelly, maple syrup, and less easily identifiable but equally gooey substances poured down over Rachel's head and robes. Lola even paused to rub syrup into Rachel's hair. The Drake girls then all ran away, laughing and high-fiving each other; while Rachel stood, dripping, her slice of toast now ruined with tomato juice and lard.

• • •

The cantrip she had learned from Gaius only removed liquids, not stickiness. Rachel ran back to her dorm and took a shower, leaving her ruined robe in the laundry bin and adding extra honey from the bottle they kept in the room for this purpose into the bowl of milk outside the door. She arrived late for her first class and sat down in the first available chair. This happened to be next to Astrid, who rewarded her with a grateful smile. Rachel, however, was forced to endure Nastasia shooting her resentful pouting glances from across the room. Rachel spent the rest of Language with wet hair, sneezing and glowering when she recalled Eunice Chase's smug, superior expression, as the older girl had stood, arms crossed, watching her minions humiliate their defenseless prey.

She spent the free period between Language and Math brushing out her hair and getting warm. Then came Math, where she would have to face the same girls who had just humiliated her in the kitchen. They snickered behind their hands when she arrived. Rachel lowered the rim of her mortarboard cap and sat down with Nastasia and Joy, who was telling everyone how the princess could solve air pollution by breathing. Zenobia mocked Joy, claiming the princess must be able to end world hunger with other bodily functions, and Belladonna laughed outright, looking down on Nastasia through her heavy mascara.

Rachel realized Joy did not say these things at the princess's behest. If anything, Nastasia was more disturbed by Miss O'Keefe's worshipful behavior than Rachel. And yet it made it harder for Rachel to like the princess when the whole world was singing her praises.

Toward the end of the class, Mrs. MacDannan closed her book, removed her mortarboard, pushed her round glasses up onto her head, and made an announcement. A black and white rat sat on her shoulder, hidden beneath her bushy ginger hair. "With the end of January comes the end of our first semester. And with that comes Moving Day. On Moving Day, anyone who would like to change dormitories may do so."

Seth Peregrine raised his hand, waving it back and forth so vigorously that it set the tassel on his cap to waggling. When Mrs. Mac-Dannan called on him, he asked, "Do a lot of people change dorms?"

"Every year is different," replied the tutor crisply.

"Mrs. MacDannan," asked Charybdis Nutt, who, like Belladonna, had taken to wearing heavy eye shadow and mascara, "why does each Art have its own dorm? Why don't people just live wherever they want to?"

"Yes, what keeps things the way they are?" challenged Zenobia

Jones. "Tradition? Stereotypes? Group loyalty? The good old boys system?"

"Group loyalty?" scoffed Zoë Forrest, where she slumped in her chair, only half paying attention. Her hair was neon orange today.

"Since when is an Art a group?"

"Yeah, isn't this some kind of artificial attempt," asked Seth, "by the school to pretend that people who practice the same kind of magic have more in common than they otherwise naturally would? Like when your mom tries to get you to play with the kids of her college chums, even though they are total losers?"

Scarlett MacDannan looked around for her glasses and then, with a sigh, remembered they were on top of her head. She slipped them back onto her nose. "Mr. Peregrine, Miss Jones, Miss Nutt, I happen to be the perfect person to answer that question. In the history of Roanoke Academy, I am the only person who has lived in all seven dorms."

She held up her fingers with their seven rings of mastery. The students were well aware of her accomplishments, and yet, it still impressed them all to see her rings, their different-colored gems glinting brightly in the sunlight streaming in the window.

"You want to know why thaumaturges live in Drake, and Enchanters live in Dare?" she continued. "Well, I will tell you. Or better yet, you will tell me. Miss Jones, what's downstairs in Drake Hall?"

"Musty hallways filled with dust?" replied Zenobia. When Mrs. MacDannan gave her a probing look, the tall young woman added meekly, "You mean the Summoning Chambers?"

"And what do you do in a Summoning Chamber?" asked the tutor.

"Oh, I know!" Belladonna raised her hand but charged ahead without waiting to be called upon. "You summon up monsters, elemental fey, demi-gods, celestial and chthonic entities—so you can get charges of their power."

"Right," nodded Scarlett MacDannan, "and what's in Dare Hall, other than dormitories?"

Nastasia raised her hand. When called upon, she spoke politely. "A theater, a music room with a small stage, and rooms for practicing instruments."

Their tutor nodded. "And can anyone tell me what is in Marlowe?"

Joy raised her hand, "Oh! Oh! I can! Some of my sisters live there. They have art rooms, clay, potters' wheels. A gallery. Things like that."

"Very good, Miss O'Keefe. And Spenser Hall?"

"I have sisters there, too," continued Joy, "Every object is labeled in the Original Tongue. Every door and stair and window has the correct word taped to them. And the walls are covered with paintings and posters of ordinary things: cats, hats, baseball bats. Each one is labeled. So if you live there, Language class automatically becomes much easier. Also, they have rooms with listening crystals, so you can hear what cantrips are supposed to sound like."

Rachel started to raise her hand to ask what the purpose of *permanent* labels was. *Oh. Of course.* She yanked her arm down again, embarrassed.

Mrs. MacDannan nodded. "De Vere Hall?"

Wolfgang Starkadder spoke up from where he sat brooding in the darkest part of the room, out of the sunlight. "My brother Beowulf lives there. The place is full of heavy doors that are always closed. Each door has three pictures carved into it—of three different fey or monsters. A rope hangs from the door. They put stuff on the rope—a stone with a hole in it, a daisy chain, a red thread. You have to know what that particular object stops—and touch it to the correct picture—to open the door. So, if you go in there, and you don't know your wardings, that's it for you." He ran his finger across his throat. "You're stuck. Beo says three students have starved to death, just in the last decade, stuck between two fire doors, unable to remember the correct combination to get out. Course, if they died rather than trying all of a whole three options, they were too dumb to live, and the dorm did the rest of us a favor."

"Thank you, Mr. Starkadder for your illuminating remarks. I am certain our days have been brightened," said Mrs. MacDannan wryly. "And Dee?"

Rachel raised her hand. When she was acknowledged, she blurted out, "Dee is a library. It's filled with books!"

Something about the way she said it must have caught Scarlett MacDannan's attention. The tutor's and Rachel's eyes met, and, for an instant, their mutual love of books ignited a bond between them.

"Very good." Their stern tutor actually smiled. "Dee was my second choice, when I was a student. I lived there for a whole year. I loved it."

"Is that where you started?" asked Astrid timidly.

Scarlett MacDannan shook her head. "I started in Raleigh. You're allowed to practice alchemy on the inanimate objects in Raleigh Hall. Or the objects that used to be inanimate. The doors all talk. Some of them are rather surly. Windows open on their own. There were four different magical methods of going up stairs. For instance, if you sit on the banister, you automatically slide up to the top of the staircase. That part was fun. Ultimately, however, I decided the place was too dangerous and distracting. Which is why I first moved, Moving Day of my freshman year."

Rachel listened with interest, curious now about the other dorms. She had loved Dee Hall since she was little. She thought of the photo of the impressive edifice that she had kept under her bed. She had been so resentful that she had been placed in Dare, with her siblings, without ever being given the chance to choose. Then she sat back in her chair, her eyes unusually wide.

Should she move?

She could be free. Free of Joy's sycophantic behavior, free of Zoë's caustic comments, free of Nastasia's petulant pouting. She could live surrounded by books, books, and more books, with books everywhere.

Gaius had wanted to live in Dee. He understood its appeal. She wished she could call him on her card or the bracelet, but she knew that he was in class and unable to converse. Reaching surreptitiously into her sleeve, she pulled out the photo Valerie had given her of a disoriented Gaius wrapped in a pink towel. She gazed at it: What would he do?

"Mrs. MacDannan, what was your first choice?" asked the tiny Magdalene Chase, who was sitting beside the silent Cydney Graves.

"I beg your pardon?" asked the tutor. "Ouch! Thorin, stop that!"

Reaching under the back of her bushy red hair, she drew out her familiar, holding him by his tail. She gave the white and black spotted rat a sharp look, as if, perhaps, he had pulled her hair, and lowered him to the table, where he sat on her Euclid, alert and bright-eyed.

"You said your second choice was Dee," Magdalene explained. "What was your first?"

"Dare Hall," said Scarlett MacDannan.

"Why Dare?" asked Sigfried.

"I liked the people."

Several students snickered.

"People such as Finn MacDannan," giggled Charybdis.

Belladonna, Zenobia, and two of the boys from Drake put their heads together and hummed a few bars of a popular tune from the band Bogus. Seth and Zoë joined them.

"My affection for Finvarra MacDannan is well-known," Mrs. MacDannan crossed her arms, looking dryly amused. "Obviously, I admire him. Otherwise, I would not have married him." More seriously, she added, "But it was more than Finn. The people in Dare were truly imaginative, and they could solve problems. In Raleigh, the alchemist students experimented a lot. They liked to try new things. But they were not particularly… effective. Their experiments were as likely to go awry as to work. So, yes. I liked Finn. But it was Finn's sister and James Darling who really impressed me. They were a very effective pair."

"You mean Ellyllon MacDannan, who went on to become Mrs. Darling?" giggled Joy.

Mrs. MacDannan shook her head.

"You mean Wendy MacDannan?" Rachel asked softly.

"Yes." Their tutor nodded briskly. "My niece, Wendy Darling, who is in your class, is named for her. In fact, Wendy—the original Wendy—reminded me a bit of you, Miss Griffin."

"Really, why is that?" asked Rachel, startled.

"She was an ace on a steeplechaser."

Rachel recalled Mr. Badger's comment: *There's no one who can outfly a little girl on a steeplechaser!* Her lips parted in awe. Could the practice room in the gym have been set up by Wendy MacDannan?

"They're both crazy?" shouted Charybdis, who had apparently missed the comment about the steeplechaser. This sparked a great deal of laughter from the Drake students.

Mrs. MacDannan gave them a long steady look. But, to Rachel's surprise, the tutor was not the only one who came to her defense.

Joy O'Keefe jumped to her feet. "Will you all stop picking on Rachel! What is it with you losers? I saw what you did to her at breakfast. Are you so lame that you have to pick on little girls half your size? You do something like that again, and your hair will turn a much worse color than puke green! It will be on fire! Right, Lucky?" She sat down.

Lucky, who had been sunning himself on the table, raised his head and blew out a long plume of red-orange flame in the direction of the Drake girls. Charybdis screamed.

A warm glow spread slowly through Rachel, temporarily driving back a little bit of the darkness. Maybe she could not talk to her friends about her memory troubles, but suddenly she did not feel as alone.

"Mr. Dragon." Scarlett MacDannan lowered her glasses and glared over the top of them. Her rat had leapt up, startled. He scampered up her body and hid under her bushy hair again. "Please behave yourself, if you wish to remain in my class."

Sigfried said casually, "Lucky's last name is Smith."

But Lucky hung his head. "Yes, Ma'am."

The Dare kids were used to Lucky talking, but the Drake students gaped in amazement.

"It talked!" cried Cydney Graves, who had not spoken in weeks, except to answer the tutor's direct questions.

"Cool!" grinned Napoleon Powers, slicking back his dark hair. "Talking dragon! Where can I get one of those?"

Recovering from her Lucky-induced fright, Charybdis Nutt waved her hand, "Ooo! Ooo! Is it true that the alchemy tutor, Mr. Fisher, was dating Wendy Darling before she went... you know... totally bonkers?"

Scarlett MacDannan pinned Charybdis with such a fierce look that the girl quailed.

"It is *not true*." Their tutor's eyes snapped with anger. "And that is quite enough. Class, please turn to *Euclid Book Two*, Proposition 18."

The class returned to their work, unwilling to push the fiery-tempered teacher. Rachel's eyes rested on the page, but she had memorized all of Euclid's Propositions two years ago. Her thoughts returned to the subject of Moving Day.

Dee Hall called to her. It was the place she had dreamed of living for so many years. It had also been Gaius's first choice. She would have bookshelves in her walls, bookshelves under her stairs, bookshelves in her doors, and libraries for common rooms. She could live surrounded by books, books, books, and more books. Should she move into this book-lover's paradise?

It was tempting, so tempting.

More than her room would change, however, if she moved. Her classes would change, too. She would be in the Dee Hall core group, with Valerie Hunt, Wanda Zukov, and Rowan Vanderdecken—the granddaughter of the captain of the Flying Dutchman and the great-granddaughter of Old Thom, the sailor ghost Rachel had helped after the Dead Man's Ball—as well as with a few other students. *Did she want that?*

She glanced over at Nastasia, who gave her a kind, encouraging smile; at Joy, who was still red in the face from her outburst but who winked at Rachel and gave her a thumbs-up; at Sigfried, who was whispering to Lucky and glaring at their tutor; and at Astrid, who usually spoke to no one, but who now gave her a timid, shy smile.

Scarlett Mallory MacDannan was correct. It was the people who made Dare Hall worth calling home.

CHAPTER THIRTY:

THE WEAPON

DEEP WITHIN OUR HEART

AFTER WEEKS OF SNOW AND FROST, THE WEATHER GREW WARM IN early February. It rained for three days straight, melting the snow that had carpeted the campus since November. There had been no sign of the Heer since he retreated to Dunderberg, so it was decided that classes should continue. Even with the great, floating umbrellas hovering rim to rim above the gravel paths, walking between the buildings meant splashing through large puddles. Everything was wet, rainy, and gray, almost as if the world itself wept with Rachel.

Even cloudy weather could not dampen the spirits of the general student body, however. The approaching ball in honor of the Year of the Dragon was fast becoming the main topic of conversation. Students rushed to find partners and assemble costumes. As the masquerade was being sponsored by the Sacred Days Club, Nastasia decided to enroll in the club, eager to become involved in the choosing of decorations and future events. Joy immediately volunteered to join, as well. They tried to convince Rachel to join them, but she was unable to muster the necessary enthusiasm.

The dark mood that enveloped her, despite her best efforts to dispel, it was not improved by the letter she received from her father. He wrote that she should not worry. He would be fine. He called her Little Dart, which he had not done since she first started flying, nearly two years before. Seeing it on the page brought tears to her eyes. It drove home the truth, that he had forgotten everything since then. At the bottom of his note, he thanked her for the origami griffin. The envelope also contained a stack of pretty origami paper that he noted came from her mother.

The Tuesday Morning before the ball, word spread among the students that the melting snow had caused the creek to flood the forest to the north, above the waterfalls, and there would be a school-wide skating party that evening.

Rachel did not feel like moving, much less trekking uphill for twenty minutes in the cold of the late afternoon. However, she loved skating. She loved the hemlock forest to the north, too. When the others insisted she accompany them, she sighed and tagged along.

They went to the gym and took skates from a large locker behind one of the doors. Like all conjured item, the skates would last twenty-four hours. Then they all trekked across campus, past Roanoke Hall, and into the forest behind it. The weather had grown cold again, and it had snowed for an hour or so earlier in the afternoon, so that a light dusting of white powder lay over everything. Rachel walked along, swinging her skates by the blades and listening to the girls chatter and the boys boast. As they headed up the hill toward the designated skating area, Rachel heard a familiar voice. Ivan Romanov strolled by her group, surrounded by several laughing college girls.

A spasm of black wrath seized Rachel. She *hated* Ivan! She *hated* his grandfather! She hated everything! How could he be so handsome and cavalier when such horrible things were done by his family!

These dark thoughts stayed with her during the long walk. Finally, her group crested the hill and came to where the creek normally flowed. The whole forest floor was flooded, as far as Rachel could see. Water spread between the hemlock trunks, quiet and dark, a striking contrast to the whiteness of the newly fallen snow.

"How can we skate on that?" asked Joy. "It's wet."

Her sister Faith, the dark haired O'Keefe who worked in the Storm King Café, chuckled, "Watch and learn, O lowly Padawan."

Two lovely Asian girls with chestnut hair walked forward and knelt in the snow at the water's edge. One was younger with a cheerful smile, her hair piled high upon her head. The older one was more somber with short bangs and long straight locks. They bore a family resemblance.

The two sisters leaned over and touched the water. Feathers of ice extended from their fingertips across the surface, forming fractals and jagged patterns. The spread of ice was slow at first. Then, with a soft crackling, it began to move across the waters and between the dark trunks until the ice spread at lightning speeds. As the effect spread downward, the surface grew opaque. Soon the entire body of floodwater beneath the hemlocks was one solid block of ice.

Gasps of delight rose from the watching crowd. The two girls stood up and bowed low. The gathered throng clapped and sat down in the snow or on the ice to fasten on their skates.

"Who are they?" Rachel asked Faith.

"The Ko girls," Faith replied, as she unlaced her pretty white skates.

Rachel's eyes grew wide. "You mean, as in Chancellor Ko?"

When Faith nodded, Rachel looked at the girls with more interest. Their father was Snireth Ko, the leader of the Parliament of the Wise. Chancellor Ko's wife, she recalled, was a frost maiden.

Faith returned to lacing her skates. Rachel noticed that, like Faith, all her friends had chosen white skates. She looked down. Hers were black. That meant that in her gloom-induced daze, she had accidentally picked boys' skates. She had no objection to wearing black skates but had she picked the correct size? Men's sizes and women's sizes differed.

Sitting down, she soon confirmed that her skates were two sizes too big. With ice skates, a proper fit was very important. They needed to be snug around the ankle. These wobbled like a Bongo Board. There was no way she could skate in them.

Rachel watched as the first few people who had taken to the ice swirled and glided. Eve March spun in a tight circle, her hands in the air like a ballerina on a music box. Her brother Joshua zipped between tree trunks with consummate grace. To the left, a college boy from Marlowe conjured a puck and a pile of hockey sticks, with the help of his familiar, a marmoset. He threw a stick to Joshua, who caught it, grinning.

Other young men gathered, and one or two girls. A group of boys from Drake joined the hockey players. Among them were the sullen dark-skinned college student with sunglasses and his friend with freckles and stringy red hair whom Rachel recognized from the battle in the Summoning Chamber under Drake Hall her first week of school. They had been among the geased students whom Dr. Mordeau had ordered to attack the campus. The boy from Marlowe scowled and told them that they needed to provide their own hockey sticks. The young man in the sunglasses objected loudly that this was unfair, as everyone knew that thaumaturges were not good at conjuring. The conjurers merely snickered.

Another young man with the Drake crowd, serious-looking and scholarly, with brown hair that hung in his eyes—Rachel knew, from the Knights of Walpurgis, that his name was Herbert Sorrows—shrugged and said that he could not do hockey sticks, but he had some experience making tools. With the help of his snake, which he carried concealed beneath his coat, he conjured long-handled pickaxes for him and his friends. Turning them upside-down, they began hitting a puck around with the metal tips and laughing raucously. The boy from Marlowe objected. The Drake boys scowled and skated off among the trees to play their own dangerous game of pickaxe-hockey with several other boys from their own dorm.

Closer to Rachel, some girls were trying figure-skating moves, gliding with one foot in the air or executing perfect turns. One girl in a pretty gold and green skating outfit even dared a twirling jump. Some of those still lacing their skates clapped, impressed. Nearby, a group of girls from De Vere—including the pink-haired Kris Serenity Wright, her roommates Rhiannon Cosgrove, and the dryad's daughter—were playing tag on the ice. Also among the De Vere girls, Rachel spotted Chalandra Druess looking snug and warm in Laurel's old winter jacket. She waved to Rachel as she skated by.

Rachel gazed longingly at the ice. Then she looked over her shoulder down the hill that she had just climbed. It would take the better part of an hour to go back, switch her skates, and come back again. She sighed, too heavy of heart to lug herself all that way.

Something soft rubbed against her leg. Rachel looked down. A small and tawny Lion, the size of a house cat, purred in the snow beside her. Rachel squatted and stroked his golden mane. The little beast felt warm and comforting, like curling up in a big chair with a favorite book. It licked her nose with its rough, pink tongue.

"Is it true," Rachel asked suddenly, "that your father made Sig-fried?"

"It is." The tiny Lion purred.

Rachel blinked. Her blood brother had been made by an emperor? Was he actually a robot? Was that why she had grown dizzy when the two of them mingled their blood during the blood brother ceremony?

"Leander," Rachel knelt and stroke the tiny feline's soft fur. She spoke in a soft sigh, "I am so tired of being angry. Isn't there…something I can do? All these terrible things that happened. I think my visit to my father went awry, in part, because I was still angry at him —from the time Gaius ended up in the Halls of Healing. I know that was Peter's fault, but, at the time, I thought otherwise. And now I can't seem to forgive my father."

The tiny Lion batted at a clump of snow. The impromptu snow-ball slid across the ice.

"It is the same thing with Ivan Romanov! I know that Laurel does not want to marry him. She has a stealth boyfriend. And yet…" She shrugged helplessly.

The Comfort Lion spoke in his rich, deep voice. The words seemed to come from both inside and outside her head. "Forgive-ness is not a simple thing, child. Some will tell you it is ignoring a slight or an injury. That is not so. You must accept in your heart that someone has harmed you. Then, you must be willing to release the pain they have caused. It will not be possible, unless you can truly release the person who has hurt you from responsibility. Remember, it is an act of kindness. It is giving a gift to someone, and a gift is not something that is deserved. It is so much harder to imagine giving a gift to someone you dislike than someone you love, is it not?"

Rachel thought about that. It made a strange kind of sense. "I guess…actually, that's not so hard. Imagining giving them a gift. I'll work on that."

The little tawny feline put its paw on her knee. Its golden eyes bore into hers. "Do not render evil for evil, or insult for insult. In-stead, be forgiving, and know that as I have asked this of you, I shall bless you. The only way to overcome evil is with good."

Rachel nodded and petted the little creature, her interest piqued by the thought that she might receive a blessing. Rising, she gazed over at where Ivan was sitting on a fallen log, lacing his skates. He seemed so repugnant, sitting there cheerfully oozing charm. Could she bear to give *him* a gift? And, if so, what?

Rachel patted her coat and robes, searching for something she could give away. Her robes contained two pencils, a small pocket knife inset with mother-of-pearl, hairclips, the key-shaped lightning charm Sigfried had given her, and a pack of tissues. In the pocket of her red wool coat, she found some lavender lip balm, two bottles of Bogey Away left from Yule, and a blue origami crane that she had made that morning with her mother's gift paper. The pencils and the lip balm had been used. He probably had his own lightning charm, nearly everyone on campus did. The knife and the lavender spray struck her as hard to explain, and she was not even going to consider the hairclips or the pink and blue package of tissues. She looked back at the crisply-folded, blue paper crane.

Should she give it to him?

But if she forgave him, she would not be able to enjoy hating him anymore.

Rachel started. Was that what she really thought? *Did she want to hate him? What a vile thing!*

Closing her eyes, she imagined walking up and handing him the crane. She imagined him smiling his handsome smile. His offenses against her, and those of his family, pressed upon her. *Were not the Romanovs the ones who had robbed her father of his memories?* She deliberately ignored these nagging thoughts and concentrated on the joy of giving.

Her hatred popped like a soap bubble. One moment, its cold harshness held her like a vise, a prisoner of dark revenge fantasies. By the next, the burden had lifted. She was not even certain why her anger had felt so important. She felt free. *It was the most wonderful feeling.*

Rachel crossed the ice in her boots, sliding carefully over to where Ivan sat. Arriving beside him, she extended her arm, straight, with the crane resting on her palm. "Sorry about being so mad at you."

He took the blue paper bird and flashed her a clean, charming smile. "Well, this is a fine gift, I must say! I apologize that my jests were taken more than lightly. I will be more careful in the future. Don't take it the wrong way, your sister's a wonderful young lady."

Rachel rolled her eyes. "She was holding out on me. She has a stealth boyfriend!"

Ivan did not seem to know what to do with that information.

"I hope you find someone almost as nice as my sister to marry," Rachel added kindly.

He nodded. "Me, too."

As Rachel walked away, she felt much lighter of heart than she had in some time. Cheered, she looked around. *Whom else could she forgive?*

Many people were on the ice now. Some glided elegantly. Others stumbled and fell or shuffled stiff-legged from tree trunk to tree trunk. Wanda Zukov skated by, followed by her mini-polar bear. She waved to Rachel. Nearby, loud snarling and barking erupted as a dog fight broke out between several canine familiars. Shouts rang out as the owners tried to break up the battle.

When the yapping and growling died away, strains of *The Skaters' Waltz* could be heard floating among the merrymakers. Glancing around, Rachel saw the Ginger Snaps—a musical group consisting of the ginger-haired MacDannans, their cousins the Darlings, and a few of their friends—were playing on the ice. Oonagh had put her tuba aside in favor of a violin. Rachel caught glimpses of Eve March, Panther Fabian, Iolanthe Towers, and other young women dancing to the music on their skates.

Rachel paused to listen to her favorite waltz. Over by a clump of birches, Eunice Chase skated with a few girls from her class. Rachel recoiled. There was *no* way she was forgiving *her*. After all the humiliations she had suffered at Eunice's hands this winter, she would enjoy hating her forever!

Then, Rachel remembered: Eunice's parents had been arrested this fall.

She looked at Eunice more closely. The older girl was laughing loudly, but her laughter sounded forced. How sad and weary she looked. It came to Rachel suddenly that this young woman might not be so mean, if she were not deeply unhappy. And Rachel, who had overheard Eunice's interview with the Agents, knew that the other girl had much about which to be unhappy. Her parents had been part of Mortimer Egg's murderous cabal.

Rachel's anger evaporated, leaving only a feeling of compassion. It would not change the way that Eunice treated her, of course, nor make the petty behavior of her minions easier to stomach, but the older girl's meanness no longer hurt Rachel's feelings. *It was a start.*

Smiling, Rachel looked around again. Her eyes fell on John Darling. Though she tried for over a minute, she could not think of a single nice thing about him. She did not feel ready to forgive him yet. Behind him, however, was someone she most certainly should forgive.

• • •

Rachel tugged at the sleeve of her sister Laurel. "I don't suppose you could conjure me a pair of skates that fit?"

Laurel turned and scowled at her. Rachel smiled, her eyes full of hope and love. Laurel's scowl died away, and she gave her little sister a big grin.

"Of course, I can! Anything for my little sister. What color would you like them?"

"Purple," said Rachel, because purple was the color of enchanters, and she wished to celebrate her new loyalty to Dare Hall.

Now that she had decided not to leave the dormitory on Moving Day, she was beginning to feel proud to be living among the Enchanters. Of the entire group of freshmen in Dare Hall, only David Jordan had decided to move. He and his familiar, a mouse named EPD (short for Electronic Pointing Device) had left for Raleigh to live among the alchemists. The rest of the inhabitants of Dare were, as Joy had put it, happy to be stuck with each other.

Laurel led her over to a fallen tree and had her sit down. Taking off Rachel's shoes, Laurel ran her hands over her little sister's feet and ankles. Then she put her fingertips together and pointed them upwards.

Laurel's first three tries looked nothing like skates.

"Oh, this is so difficult without Tormie! He's snug and warm back at the dorm, the lazy tom! Even if I could rouse him, it would take him twenty minutes to get here. Let me try again."

Tormie was Laurel's familiar. In a family where the cats all had names like Moonbeam, Starshine, Evenstar, and Mistletoe, Laurel had named hers Tormenter of Mice.

"Um… could someone else's familiar help?"

"Only if I could talk to it."

"Shouldn't be a problem." Rachel's eyes sparkled. She pulled out her mirror and called. "Lucky, could you come by for a moment."

A bolt of gold and fiery red dropped from the sky, landing next to them.

"What can I do for you, small brainy blood-sister?" asked Lucky the Dragon.

"Can you help my sister conjure?" asked Rachel curiously.

"Sure thing." Lucky looked up, as if he could see something over Laurel's head. Laurel was gaping at the talking dragon with her mouth hanging open. Rachel reached over and pushed on her sister's chin. Laurel shut her mouth with a snap.

"Talking dragon familiar," murmured her sister. "Um. Right."

This time, when Laurel said the Word of Becoming and drew her hand down, Lucky waved a silver-bottomed claw. A beautiful pair of silver skates with bright purple laces appeared out of a puff of mist just in front of her sister, who caught them and handed them to Rachel.

"Thank you, funny dragon." Laurel scratched Lucky behind his horns.

"Ah, yeah! That's the spot!" He made a noise of happy contentment before zipping off again with an, "Okay, gotta go. Boss needs me."

Rachel waved from where she sat on the fallen tree. Then, she watched as Laurel slipped the new silver and purple skates onto her little sister's feet and began lacing them up for her.

"How come Sandra was on the Student Council, and you're not?" she asked Laurel. "Is it because you're a wild child?"

Laurel paused, snorting with amusement. "When do I ever boss anyone around? No one is crazy enough to ever put me in charge of other kids. Charlie is much better suited for it."

Rachel laughed. "Me, too. I'd be a horrid delegate. Delegates have to stand in front of crowds." With a happy smile, she added, "Though Vlad says, someday I'll be one of the strongest sorcerers in the school. That'll be cool!"

"Vlad?"

"Vladimir Von Dread."

"Wait. T-the Prince of Bavaria? The scary dude who practically runs Drake Hall? Mr. High-And-Mighty-In-Black-Leather-Gauntlets? My little sister is on a nickname basis with the Lord of Evil himself?"

Rachel nodded pleasantly.

Laurel paused and looked at Rachel oddly. "You really have changed, little sis, haven't you? I... I think I saw it but just wasn't prepared. It's okay to change. But you were always the quiet one. Except when you were on your broom and bashing into things. But Father never told you to stop flying because you were his favorite. I thought it was because you always listened."

"I have changed," Rachel replied. "Things happened that... have changed me. But I don't think I was ever quiet, Laurel. Rather, I was living out grand and dramatic adventures through books and stories. My life, in my mind, was full of action and wonder, but it didn't show on my face—because my body didn't happen to be in the place where I was living, if that makes sense."

"No. But that's okay." Laurel went down onto her knees on the ice, so that she was looking up at Rachel's face. "I'm also sorry I snapped at you before, that time with Charlie. Also, so silly of me, I forgot you have a cat familiar. So, falling off a broom at a hundred feet up can't hurt you, you little crazy stunt girl," Laurel roughed up Rachel's already flyaway hair, sending black locks every which way. "Thanks to your familiar gift, you should be able to fall from any height and land safely—though, despite the popular saying, not always on our feet."

Rachel sighed. This was probably not the time to tell her sister the truth about Mistletoe.

"Next thing we know," her sister continued, "you'll be dropping out of the sky right and left, like Merlin Thunderhawk."

"You know, Father actually does that," Rachel murmured, recalling seeing her father come through the high window of Veltdammerung's underground hideout to rescue her and Sandra from Egg. It had not occurred to her that the need not worry about landing due to his familiar. Like everyone else in the family, Father's familiar was also a cat.

Laurel added. "I haven't got used to who you are now. Please, give me some time to adjust. I haven't wanted to think about it, but Peter was right. We didn't take you seriously, and horrible things happened to you. Things we could have stopped. Should have stopped. If we had listened. And now it's too late. I am sorry. So sorry. Will you ever forgive me?"

Rachel leaned forward and awkwardly hugged her. Again, her heart felt lighter.

"You didn't answer." Laurel's voice quivered. "Does that mean you think we can't be forgiven? I can understand that. I would be angry, too."

"Of course, you are forgiven!" Rachel cried. "I love you!"

Laurel hugged her back. She was shaking but not crying.

Squeezing her tightly, Rachel whispered, "You were right. I should have listened to Father... Then everything would still be...."

Rachel wept.

"It's okay," Laurel said soothingly, rubbing Rachel's back. "I am sure you did what you thought was right. Don't second guess yourself. You can only... do... what...."

Laurel's eyes began to glow with a beautiful light, golden and warm. It dispelled the biting cold of the winter evening. When her sister gazed at Rachel, it felt as if the Comfort Lion were near but even more so. Rachel had never seen such a light before, and yet she felt as if she had always known it, her whole life.

Laurel spoke, and her voice was so beautiful that Rachel feared her heart would break. Only, it did not. Instead, a musical quality in the words soothed her heartache, filling her with peace and joy and hope—as if all her pains and sorrows were but bad dreams.

"Do not despair. Despair is a weapon of your enemies. They have embedded it deep in your heart. Know you that with a wave of My hand, I have calmed the oceans. With a wave of My hand, I

parted the darkness from the light. With a whisper, I called forth all of creation. Now I cleanse you of your inner wounds. Only I, young Rachel Griffin, can see the beginning and end of all things. Remember this when you have doubts."

CHAPTER THIRTY-ONE:

FOR, LO, I SHALL OPEN A DOOR

ONCE AGAIN, RACHEL FELL INTO A VISION:

The darkness bubbling below the universe started to rise toward the world, as it had when the Lion had saved Zoë. Then, golden light fell from the heavens. Unlike the beam in her previous vision, this flash lit up everything. The darkness receded far, far below. It began to inch back up, but now it was much more like a beaten dog than a roaring tide. When it stopped, it seemed farther away than it had been before the Light came.

Rachel was herself again, standing on the ice with Laurel, whose eyes still glowed brightly with the golden light. The biting winds of February swirled around them, but where they sat, winter had no power. Peace and joy encompassed them. Rachel was reminded of being curled up in their mother's lap, eyes half open, listening to a favorite book, one whose every word she loved. She was vaguely aware that she was still bound by sadness. At the moment, however, its chilly fingers could not reach her heart.

Laurel's eyes stopped glowing. She swayed a bit and smiled. Then she shook her head. Then she blushed from head to toe, bright red.

"Sorry, I just got distracted a bit I guess. Whoa."

Laurel stood up. She leaned against a hemlock with trembling legs. Then she slid down and landed on her behind on the ice. "I... just felt something. It made me tingle everywhere at once. Sort of like.... But different. Wow."

Rachel was still transfixed with joy. "You just... said such beautiful things!"

A familiar voice spoke over her black bracelet, but it was not a voice that had spoken over it before. It was, however, a voice that she had feared she might never hear again. Her heart leapt with enraptured joy.

"Hello, Rachel Griffin. I wish to come speak with you and your sister. I have decided to warn you of my coming. I see a path in which my coming helps you and your sister become closer. But the path has a second branch, in which my coming scares her, and it disrupts your life further. I'd like to speak to her, though, so could you listen to my request?"

"Of course, Jariel," Rachel breathed softly. "Anything."

"When I appear, do not leave your sister's side and run to where I am. If you do, there is a high likelihood of that ending badly. If you stay by her side, I see a much greater chance of a good resolution. Do you understand?"

"Yes. I will stay with Laurel." Rachel blushed with embarrassment at the idea that he thought she would just run to him with no provocation.

"I will be there soon. Do not be afraid. She *cannot* harm me with her magic."

Rachel glanced over at her sister, who was still in a happy daze. Laurel sat on the ice, lost in thought. Suddenly, her sister's eyes focused on something behind Rachel's back. Leaping forward and sliding dangerously, Laurel grabbed Rachel, thrusting her little sister behind her. Laurel shoved her wrist forward and shook it. The charm bracelet under her coat sleeve rattled, causing dangling charms to chime. A shield-shaped shimmer appeared in the air in front of them. Laurel grabbed the silver wand that hung at Rachel's side and pointed it.

Rachel opened her mouth and closed it, wondering if Laurel even knew how to use the wand. She hoped her sister would not accidentally fire off the last charge of Eternal Flame.

"Monster! Stay away from my sister!" cried Laurel.

Rachel, pressed against her sister's back, heard the beat of the Raven's wings. The connection over the bracelet was still open, but, instead of words, she was receiving intuitions and empathic feelings. She felt the Raven's reaction to her sister: slightly... amused? But there was also acceptance or approval, as if Laurel's desire to defend Rachel pleased him.

Rachel hugged Laurel tightly, murmuring into her back. "It's okay. He's my friend. He protects me."

Laurel kept their grandmother's wand pointed in front of her. Her arm was visibly shaking. Rachel could feel her sister's whole body trembling. Through her sister's back, Rachel heard Laurel's heart thundering in her chest.

"Please, don't hurt her," whispered Laurel. "Please?"

"I shall not harm her," came the Raven's hoarse croak. "I shall not harm you. I am here but to speak for a time."

Peeking under her sister's arm, Rachel caught a glimpse of a great black bird with his blood red eyes. Then, he changed into an inhumanly beautiful man with black wings and a halo of light over his head. For the briefest of moments, Rachel feared that Laurel was suffering a heart attack, because the thundering in her sister's chest had ceased completely. But then, her heartbeat resumed more steadily.

"So pretty…." Laurel stared at the shining halo, mesmerized.

The Raven smiled and reached up. At his touch, the light turned into a coronet of gold. Kneeling before the sisters, he held it out toward Laurel, who looked at Rachel questioningly.

Rachel smiled and nodded. Taking her sister's hand, she gently pushed it toward the halo. Laurel touched it, making a soft, inarticulate noise. A shiver ran through her entire body. Then the tension drained from her. She sighed and spoke in a low, almost reverent tone.

"It's amazing… it feels like… what just happened. Sort of." Smiling at Rachel, Laurel giggled, "It also reminds me of you, silly."

Jariel handed Laurel the halo. She took it in her hands and sank down to kneel on the ice, staring at it and smiling. Laurel held the gold hoop out toward Rachel, who knelt awkwardly beside her older sister, her skates only half on. She laid her palm on the golden coronet.

It felt like…*diligence.*

Strange sensations poured through Rachel, like that moment of waking from a dream. They reminded her of the light that had come out of Laurel's eyes. Holding the halo, she felt a spike of sheer joy so sharp that it was like being sliced in two. For a split second, she felt very different from her normal self, as if all the universe were at her fingertips.

Memories of happy times with Laurel tumbled through her mind: playing house inside a clump of gorse bushes on the moors; shrieking with terror and clinging to her sister with all her strength, as they galloped across the lavender fields on the back of Laurel's black Arabian, Wild Child; swimming in the lake, holding their noses as they jumped off the raft; taking gymnastics together at the Gryphon-on-Dart Assembly Hall; sitting in the audience and clapping, as Laurel performed those same gymnastic moves on the back of Wild Child during a vaulting competition; at Hot Springs Beach in Thulhavn, running across the black sands that separated the oceans in Greenland from steaming waters of the hot springs.

The "light" from the halo, she realized, was "shining" on different memory chains, bringing them to mind. Without actually altering them, it downplayed any negative part of each memory, emphasizing the good. The Raven knelt beside them. Rachel glanced from him to Laurel, who sat smiling with her hand on the halo, her eyes distant.

Leaning toward him, Rachel whispered, "Can I ask questions in front of her?"

"My Father has spoken to you through her," answered Jariel. "She is sacred. Speak in front of her, if you wish. He would not choose a vessel that was impure. Nor would he speak to someone who was not destined for greatness. Not so directly, at least...."

Rachel looked at her sister with awe. Then, she asked the question that had been weighing upon her. "Does the Master of the World have the power or authority to order you to take away my Elf Rune and change my memories for real?"

"No," the Raven replied. "He believes he does, but he does not. I will not go out of my way to let him know where his control over me ends. Certain things are best left unsaid."

So great was her relief that Rachel's body sagged, as if the strings holding her upright had been cut. And yet, her anger at the Master of the World grew. How beastly of him to put Jariel in such a position.

Laurel, who was still looking at the halo, spoke absently, "Someone who stays silent, so other people jump to conclusions. I wonder who that reminds me of...."

She giggled. Rachel smirked slightly, acknowledging the truth of the comment. It pleased her immensely that her sister saw a similarity between herself and Jariel.

"About my new memories," said Rachel. "They don't agree with my friends'. If I use them, my friends will think I've gone crazy, and they'll haul me in front of the Agents again. And that is bound to go badly. If I stick with my real memories... what do I do if the princess goes home and tells her father something I've said that shows that I still have them?"

The Raven replied, "The Master and the princess's father do not see eye to eye on many things. I will speak to him. He does not approve of the kind of tricks used on you, unsuccessfully, or on your father. I think he will agree to let me follow my own judgment."

Laurel let go of the golden circlet, "Okay! Now I want to go see my Charlie. Thank you, Mr. Scary Tengu, for watching out for my sister and not killing me. I like not being killed."

The Raven said, "I am not a tengu."

She shrugged. "Whichever. I appreciate that you are not the thing I thought you were."

"I did nothing actively to be who I...."

Laurel interrupted him. "Oh, shut up! Wow, you are very disagreeable. That's where Rachel gets it! Bad influence! Bad tengu!"

She shook her finger at him. Jariel looked at Rachel, as if not sure what to say. Laurel got up and threw her arms around him. Even on one knee, he was as tall as she was. He looked resigned to his fate. Delighted, Rachel rushed forward and hugged him, too.

"Now you're in a select club," she whispered to Laurel, hugging them both. Her sister smelled of winter and lavender. The winged man bore the scent of strong winds off the ocean and warm, summer breezes. "With me and an elf. Don't know if it has any other members."

"Mortal beings who have embraced me?" intoned Jariel. "It does not."

Rachel sighed with bliss. Laurel smiled and hugged them both once more. Then, she rose and skated off, looking ridiculously happy. Jariel, who was still kneeling, watched Laurel depart.

Rachel gazed at him, her eyes lingering on his huge black wings. She recalled the forgotten page from the ancient bestiary. "If you're not a tengu... you're an *angel*, aren't you?"

"I am." The Raven's gaze still followed Laurel. "Your family cares about you a great deal. Your sister was ready to die defending you. I wonder, does that trait run throughout your family? The willingness to sacrifice yourself for another? I am not surprised my Father spoke to you and that He used your sister as His vessel."

They are like me, Rachel thought in amazement and joy. *My family—they are just like me. That willingness to die, to sacrifice ourselves for something worthwhile, something we love.* She felt closer than ever before to her parents and siblings.

He pointed his finger at Rachel's feet, and her laces finished lacing themselves. Rachel cried out with delight and glided in a circle. The fit was perfect. She felt sorry that such beautiful silver skates would be gone by the morrow.

"Know this, Rachel Griffin," Jariel said, still on one knee. He met her gaze eye to eye. "Your father now is closer to who he truly is than before."

"How so?"

"He had many false memories, used to manipulate him—to better serve the Master's ends. It made me unable to be as... elegant... in my work. The Master was very specific in what he wanted done."

"Am I... a real Griffin?" Rachel kicked off and glided backwards, her trailing foot still in the air. "Or is my family from Outside?"

"You are a real Griffin," he assured her with a kindly smile. "Your father's family goes back to Abaris of the Arimaspians, just as you have been told. Your mother's family, on the other hand... but perhaps, it is best not to speak of them here."

Rachel sighed with relief. Her beloved Grandfather really was her grandfather. She glided back to where Jariel knelt. What had he been about to say about her mother's family? If she asked him outright, he would not answer, of that she was reasonably certain. Maybe a question from an unexpected direction?

"Mrs. March, the Grand Inquisitor's wife?" Rachel twirled in a circle and stopped by moving her feet into third position, left foot perpendicular to the middle of the right one, and dragging the back skate on the ice. "She has a great deal in common with my mother: our same dissembling technique, perfect memory, unusually… um… shapely. Mrs. March even has the same slight tilt to the corner of her eyes as Sandra. I know she was supposed to have been conjured, but is Cassandra March somehow related to my mother's family?"

Jariel gazed at her keenly for a bit. "No. And yes. Of this, I shall say no more."

"Ah," Rachel murmured, disappointed, for that cryptic answer had merely caused the fires of her curiosity to burn hotter.

The Raven turned his head and gazed into the distance, the feathers of his folded wings rustling.

Fearing he might be preparing to depart, Rachel said in a small voice, "Before you go, I… have a few more questions."

"You may ask."

"Is the ability to give you orders based on rank or talent? In other words, can the younger Romanovs, like the princess, give you orders? Or only the King and his… what? Father? Brother? Cousin? Alternate self? Third Uncle Twice Removed? Can I tell Vladimir about the Romanovs' part? I think he should know. Can I tell Siggy? Can I talk to you over the bracelet? Is there anything you would like me to do? Or anyone you would like me to pass a message to?"

"Questions, questions." Jariel smiled down at her fondly. "Let me answer in order: Only the Master of the World may command me now. The ability will pass to his heir should the Master meet his end. Your friend cannot command me at this time. You may tell Vladimir Von Dread. You may tell Sigfried Smith."

Rachel shouted with joy and jumped up and down, which was difficult in skates, but she managed to keep her balance. She laughed and glided in a circle around him.

"Thank you! Thank you! I hate keeping secrets from Sigfried!"

The Raven continued, "I would prefer if you did not mention any of this to the princess. I foresee the Master will be returning shortly. It would be best were he to not have his attention drawn back to this school. For now, at least. I foresee he will speak to his granddaughter. The less she knows, the less she can betray.

"I can alter your bracelet," he continued, "so it can communicate with me, but if the person who created it were to take it back, he would know it had been changed." He touched her bracelet, and it vibrated for a moment. "You may use it as you usually would. Speak the name you have given me, and I will hear."

A great happiness suffused Rachel. She stood hugging her black bracelet to her chest and beaming, elated. Then a thought occurred that caused her smile to falter.

"Jariel." She began skating back and forth in front of him, falling into a tight figure-eight. "In November, I saw two ghosts disappear. One dissolved into shining light. That was a good thing, I think. But the other... He was pulled into the ground. Where did he go?"

"Remus Starkadder?" All traces of a smile left the Raven's face. "He is in Hell."

"The place you mentioned before? The one that is like Tartarus but worse?" She pushed off, gliding backwards in her dismay.

"A thousand times worse. It is a place of torment, where demons play with the souls of the damned, as if they were so many toys."

"That's... horrible!" breathed Rachel. "Can't something be done?"

"*And death and hell were cast into the lake of fire.*'" The Raven spoke as if quoting.

Rachel re-traced the figure-eight carefully, one blade at a time, like an old fashioned figure skater. After a time, she began to wonder if he had forgotten her. She looked around and saw other students happily skating. None of them seemed to notice the inhumanly handsome, eight-foot-tall, winged man.

Finally, he spoke. "Something will be done, in my Father's own time. For thus shall He send the Keybearers."

Rachel dropped the saw-toothed toe-rake of her right skate and skidded to a stop. "The Keybearers that I'm not a part of? Those Keybearers? I want to help! I want to go, too!"

"You *want* to go to Hell?" he asked, stunned.

"If I can help... if I can do some good," Rachel begged. "Any good at all?"

The Raven stared at her, his eyes gray now and very dark. "Rachel Griffin, you do not have a destiny, such as the Keybearers have, but you do have a future—a likelihood of what will become of you: the things you will most probably do, the family you will most likely have. I think, from what I know of you, that these things will please you."

He glanced to the left. Following his gaze, she saw Gaius, talking to Vlad and William, as they prepared to play hockey against Joshua March and some other college students.

Jariel turned back to her. "If you chose to go with the Keybearers on their mission, all this may change. That decision will open new doors. If you walk through those doors... I do not know what will occur. Your whole life, your future, may change."

Rachel moved her skates in and out, so that she slowly moved away from him and then, reversing direction, back toward him again.

She spoke very carefully. "You mean, I might not become the Librarian of All Worlds. And I might not marry Gaius?"

He nodded slowly. A rush of joy almost lifted her from the ice. So these much-desired things did await her! But joining with the Keybearers meant that her future might change. Her stomach began to tighten at the thought that she might lose these precious future things.

"Because these things would be taken from me?" asked Rachel, her voice quivering.

Jariel shook his head. "Because you might change."

"Even if I changed, I could still choose to become the Librarian of All Worlds, right?"

The Raven gazed evenly at her, "Once upon a time, four farm boys wished upon the first star of evening. Each wished for his own farm, there in the valley, with rich crop yield and fish in the river, so that they could all remain fast friends forever. Three received their wish. The fourth however, when his nation went to war, joined up and served.

"When he came home, the old dream was no longer enough for him. He had changed. He departed again and served where able. One day, he returned home, as the lord of those very lands where his old friends lived. In the end, he watched over them with a kind and steady hand."

"But he could still spend time with his friends, right?" Rachel said in a small voice.

"He could have, but the experience would have been bittersweet. You, as the daughter of a duke, know better than many how difficult it is for a lord to laze by the river and fish with his farmers, as equals. A lord has more urgent tasks."

Rachel bit her lip. She wanted the things the Raven had mentioned so very much.

A longing came over her to leave her future as it was. Gaius was Vlad's lieutenant; Rachel's job was to support the princess and Siggy. They would make great partners. They would marry and have six children and be as happy as any two people could be. She was to be a librarian adventurer and build the Library of All Worlds. She would find the information that others needed in order to do their great deeds. Her task would be in the background, but it would still be important. If she stepped forward into the limelight, *everything might change.*

She did not like the limelight. She did not want it to change!

And yet, from deep within her, another voice sang, a part of her that followed in her grandfather's footsteps. That part was fierce and majestic and devoted to justice; the blood of sixty-four generations of Griffins, great sorcerers and dukes, flowed in her veins. It formed an unbreakable bond with the family the Raven had described—where all members were willing to sacrifice themselves for each other. That part of her could not bear the idea that something was terribly wrong in the universe, and she might walk away without doing all that was within her power to set it right.

Besides, had not she made this decision already, the day she first met the Raven, when she offered her life to save the world? Was she going to back out on that now?

"That's what I want!" Rachel's voice was calm and steady, an inner fire burning in her eyes. "I want to help. Even if it means losing everything."

The Raven's eyes shone brightly. *"For, lo, I open a door, and no power beneath Heaven shall close it."*

The words echoed oddly in her ears. A strange wind blew through the hemlocks, causing their branches to dance. It ruffled his feathers and billowed her hair. He bowed his head, silent.

"I have opened the way." Jariel straightened again. "You have merely to walk towards it. And if this future should turn out to be harder than you can bear, Rachel Griffin, may my Father have mercy upon us both."

Chapter Thirty-Two:

Anything

For a Friend of Valerie's

THE SUN GREW LOW IN THE WEST, BEHIND STORM KING, AND THE daylight was beginning to fail. Here and there, so faint that at first Rachel thought it was her imagination, tiny twinkles—blue, lilac, and violet—appeared among the dark trunks of the evergreens. First a glint amidst the icy branches, then two, then four. Then dozens of points of light, all shades of blue and purple, danced in the gloom. They were some kind of will-o'-the-wisp Rachel had never seen before, floating everywhere, like fairy lights.

Rachel's lips parted in wonder. The scene was like something from a poet's vision of elfland. In the distance, other students cried out in delight.

Close at hand, Jariel stood before her, the dancing blue and lavender will-o'-the-wisps reflected in the black feathers of his wings. The evening was growing colder. Yet, standing near the angel, Rachel felt as warm as if she were snug at home, sitting before a fireplace. Despite the deepening twilight, he seemed brighter, crisper. She stared up into his gray eyes, her heart full to overflowing.

The Raven turned his head, gazing to the north. "Strange."

"Strange?" Rachel looked that way as well, though all she could see was hemlocks. "What is that?"

"The ogre has left his cave and is climbing the cliff." The Raven's eyes moved, looking beyond what Rachel could see. "The woodwose departs his wood and heads west. The trolls are coming down from their spruce-covered slopes."

"Are they headed here?" Rachel felt a sensation akin to a shiver.

"Not if the wards hold...."

"Won't they?" asked Rachel, startled.

The Raven did not heed her. His voice had a distant tone to it, as if he was not quite aware of her. "There are creatures of my world. I should be able to see all likelihoods of their actions. The fact that there is a haze, an uncertainty, is... disturbing."

"How so?"

"There are very few powers that can deceive my vision, and none of them are...." The Raven's voice trailed off. He turned back to Rachel. "I must depart."

Rachel threw her arms around him again and whispered, "I love you, Jariel."

"Thank you, little one." A smile lit his eyes. He leaned forward until his forehead touched hers, warmth spreading from him to her. "I love you, too."

Rising to his feet, he stretched his enormous black wings, scattering blue and violet will-o'-the-wisps. Without so much as a twitch of a feather, he soared upward and was gone.

• • •

Rachel glided between the tall dark trunks, tiny blue sparks dancing brightly in the glowing twilight. All the world looked like fairyland. Music rose softly, the lilting strains of *Pachelbel's Canon* contributing to the sensation of being in a beautiful dream. As the sky darkened, skaters gathered in a few central areas where the hemlocks were spread far apart, giving them room to maneuver. Girls laughed and shrieked. Boys shouted, egging each other on.

There was a joyful shriek as a laughing Merry Vesper cantered through the middle of the hockey players on the back of her white reindeer. Some of the players applauded. Others swore. Vladimir Von Dread, who again skirmished with Mrs. March's lanky eldest son, did not even look up. Rachel could not help noticing how fine both young men looked, their faces intent, their hair dark with sweat. Recalling her foolish fantasies — from the days before she knew about Sandra's secret boyfriend—about how Dread might desire a wife with perfect memory, she blushed at her own naïveté.

Darting away into the growing gloom, Rachel took advantage of a place where the trees grew close together to skate by herself. No other students were nearby; however, a pair of foxes trotted across the ice. Through the hemlocks, she also spotted a raccoon, and a lynx. From the size of the animals, she was certain they were familiars.

Rachel found a nice set of evergreens in two clumps and circled their trunks, forming a lopsided figure-eight. Her feet glided, sure and steady over the ice, but her mind was a million light-years away. A thousand, thousand thoughts chased themselves like dizzy kittens, as the many amazing things that had just occurred somersaulted through her mind: learning to forgive, hearing the words spoken through the glowing-eyed Laurel, and now choosing a more grand and dire future than the one she had originally been dealt. Then there was the woodwose and the ogre. Rachel glanced nervously to the north, but the memory of falling out of the sky on her broom when she and Sigfried flew across the line of tree trunks actually brought her comfort. If the wards could stop Vroomie, they could probably stop a few trolls.

She skated back and forth in the early twilight. Soon, she knew, all this would hit her. At the moment, though, she felt numb—no, not numb; at peace. The grace and calm that had come with the Voice that spoke through Laurel still surrounded her, cushioning her. But the sorrow and pain that had oppressed her since her father lost his memory still loomed, cold and solid, like a huge frozen block of ice. Sooner or later, the golden warmth keeping this iceberg at bay would ebb, and she would be plunged back into the emptiness and darkness.

As she skated, her blades gliding rhythmically across the snowy ice, her thoughts returned to the quandary that had been bothering her for months. Which should she pursue: *Everything or Truth?*

Truth felt right, but she balked at giving up her beloved desire to *Know everything!* But was her goal even theoretically possible? Could *any* being even come close?

The Emperor of All Things Seen and Unseen. The words rang in her heart like a song. She repeated them once, twice, and then again. She knew nothing of the Lion's father, but if he were really the emperor of all things, even unseen things, then would he not know which things were truth and which were not? That was what she really wanted—to know *All Things Seen and Unseen*, or rather to know all things *unseen*, the secrets no one else had yet discovered.

The dilemma that had been troubling her since Carthage resolved, Blackie had questioned the usefulness of knowing anything but the truth, but his example had not been of a lie, but merely of a trivial fact. Which facts were trivial, however, and which were not were a matter of circumstance. Most likely, she would never need to know about fly eyelashes—especially as she had looked it up and most flies did not have any. Yet, sometimes the most trivial fact, overheard in passing, was the one that proved crucial. With a memory like hers, any fact she learned stayed with her forever. Why not have as many facts filed away to pull out in times of need as possible?

But it would not help her to remember something that was incorrect. What she really wanted was to *know truth from lies.*

• • •

Salome's voice rang out cheerfully from the calling card in Rachel's pocket. "Yoo-hoo! Die Horribly Debate Clubbers! Clubbees? Clubbettes? Action at six o'clock. Well, six o'clock from my position. Incoming!"

Rachel skated back toward the larger gathering areas, looking for her friends. She caught sight of a streak of red and gold among the trunks and hurried over to where Lucky snaked through the air, circling above Sigfried's head. Rachel glided over to join them. Nastasia was there, dressed in a charming, fur-trimmed white outfit complete with a muff. With her and Sigfried were Joy and Valerie. Beauregard, the Tasmanian tiger, moved stiff-leggedly over the unfamiliar cold, hard stuff, while Payback, the Norwegian Elkhound, padded confidently across the ice, stopping here and there to sniff a sapling or a fallen mitten.

As Rachel joined them, they converged on where a pink-cheeked Salome waited, so eager with whatever it was that was exciting her that she was practically jumping, causing the pom-poms on her skates to jiggle and bounce. Salome wore a cute, tight-fitting, blue and white skating outfit that Rachel found shockingly immodest but which everyone else seemed to accept as normal. Gesturing for them to gather around, Salome leaned forward.

"Someone, I can't say who, of course, just convinced Eunice Chase that she should confront Vladimir Von Dread about how badly he has been treating her." Salome's luminous eyes danced with glee. She gestured toward the hockey game. "Let's watch, shall we?"

"Von Dread!" screeched a girl's voice.

Eunice Chase came storming across the ice in her boots, her hair hidden under a white crocheted hat. She charged over to where the boys and Zoë were playing hockey. Zoë's friend Seth was playing as well, though most of the others were college students. Rachel recalled that Seth had belonged to a hockey team in middle school.

Putting her hands on her hips, Eunice shouted in a voice that carried through the forest, "Prince Von Dread, I have had just about enough of you! How dare you speak to me so rudely! I may not be royalty, but I am still important!"

Vladimir skidded to a stop. He surveyed her, his hand resting atop his hockey stick.

"Chase, you will never, ever address me in this manner again." Von Dread spoke calmly, but his voice carried even farther than hers.

"I treat you very well, considering what a low and cowardly thing you are. I know about what you learned when the Agents were here. I know you remember your parents discussing the murder of your little sister in front of you. I am aware of your utter lack of concern for her, even after you remembered that information."

Around the hockey game and beyond, gasps rang out.

"She's not my sister!" spat Eunice.

"It is not for you to choose who is in your family," Dread replied. He handed his hockey stick to Gaius and crossed his arms. "Whether by the circumstance of birth or by tragedy, she was placed under your care. And you have failed utterly in protecting her. You have done the opposite, in fact, abusing her and physically assaulting her for your own petty, selfish reasons."

Eunice began to object. Dread closed the distance between them. He towered over her.

"Quiet," he commanded. "You do no longer have the right to address me. Count yourself lucky that I am not as pathetic as you. Were I a lesser man, I might strike you, to show you a small amount of what you have done to that little girl. But I am not so low as to act thus. Only the weak resort to cruelty, Chase. You are weak. Do not make me forget that I am not."

Turning his back on her, he retrieved his stick and returned to the hockey game.

Rachel stood with her mouth hanging open, a-tingle with hero-worship. Vladimir had just stood up for Magdalene in front of the whole school. And he had done it so elegantly! *You are weak. Do not make me forget that I am not.* That was sheer elegance. It was like something her grandfather would have said.

Salome took a deep breath and fanned herself. She looked flushed and excited and was almost out of breath. "It was so great. Ohhhh. It was beautiful. I think I need to take a nap now."

"I am willing to sign up for the Von Dread fan club," announced Sigfried. "Right now."

"Me, too!" said Lucky. "Dragons for Dread!"

"Is there a Von Dread fan club?" Rachel spun in a circle. "Thank you, Vlad. Thank you for looking out for Magdalene." When she spoke his name, she casually changed her emphasis to activate the black bracelet, so he would hear her.

"Um, hello?" objected Salome. She waved her pretty blue and white fingernails in the air and pointed them back at herself. "What about the Salome Iscariot fan club?" She spread her hand outward again. "I got all of this done for you. At the peril of my own boredom!"

Valerie, who was holding Siggy's arm, perhaps helping to hold him up, perhaps letting him hold her up, Rachel did not know, shook her head. "Salome, I love you, and you are my best friend. But that 'peril of your own boredom' thing made no sense."

"Oh, you know what I mean!" Salome replied gaily. "I am totally your spy in among the thaumaturges, aren't I? I think we need a secret language. Something easy to learn. Wait, no. Learning it would probably take, like, days. That sounds boring. Let's just have secret meetings and wear dark cloaks. Er, darker than the robes that we're already wearing..."

"Darker cloaks would be hard. Maybe the ones we have will have to do," said Sigfried seriously. "But I'll join the Salome Iscariot fan club. So will Lucky!"

"Dragons for Scantily Clad Thaumaturgesses!" cheered Lucky.

Joy snorted, "Can't say who, of course.' Very subtle."

Salome looked unduly pleased.

"I can't join your club," Joy continued. "I like you, but you're obviously evil."

Salome laughed and tossed her head. "Yeah.... Yeah, I am."

"She's not evil!" Valerie rolled her eyes. "She just likes to annoy people. That's not evil. It's just a little mean."

"Duh, Valerie! I am in Drake!" replied Salome. "We're all eeeeeeevil. Capital-E EVIL actually. Strangle puppies, punt kittens, all that good stuff."

"I am confused, Miss Iscariot," said Nastasia, who had been standing quietly, watching the others with a slight frown. "Why did you do this?"

"For Rachel, of course," exclaimed Salome.

"Wha–what?" Rachel gaped at her. "For me?"

But she had just forgiven Eunice! Or tried, anyway.

"Sure thing!" replied Salome. "Chase was giving you such a hard time, with all her little minions scuttling around, chucking stuff at you, and throwing out your math homework." She wiggled her blue and white fingernails to indicate the scuttling of the minions. "I figured the time had come to stuff a cork in her." She grinned, bubbling over with sheer delight. "As I told you, anything for a friend of Valerie's!"

CHAPTER THIRTY-THREE:

THE MOST-FAVORITE PERSON CONTEST

RACHEL'S BRACELET VIBRATED.

Vladimir's voice spoke beside her ear. "I did not protect the younger Miss Chase for your sake, Miss Griffin, but you are welcome nonetheless."

"Perhaps not," replied Rachel softly, smiling. "But I was the one who asked you to protect her. So I feel well served, even if that was not your intention."

"I will not abide women being abused," Vlad's voice stated. "My mother was abused for most of her life by mundanes and Wise alike. I will not tolerate such things in my presence."

Rachel knew nothing about the late Queen of Bavaria—except that she had died years ago, and Vladimir had gone to the memorial gardens on Samhain to light a candle for her—but there was something most noble about his sentiment. It made a warm coal glow in her heart.

She said, "Could you let me know if you have a time when you are not busy and could talk in person, Vlad? I have something direly important to tell you."

He paused. "Is the matter time sensitive?"

"As in immediate? No."

"As soon as the game is over," came his reply, "I will find you."

Rachel left her friends, who were still squabbling over who was or was not evil, and skated through the darkening forest. The sun had disappeared behind Storm King. Above the trees, the sky was a deep periwinkle blue. As the twilight grew darker, the blue, lilac, and violet wisps flickered more brightly among the trunks, their glowing colors reflected in the surface of the ice, so that they seemed to float both above and below.

Rachel twirled amidst the sparkling lights, aglow at the wonder of the winter wonderland. Then she glided across the ice, her hands clasped behind her back, her feet moving smoothly, one and then the other—though occasionally, she had to jump to avoid a stump or the stalks of dry reeds protruding above the frozen surface or swerve to avoid someone's runaway familiar. She spun around and skated backwards for a time, glancing over her shoulder, and then using her perfect memory to recall where the trees and obstacles were behind her.

It was great fun, almost as much fun as flying. She was glad she had decided to come.

But as the sky darkened, so did her mood. The thought of the ogre and the other denizens of fey leaving their accustomed haunts to move across the island spooked her. Also, this recent incident with Eunice was disturbing, or rather, Salome's part in it. Salome seemed so exuberant, so sheerly joyful. And yet.... Rachel shivered. She did not want other people fighting her battles for her, especially people who did creepy things—like upsetting someone until they challenged her to a duel or yelled at the imposing Prince of Bavaria in public.

A cheer rang out from the hockey game. Rachel turned and skated closer, pausing to watch her boyfriend in action. He was shorter than the other boys, except for Seth Peregrine, but he was quick and wiry. Her hand resting on the trunk of a large hemlock, Rachel waved to Gaius, who blew her a kiss. This led to a great deal of hooting from the college students, whom Rachel would have expected to know better.

"Dating a toddler, are you?" called one of the goalies, a college boy from Persia.

Raucous laughter followed, along with some leers, as the older boys looked her over in a way that left Rachel feeling uncomfortable. Her cheeks grew hot, but Gaius just chuckled and grinned his lazy grin.

"Upset are you, Ishkandar, because your girlfriend can't hold a candle to the sun of cuteness that is mine?" he replied airily, as he sent the puck between Ismail Ishkandar's legs and into the goal.

Both his team and the crowd went wild, cheering. Rachel took advantage of the excitement to slip away. A few boys in the crowd were still watching her, including one or two rather good-looking high school boys. Rachel ducked her head and gazed studiously forward, until she had skated out of sight.

Thinking over the incident, she smiled. She was pleased Gaius believed her pretty enough to boast about her. She was also proud of herself for ignoring the admiring glances of the boys. She was proving to be a loyal girlfriend. She had always wanted to be the kind of girl who would be a loyal girlfriend. It pleased her that she never so much as looked at any boy but Gaius.

"You're not that cute," an older girl exclaimed caustically behind her. "You're not half as pretty as I am. What does he see in you?"

Rachel spun around to find Tess Dauntless sitting on a fallen log, swinging her skated feet. Tiny lilac and blue sparks glinted in her wavy blond hair.

Tess continued, "He gets so much grief for dating a thirteen-year-old, a lesser man would be crushed like a bug. If he were my boyfriend, I'd have pity on him and break up with him, rather than put him through that."

Rachel said nothing, embarrassed that she had had no idea that Gaius was being teased because of her. The older girl's eyes raked over Rachel's girlish form. "At least until I developed a little.... " She gazed pointedly at Rachel's lack of curves.

"He likes me because I'm clever," Rachel crossed her arms and thought of the many things she had done that had wowed her boyfriend, things she could not speak of aloud. "And apparently, he thinks I'm twice as cute as the goalie's girlfriend. Maybe that's cute enough."

"Anyone can be cuter than Petra Volonski," Tess shot back. "Her older sister Medea is much prettier than she is."

Rachel assumed that this Petra person must be the girlfriend who was the candle to her sun of cuteness—the phrase amused her. It took all her dissembling skills not to giggle in front of Tess. Gaius was such a sweetie.

Her bracelet vibrated again. Dread's voice spoke in her ear.

"The game has ended. I am free to converse."

"Coming!" Rachel cried. Glancing over her shoulder, she waved to Tess. "Nice speaking with you. Must go."

Tess wiggled her fingers in a half-hearted good-bye. She looked glum.

• • •

Vlad met her by a fallen log, where he had bent down to tighten his laces. He was wearing heavy black and brown hockey skates. They looked well-used, quite different from her conjured ones.

"Did you play hockey in the Olympics?" asked Rachel.

He shook his head. "Fencing, skiing, speed skating, swimming, shooting, septathlon, and fulgurating. I could not participate in any sport that required practicing with a team, as I spent too much of my time here."

"That's quite impressive!" Rachel knew most of this but hearing him say it still awed her.

He nodded, accepting the compliment graciously. "I have been granted many advantages. It is my duty to look out for those who have not."

Wishing to reward him for his chivalrous sentiments, Rachel smiled up at him. "F.B., I thought you'd like to know that my mother is on your side."

"F.B.?" He raised an eyebrow.

"It is short for F.-B.-I.-L." She drew the dashes for brother-in-law in the air.

He thought for a moment and then nodded again, as if accepting a compliment, a ghost of a smile haunting the corners of his lips.

"Mother told Sandra that she was going to talk to my father on your behalf. Of course, that was before..." Rachel's voice trailed off.

Vladimir stood up. "Before what?"

He pushed off, and the two of them began skating side by side, heading by wordless agreement, toward the outskirts of the ice. Overhead, a large great horned owl flew by. Rachel recognized it as a familiar from De Vere.

"Before my father lost his memory," replied Rachel, keeping pace beside him. "I suspect my mother has more immediate concerns now."

"Then we should get your father's memory restored as soon as possible." He examined her closely. "Right?"

"I'd never spoken to my father about you. I have no idea if you have a better chance with Old Father or with this new one."

He paused for a moment and then gave a shake of his head. "It does not matter which one I would have better chances with, does it? If your father was injured, we should work to heal him. I will deal with him either way."

Rachel smiled, quite pleased. Then her face crumbled. Grief over her father's fate threatened to overwhelm her calm. She turned her head abruptly away and blinked her eyes, until she drove back the threatening tears. "B-but how can anyone help him, when no one is allowed to know what's wrong?"

"Ah. It is as I somewhat expected," he said gravely. "This is a hard situation. I will have to consider it for a while before suggesting a solution. Do not give in to despair, Miss Griffin. As long as he is healthy, we have time to make plans and figure this out."

"It's my fault," Rachel admitted softly. She looked up at him. "Thank you for that. I must admit I have felt quite in despair, but I will endeavor to less despondent." She added, "This is the second time today, I have been told not to despair."

She recalled the words spoken through Laurel. Even the memory of the event lightened her heart.

He clasped his hands behind his back he skated. "You cannot help how you feel. But we have not lost, the world endures, and we have struck a blow or two against our current, visible enemies. The future, of course, is unknown. Now is the time to rest and recover from our wounds. You did well this fall. You should be proud of yourself. No one else can claim the accomplishments that you have achieved over the past six months, myself included."

Rachel ducked her head shyly. "I do my best."

"The world persists." He gestured towards the trees, the ice, and in the distance, the laughing skating students. "We have not failed."

His answer heartened her. If she had not adored Vlad before, she would now.

They skated for a time in companionable silence, but his words kept echoing in her mind. *You cannot help how you feel.* His calm acceptance of her dilemma lifted a weight from her shoulders that all the comforting words of her friends and family had not. As this burden departed, something astonishing happened.

With the swiftness of breaking ice, a crack appeared in the despair that had imprisoned her since her trip to London. With this came sudden enlightenment. Vlad was right! She could not help how she felt. But her attempts to deny her feelings had led to her misunderstanding the nature of her distress. All this time, while she had been in despair—unable to eat or to concentrate in class—she had thought she was distraught about her father losing his memory.

But it was not that at all! True, she was upset about her father, but that just made her want to rush out and find him a cure. No, there was only one thing that could cause her to act like a puppet with broken strings, or—more to the point—a ship with no rudder.

She was extraordinarily, tremendously angry at Gaius.

Rachel's mind balked. No. It could not be. Gaius meant everything to her. He was her most-favorite person, the center of her universe. He cheered her up and kept her calm. She could not be angry with him. It was impossible.

And that was why she was so upset. His response to the secrets she had shared in her special room had hurt her, deeply. But her mind had rejected this information, thrust it away so as not to acknowledge it. Instead of being angry at the person she most trusted, it had shut down.

How dare Gaius side with her father!

Fury pulsed through her like an electrified knife. Did he have any idea how difficult that day had been for her? Who did he think he was, telling her what was reasonable for a thirteen-year-old? Who did he expect think was going to save the world? *Him?*

Worst of all, where did he get off browbeating her about throwing herself upon the Raven's mercy—as if she had committed some kind of act of treason? She had been lost and hurt and bereft, but her boyfriend had been too overwhelmed by the strangeness of it all to support her. She had needed comfort, a stalwart shoulder to lean upon, but, like a sapling before a gale, he had given way beneath the strain.

Gaius had failed her.

As quickly as it had flared, her anger began to fade. *You must accept in your heart that someone has harmed you. Then, you must be willing to release the pain they have caused.*

That had been her mistake. She had not accepted that she had been hurt. Now that she understood, it was easy to begin forgiving him. Gaius had not meant to hurt her, that she knew. His words had been thoughtless, not malicious. As far as letting her down, it was not his fault he had found it all overwhelming. It was a tremendous amount for a sixteen-year-old boy to take in. She should be glad he had recovered at all.

She had been asking too much. He was a very good boy, but he was just a boy.

Rachel forgave Gaius for his complaint that she should have been more obedient, for his concern about her facing danger at a young age, and for his temporary uncertainty in the face of overwhelming oddness. Try as she might, however, the fact that her boyfriend did not understand her love for the Raven still smarted.

As long as she was being truly honest, his lack of understanding about the Raven did far worse than smart. It radiated agony, like trying to walk on a broken leg. She had no idea why this one thing hurt so much, but she could easily forgive him for the rest of it.

Standing on the ice, surrounded by dancing blue and violet will-o'-the-wisps, Rachel owned up to how difficult the last couple of weeks had been for her. She had dwelt in a haze of gloom. She had hardly eaten for days. All her clothing was looser on her now, and she had been slender to begin with. She had even missed a class!

She could not risk this happening again. She needed someone at the helm of the ship of her soul who would not bend before the winds of adversity. She needed to choose a new most-favorite person.

Rachel looked up at Vlad, who still skated beside her. *Could it be him?* He did remind her of her grandfather, who had been the first person to hold this position. Much as she admired Vladimir

Von Dread, however, he would not do. He might seem confident and impressive, but he was only nineteen. He was not omniscient. Because that was what she needed. Someone who knew so much that, if he gave her an order, she would actually believe he understood the situation better than she did.

Gazing through the trees as they glided along, Rachel's eyes came to rest on the place where she had skated out a figure-eight while asking Jariel about the fate of Remus Starkadder. *And suddenly, she understood.* She knew exactly why Gaius's siding with her father had hurt so much. Her boyfriend had chided her for favoring the one person whom she most loved in all the world—not in a romantic fashion, as she loved Gaius, but with a pure love, joyous and deep.

Thank you, little one, the Raven's voice whispered in her memory, *I love you, too.*

Rachel took a deep breath and let it out slowly. As she exhaled, she felt the helm of her soul pass out of the hands of Gaius Valiant, much as she adored him, and into those of the one she now realized that loved more than any other—the tall, winged Raven who had risked the world to let her remain herself.

CHAPTER THIRTY-FOUR:

PLUNGING PELL-MELL

INTO THE OCEAN OF THE HEART

A BLAZE OF LIGHT ILLUMINATED THE DARKENING FOREST. Wisp-sculptures shaped like large hanging lanterns—made of domestic golden-white will-o'-the-wisps—ignited above the skaters. These, too, were reflected in the ice below, so that the glowing purple, blue, and white-gold points all danced like living glitter around the skaters, who now seemed to float amidst the twinkling. The entire frozen forest looked like an enchanted ballroom.

Rachel and Vlad skated along the outside of the impromptu rink. Away from these central wisp-lanterns, the evening was rapidly growing dark. Occasionally, they navigated too close to branches, and the short, soft, flat needles of the hemlocks brushed their hair and faces. The scent of evergreen filled their nostrils.

They came to a fallen trunk. Rachel slowed, preparing to cautiously step over it. Vladimir, however, sped up. He leapt into the air and, bending his knees so as to bring up his feet, and sailed over the obstacle. Straightening his legs on the far side, he resumed skating, as if his blades had never left the ice. Rachel gawked, impressed. He had done this quite casually, as if it were the most natural of things to jump effortlessly over logs while on skates.

The roar of rushing water distracted her from her admiration of her future brother-in-law. She turned, searching for the source of the sound.

"I thought the Ko sisters froze everything," she said.

Von Dread shook his head. "Only the floodwaters. The creek is still running underneath. What we are hearing is the waterfall.

Shall we head that way?"

He offered his hand, and Rachel shyly took it. They skated side by side through the dark trunks. The sky was now a deep blue, with feathery clouds of dove gray and smoke gray hovering in the ever darkening sky. They heard the roar of the falls before they saw the brink over which the water plummeted. Curious, Rachel let go of his hand and skated closer.

"You should be careful, Miss Griffin," Von Dread advised. "The ice is thinner where the water is running."

"Oh, I know." She flashed him a pixy-like half-smile over her shoulder. "We have a lake at Gryphon Park with its own stream. We know to stay away from the dam when skating. But here, unless I am over the creek itself, even if the ice broke, I'd only fall a foot. And I can see that it is frozen all the way down."

She peered at the milky ice beneath her feet, catching glimpses of imperfections here and there to a depth of about a foot.

Vlad nodded thoughtfully. "We could also walk on the snow, if you wanted to look out over the edge. There is a boulder right there—by that large hemlock—that offers a good vantage point for gazing down at the falls."

The two of them stepped from the ice and walked carefully on their blades, leaving long marks in the newly-fallen snow. When they reached the boulder, Rachel brushed snow from the large rock and leaned over it. She lay on her stomach with her silver skates kicking in the air and peered over the edge at the waterfall. Frozen fingers of ice hung down, forming jagged, lace-like formations, below which water flowed freely. The whiteness of the ice seemed to glow in the near-darkness. From the brink to the small pool below was a drop of twelve feet. Leaning over thus, Rachel listened to the nigh-deafening noise of the water. Staring down, she felt as if she were about to plunge into the icy waters of the pool beneath, even though she knew she was safe on the boulder.

"Miss Griffin, a pair of asrai live here." Vlad's first word was hard to hear over the roar of the falls. As he spoke her name, however, her black bracelet vibrated, and she could hear his voice perfectly in her ear. "Any sign of them?"

Rachel shook her head, her attention focused on the pool below. "This is the uppermost falls of Roanoke Creek, right? Do they live in all four waterfalls? Or only this one?"

"I have not seen them at the others." He stood behind her, one hand resting on the branch of the large hemlock. "I have seen them here, upon occasion, when I came up here from the boardwalk."

Rachel turned her head, staring down the creek to the south, but she could not see the boardwalk from here. "I never see anyone on the boardwalk when I fly by it. Why is it there, if no one uses it?"

"It was originally a bridle path," he replied. "Back when horses were still part of the academy's curriculum. When the school modernized in the seventies and dismantled the stables, the bridle path was turned into a boardwalk. It was quite popular, I am told. After the Battle of Roanoke, however, the entire campus shut down for a few years. When the school started up again, about twenty years ago, none of the new students were aware of the boardwalk's existence, so very few people come here anymore."

Rachel crossed her arms on the cold boulder and rested her chin on them. Almost no one used the boardwalk, and yet Vlad had come this way often enough to have seen the elusive water fey who lived in the falls—not just once but "upon occasion." Rachel herself had been on the boardwalk only a few months ago. She had come with... Sandra.

Oh, of course. That must have been how Vlad and her sister carried on their romance without Peter or Laurel knowing about them. They probably spent quite a bit of time on the boardwalk—where they could be relatively certain no one would disturb them. It must have been their own intimate romantic retreat, rather like Rachel's private hallway and her secret hexagonal room. So when Sandra wanted a private talk with her little sister, she had automatically taken Rachel to the place that she herself had habitually gone when she wanted privacy. Or perhaps, her sister had wanted to see the special place she had shared with the boy she loved and had merely taken her sister along because Rachel happened to be there.

"Do you ever see an asrai?" asked Vlad, his voice still speaking right beside her ear.

Rachel shook her head. "I'm surprised they allow river nymphs so close to the school. Aren't they dangerous?"

"Asrai? No. They are very shy and retiring. It is quite an honor to see one."

"Oh!" Rachel peered more closely at the frozen curtains of ice. Nothing moved. She tried remembering back, but she still saw no sign of motion in the waters. "What do they look like?"

"Lovely young women made of wind and water."

"Then they are like river nymphs, only not murderous."

"Murderous?" Vlad's voice rose. "Do you know of many murderous nymphs?"

"I live along the River Dart. By ancient covenant, Dart's allowed to claim one human life a year."

"And your father allows this?"

Rachel shrugged. "What can he do? It is his duty to uphold the covenants. It used to be worse, centuries ago, before she was bound."

"She kills a person a year?"

"Not always. If she can grab someone in the winter months, she gets away with it, but if she has not killed by the Spring Equinox, we make a man of straw and hold a huge ceremony, where we mourn and wail and carry on—so that it seems as if she has taken something of worth from us. Then one of the townspeople pens an article for one of the mundane papers, saying how so-and-so has died and how tragic it is. And isn't it good that Dart took someone early this year, so we are all free to enjoy her waters for the rest of the months? And it's done."

"Why put an article in the Unwary papers?"

"Even the Unwary believe that Dart kills. They have a saying that goes: 'Dart, Dart, cruel Dart, every year thou claim'st a heart.' It's their local legend." Rachel turned to look at him over her shoulder. "Don't you have murderous river maidens in Bavaria, too? I thought the Rhine was famous for them. What about Lorelei?"

"We have many legends about Rhine Maidens, but no one has seen Lorelei in many, many years. I believe the last reported sighting was in the time of my great-grandfather, and the members of my family are very long-lived. We do have a statue of her though."

His voice sounded thoughtful, but it was dark enough now that she could not quite make out his features.

Rachel climbed onto her feet and began making her way back across the snow. Vlad fell in beside her. Stepping from the shore to the ice was always tricky, but soon they were gliding across its smooth surface again, back toward the illumination of the wisp sculptures.

"What does she look like?" Rachel reached out and slipped her hand into Vlad's again.

"The statue of Lorelei?" he asked. "It looks like Lorelei Wednesday."

"You mean our Rory Wednesday?" Rachel exclaimed in surprise. "The most beautiful girl on campus—except for the princess? That Miss Wednesday? Do you think Rory could actually be the Rhine Maiden?"

"She could be a descendant, I would think," replied Vlad. "I hardly think she is the Rhine Maiden herself. That would be decidedly strange."

Rachel looked up at him. "Stranger than you actually being a Gypsy swan king from another dimension?"

Vlad gave a short, sharp laugh. "Perhaps not." He paused. "You mentioned that you had something of dire import to discuss? Or have we already spoken of that?"

"I do." Rachel looked around nervously. "And, no, not yet."

Von Dread looked around at the trees and ice. A few blue and violet wisps floated nearby. The other skaters all seemed to be gathered beneath the lantern-shaped wisp-sculptures, where it was bright enough to see the ice.

"We are alone," he observed, letting go of her hand and crossing his arms. "There may be methods to spy on us that I am unaware of, though. Such as some of your methods. I assume you will not be spying on us while we are speaking?"

"No." Rachel snorted with mirth. "Vlad, I'll try to explain the situation without saying too much. My father is not the only one whose memories were changed. Mine were changed, too. Only I also recall my original memories. But I am afraid to let in front of anyone who..." she pursed her lips together, and looked around nervously, "... might be related to anyone who might have wanted me not to have my real memories."

She watched his face very carefully. He looked a little confused, which was a first.

"Might be related...." Dread frowned. "Wait, why change your memories? How does that make any sense? Wouldn't your friends just remind you? How ridiculous. If the being who tried to change your memories is the one I think it is, I assume it might have known it would fail. Unless I am not guessing correctly, which is a strong possibility, since I do not even begin to claim that I can guess from whom you are getting your information. My father would be impressed. He is not easy to impress."

Enough of the gold-white light reached them where they skated now for Rachel to be able to make out his expression. He looked slightly sad, as if he really were a nineteen-year-old boy who wished he could impress his father.

Rachel bit her lip, touched by this glimpse through the chink in the wall of the fortress that was Dread. She had never seen him look vulnerable before. This glimpse into his inner world went to her head like wine. She felt as if she were back by the waterfall staring down at the pool—only as if the drop was much deeper, and the pool much larger, a veritable ocean above which she teetered dangerously—as if she were standing on a tiny platform that might, at any moment, pull free of its few restraints and plunge down into the dark purple waters of the ocean of the heart.

Sternly, she pulled herself back from this particular brink. She had the best of boyfriends, after all, and she was hardly going to try to win Vlad away from her own sister. As long as this was a day for brutal honesty, however, she had to admit that she had been wrong when she congratulated herself for not looking at any boy but Gaius. She had forgotten that there was one other boy who occasionally came dangerously close to turning her head.

Vladimir straightened and became the Dread everyone knew again. "I can control information leaving the school in many ways. But I cannot stop someone from stepping into a dream. Perhaps you could speak to the power that implanted the false memories?"

"There are two powers involved," Rachel said slowly. "We can call them the Dark Angel and the Master of the World. The Master is the one I am worried about. The other one...." She smiled and murmured softly. "That one can do no wrong in my eyes."

"This second one, this so called Master, is a man?" Vlad asked imperiously. "If so, he will be reasoned with or dealt with. He should elect the former."

Rachel actually smiled, a real smile. "Thank you, Vlad. That makes me feel much more cheerful. And safe."

He nodded grimly, but Rachel could tell that her words pleased him. He was gratified that his presence made her feel safe. She suppressed a girlish sigh. He was so *cute*! It was a very good thing that she liked Sandra so very, very much. No lesser woman would deserve him!

Skating closer, she tugged on his sleeve until he leaned toward her. She said softly, "The Master of the World is the one who took my father's memory away. He made the Guardian do it. He can order the Guardian around."

Vladimir's pupils widened. "That is...something. Do you know why he did it? Was it something to protect the world?"

"My father broke a covenant he had made with him. Father thought... he misunderstood what I was saying and thought the Guardian had tried to hurt me. So Father... did something to get the Guardian's attention. Something that affected the Wall that protects the world."

Dread stood a little straighter. "What did he do? No." He raised his hand. "It's better not to know. Perhaps.... Are you going to try and heal your father? Or should we leave him as he is? It is up to you."

Rachel's voice shook slightly. "I'm afraid of the Master of the World."

Feeling suddenly exposed, she peered into the darkness beneath the trees, recalling the woodwose and the troll and the other creatures that the Raven had said were aprowl. She caught no sign of anything untoward. Sternly, she reminded herself that, whatever those nasties were about, they could not enter school grounds. The tension in her chest eased slightly.

"He is an unknown. And he is powerful." Vladimir nodded. "He has control over our lives, and we know nothing about him." He paused and then continued with calm determination. "We must discover more. His interests. His weaknesses."

"Vlad, there *is* more. The Master of the World...." Rachel took a deep breath and tried to keep her voice from trembling. It had been this final piece that had stunned Gaius. If Von Dread went into shock as Gaius had, she did not know how she was going to bear it. "The Master of the World is the head of the Romanov family. He's the father of the King of Magical Australia."

The Prince of Bavaria blinked twice. "That is unexpected."

Rachel waited, peering at him carefully, but Vladimir merely looked grim. She let out her pent-up breath. What a relief! Finally, there was someone to whom she could speak candidly—without reducing him to an inmate at Bedlam!

That was unkind, she noted with chagrin, one of the first such thoughts she had ever had toward her boyfriend. Well, other than the part where she had been enraged at him, but she had already forgiven Gaius for that, for the most part. She could not help wishing, however, that Gaius had been the strong one, the one who took the news well. She did not like being the stronger of the two of them. It did not feel right.

"I do not want to declare outright war upon this Romanov yet," stated Vladimir, his arms still crossed. "I need to find out more about him first. It is unfortunate the princess dislikes me so, but knowing he exists helps a great deal. Now we must figure out how to investigate further, without letting him know that we have learned of his existence."

Rachel felt so grateful to have an ally, someone else willing to take up this fight, that she found herself at a loss for words. They skated back toward the dancing lights in silence. Ahead, the skating party was beginning to break up, due to the failing light. Students were starting to leave the ice in search of their boots.

"Gaius was worried about me telling you even this much," Rachel said finally. "He's afraid of you losing your memory. He says we need you. I think he's right. But the Rav...the Guardian said it would be okay if I told you. And I didn't want you accidentally angering the Romanov princess again, without knowing the risks."

"I thank you for telling me," Dread replied. "I... would rather know."

Rachel smiled shyly. His calm, no-nonsense approach to the dangers she described was so much more than she had hoped for. She suddenly felt lighthearted, so lighthearted that she was not sure her feet were touching the ice.

"I am going to work on how to help Father, so he can get better," Rachel spoke firmly. "So I can convince him of what an excellent son-in-law you'll be."

"I would appreciate that," he replied sincerely.

She gazed up at him, as he loomed above her, blue sparkles floating about his head. He gazed back at her solemnly. Standing so, she could almost hear the snap of yet another of the imaginary supports keeping her from falling into the ocean of love. She felt so close to him when they spoke together like this, as if they could calmly and rationally discuss any topic. They might actually have suited rather well as husband and wife, she thought wistfully. It would have been like marrying a young version of her grandfather.

"I'd marry you myself," the words were out before she realized she was speaking, "if we didn't both prefer someone else."

"Were you older, I might have met you first," he replied. "At this point, I would prefer not having to duel Valiant again."

A shiver of pleasure ran through Rachel. *That was not what she had expected him to say.* Overcome with girlish delight, she impetuously tugged on the prince's coat sleeve. When he leaned down, she balanced on her toe-rakes and kissed him lightly on the cheek.

Vlad smiled. It made him look quite handsome, even more so than he ordinarily did. Leaning forward, he wrapped his arms around her and lifted her from the ice. He pulled her against his chest and held her tightly. Rachel gratefully hugged him back. His body was both unyielding and unexpectedly warm.

"Do not let people know I am hugging anyone," he whispered in her ear. "If they find out, I'll have to give them out to everyone."

"Most certainly. That would ruin your reputation." Rachel managed a cool tone despite the waves of giddiness that assailed her. She pictured the Knight of Walpurgis' meetings, if all the girls who fancied the prince thought he was fair game for hugging. A brief giggle escaped her lips. She whispered, "It will be our secret."

Von Dread balanced her carefully on her skates again. Then, he bent down and kissed her on the cheek, just beside her ear. A most glorious sensation blossomed through her body, tingling from the top of her scalp down to her toes. It was a very grown-up feeling, but, oddly, it felt *right*—not awkward and too mature, as when Gaius kissed her in the same spot.

The same spot? It could not be an accident. This by-the-ear-kissing must be a trick that boys knew about, at least these two boys, who were friends. Vlad had kissed her there quite deliberately, which meant: he must have *wanted* her to feel this way.

Snap. The last teetering restraints suspending her above the vast ocean of the heart broke and she *fell...*

in...

love.

"*I love you!*" she blurted out. Before he could reply, she spun and skated off, calling over her shoulder, "Bye!"

CHAPTER THIRTY-FIVE:

SPARKS IN THE DARK

CRACK!

Flash!

Kaboom!

It took Rachel a moment to realize that the clamor came from real lightning flashing across the dark twilight sky and not from the chaotic state of her thoughts. In the brilliant illumination, tiny flakes drifted amidst the twinklings of the blue and violet wisps. It had begun to snow. It was strange to have lightning and snowflakes. Thundersnow was a rare occurrence.

Another lightning bolt jagged across the sky, so low it seemed to clip one of the taller trees as it continued to race by, which was, of course, impossible.

In a burst of orange flame, the top branches of that tall hemlock ignited. Rachel blinked in confusion. Lightning could strike a tree, but it could not clip it as it flashed past. Another lightning bolt careened madly around the sky, striking three trees, two of which blossomed into balls of orange flame.

Lightning imps!

High in the sky, a trumpet sounded. A dark child-like shape, with a horn, white cap, and doublet and hose, flew by overhead.

The Heer of Dunderberg had crossed the warding wall!

Rachel shoved aside her confusion over the state of her heart and pulled from her pocket the oak key amulet that Sigfried had made for her. She slipped it around her neck. Shouts rang out and a few screams, but they sounded more startled than afraid. By now, all the students had made anti-lightning amulets. Some skaters hurried away from the flaming trees, but upperclassmen were already dousing the fires—an easy task for a canticler of any skill.

Ahead, proctors were herding the students into the central area of ice lit by the wisp sculptures. Familiars barked, screeched, or howled with excitement. Through the late twilight and the falling snow, Rachel spotted Ivan, Marta Fisher, Yolanda Debussy, and Agravaine Stormhenge, four of the five students who were members of the secret organization called the Brotherhood of the White Hart. They moved about briskly, helping the proctors by conjuring boots or dousing fires. She did not see their fifth member, John Darling.

A fountain of golden sparks ignited in the darkness, accompanied by rousing music and a chorus of "Ahh!" from gathered students. Rachel recognized the tune the Ginger Snaps were playing, a type of protective enchantment called a *Sacred Ring*. The spell formed a ring of bright golden sparkles that no harmful entity or power could cross. Rachel had never seen a *Sacred Ring* cast by such a large group of musicians. She was impressed by the size of their twinkling circle; it had a diameter of well over a hundred feet. As John Darling was a member of the Ginger Snaps, that accounted for the fifth White Hart.

"Everyone?" William's voice came calmly over the black bracelet. "Vlad? A spruce troll is approaching the skating area."

A spruce troll? Then it was not just the Heer and his minions. The wards had been breached. *Roanoke was under attack!*

Dread's voice rang out over the bracelet, cool and in command. "Spread out. Head north. The trouble seems to be coming from that direction. Be on your guard. There may be worse things than spruce trolls heading our way."

"The ogre is coming, too," Rachel announced over the bracelet. She was pleased with how even her voice sounded. It hardly shook at all. "And the woodwose and more."

"That is ill news," replied Dread. "We must see that the ogre does not make another kill. Evans, Dare, Westenra: Look for students who may be in danger. Locke, Valiant, Coils: The breach in the wards must be located immediately. And, everyone, avoid the proctors. Their duty to protect students will compel them to impede our progress. Go."

"Aye, aye, boss," drawled Gaius cheerfully.

Rachel was relieved when her heart did its normal little dance at the sound of her boyfriend's voice. Whatever treacherous affections she might feel towards Vladimir, Gaius definitely still came first.

Vladimir had not been addressing her, but Rachel longed to follow his instructions. Despite her trepidations about the wild fey being on the move, she, too, wanted to help make sure everyone was safe. She skated well and did not lose her head when in danger. That made her just the sort of person who could be helpful in an emergency. And it would make her feel closer to Vlad and Gaius if she could act as one of their exclusive group.

Alas, she was not one of their group. Instead, she was a fresh-man who had promised herself that she would be more careful—now that she knew how worried her father was for her. Reluctantly heading for her boots, Rachel cast one last glance back into the beck-oning darkness.

"Help!"

Instantly, she became motionless as a fawn, listening. Had she heard a cry? Was it her imagination? Or a fey creature seeking to trick her?

"Somebody! Help me!" The voice sounded faint but definite. Rachel cupped her hands around her mouth. "Hallo?"

"Rachel, is that you?" cried a familiar, frightened voice. "It's me! Astrid!"

Rachel peered into the blackness and then glanced toward the bright, gold-white wisp lanterns. Technically, she should go fetch a proctor, rather than skate off into the fey-filled night like—well, like Gaius and his friends. But, there were very few proctors and tutors in proportion to the number of students, and it would take time to go find someone and come back, time Astrid would spend alone in the dark. If that *was* Astrid.

She gazed in the direction of the cry, but the night was now totally black. She could make out nothing, except a few stray lilac wisps, hovering like spots before her eyes. Luckily, however, she had skated through this area earlier in the evening. Relying on the map provided by her memory, she pushed off and began to adroitly avoid the stumps and fallen logs that had been visible earlier.

"Are you all right?" Rachel called, skirting to the left to avoid a sapling. She shot forward and then dragged her toe-rake, gliding to stop before a prone figure she could barely make out in the dark.

"I'm all right. Except for my pride. I think it may be a little crumpled. Or maybe that's my nose." Astrid's gentle voice was closer now. She sounded frightened but plucky. "I fell."

"I fell, too." Rachel pressed her hand against her chest, above her disloyal heart. She glanced, as she did so, back toward where she had skated with Vladimir. She did not bother explaining to her roommate that she meant a different kind of fall.

Another lightning bolt cut across the sky, illuminating the ice. Astrid shrieked.

In its momentary flash, Rachel saw her roommate splayed on her stomach, a trickle of blood running from her nose. Snowflakes dusted her back and hat. Around the fallen girl's neck was the purple, tasseled scarf Rachel had given her as a Yule gift. Rachel smiled, touched.

Then, it was dark again.

This was *the real Astrid*. No fey out to trick her would have added the purple scarf.

The night seemed even blacker and colder after the brightness of the lightning. Rachel drew her coat closer around her and donned her furry mittens and her snowman hat. Then she knelt down beside her roommate.

Astrid's voice trembled with fear. "I-I don't h-have...."

"Shh. All is well," Rachel murmured. "It's going to be okay."

"I-I didn't b-bring my lightning c-charm," Astrid's voice was still shaking—whether from fear or the cold, Rachel did not know.

Bracing herself against a trunk, Rachel grabbed Astrid's outstretched hand. Her roommate gamely began trying to regain her feet. Astrid's skates slid several times. It did not help that Astrid was one of the taller girls in the freshman class, significantly taller than Rachel. Once she nearly tumbled over Rachel's shoulder, but the two girls refused to give up. Finally, Astrid stood shakily on her skates, holding tightly to a slender hemlock sapling.

Another flash of lightning. Astrid screamed again.

"You must think me such a ninny," she apologized shyly, ducking her head as she clung to the evergreen. "I-I've always been nervous during thunderstorms. My uncle d-died by being struck by lightning."

"Oh! I'm sorry!" Rachel cried. "Were you there when it happened?"

"No, it was b-before I was born. But I have been told about it my whole life."

"Oh. I guess that might make it scarier."

"Yes. I think it does."

"Here!" Bending away in the dark, Rachel pulled her own oak key from her neck and slipped it into Astrid's hand. "Wear this one."

"Oh! You brought an extra one!" The tall, slender girl sounded so relieved. "How smart!"

"Siggy made me that one," Rachel replied.

She did not add that she had not thought to bring the one she made herself in class, so she was now without protection from the lightning.

Together, the girls started their trek back through the ice-covered forest. Astrid was a poor skater. She had only worn skates twice before, she explained, while visiting Rockefeller Center Skating Rink with her family. It did not help that as soon as they started moving, she gave a little cry and lifted her left foot.

"I... seem to have hurt my ankle."

"Sprains are easy to heal with enchantment," Rachel replied cheerily, hiding her dismay. She wished she knew some healing enchantment and wondered if she should use her bracelet to call for Jenny. "If we can get you to the others, I'm sure someone can have you on both feet in no time!"

"I-if I can get t-there." Astrid's teeth chattered.

"I've got a jolly idea! I'll pull you," exclaimed Rachel. "We've played this game at home loads of times. Stand behind me and put your hands on my shoulders."

Rachel stood with her back to Astrid, who grasped Rachel's shoulders with both hands. The difference in their heights made this more difficult, but Rachel was able to pull the taller girl. Astrid held one foot gingerly in the air, gliding on her other blade, as Rachel drew her slowly forward.

They moved through the blackness. Rachel was glad that she remembered the way, because the reflections in the ice of the golden-white lanterns and the sparkling sacred ring made their exact location confusing to the eye. Flashes of lightning gave glimpses of the landscape ahead. Occasionally, tall beams of white light, stretching from the earth to the sky, lit up the night as well. Someone was jumping—probably Dread.

Sure enough, in the next flash of lightning, Rachel caught a glimpse of him, falling with the snow, as he blasted the Heer of Dunderberg with Eternal Flame from his wand. When Vlad approached the ground, he turned into a tall beam of light and reappeared high in the sky, well above the storm goblin, and the whole thing happened again.

Rachel's heart skipped a beat every time she saw him falling.

She drew her eyes away from Dread's battle and brushed snow from her face. A layer of fine white powder was forming across the ice. The two girls glided silently through the darkness. Their breath formed misty puffs. Behind her, Rachel could hear the roar of the waterfall growing fainter. Astrid stumbled, scratching her face against low-hanging branches. Rachel did her best to avoid such branches, but she had not glanced high enough, earlier in the afternoon, to recall what was there at Astrid's level.

"Ouch!" cried Astrid. "Something hit me!"

"Ow!" A sharp pain went through Rachel's head, like having a hair plucked. It smarted. Tears stung her eyes.

"Something just stung my cheek!" cried Astrid. "Oh! And my arm."

Ouch!

Sharp pain struck Rachel's ear. She clapped her hand to the spot, accidentally knocking away something that buzzed like a dragonfly.

"*Aroint you, giantesses! This is our forest now!*" came a high, sweet voice in the vicinity of Rachel's ear.

"Pixies!" Rachel declared fiercely, moving closer to Astrid, who grabbed her shoulders so tightly that it hurt.

"Yes, Sir Thistlewhip!" cried another even higher voice. "For fair is foul, and fowl is fare. And we would have royal fare tonight! Let us take these giantesses captive and force them to cook us a feast."

Other tiny voices, high and sweet, called out from the darkness nearby.

"They can bake us honeysuckle pie and roast nightwings, sweet cakes of spiderweb and a thousand lovely delicacies!"

"Let us make the giantesses our slaves!"

"Slaves, Sir Rosethorn? Poppycock and dimwhittle! Let us pluck their heads till they are bald, and use their purloined locks to fleece our beds! We shall sleep like princes snuggled amidst locks such as these!"

"That hair's mine!" objected Rachel, as a second lock was yanked from her head.

Astrid tugged her hat closer over her ears. She murmured wryly, "I'm not sure they would want my hair. It seems to have a mind of its own. I don't think it would be good for pixie beds—unless they want it for bedsprings."

Rachel smiled but then cried out again, as something jabbed her in the back. She swatted at the darkness. Her hand encountered nothing.

"Move hence, giantesses!"

The sharp pain prodded her again. She jumped, nearly losing her balance. Astrid cried out in pain, whether from a thorn or because she had put weight on bad foot, Rachel could not tell.

"We can make them dance for the redcaps, who will give us, in return, some of their stormy, sleep-causing rum!"

Sir Thistlewhip called, "With which we can play tricks on mortals, Sir Eglantine!"

At this, the high, sweet voices all laughed together, a sound as melodious and as eerie as a Wagnerian chorus.

"Let us trade them to Big-Ugly in the cove for sparkles!" cried Sir Rosethorn.

"No good! No good!" cried Sir Thistlewhip. "That one will as soon as eat us! Our weapons, so sharp and fierce, mean nothing to it! That one only fears the lightning-throwers!"

"Let us spirit the giantesses away, comrades-at-arms!" cried Sir Rosethorn. "So far that no mortal will ever regain them!"

The voice of Sir Eglantine replied, "Yes! They shall not find them, not unless they have in hand the star from the crown of the First of Kings, stolen nigh these two hundred years from our Heer!"

"Let us punish these children for the crime of those!"

"Charge!"

Rachel found herself beset on all sides. She twisted and swatted, to no avail.

"Ow!" Astrid cried. "They're poking me. They're everywhere! Mean little buggers!"

A flash of lightning illuminated the forest. Tiny knights with dragonfly wings and lances tipped with thorns surrounded the girls, hovering amidst the twirling snowflakes. They wore armor of bark and helmets made from acorn caps. Their faces were fierce and fey.

Then it was dark again.

Rachel waved her hands around but could not catch a single one.

"Oh! I can't see them!" cried Rachel. "I can't paralyze them if I can't see them."

"Ow!" cried Astrid again, frightened.

Rachel kept up a brave front for Astrid's sake, but she was frightened. It was tremendously disorienting to be surrounded by tiny sharp things she could not see. She kept fearing they would stab her in the eye or cause her to trip or just keep them from reaching safety until the two girls froze to death. Her breath caught in her throat.

"What would we do at home?" she murmured, her voice warbling. Then, suddenly, she laughed. "Silly me."

"Silly...? Why?" Astrid's gentle voice was tinged with hope. "You know what to do?"

Reaching into her coat pocket, Rachel pulled out the two small bottles left in her pockets from the Yule holiday and put one into Astrid's hand. "Here. Spray them."

The swish of spray bottle pumps sounded in the darkness.

"Och! I am slain!" cried Sir Thistlewhip, though he sounded perfectly hale.

"*Flee, flee!*" cried Sir Rosethorn, "*before the putrid miasma bears down the rest of us!*"

"*But what of the delicacies!*" inquired Sir Eglantine. "*The strapping giantesses?*"

"*Flee! Flee, I say!*"

With buzzing and high, sweet cries of knightly woe, the pixies fled into the snowy night.

"And good riddance!" Astrid shouted into the darkness. Then, she grew quiet and ducked her head, as if startled by her own show of pluck. After a moment, however, she sniffed the cold air. "Smells like..." she breathed more deeply, "... lavender?"

"Lavender is useful for many things," Rachel replied gaily, giving the little bottle of Bogey Away an extra squirt before she returned it to her pocket. She, too, breathed in the mingled scent of lavender and snow. "The First of Kings? I wonder who they meant."

"Do you think maybe they meant the one we learned about in True History, King Alulim of Sumer?" mused Astrid. "And who were the 'other children'?"

"Other children?" Rachel stared.

Astrid hesitated, as if suddenly uncertain of herself. Her teeth chattered a little "They s-said something was s-stolen nearly t-two hundred years ago, and that 'these children'—meaning us—should pay the price for the others. I assume they meant the thieves."

"Oh! They did, indeed. Good catch, Astrid! You're quite sharp!"

"Thanks," Astrid sounded embarrassed but sweetly pleased.

"We could use someone like you in the Die Horribly Debate Club," mused Rachel. It occurred to her that she had just heard Astrid speak outside of class more in the last fifteen minutes than in the whole rest of the school year put together.

"I-I... don't think the princess wants me there." Astrid ducked her head again.

"Nastasia?" Rachel asked, surprised. "If it were up to her, everyone would be a member! If she seems standoffish, it's because she's so annoyed not to be able to share information with everyone. But... it's dangerous, some of what we do."

"Like falling out of dreamland in T-transylvania?" Astrid gave a mock shudder. "No thanks! I'm m-more of an R&D person, anyway."

"R&D?" asked Rachel, puzzled.

"Research and D-development."

"Ooh! Science stuff. Like Gaius and William," Rachel cried enthusiastically. "You were an intern at O.I. last summer, weren't you?"

"Y-yes." Astrid's teeth chattered audibly now.

"Oh! I am so sorry! You're cold!" Rachel turned back toward the bright central area where the wisp lanterns hung above the ice.

"Oops."

"Oops."

"Oops... what?" Astrid asked nervously.

"I'm... turned around. I—don't know where we are."

"Can't we just move toward the bright spot?"

Rachel wet her lips, which only made them feel more chapped. There was no way to explain the problem to Astrid—that she no longer knew where the stumps, fallen trunks, and low branches were—without revealing the secret of her perfect memory. This hardly seemed the time for that. Rachel blinked in the darkness, hoping to recognize a shape, a branch or tree. Near at hand, however, the only object her eyes could distinguish was a single, lone, blue wisp. Astrid must have been looking at the same twinkle. She sighed wistfully. "It's a shame neither of us brought an instrument. We could play that song we had to perform back in October for our first quarter review. The one that summoned wisps."

"What a good idea," Rachel blinked in the darkness. "I wonder...."

Using her mother's technique, she made her entire face as still as a mask. Then, keeping her features as motionless as possible, Rachel began to whistle the tune they had practiced in class. The piece was much longer than the short three notes of the hexes she normally whistled. Her first two tries, she lost control of the magic. Miniscule indigo summoning sparks ignited in the darkness, fizzled, and vanished again. Rachel's lips and cheeks buzzed and tickled. It felt both strange and uncomfortable. But she hated to give up.

Rachel pulled out the lavender lip balm from her pocket and moistened her lips. Then, closing her eyes, she tried again, more slowly. Twinkling, bright points shown through her eyelids, and the smell of apples filled the air.

There! Astrid gasped in awe. Into the silence of the night came a soft, nigh-inaudible sound. It grew louder until it became the whisper-hum of wisps. Rachel opened one eye.

Tiny points of wisp light — blue, violet, lilac, and gold-white — danced around the girls. The wisps circled their heads like a twinkling mobile, illuminating the darkness and the falling snow with their colorful glow. Rachel moved her hands; the little sparkles moved with them.

It was utterly beautiful, as if the stars had come down to earth to bow and dance. Spreading her arms, Rachel threw back her head and twirled on her blades, laughing with joy. Astrid could not twirl. She held firmly to a hemlock branch. Yet her face, too, was filled with wonder, blues and purples playing over her features.

With a cry of delight, Astrid exclaimed, "This must be how the planet Jupiter feels, surrounded by its moons!"

Basking in the radiance of their personal galaxies of whirling wisps, the two girls moved forward. Rachel skated, pulling Astrid behind her. Skating to the whisper-song of the wisps, they eventually came to the edge of the ice.

"Let's see if you can step on your foot now," Rachel suggested.

Astrid gazed at the snowy bank. "I-I guess I take off my skates and walk in my socks?"

"Not at all," insisted Rachel. "Just walk on your blades."

"But... there's no ice."

"Just walk normally. Like this." After helping Astrid to hold onto a tree, Rachel stepped carefully off the ice and then stomped around, demonstrating. "Just make sure you place your foot straight down each time, and you'll be fine."

"Really?" Quite hesitantly, Astrid tried stepping from the ice onto the snowy bank. "Hey! That's easy! Why didn't anyone ever tell me that you could do this in skates?"

"Don't know," Rachel laughed. "How's your foot?"

"Smarts, but it's not as bad as it was. I think I can hobble."

Another lightning flash illuminated the snowy scene. Astrid let out a soft squeak and grasped the oak key that now hung around her neck.

"Hallo? Someone there?" Ivan Romanov's voice floated out of the darkness.

"Yes!" Rachel called out. "Over here!"

"What do we have here?" Ivan came forward, a ball of *lux* light hovering at his shoulder. He had traded his skates for high leather boots with gum soles and moved confidently across the snow-covered landscape. He stopped, however, as if startled. Or, perhaps, he was charmed by the sight of two young women surrounded by will-o'-the-wisps—an aura of gold-white, violet, blue, and lilac dancing around them. For he stood gawking, his mouth open. "Are you...human? Or...."

"Quite human." Rachel fought not to laugh.

He stepped forward, grinning his princely grin. "Hallo, Rachel and... Anghared? Agnes?"

It took Rachel a moment to grasp that he did not remember her roommate's name.

"Astrid. Astrid Hollywell," she replied dryly. "Your sister's roommate?"

"Yes, of course. Sorry, Astrid." He flashed her a good-natured smile. "What seems to be the trouble? Leg hurts?"

"I fell," Astrid said sheepishly. "I-I hurt my ankle."

"Cold, too, by the sound of it. No worries. Let me give you a hand, shall we?" he asked.

Bending, Ivan lifted Astrid and carried her across the snow, striding as easily as if his arms were not filled with a tall fourteen-year-old girl. In just a few steps, he was more than ten feet ahead of Rachel, who had to place each skate carefully to walk.

"Coming, Mini Griffin?" he called over his shoulder.

"Um. Yes, but I think I'll skate," Rachel called back. "Faster that way."

Returning to the ice, she skated backward, waving until they were out of sight.

Chapter Thirty-Six:

Wilis at the Water's Edge

"Yoohoo!" Joy O'Keefe's voice came over the calling card in Rachel's pocket. "Does anyone know how to get rid of Wilis?"

Rachel, who was a mere hundred feet from the crackling, sparkler-like edge of the sacred ring, slowed down. Wisps twinkled around her like multi-colored stars. Their familiar whisper-song made the darkness more comforting.

Wrestling her card out of her pocket, she spoke into it. "Wilis? Don't they mostly bother boys? You should be all right, so long as you aren't heartbroken."

"They have surrounded Mr. Smith. At least two dozen," the princess's voice replied. She sounded urgent. "And I am afraid he's starting to dance. No, maybe he's trying to stomp on their feet. Either way, do you recall how to stop them? I know we covered repelling them in Music, but I didn't bring my sheet music."

"Griffin, you're the walking encyclopedia!" Valerie's voice joined Nastasia's. "Siggy tried his trumpet and some cantrips, but they won't go away. Was it salt? Hot pepper? Either way, I don't have it on me."

As she listened to the calling card, Rachel turned around in the freezing darkness, hugging her coat close and tried listening for Valerie's voice out there in the darkness. She could hear distant, eerie, ethereal music, the Ginger Snaps playing their enchantment, the crackle of the sacred barrier, shouts, cantrips, and the yaps and squeals of familiars, but not Valerie. Wherever the others were, they were out of voice range.

An eerie chill scampered up her spine. *The ogre!* Sigfried had gone searching for the ogre. Rachel was certain of this. He had headed off in to the darkness, taking the other girls with him—or they had insisted on tagging along. He must have headed north and, thus, run into the Wilis William had mentioned. But if Siggy located the man-eating brute, what could he possibly do to stop it? Of course, mere practicalities such as this had never stopped Sigfried.

"How about Lucky?" Rachel asked aloud, "Aren't they afraid of him? He seems to be able to burn supernatural things."

"Lucky is not currently available," quipped Valerie.

"Um…. Okay. You said no salt, right? Doesn't Nastasia have any in her purse-house?"

"No good," came Valerie's reply. "Siggy already dumped all of it to stop a thing moving in the dark. Only, it turned out to be someone's familiar."

"Oops." Rachel paused, absentmindedly waving her mitten through the air, watching the swirl of dancing blue and violet and occasional gold-white—as the wisps followed her hands.

In Music class, they had studied a song to dispel Wilis, but it was long—much longer than the wisp song that had been so hard for her to whistle—and no one she knew in their class had mastered it. However, they had also covered Wilis in Math.

"Running water!" she cried. "They can't cross running water without a special bridge."

"It's February, in case you hadn't noticed," Valerie replied dryly.

"We don't exactly have a surplus of running water!"

"Yes we do!" Rachel silently thanked Vlad. "You're to the north, right? Just head south. The creek is still running under the ice. That should do it."

"Okaaay." Valerie sounded dubious, but Rachel could hear her calling to Siggy to back up, and the princess's voice murmuring, "Oh, running water. Very wise."

Joy's voice came again. "Hey, Griffin, how'd you know we're to the north?"

Rachel shrugged. "You're with Siggy. Where else would Sigfried the Dragonslayer head but toward the trouble?"

⁂

Putting her card away, Rachel hurried northward, hoping to find them. The eerie feeling that had sent a shiver creeping down her spine remained with her. The feeling slowly grew into a sense of foreboding. Something bad was going to happen if her friends stayed out in the darkness. She felt sure of this. She had to get them back to the safety of the proctors before Sigfried found the invulnerable monster.

She reached the northernmost edge of the ice without encountering anyone. Farther east, she could still hear the faint roar of the waterfall. Heading west, she skated along the edge, searching for her friends—until she recalled that the woods were full of rogue fey. Then she darted southward, moving close to the outer edge of the Ginger Snaps' sacred circle.

The snow was still falling. White flakes danced amidst the golden sparkles of the circle. Her blades left a trail in the white powder coating the ice. As she skated, she veered northward again, hoping to avoid the notice of the proctors. Away from the bright lights of the center, the glow of her entourage of twinkling wisps illuminated the darkness. They glistened beneath her, blue, lilac, and gold-white reflecting off icy patches and, more mutedly, off the snow.

Overhead, lightning flashed, temporarily brightening the landscape. Another white flash, this one vertical, indicated that Dread's fight against the Heer had moved to the east. Rachel's heart skipped a beat. She quickly looked away. It was too nerve-racking to watch him fall, but she smiled, impressed by his valor.

Where was Gaius? Facing lightning imps? Ogres? She wanted to call him but felt she should not, in case he was in a dangerous situation. She did not want to distract him at a crucial moment. Still, it made her just the tiniest bit sad that he had not taken a moment to check on her.

Through the trees came an eerie, pale glow. It was precisely the same glow as the white gowns of the Wilis that she had seen on All Hallows' Eve. Then came the blare of Siggy's trumpet. Coming around a clump of hemlocks, Rachel saw them: tall, veiled women in white, flowing, phosphorescent gowns. Some had sickly, unpleasant, green flames hovering over their outstretched palms. The ghostly women had paused at a random spot on the ice and seemed to be unwilling to go farther, as if restrained by some invisible wall.

They reached out with their long arms, beckoning and calling to the handsome Sigfried.

Rachel circled south, until she was on the far side of the invisible wall, no doubt marking where the creek ran beneath the ice. Soon, through the dark trunks, she caught sight of a ball of *lux*-light hovering over the princess's shoulder. Sigfried, Joy, Nastasia, and Valerie stood on the ice, facing the Wilis. Payback growled beside Valerie, who had a tight grip on the elkhound's collar. Relieved to have reached them, Rachel darted toward her friends.

"What's that?" gasped Joy, pointing in Rachel's direction.

Rachel glanced over her shoulder but saw nothing unusual in the darkness behind her.

"Fey or ae?" called Nastasia.

"I think that's Rachel," said Valerie, shading her eyes. "Do you realize you're sparkling? Tell the truth now, you're really a fairy duchess, not an English one, aren't you?"

"I'm not a duchess, just the daughter of one," Rachel replied cheerfully. "And these are wisps."

Catching on immediately, the princess clapped her hands with delight. "You played the song! The one we practiced in Music!"

"Yes, exactly."

The two girls smiled at each other, happily.

"Our magic doesn't work on these wily women," Siggy scowled, glaring at the pale women. "What good is magic if it doesn't work against bad things?"

"You tried the song for repelling Unseelie?"

"What? That thing? It goes on forever! Who has time to learn all that?"

"People who want to live," Rachel replied dryly. "Did you try a Glepnir band? They're supposed to be useful against the supernatural."

"Oh. Didn't think of that." Sigfried raised his hands and performed the cantrip. "Argos!"

A band of golden light appeared in mid-air, its glow glinting off the falling snow. It encircled the lead Wili. The rest of the ghostly women backed up, hissing. Sigfried cheered and punched the sky.

Payback barked excitedly. Being the well-trained dog that she was, she stayed obediently beside her mistress.

"Yes! Take that, creepy, dancey, freak-women!" Siggy shouted. "Who's going to make who dance now, hmm?"

The Wilis backed away, dragging with them the one Sigfried's Glepnir band had trapped.

Rachel watched them go with relief. She glanced nervously at the dark around them, but saw no sign of motion. For the moment, all was quiet, which meant that now was the time to get her friends back to safety.

"Well done, Blood Brother. Hey, let's head this way! I thought I heard something that might have been a cry for help," Rachel lied casually, as she started moving back toward the central wisp-sculptures.

Nastasia and Joy followed her. Siggy lingered behind shouting at the Wilis, but Valerie took his arm and began dragging him after the girls. Rachel allowed herself a secret smile in the darkness. It looked like she would be able to lead them back without Sigfried realizing what she intended.

Ahead through the trees, the brilliant wisp-sculptures and Ginger Snap's golden circle were but a distant gleam. Rachel judged that she and her friends were at least a quarter mile away from where the proctors were collecting students to bring them back to campus.

As Payback trotted past her, Rachel glanced around. "Where's Beauregard?"

Nastasia held up her purse. "I put him in the house. He did not care for so much ice."

"That makes…"

Three white columns of light flared momentarily against the northern sky. Then they were gone. Someone had jumped. Rachel judged the beam of light to have been far enough away that the people were likely not on school grounds.

"Aw!" Siggy swore, sliding to a stop. "They escaped!"

"Who escaped?" asked Valerie.

"The baddies! The people who opened the wards."

"What?" Rachel asked. She peered northward. "Could you see them from here?"

He shook his head, disgusted. "No. They are out of my range. Lucky went to check out the wards, to see where the break was. He's been circling the property. He came to that spot up there—where that light flashed—and found three people, but now they got away. They were at one of those breaks in the tree wall with big rocks."

"A ward-lock?" Rachel prompted. There was a ward-lock due north, just about where those pillars of jump-light had appeared. "I bet Gaius would be interested in hearing this." She spoke her boyfriend's name with the intention of calling him.

"Yeah, whatever." Sigfried shrugged, unconcerned with the proper name for the breaks in the trees, or maybe that was his re-action to her mentioning Gaius. "The three people dug up one of the big stones. Only they had bags over their heads or hoods or something. Lucky couldn't see their faces."

"Hoods like Veltdämmerung?" asked Rachel. She tried to start skating again, but Sigfried was standing still, looking northward into the night.

Siggy shook his head. "More like black pillowcases with eyes cut in them."

"Oh." Rachel blinked. "I have no idea who that might be."

"What were they wearing?" asked Valerie. She pulled out her notebook, but it was too dark for her to see the pages. Twice, she tried the *lux* cantrip, but she produced only a tiny fizzle of light. Sighing, she glided over into the illumination of the floating light ball that hung beside Nastasia's shoulder. "Sorry. Reporter Girl habits require note taking. And my flashlight doesn't work on cam-pus. Sigfried, describe what Lucky saw, now, before you both for-get the details and report that you saw giant frogs carrying toy heli-copters."

"Now that you mention it, they were rather frog-like," Siggy be-gan.

Valerie glared at him.

"Ouch!" Sigfried exclaimed gleefully, throwing up his arms, as if to parry a blow. "Looks really can wound! Wow! Okay, Fearless Re-porter Girl, far be it from me to mislead the press. They were dressed like us, in school robes, only with black pillowcases with holes cut in them over their heads. They were kind of tall, so probably college kids or adults, not our age."

"They must have been on our side of the wall," Rachel murmured. "Or else even physically removing the stones would not have opened the wards *at the ward-lock to the north of us.*" She spoke the last phrase clearly for the sake of her hopefully-listening boyfriend.

Nor was she disappointed. Over the bracelet, Gaius's cheerful voice spoke in her ear. "Thank you, Miss Griffin. We're on it!"

Amidst her nimbus of blue and violet wisps, Rachel smiled happily.

"We should head back," Nastasia said primly. "The proctors are conveying students back to campus. They've brought kenomanced bags and a few flying umbrella carriages."

No. No! Rachel mentally pictured herself waiving her hands furiously in front of Nastasia, *don't bring it up so directly! I had him heading back!*

"But we haven't found the ogre!" objected Siggy. "Lucky saw him around where we found the Wilis."

Sigfried turned left and right, as if suddenly realizing that he had been skating away from his goal. Then he stopped moving and inclined his head. Rachel guessed that meant he was scanning the area with his amulet.

"The ogre!" cried Joy, frightened. "You didn't tell us the ogre was on campus! It has a charmed life! There's nothing we can do!"

"Charmed by Baba Yaga, right?" countered Sigfried. "Then there's definitely something we can do. We just don't know what it is."

"What do you mean?" asked Joy uncertainly.

"Baba Yaga's magic can be overcome," replied Siggy. "Otherwise, she never could have been defeated by a dancing girl and some mermaids."

"And a sword that no longer exists," quipped Valerie, wryly.

"And the sword that I should have re-forged," nodded Sigfried.

Rachel said, "Baba Yaga was defeated — which means her charms can be overcome. I wish we had asked Varo more questions about how the sword *Nothor* was able to harm her."

The princess sighed in exasperation. "Really, Mr. Smith, this behavior of yours is a dereliction of duty. The brute might not have had a chance to escape, if you had shared what Lucky told you with the rest of us right away."

"If we'd waited, the ogre might have gotten away!" cried Sigfried.

Nastasia made a ladylike noise of frustration. "But the ogre *did* get away, Mr. Smith. From us and from the proper authorities—whom we failed to inform. We were right beside two members of the Brotherhood of the White Hart before you led us in this direction. We could have notified them immediately, instead of heading off on this foolish wild dragon chase! I suspect we are probably breaking six different rules just being out here in the dark by ourselves. Let us head back, before we compound our infractions."

"If we stay, we might be able to break twelve rules! Or thirty-six!" Siggy crowed happily. "What's the record?"

"Really, Mr. Smith. This is unacceptable," the princess exclaimed, exasperated. "Miss Griffin, will you please help me explain why, in the interest of everyone's safety and well-being, rules must be obeyed?"

Siggy, meanwhile, was looking off into the distance. "Come on, Griffin, get your broom. If we hurry, we might make it to the ogre's lair before it gets back."

Rachel suddenly wished she had brought her broom. They could have slipped through the open ward-lock and flown to the far end of the island, while the monster was here, attacking the school. After all, once the ogre had already invaded the campus, the bargain about leaving its belongings alone would be void, right? She shook her head, chagrined. She was supposed to be getting her friends back to safety, not rushing off into the dark. The feeling of foreboding that had troubled her earlier had suddenly returned a hundredfold. She shivered.

Looking around, she realized that the princess was still gazing at her expectantly. Rachel groaned inwardly. Now if she moved toward the wisp-sculptures, it would seem as if she were backing Nastasia, and Sigfried would feel she had turned on him. She hated being thrown in the middle of her friends' arguments. More and more, they seemed bent on pulling her in two.

"Um...." She threw Siggy's girlfriend a pleading look.

Coming to the rescue, Valerie slipped her arm through his. "Come on, big guy. This police detective's daughter thinks that six is the maximum number of rules she can violate in one day."

Rachel breathed a quiet sigh of relief.

The five of them continued skating back through the falling snow, with the princess's shimmering ball of *lux*-light illuminating the way. Snowflakes danced in the pale gold light. Siggy and Valerie skated very close together, Payback trotting close beside them. The dog's presence comforted Rachel. If something bad approached out of the night, surely the dog would smell it.

It was much more pleasant to skate through the night with Nastasia's ball of *lux*-light illuminating the trunks and branches than it had been to rely on the fainter wisp-light, but it was scarier, too. She could not see much beyond the ball of light, and with all the noise her friends were making, she feared she would not hear something approaching out of the night. As the darkness grew more oppressive, Rachel sought a topic to discuss to distract her.

"By the by," she declared suddenly, as they glided through the dark trunks, "I talked to the Comfort Lion about Siggy."

"Did he tell you that I was a robot?" Sigfried crowed. "His father the emperor made me."

"He didn't really make you, Sigfried." Hearing Valerie's voice, Rachel could perfectly picture the Fearless Reporter Girl's eye roll, even though it was too dark to see her.

"Actually, he did," Rachel insisted. "Leander told me so."

"The Comfort Lion's father?" asked Valerie.

Even in the darkness, Rachel could hear the other girl's skepticism.

"I don't think he's *really* a Lion," Rachel said slowly as she glided along. "Any more than the Raven is really a raven."

Ahead, something growled in the darkness. Rachel could make out a motion, low to the ground. Payback barked and would have lunged forward, had her mistress not grabbed her collar.

Valerie pressed closer to Sigfried, pulling the elkhound with her. "Whatever that is, it must be able to cross running water."

"Do your thing, human encyclopedia," Joy squeaked. She also skated back to hide behind Siggy. "Tell us what it is!"

"Um...." Rachel balked, her heart hammering. Her mind raced back to Mr. Tuck's lecture and the drawings she had hung on the wall of 321. "Based just on a growl? Water Panther or *Mexaxkuk*, maybe? Too low to the ground for the ogre, and most of the others don't growl. Unless it's the phooka. One can never tell what a phooka will look like."

"Wow!" Valerie sounded impressed. "You're good! I'm going to pay more attention to this stuff in the future."

Rachel shrugged and glided closer to the others. "Dartmoor can be a dangerous place, if one isn't careful. It's important to know your fey."

Siggy said, "It's a snaky thing. Like the bastard child of an alligator and a giant anaconda with the horns of a horned toad. I can also tell you what it looks like from behind or underneath."

"That would have been the *Mexaxkuk*," said Rachel. "Man-eating horned lizard."

"What stops a... whatever it is?" asked Joy nervously.

"Um? Fresh bread, maybe?" said Rachel. "Though I don't think things that growl eat fresh bread. Rowan branches? Almost everything is stopped by salt or cold iron."

"Siggy used all the salt. Don't think we have any iron," Joy's voice broke. "Unless the princess has some in her house. Do you, princess? You have everything, right?"

Nastasia replied somberly, "No, I don't. But if we make it back alive, I will remedy that."

"We so need a friend from De Vere," muttered Valerie. "Do our steel knives count?"

"I'd be perfectly happy to introduce them to my knife!" cried Siggy.

"Stop!" cried Valerie. "Don't you dare get that close to them!"

"Iron, smiron," scoffed Sigfried, sounding not the least bit disturbed. "I bet this stops it."

He pulled out his trumpet and played a trill. A whoosh of silver sparks lit the darkness, revealing a horned lizard at least twice as big as Lucky squatting on the ice in front of them. With a vanilla-scented *whoosh*, Sigfried's sparkly wind picked the creature up and threw it through the air. It made an odd, sad cry as it sailed off into the darkness.

"Good blowing, Tex!" Valerie punched her boyfriend's shoulder fondly.

"That's why you keep me around," crowed Siggy, sounding quite pleased with her compliment. Turning his head, he called, "Lucky, the yellow-bellied monster turned tail and ran, that coward! It's running right toward you. Get that thing!"

They continued skating through the dark trees. Rachel gauged they had covered half the distance, putting them about an eighth of a mile from their destination. The cheery lights ahead were closer now, though so were the dark shadows cast among the trees. Only a little longer and they would all be safe. With a happy little sigh, she began to breathe more freely.

Payback startled a tiny silver fox out of a bush. Rachel recognized it as a familiar from Spenser Hall. The little thing ran from them, hiding in a thicket, but Nastasia, thanks to the Gift of Moira, could be understood by any creature. When she called to it gently, it came creeping out. Joy picked it up and climbed awkwardly into the princess's house to keep it safe.

"Um, princess?" asked Valerie. "Can Payback go in the house with Joy? She doesn't have an anti-lightning charm, and I'm afraid she'll run after something that can hurt her."

"Of course, she's a good girl, isn't she?" Nastasia opened her bag and smiled at the elkhound, petting the dog's forehead. Valerie spoke a word and pointed. Wagging its curly tail, the silver and black hound ran down the staircase to join Joy, the fox, and Beauregard.

Only four of them remained. Valerie and Siggy skated close together. That left Rachel and Nastasia. The princess moved closer and linked her arm through Rachel's. She offered her muff, and both girls stuck their outside hands into the white furry softness. Some of Rachel's wisps had wandered off, but a halo of lavender and pale gold still surrounded both girls.

The princess sighed sadly. "Rachel, I am beginning to worry about Mr. Smith. He seems to be getting... wilder."

Rachel laughed and squeezed her friend's arm. "No. He's always been that way. The first time I ever spoke with him, he wanted to put bombs on brooms, so we could blow up lecture halls if the classes were too boring."

Nastasia was silent for a moment, and then she began to giggle. She pressed the hand that was linked through Rachel's arm against her lips. "Oh, my. Yes, I guess you are right."

"It's just his way of expressing himself. The world seems cold and arbitrary to him. I think he likes to think that he can take everything that comes his way."

Before Rachel could say more, tall pillars of light began flashing in the distance, first to south, then the east, then the west.

"What's that?" called Valerie, pausing in an attempt to take a photo of the flashes in the dark. Rachel and Nastasia skated over to join her and Sigfried.

"Agents," replied Rachel with confidence. "They are checking on the ward-locks. As soon as they find the damaged one, they will—"

Sure enough, one, two, and then five pillars of light flashed to the north, where the broken ward-lock was. Rachel gestured to the north and smiled.

"Agents of the Wisecraft," sighed Valerie, wistfully. "I'd like to be an Agent."

"You should!" replied Rachel. "They always need more good people."

"Are you going to be an Agent?" Valerie asked curiously.

"And follow directions all the time?" Rachel shuddered. "Not for me!"

Lightning flashes lit the entire sky, illuminating something the size of a boulder flying through the snowy sky.

Boom!

The earth shook.

Crack!

The sound of breaking ice spread to their left.

Rachel's heart leapt into her throat. She tightened her hold on Nastasia's arm. Not now. Not when they were so close!

"What was that?" yelped Valerie in surprise.

Nastasia squinted upward, "I believe the Heer or his servants are tossing boulders."

"Ace!" exclaimed Siggy. "Incoming!"

"That's… not good." Valerie looked up nervously.

"We have nothing to fear from boulders," Nastasia replied. She pulled her hand out of her muff, preparing herself to cast cantrips if needed. "*Nothor* will deflect any flying object."

They glided forward more quickly. Another flash of lightning illuminated the sky, and then a third and fourth. Twice more, the ice trembled and cracked. Then, it was quiet for a bit. The central lights grew close.

Suddenly, as another dark boulder sailed through the snowy sky, there was white light and crackling almost directly overhead. A lightning imp hovered high above them, amidst the swirling snow. It gazed down at the students, its eyes dancing with malicious glee. The little creature seemed to be made of lines of blue-white electricity, all buzzing and bright. Its javelin crackled in its hand. It gave an impish grin and drew back its arm to strike.

"Do your worst!" Sigfried shouted at imp. "I'm properly grounded!"

The imp laughed and cast its javelin. Nastasia and Valerie grabbed the protective oak keys hanging from their necks, but Rachel had nothing to grab.

She had given hers to Astrid.

Chapter Thirty-Seven:

Spells and Cantrips

Against the Lightning

Rachel had only a split second to act, or she would die.

A split second was enough. Suddenly, her comprehension of the scene shifted. Instead of a lightning bolt coming at her, she saw a thrown javelin, an object flying through the air.

She could do this. Her hours of relentless practicing and the physics that William and Gaius had taught her paid off. Without hesitation, she gestured from the crackling bolt to the dark form of the boulder traveling across the sky, directing the inertia of the lightning javelin into the flying rock.

"*Turlu!*"

The javelin stopped moving and then dropped straight down. The spearhead impaled in the snowy ice and trembled there, crackling. Overhead, the lightning imp cursed and sped away.

"Woohoo!" crowed Sigfried. "Yeah! Don't mess with us! We'll take the *voom* right out of your voomerang!"

"That... doesn't make any sense," murmured Valerie.

KABOOM!

Fire blossomed in the distance, on the slopes of Stony Tor. Rachel frowned, wondering what could have caused such an explosion. Then, an eerie horripilation spread through her until the hair along the back of her neck was standing up straight. The orange flames were in an exact straight line from where she had cast the force from the lightning javelin into the boulder. Had her cantrip caused the boulder to fly more than half a mile to collide with the tor?

There would be time to worry about that later. They were nearly back.

"Quick, let's keep going!" she called.

"Help!" A high-pitched cry came from their left. "An ogre! It's got Kris!"

"Ah! There's the target!" cried Siggy, gleefully.

The ice beneath them shook. Something huge came crashing through the trees, into the range of the princess's golden *lux*-light. An enormous humanoid creature pelted across the snowy ice. It towered well over a dozen feet tall, with horns, tusks, and stony skin. Over its shoulder, it carried a girl whose legs were kicking wildly.

Rachel's heart hammering so loudly that she could hardly hear, she grabbed her wand and pointed it at the monster.

"I'll save the damsel in distress!" shouted Siggy. Lifting his head, he called, "Come on, Lucky! Stop dawdling with that *Mexaxkuk*!"

"You can't save her!" Valerie shouted back. "Look at the size of that thing!"

"The ogre's going to eat that girl. I can't just stand here!" Sigfried looked over his shoulder, the crazy humor gone from his eyes. "Besides, I vowed a vow."

Siggy blew his trumpet. Nastasia, who had her violin ready, drew her bow across the strings. The night glittered with a *whoosh* of dancing silver sparkles and fresh, pleasant scents. When they struck the ogre's back, however, they flared oddly and winked out.

No wind pushed the monster. Rachel gulped. Everything she had feared was coming to pass. Her wand would not help. Neither would whistling. All she had left was her tiny frame, which would offer no resistance to the muscle-bound brute.

Suddenly, she nearly laughed aloud. What was the point of having all these powerful protectors, if she did not call them when she needed help!

"Gaius!" she called softly, her hand on her black bracelet.

Her boyfriend's voice spoke in her ear. He did not sound panicked, but she heard a distinct note of alarm. "Rather busy here!" His voice rose, shouting, "Hold still, Topher! I'm coming! Vlad! We need you! Now!"

To the east, a pillar of light flared in one part of the sky and then another. Rachel's heart sank. No help would be coming from that quarter, not anytime soon anyway.

Around her, her friends were backing up, except for Sigfried, who stood his ground, staring back at the brute that stood glaring at him with its beady eyes. The monster was enormous and entirely immune to their magic. There was nothing she could do.

Should she run? After all, Sigfried had asked her to vow with him to stop the ogre, but she had never answered. She was not bound to stay and fight a battle she had no way of surviving. She could flee and live.

With a disdainful snort, Rachel thrust that thought aside as unworthy of her. She would never desert her friends. There must be something they could do. Some hint she had picked up from Darling Northwest, some clue that Mr. Fisher had given them. As she searched her pristine memory, the voices of the pixies rang out in her mind: *Let us trade them to Big-Ugly in the cove for sparkles! No good! No good! ... That one only fears the lightning-throwers!*

The ogre was a member of the compact of fey who wanted to keep the Heer imprisoned, and he lived in Dutchman's Cove. *Could the Big-Ugly in the cove mean....*

"The javelin!" cried Rachel. "The ogre's not immune to lightning!"

"If only we could pick it up!" said Nastasia. "But we would be killed."

"Never underestimate a robot, human!" declared Sigfried.

Pulling a nettle cake from a pocket, he shoved it into his mouth. Then he charged forward, practically running across the ice with his skates. Only now, as she watched him—his ankles turned at an awkward angle, his feet moving in a straight line instead of in a V formation—did Rachel realize why he and Valerie had been skating so close together. Sigfried had needed stabilizing. This was probably his first time on skates.

He raced across the ice. Instead of gliding, he relied on sheer brute strength to run across the ice. At any given second, he was an inch away from a very hard fall. It was only by dint of extraordinary athletic abilities that he kept going. *Maybe he really was a robot!*

Sigfried grabbed the abandoned lightning javelin, where it crackled in the ice, and pulled it free. Continuing his awkward rush, he charged forward, striking the ogre in the only place he could reach without hurting its prey, its ample, meaty backside.

The javelin crackled. Blue-white lightning leapt up and down its length. The ogre let out an enormous, angry roar and stumbled. The girl screamed.

"Oh yeah!" Siggy vaunted. "Pays to be a robot!"

The crackling spear bounced off the brute's pebbly flesh and fell to the ground.

"Oops," murmured Sigfried.

The spearhead had not hurt the brute, but the lightning had discomforted him. Kris's limbs, unfortunately, twitched as well. Rachel's heart leapt into her throat.

Sigfried stabbed at the ogre again and a third time. Electricity crackled over its pebbly skin. The ogre bellowed in pain and tossed his prize aside.

The pink-haired girl flew high into the snowy air. Whipping out her grandmother's silver wand again, Rachel caught the falling girl with a charge of *tiathelu* and lowered her to the ground near where two other girls from De Vere waited. The other two girls quickly helped her up. Rachel was gratified to see that Kris was able to stand and take a shaky step.

The ogre spun and bore down on Sigfried, who tried to run —on skates. The ogre thundered after him, cracking ice with his huge ponderous steps. Despite the fact that her sorcery kept fizzling out when it struck the monster's skin, Nastasia continued playing, attempting one spell after another. Valerie, desperate to help her boyfriend, tried several cantrips, but they had no effect. Rachel, too, tried a few spells from her wand. Nothing.

Siggy dashed behind a tree. The ogre pulled up the tree. The ice from which the tree had been plucked broke, cracks spreading rapidly outward. Luckily, the water, which was only about a foot deep, was entirely frozen.

Siggy lunged behind another trunk. That tree, too, was uprooted. Siggy skated toward a large boulder and tripped over the cracked ice. His skates flew out from under him. Unable to rise, he began scampering backward, sliding on his behind with his hands and skates pushing him frantically along in his effort to get behind the boulder.

The ogre lunged and caught him by his skates.

"Siggy!" shrieked a terrified Valerie. "Wh–what do we do? That th–thing has a charmed life! We'll never stop it!"

Holding the boy by the blades of his skates, the ogre flung Sigfried into the air and then smashed him toward the ice. Siggy could do nothing to save himself. This did not stop him from trying. As his body swung toward the ground, he crunched his stomach muscles, performing a sit-up in mid-air, so that his head escaped the brunt of the impact. At the same time, he did not cease from shooting the ogre in the face with ineffective spells from his wand, drawing his knife and—after not being able to reach the ogre's hand to stab it—throwing the blade at the monster's face, and spitting at it.

Bellowing like an enraged boar, the ogre shifted his grip and slammed the boy's head against the ice, twice. Siggy's body went limp.

Valerie screamed. In her panic, her skates went out from under her, and she tumbled to the ice.

The ogre stood over Sigfried, its chest heaving. It looked as if it were contemplating whether or not to eat him. Nastasia played more frantically, even though her spells continued to do nothing. She sawed her bow so hard that a string broke. Rachel, too, felt panicky. She had *known* something bad was out there tonight. Now, Sigfried's life was on the line, if he were even still alive, and she could think of nothing to do. A scream threatened to leap from her throat.

No. She would not panic. Losing her nerve would do Sigfried no good.

Her grandfather's words echoed in her mind: *Fierce as a tiger. Calm as a lake in August. And cool as ice—when you are not as fiery as a furnace.*

Rachel took a deep breath and calmed her thoughts. There was one thing she had not tried. Closing her eyes, she recalled her meeting with Kitten's familiar in the Memorial Garden on a chilly day in early November. In her memory, the Comfort Lion sat beside one of the tall shrines. Tilting his head, he spoke: "*Ye shall know the truth, and the truth shall make you free.*"

Oh. Rachel's shoulders slumped. That had not worked. That was the same thing he had said last time. *Except....*

Rachel carefully compared the two memories — the time she had recalled him when she was before the burning furnace in Carthage, and this memory now. In one, the little feline stared directly at her. In the other, he had cocked his head to the side. *The memories were different.*

Time seemed to stop.

Only for a split second but, in that slice of eternity, a tremendous sense of peace settled over Rachel, as if whether she lived or died was immaterial. In the way of visions, she suddenly knew that these words were meant to remind her of her contemplations earlier that evening about the same verse: *Most likely, she would never need to know about fly eyelashes.... Yet, sometimes the most trivial fact, overheard in passing, was the one that proved crucial.*

As certain as a dream, she understood the message. *Somewhere in her memory were the clues she needed to save her friends. Somewhere.*

Rachel stood motionless on the ice in the falling snow, listening to the steady beat of her own heart. Everything seemed unusually crisp and clear. A nimbus of bright, tiny wisps illuminated the air around her. Beside her, Nastasia was helping the trembling Valerie to her feet. Both girls shook with fear. Ahead of her Sigfried lay on the snow, a dark puddle spreading onto the ice behind his head. Somewhere behind him were Kris Serenity Wright and two of her friends, unless they had run. She hoped that they had run.

Between her and Sigfried, breathing slow, labored breaths, loomed the man-eating ogre. The brute was at least three times wider than any man and twice as tall. His eyes were small and beady and bright with malice, his mouth an enormous gash across his ugly face. His thick top-knot of black, oily hair was adorned with bones. Even where she stood in the cold, Rachel could smell his fetid breath. The stink of it made her want to run.

Her legs trembled, but she stood her ground.

How did one revoke a charmed life? She rapidly rifled through the library in her mind, searching for any clue that might help.

The sword *Nothung* had slain Baba Yaga. The dragon in the sewer claimed it had a charmed life, but Sigfried had defeated it. The wraith they had fought during their first week of school had seemed invulnerable until....

Oh. Of course!

Glancing northward, Rachel could see nothing in the dark. Calculating times and distances in her head, based on speed, motion vectors, and her experience flying her broom, she guessed that they still had two or three minutes to wait.

"The ogre can be defeated!" she cried to the other girls, "But we need to stall him!"

"On it!" cried Valerie.

Valerie's voice was panicky, but her actions were brave and sure. She dashed forward, skating recklessly across the broken ice. As soon as she was barely parallel to the ogre, who was leaning over the fallen Sigfried and licking its lips, she lifted her camera and set off the flash.

Brilliant, white light illuminated the darkness, leaving everyone temporarily blinded. The ogre yowled and threw its arm in front of its face to protect its tiny, pig-like eyes.

The flash faded. The ogre growled and blinked. Then it lunged forward, grabbing at Valerie. Valerie turned and skated away. Unlike Siggy, the Maine-borne girl was a natural on skates. Even in the near darkness, she avoided the cracks and trunks with ease.

And yet, the ogre was gaining.

"Miss Hunt!" cried Nastasia. "Brace yourself!"

The princess ran her bow across her instrument. Despite the broken string, beautiful silver sparkles illuminated the darkness. With a *swoosh*, they danced across the intervening distance and struck Valerie, imparting a tremendous burst of speed. Valerie flew forward several dozen feet, arms windmilling. Then her found her balance again. Pulling her left foot in fast, she went into a tight backwards spin and barely missed slamming into a tree.

The ogre paused, breathing heavily. Valerie was quite some yards away now. It glanced back and forth between the supine Sigfried and Nastasia with her violin.

Sigfried and Nastasia were both in danger. Both needed saving. Both suddenly seemed irrepressibly dear to Rachel. She could not bear the idea of the monster harming either of them.

Where was he? Rachel looked northwards over her shoulder but saw nothing. Yet, she knew for certain he was coming. He would save Valerie and the princess, and Sigfried, if Siggy were still alive. All she had to do was stall the ogre.

But how? Rachel had no idea what to do. Yet, she could not bear the idea of the parents of one of her friends receiving the same message Tommy Check's parents must have received. She had met both the King of Australia and Detective Hunt, and as for Sigfried, he had Lucky. She pictured her friends' fathers' faces becoming pale as they learned the news; their child—their precious one—gone forever. She imagined their grief feeling much like her father's agony, which the Raven had shared with her, only a thousand times worse. The thought was so painful, so wrong, that something deep inside her rebelled.

She *had* to distract the monster until he could be killed.

It was time to act.

Barreling forward, she skated directly towards the ogre. A mere dozen feet from the hulking brute, she turned her blades sideways, sliding to a stop.

"What are you doing?" Valerie screamed in terror, grabbing hold of the nearest tree. "Get away! He'll kill you!"

"Rachel!" the princess cried simultaneously. She started forward as if to join her and then halted, terrified and uncertain. "Back up! He is utterly enormous! There is nothing you can do! Run!"

The creature *was* enormous. A mere step and its thick, ropy arm could reach out, grab her head, and squeeze it like an orange. But Rachel could not think about that now. It did not matter whether she lived or died, only whether she stalled him long enough to save her friends.

Donning her mask of calm, she drew a deep breath and cast out the net of her thoughts, looking for something, anything of use. In her memory, Kris Serenity Wright's voice repeated: *He said the ogre came from far away and didn't fit in well with the local spirits. How* far away? As far as the Steppes of Russia, or wherever it was that Baba Yaga and her wandering hut had come upon an ogre?

Hoping against hope that this monster might recognize the only ogre name she knew, she shouted, "Mambres!"

The ogre tipped its ugly head one way and then the other, cracking its neck joints with loud pops. "Who calls my name?"

Dear gods! It had worked!

Only now the brute was looking *right at her.* Well, she might as well die with courage as die a coward. Tipping up her chin, she met its gaze squarely. "I am The Lady Rachel Griffin."

"I have heard of you, Rachel Griffin. You are the Raven's pet."

What?

Rachel had never felt so terrified and so delighted at the same time.

Desperate to keep it talking, she blurted out, "Is it true you're the brother of the Ogre of Smeeth?"

A strange change came over the monster's face. He looked almost... human?

"My brother, Jannes!" He breathed, a heavy snort of breath misting the air before him. "I have not thought of him in many a century. We were the greatest of sorcerers once, before that le Fay woman stole our book!"

Random bits of trivia clicked together in her mind with lightning speed. Rachel almost smiled. "You are from Egypt."

"Egypt?" murmured the princess behind her, puzzled.

"Yes," grunted the monster who had once been a man. "We served the great Pharaoh Menthesuphis, called Merenre Nemtyemsaf II. We were the greatest sorcerers who ever lived!" He snarled. "Until the one drawn out of water ate our enchanted staffs with his."

Rachel's eyes narrowed. She recalled a tale she had read in one of her grandfather's history books. "I've heard that story. There was a slave revolt. They had a powerful sorcerer who prevailed for a time—sending plagues. In the end, however, his sorcery failed, and he and his entire tribe were drowned in the Red Sea." She frowned slightly. "Though some historians say that the Gypsies are descended in part from these people, so some of them must have lived."

"Is *that* how they tell it now?" The great hulking monster seemed almost alarmed. Then he laughed, a very grating and unpleasant sound. "The world has gone mad! Dark and awful changes have been made to the minds of men. They have forgotten all the truths that kept the darkness at bay." He leered at Rachel menacingly. "Not so gray anymore, is he?"

"I beg your pardon?" asked Rachel, puzzled.

Mambres stomped toward Rachel, reaching for her head with his long, ropy arm, bulging with muscles. Her mind shouted at her to flee, but she held her ground, glaring back at him. Only a little while longer, and her friends would be safe. She was certain of it.

But how to stall him? She was pretty sure that spraying him with Bogey Away would not cut it.

"You should not trouble Miss Griffin," Nastasia announced clearly. She skated up beside Rachel, hooking her arm through her friend's. Rachel had wanted her friend to flee to safety, but she gave her a grateful smile.

From the trees, Valerie called, "The Raven will come save her, you know."

"He will do nothing," scoffed the ogre. "I am here by invitation. He will not bend his precious rules, that one."

Rachel swallowed. She knew what the brute said was true. Jariel would not act to interfere with any worldly things where men were involved.

The princess's voice snapped with authority. "Invited? Within the school wards? Under whose authority?"

That was a good question! Rachel threw her friend an admiring look.

Mambres chuckled darkly. "By the authority of one who has agents inside this establishment, and who means it harm. An old enemy seeking revenge. Who are you who asks?"

The princess stood ramrod straight. "I am Nastasia Romanov, Princess of Magical Australia."

"Romanov!" The ogre actually took a full step backward, startled. Rachel's heart leapt with hope. Then its face split into a terrible, eager, hungry grin. "Why heckle the servant when you can heckle the master?"

He lunged toward Nastasia. His footfalls slapped the ice like thunder.

"Graarr!"

With a noise like a falling sequoia, the ogre fell flat on his face. The ice beneath him broke with a cannon-like *crack*. In the faint light of the wisps, Rachel could see that his thick, stump-like legs were entirely entangled by roots that had mysteriously broken through the ice.

Behind him, Kris Serenity Wright stood among the trees. Fox ears had sprouted from her head, and a thick cloud of wisps swarmed around her. At first, Rachel wondered if Kris had played the song they had learned in class. Then she remembered what the De Vere girl had said about the fey-born having special talents. In Japan, wisps were called *kitsunibi*. Most likely, even the domestic ones would obey to the kitsune's daughter.

In the lavender glow of the wisp-light around Kris, Rachel could see Hekpa the dryad's daughter, glaring at the ogre, her arm outstretched. Around her, the trees swayed back and forth, as if an angry wind blew through their branches, but no other trees, anywhere else, were swaying. Following the young woman's outstretched hand, Rachel saw the tree roots moving and growing around the ogre's legs, seeking to bind them. Rachel gave a soft cheer.

The ogre ripped through the roots, breaking them.

Hekpa shouted in wrath. "Tree murder!"

The ogre climbed to its feet and lunged toward the princess again.

"Eeeyyaahhh!" Out of the darkness, Sigfried leapt onto the brute's back, stabbing it repeatedly with his knife, which he had somehow recovered in the dark. The knife skittered off the ogre's skin. Still, despite the blood running over his eyes, Siggy did not give up.

"You're alive!" cried Valerie, tears of joy on her cheeks.

"Incoming!" A red and gold dragon dropped from the snowy sky, fire billowing from his mouth.

"Finally!" cheered Rachel, jumping up and down on her skates.

Bellowing with rage, the ogre uprooted another hemlock and swung it at Lucky. The dragon lithely ducked out of the way of the tree-club. Swooping low, Lucky scorched the ogre, red-orange flames curling over the brute's head and shoulders. There came a loud *Pop*. The monster let out a strange, strangled cry.

"Get him!" cried Rachel. "His life's no longer charmed!"

"Die, monster!" shouted Sigfried, stabbing it again.

His knife sank into the creature's flesh up to the hilt. At the same moment, Lucky set the brute's top knot on fire.

The girls attacked. Rachel whistled a stream of blue sparks. Nastasia knocked the monster over with a powerful silvery wind. Valerie shouted out the Glepnir cantrip, binding the monster with a band of glowing golden light. Farther away, Hekpa, Kris, and Rhiannon cast spells as well, though Rachel could not see what they were doing.

The ogre let out a loud bellow of pain and alarm, his agonized face lit by the light of his own burning hair. Then Sigfried, still clinging to its back, reached around and, using the Bowie knife that Valerie had bestowed upon him—which he had apparently recovered from where it had dropped on the ice—he slit the ancient monster's unprotected throat.

Valerie's camera flashed.

Gargling, Mambres tried vainly to raise his trapped arms, but the glowing Glepnir bond restrained him. With an enormous crash, the great body fell to the ground, dead.

"Way to go, Luck!" declared Sigfried, fist bumping his dragon.

"Nice work."

"Sorry about that," said Lucky, in his gravelly voice. Rachel noticed that his fur was a bit charred. "That *Mexaxkuk* proved surprisingly wily. Then I had a run-in with lightning imps. Nothing to worry about."

"Is it really dead?" cried the young woman they had rescued. Her pink hair looked lilac in the glow of the lavender wisps. Her fox ears twitched as she turned her wide eyes toward Sigfried and bowed low, Japanese-style. "Thank you very much for saving me."

"It was nothing," announced Sigfried, his hands on his hips, a dark stain dripping down the side of his face. "I kill ogres every day, just for kicks. Besides, I did it for Valerie."

Then he fainted.

CHAPTER THIRTY-EIGHT:

FORGIVENESS IN THE SNOW

"RACHEL," VLADIMIR'S VOICE SPOKE IN HER EAR. "GAIUS INDICATED that you might need help?"

"It's all right, Vlad, we're...." Rachel looked at the fallen Sigfried, six girls kneeling around him, including a frightened Joy—who had come out of the princess's purse-house to fuss over Siggy—and a worried Lucky licking his face. "Actually, one of our party is badly wounded. Can you help get him to the infirmary?"

"I am coming."

A tall pillar of bright light reached toward the sky, illuminating the snowy night. The dark puddle and stain on Siggy's head suddenly flashed blood red, causing two of the girls to gasp in fear. The light swirled, instantaneously forming bones, organs, and then flesh, all of glowing whiteness. Then color filled in, and Vladimir Von Dread stood on the ice beside them, his arms crossed.

Vlad immediately stepped forward and knelt beside Sigfried, girls scattering before him like frightened doves. "What happened? Has he been moved?"

"He was standing just a moment ago." The princess addressed the prince with chilly formality. She still knelt by Sigfried, cradling his head in her lap and trying to stop the bleeding with her handkerchief.

Valerie, who also sat beside her boyfriend, holding his hand, said, "The ogre slammed Sigfried's head against the ice, twice. I... don't understand how he can be alive, much less how he was able to wake up, stand, jump on the ogre's back, and slit its throat!" She shook her head, amazed. "If any one of us had taken that kind of trauma to the head, we'd be dead!"

"Maybe he really is a robot," murmured the princess, faintly.

"If he has been walking around and fainted, I can move him."

Vladimir scooped Sigfried up into his arms and stood up, as if the tall, muscular boy weighed no more than a toy poodle. Lucky darted forward and wrapped himself around Siggy's body, forming a fuzzy stole. "I shall bring him to Nurse Moth."

Vladimir's eyes traveled over the scene, taking in the girls, the fallen trees, the cracked ice, and the dead ogre, but his face betrayed no reaction.

"Um... may I come along?" Valerie clambered to her feet, balancing again on her skates, and grabbed the stern upperclassman's sleeve.

Dread turned to regard her. She let go and nervously slid away from him.

"Of course, Miss Hunt," he replied. "Put your arm through mine."

Valerie did so, relieved. Gazing at him, so tall and impressive amidst the blue and lilac wisps, Rachel could not help feeling the least bit wistful, regretting that she was not the one with the reason to stand so close to Vlad. She quickly glanced away, glad that her blush would not show in the faint lavender light.

"Gaius... and Topher?" she asked, determined to be loyal to her boy. "Are they all right?"

"They are well. Topher may have broken his arm, and Gaius has a few minor scratches, but they will recover."

"Oh," Rachel mouthed, wide-eyed and curious. She could not wait to hear what adventures had befallen her boyfriend, but she asked no questions. Gaius would have to tell her himself.

With a nod to the rest of them, Vladimir jumped. The pillar of light briefly illuminated the brilliant red bloodstain on the ice. Then it faded, leaving them all temporarily night-blind.

"Is it really dead?" Kris Serenity Wright walked over and kicked the ogre's body several times with her booted foot. "Good!" Then, she frowned. "Oops. That's going to be hard for Grandda to explain. The Concords that keep peace between us and the fey depend on us not troubling them. Of course, the ogre did invade our wards and kidnap me! So maybe he was fair game."

The princess came up beside Kris and said kindly, "You seem quite collected, Miss Wright, considering the remarkable circumstances."

Kris laughed and shook her head. Her pixie-short, pink hair bounced around her face. "Actually, I'm totally freaking out. But it hasn't caught up with me yet. Just watch, though. I'll be screaming like an *uwan* any moment now!"

Her two roommates came up beside her. Rachel noted that the three wore their boots. The ogre must have grabbed Kris as she was returning to campus. Rhiannon gazed apprehensively at the ogre, as if she were afraid that it might leap up and grab her friend again. Hekpa, on the other hand, looked more angry than scared.

"I tried to save you!" she said to Kris, her tiny mouse peeking out from her fur-lined hood. "Two hemlocks helped. They moved to trip your captor when I called to them, but that brute just ripped off their branches! Poor things! And after they tried so hard. It takes great effort for trees to move like that!"

Stomping over to the fallen hemlock that the ogre had used to try and club Lucky, she sorrowfully laid a hand on its shaggy bark, shaking her head sadly.

Kris patted herself down from head to thigh. To Rachel, she said, "Everything seems to still be here. I guess I'm all right. Thanks all of you and Mr. Smith. Good job!"

"And Lucky," murmured Rachel. "It was Lucky who saved us all."

"Lucky?" asked the princess, rising to her feet and brushing off snow. "How so?"

"He broke the enchantment maintaining the ogre's charmed life," said Rachel.

"Ah!" the princess nodded, suddenly understanding. "That's what we were waiting for."

Rachel nodded. "He had popped the protection on the wraith in September, and Siggy had mentioned that he and Lucky attacked the dragon in the sewer together. Sigfried's first blow bounced off, but, by the second blow, he was able to strike the creature. That second blow was after Lucky breathed on it. Also, according to Siggy, the sword that slayed Baba Yaga had been forged in dragon fire."

She did not add that the Comfort Lion had promised her that she had the clues she needed within her memory. Explaining how she had received that message would be too complicated.

"Very clever, Miss Griffin. I commend you." The princess smiled kindly, her eyes crinkling.

"Wow!" Kris said, still gazing at the supine brute. "Without Lucky, we would all have been ogre chow! I've got to thank him and Siggy somehow."

Rachel smiled. "They like food."

"You were pretty brave yourself," said Kris, grinning at Rachel. Rachel ducked her head, embarrassed.

"What happened?" Joy joined them. "The ogre just grabbed you?"

"He was angry with my grandfather, for binding him. Making him not eat humans," said Kris. "I guess he wanted me as a hostage or something."

"So, he hunted you down?" asked Joy with a shiver. "Picked you out from everyone else? That's... scary!"

"Grandfather was v-very angry about the boy that got eaten," said Kris. Her teeth started to chatter, and her body had begun to tremble. "H-he made sure the o-ogre felt his wrath. I-I th-think it wanted rev-revenge."

Nastasia sent Joy into her purse to bring up a blanket. When Joy did, the princess wrapped the fluffy pink comforter around Kris's shoulders. "You are showing signs of shock, Miss Wright. Why don't you go inside, where it's warm."

Nodding mutely, Kris climbed inside and headed down the stairs, helped along by her two best friends. Rachel could hear Joy below, offering encouragement. Once Kris was settled, Nastasia closed her bag, and only Rachel and the princess remained.

• • •

Nastasia held out her arm and offered her muff again. Rachel accepted, slipping one arm through her friend's elbow and the other into the warm fur. The two girls smiled at each other.

"Did you understand what the ogre meant about something not being gray any more?" asked the princess, presently.

"Not at all," replied Rachel, truthfully. "I'm not even sure to what category of thing he referred."

"How did you know that it was from Egypt?" asked Nastasia.

"It was just a guess, something to keep him talking. He said that Morgana le Fay had taken their book," replied Rachel. "Mr. Fisher told us at the beginning of the year that Morgana had made herself immortal using *The Book of Going Forth by Day*. The other name for that book is *The Egyptian Book of the Dead*."

"Ah! Interesting. You were very quick on your feet there, Miss Griffin. I admit, I am impressed. I don't think I could have kept him distracted as long. It was only because you showed such spirit that I was able to rally."

"I was grateful for your support," Rachel replied loyally, not adding that she had wished that the princess had fled and not risked both of them.

"Mr. Smith conducted himself quite handsomely, as well." The princess sighed. "I have been thinking about what you said earlier. Perhaps, I am too hard on him. Being at school is much more difficult than I expected, too."

Rachel recalled how she had felt that the princess, too, had seemed withdrawn during the last few months. Perhaps, now that she herself was not so depressed, it was time to begin thinking about others, to try to find out what was bothering her friend.

"In what way is school difficult?" Rachel prodded gently.

The princess sighed again. "I had thought that the work would be hard but that being with other students would be pleasant. The work is difficult, yet it's fascinating, but...."

"Is it the secrets?" asked Rachel. "That make it hard, I mean?"

Nastasia was silent for a bit, then she let out a long sigh and nodded. "Wulfgang came to talk to me again. While we were skating. Again, he asked that we might be friends. We talked just a little. It was pleasant talking to a boy of my own rank. Too pleasant, in a way."

"You mean you like him," Rachel teased happily.

The princess shook her head somberly. "I mean that I nearly forgot myself and spoke of things that are secret." Nastasia stopped skating and turned to face her friend. Rachel stopped as well. "I...

just cannot do this. I cannot be his friend and remember what not to say. I am not like you, with your gift of memory."

Now it was Rachel's turn to sigh. "My memory does not help me with that sort of thing. I say the wrong thing often." She thought but did not add, *You would be amazed how often.*

"I must make it clear to him that we cannot be friends at this time," the princess said sadly. "We cannot risk the whole world for the sake of our own pleasures."

"That's... rather sad," Rachel said softly.

Nastasia was silent. Their blades zipped along the snowy ice.

Suddenly, the princess announced, "I am sorry, Rachel. I know you will be angry with me, but I am *happy* that I did not bring you and Sigfried with me when we took Illondria home."

"What?" Rachel cried, as if stung. "Why?"

The words burst from Nastasia like the whistle of steam from a boiling kettle, as if she had been holding them in for far too long. "Because I might have lost you, too!"

Rachel's mouth formed an O, but no sound came from her lips. Then, sniffing slightly, she smiled. "I'll forgive you, if you forgive me for this."

Despite Nastasia's dislike of intimacy, Rachel threw her arms around her friend and hugged her. With a happy little laugh, the princess wiped away a tear and hugged her back.

. . .

The two girls started skating again. The tension that had been growing between them, ever since the princess had brought the Elf home, evaporated. It was a day for forgiveness, Rachel decided, with her hand snug in the furry white muff, and forgiveness brought a lessening of burdens. She felt so light; she wondered if her skates were still touching the ice. Maybe Nastasia's arm, tucked through hers, was the only thing that kept her from floating away.

"Joy? Joy?" girls' voices called from the darkness.

"My sisters!" cried Joy, from the bag. "Oops! They sound worried. Um... you'd better let me out."

Joy climbed out of the purse and skated toward where several of her sisters were searching for her. A moment later, Ivan Romanov's voice called, "Nastasia, is that you? Where have you been? Alexis is frantic."

"Better go," Nastasia gave her friend a kind smile and skated toward her siblings.

Rachel waved as the princess went. To the right, beneath the bright wisp sculptures, she spotted Gaius. She zipped across the ice toward him, the last of her dwindling wisp entourage departing to join their fellows. Gaius's face split into a big grin when he saw her, and he gathered her into a tight hug. She lightly ran a finger over his bandaged cheek.

"It's nothing," he scoffed. "Just a scratch. We got into a scuffle with some red caps and a trow." He paused and hugged her more tightly, resting his chin on her head. "I would have been much more scared, if I had realized that my girlfriend was facing off against the ogre! You should have called me! We could have spared Vlad, especially after William arrived."

"It sounded as if you two were in trouble."

"Topher was being dragged across the ice by his foot and had become lodged between two trees," explained Gaius, "but the buggers kept pulling."

"Was that how he broke his arm?" asked Rachel.

"Nooooo." Gaius looked as if he was trying not to laugh. "That was when he finally got to his feet and tried to chase after the red caps, shouting at them... and he skated over his own lace and fell flat on his face." Gaius winced, but then he just gave up the struggle and burst out laughing. "I love Topher, but, man, that boy can be a klutz."

Rachel also struggled not to laugh at the other young man's mishap. "Isn't Topher from Alaska, where they skate all the time? Maybe the fey were responsible for his laces being untied. They do things like that."

"Maybe," said Gaius, more seriously.

Then he burst out laughing again.

Rachel stepped away so she could see her boyfriend more clearly. Before she could speak, however, something came flying at her, coming out of the dark at high speed.

"*Dongsaeng!*" Her sister Laurel grabbed her up in a huge bear hug. Over her shoulder, she called in a cheerful singsong. "See, Peter, I told you she'd be all right. Everything is wonderful today. It's like the world is surrounded by golden light."

"Um... I better go." Gaius winked at Rachel.

Rachel, who was still hugging Laurel, smiled brightly and winked back. Over the black bracelet, she whispered, "By the way, Gaius, you saved my life. Thanks to what you and William taught me about physics and *turlu*, I lived... when I otherwise would have been fried alive."

Gaius's face lit up. He threw her a huge grin and a thumbs up as he skated away.

Peter arrived, breathing heavily, as if he had been skating very fast. Reluctantly, Laurel let go of her little sister, but she stayed close beside her, leaning an elbow on Rachel's shoulder.

"Rachel, you should not have scared us like that." Her brother wagged his finger at her sternly. "I was beginning to fear that you had been eaten by the ogre."

"The ogre's dead," Rachel replied seriously. "Siggy killed it."

"What, really? The ogre with the charmed life?" cried Peter. When Rachel nodded, he asked, "And Sigfried Smith killed it?"

"He did."

"Jolly good of him!" Peter looked quite impressed. "I say! Maybe we should all adopt this orphan boy as our blood-brother!"

"The bigger our family, the better," sang Laurel, dreamily. With her brother and sister beside her, Rachel found her boots and changed into them. Her siblings told her to abandon the conjured skates, which would vanish after twenty-four hours, but she refused, holding them close to her chest as they walked through the falling snow. The three of them trekked back toward the school, as part of a large group of students, surrounded by proctors and some of the White Hart members. The group chattered loudly, everyone excitedly exchanging stories. Most of their tales were of possibly having seen a pixie or of a boulder that whizzed by overhead. No one else reported having gone off into the darkness. Rachel stayed quiet, too overwhelmed by the evening's occurrences to speak.

The snow was still falling, but the thunder had stopped. There was no sign of the Heer or the lightning imps. The students arrived safely back on campus, with only one run-in with a stray spruce troll that ran away as soon as it saw their lights.

Upon reaching Roanoke Hall Rachel was shocked to realize that it was only seven o'clock. She headed inside with everyone else for a late dinner and a steaming cup of hot chocolate. Someone had enchanted the central fountain, so that flames leapt from it instead of water. Chilly students had gathered around it for warmth. Taking her hand, Laurel pulled Rachel over to the fire, and the three Griffins joined in toasting marshmallows and making s'mores.

CHAPTER THIRTY-NINE:

FORGOTTEN THINGS

THE NEXT DAY, CLASSES WERE CANCELED, AND ALL DORMITORIES were locked down, due to the danger of the wild fey free on campus. Rachel and her friends headed downstairs to study and talk in front of the fireplace in the cellar common room of Dare Hall. Sometime during the afternoon, to everyone's relief and delight, the proctors brought Sigfried back to the dorm, his head swathed in bandages.

When Rachel returned to her room that evening, she noticed something unexpected leaning against the wall beneath the arched window. Despite all laws of sorcery to the contrary, the conjured silver skates with purple laces that Jariel had sized so perfectly for her were still there. Looking at them, Rachel somehow knew that they would never vanish.

A single black raven feather lay beside them. Rachel kneeled and snatched up the feather. Brushing its softness against her cheek, she recalled her most recent conversation with its owner.

• • •

Sneaking away from where her siblings had been singing campfire songs and roasting marshmallows the night before, Rachel had slipped out of the dining hall and gone to sit on the great staircase leading to the second floor, one of the very few staircases in Roanoke Hall that was not a spiral. It was chilly here, and the stone seemed to suck the heat out of her body. Seated on the marble, she hugged her arms and spoke over the bracelet. "Jariel, I have a question."

"Yes, Rachel Griffin?" The Raven's voice spoke just beside her ear.

"So, the awful truth about all this forgetting is that...." She took a deep breath, "You're the one responsible, aren't you? For all of it."

"Responsible?"

"For things like why we can't remember from whom the original founders of Roanoke Island were running? And all the other forgotten things, too. Like saints and steeples and friars and the disappearance of the wings on the statue of the angel? Those are all things you've made the world forget."

The Raven replied solemnly, "The answer to all those questions is yes, Rachel Griffin."

"Wh–why?" she asked, her voice warbling. "To fit people in? When you told Illondria that you changed memories to protect us, I–I assumed you meant things like making people forget that Gaius's farm did not use to be there. Not... all this. Was it all to protect the Walls?"

"I—may not reveal any of his doings."

"The Master of the World's behind orphaned words, too!" Rachel cried. "He's made you change the whole world?"

"Speaking on this subject would be in direct disobedience of my orders. But I can say this, that all the memories I have changed were at the behest of the one you call the Master of the World—directly or indirectly—or to protect the Walls. Save for one."

This answer came from higher up and slightly to the right. Rachel spun around. Jariel stood at the top of the first flight. He was shirtless, holding his halo in one hand. His black wings, half-spread behind him, filled the entire landing. His eyes were red as blood. Rachel scampered to her feet and ran upstairs. She passed the landing and continued four steps up the next flight, until she was closer to his height.

"Except for one?" she asked, breathlessly. "Can you tell me about that one?"

"Coracinus Moth learned something too dangerous for him to know."

"*Cousin Blackie?*" Rachel felt oddly let down. She had so wanted to be able to hate the Master of the World on Blackie's behalf. "You cannot just protect him, as you protect me?"

"I cannot take the chance, lest any of my lower brothers should look into his mind."

"Lower brothers?" Rachel gazed at him carefully. "You mean demons?"

He nodded solemnly.

"What did Blackie find out?" She stepped down two steps to be closer to him, looking up. "Can you tell me?"

The Raven gazed at her for a time. "I cannot tell even you. The knowledge is too dangerous. But I can tell you what the matter concerned. Perhaps, then, you will think less harshly of me."

"Yes?" Rachel leaned forward eagerly.

"He discovered where Moloch sleeps."

"Oh!" she whispered, both astonished and a little envious of Blackie. She had been working diligently to learn that information herself.

Jariel turned his head, gazing toward the northeast. Rachel followed his gaze. She knew in that direction lay the dining hall and, a few miles beyond that, the sharp crescent peak of Stony Tor. He might have been glancing at the tor, or he might have been looking across the ocean at Iceland or Moscow. There was no way for her to tell.

"I understand that Moloch is one of the worst of the worst, and we don't want him to wake, but why remove so much of Blackie's memory?" she asked. "Why not remove only the offending information?"

"I tried. Twice. He reproduced his results, discovering the same secrets a second and then a third time."

"Oh," she murmured again.

The chill of the evening on the ice had taken its toll on her. She shivered and rubbed her hands together, trying to warm them.

"If a person has too much proof of a hidden thing, the world sides with them," said Jariel. "The evidence reappears."

"Like Great-Aunt Nimue and the rattle?" Rachel asked, her eyes trained on his face.

Jariel smiled slightly, as if her perspicacity pleased him. Rachel noticed that his eyes were now as gray as the clouds around the moon. He nodded. "Nimue Griffin Moth recalled that the child of Ellen Griffin would be named after the pretty girl who was to have married her favorite nephew. Nimue had been hard on that girl when they first met, thinking that she could treat the young woman more kindly later. Later never came."

Rachel climbed up several stairs again, until her head was even with his. "You mean, like the way she was kind of mean to Gaius, saying she didn't trust short men, but she secretly liked him?"

"Very like," he nodded. "Only your mother's friend did not know your great-aunt well enough to see through her gruffness. Your great-aunt regretted this. She confessed it to Gilbert Ashley, the silversmith, when she ordered the rattle. Whenever she thought of this chain of events, remembering how she had discussed with the silversmith why the baby was to be named Amber, the S I had placed on the rattle vanished, returning to an A. I could not keep her from remembering this without changing Amber Benson's name. But too many people knew the name of the dead girl for me to hide it easily. I hate to change them more than I must."

When he finished, she swallowed and met his unearthly gaze with a challenge.

"Why did you hide the existence of my dead sister Amber?"
"Because your sister Amber is not dead."
"Wha—what?"

Rachel's boots slid out from under her on the slippery marble. Her arms wind-milled. She would have fallen had he not stepped forward and caught her elbow. He set her on her feet again, upon the landing. He then squatted down on one knee, until he gazed at her eye-to-eye.

"You have three sisters, not two," he said. "One was taken from your family as a baby, before you were born. By the Master. Your father and mother agreed to this, but, to my shame, it was because I had already changed them to fit the Master's needs. I...."

Pain contorted his face. He pressed his hand on his chest.

"I-I cannot tell you more," he gasped. "It directly affects him, and I am constrained from telling you his plans. Even what I have said is... painful. I cannot risk destroying myself."

"No! Don't hurt yourself!" Rachel cried, rushing forward until she was right next to him. His feather radiated a heat that felt so good to her chilled body. "You must take care of yourself. Do not tell me anything you cannot. I... I understand what that is like—not being able to tell people things." She put her hand on his shoulder.

"Is that an oath that's hurting you? Like when people swear on the waters of the River Styx?"

"Very like," Jariel repeated, nodding.

"My parents—" Her voice failed. She tried again. "My parents—from my family, whom *you* claimed would sacrifice anything to keep each other safe—*gave up their baby girl?*"

She could not even express how wrong that seemed.

Jariel closed his eyes. When he opened them, they were again blood red.

The Raven spoke. "I can change the fate of this world, if you wish. Not on a grand scale, because it would go against my orders. But I could make it very likely that your sister Amber returns. Would you like to meet her? I do not know what has happened to her. I have seen glimpses of her from afar. She is involved in other things. Things which are a distraction to me. I do not know what the Master has told her about her parents. Your parents and siblings do not remember her."

"Yes," Rachel replied in a small voice. "I would like that very much."

Or, at least, she had planned to say that. She felt too shocked to be sure of what she actually said.

He looked off, as if into the distance. "Many paths I see stretching into the future. I choose one, and I say it is destined to be so.... And it is done. She will come."

Rachel was quiet for a time, too full of pain and awe to speak. She shook her head, whispering, "The Master of the World made you make us forget so many things!"

"No. Only one thing did he bid me to make your world forget and one thing alone. The rest merely followed."

"I'm... not sure I understand."

The Raven winced in pain again and pressed his hand against his chest. Sorrow haunted his perfect features. "I can say no more." "Okay."

Stunned by what she had learned, Rachel nodded kindly and gave the tall winged being a quick hug. Then she started down the steps, back toward the dining hall and warmth. When the Raven called her name, she turned back.

"Yes, Jariel?"

The Raven stood at the top of the first flight of stairs, his eyes as scarlet as newly-spilt blood.

"Know this, Rachel Griffin: nothing left in this world is as important as the one thing I have caused it to forget."

Here ends *The Awful Truth about Forgetting*.

Our heroine's adventures continue in the Fifth Book of Unexpected Enlightenment:

THE UNBEARABLE HEAVINESS OF REMEMBERING

Subscribe to the *Roanoke Glass* at https://goo.gl/UEdUKW to be kept up-to-date on all things *Unexpected* and the further adventures of Rachel Griffin.

For more information about the Roanoke Academy for the Sorcerous Arts, see the school's website: http://lampwright.wixsite.com/roanoke-academy *or join the Facebook group at* https://facebook.com/groups/RoanokeAcademy

GLOSSARY

Agents—Magical law enforcement. Agents fight magical foes, both human and supernatural.

Alchemy—One of the Seven Sorcerous Arts. It is the Art of putting magic into objects.

Bavaria—A country that exists in the world of the book but not in our world. It is known to both the World of the Wise and the Unwary. It is ruled by the Von Dread family.

Canticle—One of the Seven Sorcerous Arts. It is the Art of commanding the natural and supernatural world with the words and gestures of the Original Language.

Cantrip—One word in the Original Language, *i.e.* a canticle spell.

Cathay—The Democratic Republic of Cathay, a country that exists in the world of the book but not in our world. It is known to both the World of the Wise and the Unwary. It is ruled by an elected council.

Conjuring—One of the Seven Sorcerous Arts. It is the Art of drawing objects out of the dreamlands.

Core Group—A group of students, usually from the same dorm, who attend all their classes together.

Dare Hall—The dormitory at Roanoke Academy that is favored by enchanters.

De Vere Hall—The dormitory at Roanoke Academy that is favored by warders and obscurers.

Dee Hall—The dormitory at Roanoke Academy that is favored by scholars.

Drake Hall—The dormitory at Roanoke Academy that is favored by thaumaturges.

Enchantment—One of the Seven Sorcerous Arts. It is based on music and includes a number of sub-arts.

Fulgurator's wand—A wand with a spell-grade gem on the tip that is used by Soldiers of the Wise to throw lighting and to hold other kinds of spells.

Gnosis—One of the Seven Sorcerous Arts. It is the Art of knowledge and augury.

Heer of Dunderberg—Storm Goblin locked up with his Lightning Imps in a cave in Stony Tor on Roanoke Island.

Jumping—A cantrip that allows the practitioner to teleport.

Magical Australia—A country that is only known to the Wise. It is ruled by the Romanov family.

Marlowe Hall—The dormitory at Roanoke Academy that is favored by conjurers.

Morthbrood—An ancient organization of practitioners of black magic. During the Terrible Years, the Morthbrood served the Terrible Five.

Mundane—Without magic. Refers both to the modern technological world and to those who cannot use magic. It is possible to be mundane and Wise, if one has no magic but is aware of the magical world.

Obscuration—A subset of Warding. It allows for the casting of illusions that hide things and trick the Unwary.

Original Language—The original language in which all objects were named.

Parliament of the Wise—The ruling body of the World of the Wise.

Pollepel Island—The name the Unwary call the island they see in place of Roanoke Island. It is also called Bannerman Island.

Roanoke Academy for the Sorcerous Arts—A school of magic on a floating island that is currently moored in the Hudson near Storm King Mountain.

Scholars—Practitioners of the Art of Gnosis.

Sorcery—The study of magic.

Spenser Hall—The dormitory at Roanoke Academy that is favored by canticlers.

Terrible Five—The leaders of the Veltdammerung, who terrorized the World of the Wise during the Terrible Years. They consisted of: Simon Magus, Morgana le Fay, Koschei the Deathless, Baba Yaga, and Aleister Crowley.

Thaumaturgy—One of the Seven Sorcerous Arts. It is the Art of storing charges of magic in a gem.

Thule—A country that is known only to the World of the Wise. It occupies the section of Greenland that is, in our world, occupied by the world's largest national park (larger than all but 32 countries).

Transylvania—A country that exists in the world of the book but not in our world. It is known to both the World of the Wise and the Unwary. It is ruled by the Starkadder family.

Tutor—The term used for professors at Roanoke Academy.

Unwary—One who does not know about the magical world.

Veltdammerung—Twilight of the World. The organization that served the Terrible Five during the Terrible Years. It consisted of the Morthbrood and of supernatural servants.

Warding—One of the Seven Sorcerous Arts. It is the Art of protecting one's self from magical influences.

Wise—Those in the know about the magical world (as in the root of the word 'wizard').

Wisecraft—The law enforcement agency of the Wise. The Agents work for the Wisecraft.

World of the Wise—The community of those who know about the magical world.

Acknowledgements

Thank you to Mark Whipple, John C. Wright, and William E. Burns, III, who breathed the life into the original story.

To Virginia Johnson, Erin Furby, Anna MacDonald, Brian Furlough, Bill Burns, and Jeff Zitomer, who helped iron out the bumps, and to my sons, Orville and Justinian for playing along and particularly to Juss, for wearing a lightning imp under his cat.

To Erin Furby, Kiara Lingenfelter, Joel C. Salomon, Meredith Dixson, Mark Thompson, Allan Lakner, Anthony Regan, and Bruce and Billy Carlton, for slogging through the early drafts, and to Sue Sims for catching "Americanisms".

To Jim Frenkel for the gift of editing, for which Rachel will be forever grateful.

To Anna "Firtree" Macdonald for making it readable.

To Joel C. Salomon for making it so that other people can read it.

To Dan Lawlis and Danille Ackley-McPhail for making it presentable.

To my mother, Jane Lamplighter, for listening and making dinner on Wednesdays, so I could write. This volume is dedicated to her.

About the Authors

L. JAGILAMPLIGHTER is also the author of the Prospero's Children series: *Prospero Lost*, *Prospero In Hell*, and *Prospero Regained*. She is an assistant editor with the *Bad-Ass Faeries* anthologies. She is also a founding member of the Superversive Literary Movement and maintains a weekly blog on the subject. When not writing, she switches to her secret identity as wife and stay-home mom in Centreville, VA, where she lives with her dashing husband, author John C. Wright, and their four darling children, Orville, Ping-Ping, Roland Wilbur, and Justinian Oberon.

To learn more, visit http://ljagilamplighter.com
On Twitter: @lampwright4

MARK A. WHIPPLE grew up in Croton-on-Hudson, which is not far from Roanoke Island. He then attended St. John's College in Annapolis, the mundane sister school to Roanoke Academy. Until recently, he has spent his free time, when not busy torturing Rachel Griffin, protecting the world from video game threats. Now, however, he volunteers with Stillbrave, a charity devoted to helping the families of children with cancer.

Unexpected Charity: 30% of the authors' proceeds from the *Unexpected Enlightenment* series goes to charity. Current charities of choice:

Mark's choice: Stillbrave Childhood Cancer Foundation – helping families of children with cancer.

Stillbrave Childhood Cancer Foundation
6731A Edsall Road
Springfield, VA 22151
https://stillbrave.org

Jagi's choice: All Girls Allowed – fighting for the rights and dignity of girls in China, and St. John's College – which, as the Wise all know, was started by two students from Dee Hall.

All Girls Allowed
101 Huntington Avenue, Suite 2205
Boston, MA 02199
http://allgirlsallowed.org

St. John's College
60 College Avenue
Annapolis, MD 21401
http://www.sjc.edu

Made in the USA
Lexington, KY
26 March 2018